# PRIMAL
# INSTINCT

# Also by Tara Wyatt

*Necessary Risk*

# PRIMAL
# INSTINCT

## TARA WYATT

FOREVER

NEW YORK   BOSTON

Copyright © 2016 by Tara Wyatt
Excerpt from *Necessary Risk* copyright © 2016 by Tara Wyatt
Cover design by Christine Foltzer
Cover illustration by Tony Mauro
Cover copyright © 2016 by Hachette Book Group, Inc.

Forever
Hachette Book Group
1290 Avenue of the Americas
New York, NY 10104
forever-romance.com
twitter.com/foreverromance

First Edition: May 2016

Forever is an imprint of Grand Central Publishing.
The Forever name and logo are trademarks of Hachette Book Group, Inc.

The publisher is not responsible for websites (or their content) that are not owned by the publisher.

The Hachette Speakers Bureau provides a wide range of authors for speaking events. To find out more, go to www.hachettespeakersbureau.com or call (866) 376-6591.

ISBN: 978-1-4555-9028-5

Printed in the United States of America.

OPM

10 9 8 7 6 5 4 3 2 1

*To my parents, Gerry and Catherine. Thank you for letting me read whatever I wanted growing up. Questionable parenting for the win!*

# ACKNOWLEDGMENTS

Thank you to my family for all of your continued support—my parents, Gerry and Catherine; my husband, Graham; my brother; my extended family; and my puppy, Schroeder. I wouldn't be doing this without your encouragement, and your tireless enthusiasm means everything to me. I love you guys so much.

A big thank you to my friends Amanda, Robin, and Sarah, for cheering me on, even when it felt impossible. I'm so lucky to call you wonderful ladies my friends.

Thank you to my agent, Jessica Watterson; my editor, Alex Logan; and everyone at Forever. As well, a big thank you to my coworkers at HPL, especially Stacy, Liz, Gina, Joe, Janette, and Antonella. Your support means so much to me, and I'm so grateful to work with such a fantastic group of people.

A very special thank-you to my critique partners Erin Moore and Harper St. George. I couldn't do this without you, guys. I love you both.

Thank you so much, Sarah Emery, for answering my tireless Army Ranger questions and for allowing me to pick your brain. You were so helpful, and I'm so appreciative of the time you took to answer my questions.

I'm incredibly lucky to be part of such an amazing community of writers, without whose support and encouragement I would be completely lost. Thank you to Brenna Mills, Amanda Heger, Jenn Burke, Kelly Jensen, Kelly Siskind, Victoria Austin, Samantha Joyce, Shannon Richard, Heather Powell, Colleen Halverson, Emily Albright, and many, many others (I'm so sorry if there's someone I've forgotten!). I'm so glad to know each and every one of you, and I mean that from the top of my head to the tips of my toes.

Finally, my Toronto Romance Writers tribe. You ladies are smart, kind, hardworking, supportive, and some of the best people on the planet. Thank you to Juliana Stone, Eve Silver, Morgan Rhodes, Maureen McGowan, Molly O'Keefe, Elly Blake, and (my bae) Nicki Pau Preto. You guys are the best. The absolute freaking best.

Additional shout-outs: wine, chocolate, and classic rock.

# PRIMAL
# INSTINCT

# CHAPTER 1

Taylor Ross needed it to happen tonight.

If she closed her eyes, she could even pretend to feel it, almost taste it, the way she used to. And then the dry spell would end, and things would go back to normal. Tonight. What she needed shimmered around her, in front of her, and if she reached out her fingers, if she touched the gauzy inspiration floating in the air, she might finally be able to write music again.

She drummed her fingers against the table, the red tablecloth absorbing the restless rhythm she tapped out. She blew out a breath and reached for her Jack and Coke, staring at the blinking light on her phone that lay on the table in front of her. She took a sip of her drink and then ran her finger across the screen, frowning at the numerous text messages, e-mails, and Google Alerts all begging for her attention. She took another sip and pushed her phone away, then flipped several pages of the notebook that lay open on the table in front of her, scowling at the scribbled and hastily scratched out chord progressions and lyrics.

She didn't want to think about any of it—breaking up with Zack, getting booted off a plane and the subsequent viral video of her in-air meltdown, or her inability to write. If her life was a sentence, the past few months had been a semicolon. An interruption, a pause. The past and the future linked by a tiny, little wink in time. She was tired of standing still, so for tonight, all she wanted was to catch a buzz so that she could numb the pain, the doubt, and the loneliness that were always simmering just below the surface.

She rested her chin in her hand as she scanned the dim interior of the Rainbow, a favorite LA hangout for rockers, groupies, some locals, and the occasional tourist. Red vinyl booths lined the walls, which were covered with rock paraphernalia. Autographed pictures, gold records, and vinyl albums, all encased in glass and staring down at her. She knew, if she wandered over the garishly carpeted floor to a corner near a window, she'd find a picture of herself and two assholes, all glaring moodily at the camera. She remembered autographing that picture. Hell, she remembered posing for that picture, full of the kind of cocky swagger only a twenty-two-year-old with a hit record can pull off.

How had ten years gone by so damn fast?

She glared up at the plants lining the ceiling, a row of lights shining from underneath them. Frustration rolled through her as her eyes landed once again on her phone. She was gripped by a sudden urge to hurl it across the room, but she forced herself to pick up her drink and drain it instead. She certainly wouldn't be the first musician to throw a tantrum at the Rainbow, but it wouldn't accomplish anything.

She shook her head and forced herself to focus on the blank page. Her brain scrambled for an idea, a melody, a lyric, a hook, *anything*, but the harder she tried to pull a song out of her brain, the more she felt like she was spinning her wheels in mud. Sweating and working and stressing and getting nowhere fast. The album was already six months overdue, and she needed something to show the label within the next week, otherwise they'd dump her, and she'd be out on her ass. And then what? If she wasn't a musician, a performer, then who was she? It was how she'd defined herself for over ten years now, and if she lost that part of herself, she didn't know how she'd stay whole.

It wasn't lost on her that her fame had dwindled to the point where she was able to sit in a bar, alone, without anyone even noticing her presence. But it wasn't the loss of fame that bothered her. It was the loss of the music. The fame was simply a perk that came with making something that people connected with, of performing on a stage, guitar in hand, feeding on the crowd's energy.

She sifted through the scraps of ideas littered throughout the notebook. She'd hoped maybe coming to the Rainbow where so many greats had hung out would inspire her. As if sitting in a sticky vinyl booth would somehow miraculously move her to finally write a new song. Lips pursed together, she shook her head again. She had nothing. Her brain spun emptily, filled with nothing but frustration and disappointment and fear.

Shoving the notebook aside, she scrolled through a series of texts from Jeremy Nichols, her manager, and then opened her phone's web browser and navigated to a video of her disgrace at thirty thousand feet.

Like pressing on a bruise, she pressed Play. She'd already watched it several times; she couldn't seem to stop watching it, and she couldn't stop herself from cringing every time she did. She'd been trying to make herself numb so that she wouldn't *hurt* so much. And God, she hurt. Several months ago, she'd started casually dating bodyguard Zack De Luca, and much to her surprise, she'd fallen fast and hard for him. For the first time in years, she'd wanted something more than casual. But Zack hadn't, and even though he hadn't meant to, he'd broken her heart.

So, to numb the pain of walking away from Zack, she'd joined the mile-high club with a cute guy she'd met earlier in the airport lounge. They'd flirted, had coffee, and gone their separate ways. When she'd boarded the plane and found her first-class seat, she'd been pleasantly surprised to discover that cute coffee guy was right across the aisle from her. The flirting had resumed, and she'd moved over to the empty seat beside him. One thing had led to another, and after about forty-five minutes, they'd wound up in the bathroom together. As soon as they'd emerged, they'd been confronted by the flight attendant, who knew exactly what they'd done, and threatened to have them arrested when the plane landed. When Taylor had started to apologize, the woman had turned on her, calling her a dirty slut. Livid and with no patience for bullshit double standards, Taylor had had a few choice words for the woman. The air marshal had come over to see what the commotion was about, and the flight attendant had called Taylor a white trash whore. So she'd slapped the flight attendant across the face, and the confrontation had devolved into flailing limbs and hair pulling. The air marshal had had to separate them, and she'd accidentally caught him in the throat with her elbow.

Not her finest moment.

She'd been escorted off the plane, and the video of the whole thing had gone viral almost immediately.

She shook her head and closed the video. Her pulse throbbed ominously in her temples, warning her of an oncoming headache. Everything was falling apart, and hell if she knew how to fix it.

A gawky guy with a slim build approached her table, and as his eyes met Taylor's through his thick horn-rimmed glasses, a chill crept over her skin. His dark brown hair was long on top and shaved close on the sides, his plain white T-shirt and jeans boring but clean. A surge of something weird, something cold, pushed up through her chest, and she forced herself to take a breath. He was probably just a fan looking for a picture. She should be grateful she still had fans. And yet something about this guy set her on edge.

"Hi, um, Taylor? Taylor Ross?" His voice was higher than she'd expected.

"Yeah, hi," she said, wanting to get this interaction over with.

"Can I, um, get a picture?" His eyes darted around the bar, oddly bright, and the hairs on the back of her neck prickled. He pushed his glasses back up his nose and made an awkward, fluttering gesture with his hand before shoving it in his pocket. She glanced around, trying to figure out what he was looking at.

She plastered a smile on her face that she hoped didn't look as fake as it felt. "Sure." Pressing her palms against the table, she stood from her booth.

He slipped his arm around her, and another chill shivered down her spine, making her shrink away from him a little. Raising his phone in front of them, he took the picture. Relieved, she started to move away from him, but his arm tightened around her. He smiled shyly.

"One more." She held still for the picture and didn't smile this time. As soon as he'd clicked the button, she pulled away. He let her this time, his fingers trailing over her waist and leaving her feeling as though she'd been slimed. "You shouldn't be here by yourself. I can keep you company."

"No thanks." She turned away and moved to slip back

into the booth when he tapped her on her shoulder. She spun, ready to tell him to fuck off, but froze at the look on his face, his eyes blazing, his lips curled into a thin sneer.

When he spoke, his voice was quiet and determined. "But I want to. You have to let me."

Anger melted her fear, and she scoffed out an impatient laugh. "I don't have to let you do sh—" But the rest of her words died as he grabbed her, curling a surprisingly strong hand around her arm, and her heart leaped into her throat. There was a time when she hadn't gone anywhere without security, but that level of fame was long behind her.

"Get off me," she growled through clenched teeth, jerking away from him. His fingers dug in harder, and she raised her knee, ready to hit him in his tiny balls.

"What's going on here?" At the sound of the deep voice, the creep released her.

"Nothing." The creep stuffed his phone back into his pocket and stalked away toward the exit, disappearing quickly into the crowd. Taylor let out the breath she'd been holding, her shoulders slumping slightly. Her skin itched, a physical remnant of the anxiety.

"Are you okay?" The man's voice was deliciously warm and rumbly, washing over her and chasing away the chill the creep had left behind.

"Yeah, I…thanks." Taking another deep breath, she ran her hands through her hair and turned to face her rescuer. For the second time in as many minutes, her heart was in her throat, but for an entirely different reason now.

Taken individually, the man's features were all so pretty. The intensely green eyes with the long lashes. The perfectly formed nose. The high, sculpted cheekbones. The lush, tempting mouth. The thick, short, light brown hair. And yet together, all prettiness disappeared, coalescing into the most handsome male face she'd ever seen. Her eyes scraped down his body, and she took in the way his black Led Zeppelin T-shirt was stretched tight over strong, broad shoulders and hugged his thick, muscular biceps. His right arm was covered in a sleeve tattoo, consisting entirely of intricate, detailed feathers overlapping each other, muscles rippling beneath the ink. The T-shirt fell straight down over his flat stomach and narrow waist, leading to well-built legs clad in denim.

He looked...sturdy. Like he'd been made to lean on.

She couldn't remember ever having that initial impression of a guy before. Hot, yes. Sexy, sure. But sturdy? That was a new one.

"I...need another drink." Taking a deep breath and trying to get her heart to slow down, she grabbed her purse and jacket out of the booth and made her way toward the bar at the back of the room. Her rescuer followed a few feet behind.

"Jack and Coke, please." She tipped her head at the bartender and could feel the gorgeous guy's eyes on her, leaving her skin tingling with excitement.

"You sure you're all right?" He turned sideways to face her, leaning one arm on the bar. Never had a man looked so good in an old T-shirt and jeans. Never. And never had a man been so immediately appealing. It was the model-worthy face paired with that deep, rumbly voice; the strong, muscular body with the relaxed, confident posture; the alertness in his gaze with his slow, easy smile.

"I'm fine. Really, he should be thanking you. It's because of you that his balls are still intact."

He chuckled, the sound low and warm. "Trust me, there isn't a doubt in my mind that you can take care of yourself."

She arched an eyebrow, twirling a finger around the rim of her fresh Jack and Coke. "So why'd you come over?"

"I was worried about the guy's balls." He winked, and she found herself smiling as her heart flickered in her chest.

The man scrubbed a hand over his hair and smiled, flashing a row of straight, white teeth, and the skin around his light emerald eyes crinkled in a way that had her stomach doing a slow turn. The bartender pointed at him, and he nodded.

She sat down on the barstool, crossed her legs, and ran her hands through her hair again. "I'm Taylor."

He nodded and picked up the bottle of beer the bartender had set down in front of him. "I know." He took a swig of the beer, and she watched his Adam's apple bob as he swallowed. A faint layer of stubble covered his jaw, and she found herself wondering what that stubble would feel like beneath her fingertips or against her neck, rasping over her skin. "I'm Colt."

Her heart gave a little kick against her ribs. "Thanks again for stepping in." She signaled to the bartender and pointed at Colt's beer. "You can go ahead and put that on my tab."

He smiled at her again, a cocky half grin that sent heat chasing over her skin. "You don't have to do that. That asshole crossed a line with you, and I just wanted to make sure you were okay."

She shook her head, returning the smile. "I'm trying to say thank you."

"Well, in that case, you're welcome." He leaned in closer. Jesus, he smelled good. Like warm leather and something else both mouthwatering and masculine. She bit her lip and looked down into her drink.

"Anyway. Thank you for the drink. I should let you get back to whatever you were working on," he said, tipping his head at her notebook.

It was her turn to lean in, and she smiled sweetly, looking up at him through her lashes. "Nah. You vanquished a creepy nerd for me. Have a seat."

He touched his thumb to his lips as his eyes traveled up and down her body and a slow smile turned up the corners of his mouth, his eyes crinkling once again. "Yeah. Okay."

He sat down on the bar stool next to her, pulling in close, his broad body angled toward her, but instead of feeling crowded, she felt sheltered. Her eyes slammed into his, and heat flared through her.

*Oh, holy hell, but this man is trouble.*

"So you didn't know that guy?" The way his low voice rumbled over the words sent a warm shiver down her spine and curled her toes.

She shook her head. "No. Just a fan, I guess."

"Lucky you."

She chuckled down into her drink and then met his eyes again.

Lucky her, indeed.

\* \* \*

Colt Priestley took a long pull on his beer, his eyes once more roving over Taylor's long, lean body. She was so tall, almost as tall as him, and as he was six-two, that didn't happen very often. His eyes kept sliding down to her long, slim legs, wrapped in black denim. For now. Soon, they'd be wrapped around him, if he got his way. And when it came to women, Colt almost always got his way.

Huey Lewis began thumping through the bar's speakers, and Taylor made a face, scrunching her cute little nose. "I thought this was a rock bar."

"Hey, don't rag on Huey Lewis. He had some great hits."

Colt smiled and bopped his head with cheesy, put-on enthusiasm in time to the music. She touched her fingers to her mouth and stifled a laugh before her eyes found his, and suddenly, her hand was on his chest. Hopefully she couldn't feel his heart pounding harder than a damn kick drum.

"I would've thought with this"—her fingers traced over the Led Zeppelin logo on his T-shirt—"and this"—the fingers of her opposite hand trailed up his right forearm and over his tattoo—"you'd have better taste than Huey Lewis."

He tried to think of something sexy, something flirty to say back, but his eyes were glued to her mouth, and goose bumps were trailing up his arm where she touched him. He cleared his throat and flashed her a smile.

She bit her lip and looked up at him, amusement flashing in her huge, blue eyes. "Did you know that Huey Lewis and the News were originally called Huey Lewis and the American Express? They had to change it when the credit card company threatened to sue them."

"Now who's hip to be square?" He shot her a teasing smile.

She flung her head back and laughed, a throaty, husky sound that sent blood flowing straight to his already heavy cock.

"Touché," she said, taking another sip of her drink.

God, he couldn't take his eyes off of her. The bar could've been on fire and he wouldn't have noticed. He wanted to fist his hands in all that blond hair and pull her close, taste her mouth, feel her skin against his and lose himself in her. But just for tonight.

It was all he could offer. All he had any right to want.

He watched her as she took another sip of her drink, trying to memorize the exact way her hair was falling over her shoulders, the precise shade of blue in her wide, bright eyes, the sound of her laugh.

"So why feathers?" Her fingers still trailed over his arm, sending little sparks of lust shooting through him.

Fuck. Nope. Not talking about that. Not with her, not tonight. He'd come here not to think about all of that shit. He'd come here to find a woman, or get drunk, or to start a fight. Colt knew that as long as he kept the demons fed, he wouldn't have to feel anything he didn't want to feel.

And there was a lot he didn't want to feel.

"You like it?" he asked, dodging the question. If she noticed, she didn't seem to mind.

"Mmm. I do." Her voice was beautiful, rich and sultry with a slight rasp to it, and he couldn't help wondering what she'd sound like moaning out his name. He was already imagining the feel of her fingers digging into his shoulders, her heels pressed into his ass as he sank himself deep inside her.

He forced himself to take a breath and a swallow of beer.

"You have any?" he asked, relieved she hadn't pressed him about the meaning behind his own ink.

She slipped out of her leather jacket, rolled up the sleeve of her denim shirt, and flipped her arm over. A swirled line of black stars decorated the inside of her right wrist. "And," she said and swept her hair up, showing him the Egyptian ankh on the back of her neck, just below her hairline. "I have a couple of others." She let her hair drop back around her shoulders, the blond waves fanning out around her.

His eyebrows rose. "Oh yeah? Where?"

She took one of his hands in hers and pressed it against her rib cage. Instinctively, his fingers flexed into her, and her eyes fluttered closed for a second. "Here." She felt warm and soft through the fabric of her shirt as he moved his hand down her side toward her hip in gentle strokes, still not quite able to believe that this wasn't a fantasy.

"Where else?" His eyes held hers. She slipped off the stool and stood between his legs, erasing all distance between them. She slid his hand up and around to her shoulder blade.

"Here." Her warm breath tickled his ear, and he clenched his jaw against the need to bury his face in her neck, right here at the bar. "What about you? Any others?"

With his free hand, he took one of hers, placing it over his heart. "Here."

Her long fingers curled into the cotton of his shirt, and heat crackled in the air around them. His stomach flipped, and if he was reading her right—and he would've bet a bottle of fifty-year-old scotch he was—she wanted him as much as he wanted her.

Damn, but he needed this. Needed the release. Needed the temporary oblivion of hot sex with a gorgeous woman. He didn't want to think. Not tonight. Hell, not most nights.

Time to test the waters.

He slid a hand up to her face and grazed his lips against hers, a tease of a kiss. She held stone still, her eyes fixed on his mouth, her lips slightly parted. All of the noise around him seemed to drop away, and in that moment, Taylor was all that existed for him. Well, her and the erection doing its damndest to bust free of his jeans.

He closed his mouth over hers and felt the vibration of her sigh against his lips. He fought back a groan when she slid her tongue against his, and heat exploded over his skin as he tasted her, drinking in the soft warmth of her mouth.

He couldn't remember the last time he'd been so aroused from just a kiss. His chest tightened, and as he deepened the kiss, he pressed down the cold, hard knot of fear eating at him. Already, he knew sticking to his one-night rule would suck big-time. She felt so good, so perfect, so fucking *right* kissing him, as her fingernails scraped lightly down his back.

She opened her mouth to him a little more, which he immediately took full advantage of, greedily claiming everything she offered him. He caressed her mouth with his tongue, and she moaned softly, her hips nestling snugly against his. He wove his fingers into her hair and crushed his mouth against hers as arousal and lust and need all sang through his veins. Lips and tongues melded together with increasing urgency, and the kiss seared through him. She rocked against him and bit gently at his lower lip.

Fuck, this was going to be good.

"Get a room, why don't ya?" The bartender chirped at them, and Taylor broke the kiss, pressing her forehead against his. For a second, he just stood there, trying to breathe.

She was pretty much a total stranger, and yet the intensity of that kiss had been off the charts. Hot, and bruising and so, so promising.

He swallowed, trying to find his voice. "Come home with me."

She nodded against his forehead, and his dick rejoiced.

* * *

From his little table in the corner, Ronnie adjusted his glasses as he watched Taylor walk out of the bar, her fingers laced with those of the brute who'd intruded on them earlier. He finished the rest of his Coke and slammed the empty glass down. Possessive anger coupled with an almost blinding jealousy churned through him. It'd been hard to watch that interaction, and now she was leaving with him? He'd been much happier watching her while she'd been alone, even if she'd looked sad.

He knew he shouldn't have gone over and talked to her, but he couldn't help himself. He'd been warned, but no one knew what they were talking about. They didn't see. They couldn't see. He loved her, and she loved him. Soon, everyone would know, and everyone who'd called him crazy and obsessed and delusional would fucking see.

Ever since he'd first heard her sing, he'd known he was listening to the future mother of his children.

He dropped a five on the table and pushed his way out of the bar, getting in his car just in time to follow Taylor. He had to. He couldn't let her go off alone with that brute, unprotected. And if she was going to betray him, he needed to know. He needed to see.

Because Taylor was his. Every part of her. Her gorgeous blond hair, those huge, blue eyes, the long, lean body. The incredible voice. The skilled hands. Her mind. Her soul. Her body.

She belonged to him.

# CHAPTER 2

Colt and Taylor stumbled into Colt's dark bedroom in a tangle of limbs, their mouths fused, their tongues playing. He knew he should turn a light on or, fuck, just stop kissing her long enough to get her onto the bed, but he didn't want to. Knowing that he only had tonight with her, he couldn't bring himself to break contact with her for even a second.

"You are so fucking sexy," he rasped against her mouth, nipping at her bottom lip as his heart pounded furiously against his ribs. In response, she made a melodic humming noise that went straight to his aching dick.

She wove her fingers through his hair and pulled his mouth hard against hers, her teeth scraping against his lips. He groaned and pulled her tight against him, still moving her toward the bed. He broke the kiss just long enough to yank his T-shirt up and over his head with one hand, then drop it to the floor and circle his arms around her waist.

Her fingernails scratched lightly down his back, and she leaned forward and licked a slow, hot path from his collarbone to his ear. She inhaled deeply before sighing. "Oh, hell yes." She pulled back slightly, her fingers tracing over the tattoo covering his left pec. "What's this one?" she asked, studying it, her palm sliding over his nipple.

"It's the Army Ranger shield and insignia."

Bringing his mouth back to hers, he walked her the last few feet to the bed as his fingers began working on the buttons of her denim shirt, amazed at his ability to slip them free. Amazed he had blood anywhere in his body besides his throbbing dick. She'd taken him from zero to sixty with just her mouth on his, slashing his brake lines in the process, and he didn't give a shit if he crashed. Her shirt fell open, and as the backs of her legs hit the foot of the bed, he knew it'd be worth it.

She turned and climbed onto the bed, rising up onto her knees as she pulled her shirt off and tossed it to the floor. The room was dim, the only light coming from the streetlamp outside his open window, but her eyes met and held his as she reached behind her and unclasped her bra. Her breasts spilled free, and he joined her on the bed, his mouth on hers again, his hands skating up over her ribs and palming the soft, heavy flesh of her breasts. His skin tingled at the delicious contact, and he trailed hot, open-mouthed kisses down her throat as his thumbs traced over her hardened nipples.

She moaned and tipped her head back, pressing into his touch. "Oh fuck, that feels good. Yes, Colt."

He smiled at the sound of his name on her lips, and the smile grew when her hands moved down over his chest and arms, tracing the contours of his pecs, his abs, his biceps, until she reached his pants. With sure fingers, she undid his belt buckle and popped open the top button of his jeans.

"Someone's excited," she said, rubbing her palm over the ridge of his cock through his jeans.

He cupped her cheek with one hand while tracing the other down, through her hair, over her shoulder, across her collarbone, dipping into the valley between her breasts. "Fuck, Taylor. Look at you. I'm about ready to die, here." He buried his face in her neck, kissing and nipping at the skin there. "I want to spend all night finding out exactly how to touch you, how to kiss you, how to get you to scream out my name. I want to tease you and taste you until you beg me for more. I want to fuck you until neither of us can move."

"You have a dirty mouth," she whispered, her teeth teasing against the shell of his ear, and he smiled against her skin, shaking his head slightly.

"Oh, sweetheart. You have no idea."

"Put your money where your mouth is and educate me."

He laughed and guided her down onto the mattress on her back. Still on his knees above her, he undid her jeans and began working the tight denim down her long, slender legs, stopping to yank her boots free and toss them over his shoulders. Once her jeans were on the floor, he pulled her panties down, too, adding them to the growing pile of clothing. She stretched her arms above her head, and at the sight of Taylor, naked and spread beneath him like a feast, he had to remind himself to breathe.

"Where should I put my mouth?" he asked, easing his weight down on top of her. "Here?" He closed his mouth over her nipple, sucking it into his mouth and swirling his tongue over and around it. Taylor let out a gasping moan that filled him with satisfaction. After tormenting her for a minute, he moved to the other nipple. "Or here?"

"Oh, shit," she moaned, arching her back off the mattress, her fingers digging into his shoulders. He bit at the swell of her breast and continued his downward path, tracing his

tongue down the center of her stomach and then kissing his
way over her hipbone until he was right between her thighs.
He paused for a second, deliberately teasing her.

Her head came up off the bed. "Colt? What are you—"

But she didn't finish her question, because he'd sat back
on his knees, put his hands on her calves and pushed her
legs back, her knees almost at her shoulders. "Is this where
I should put my mouth?" He bit one of her cute little butt
cheeks and then kissed her wet folds. "Here?"

"Oh God, please, yes."

"I told you I'd make you beg." He licked a slow path up
across her drenched pussy, and he was beyond satisfied at
how wet she was for him.

She made a sound that was half moan, half scream, and
he pressed her legs back a little bit farther, spreading her
open and swirling his tongue over her clit. Her legs trembled, and he tightened his grip on her.

"You taste so fucking good." He let out a low, approving
groan and began to move his mouth against her in earnest,
through with teasing. As he worked her slick flesh with his
lips and tongue, sucking and licking and kissing, he slid his
right hand down from her leg and eased two fingers into her,
curving them up.

"Holy shit, you're good at this."

He smiled against her as her hips shook, and he drank her
in, savoring every second of having Taylor's wet, hot flesh
beneath his mouth and around his fingers.

"You're gonna make me come." Her voice shook a little,
high and breathy.

He said nothing but kept up his steady rhythm, paying attention to the way she clenched around his pumping hand,
to the way her hips jerked and her breathing faltered. She
tensed, her entire body one long, slender, taut muscle, and

then she came. Hard. Her hands fisted in the sheets of his bed, her body shaking as she moaned out his name and a string of curse words. His cock jerked, pulsing and desperate to get in on the action.

He eased her legs back down and slipped off the bed, shucking his boots, jeans, and boxer briefs. He grabbed a condom from the bedside table, forcing himself to think about football, cars, beer—anything nonsexual—trying to cool down enough so he'd last more than thirty fucking seconds when he got inside her.

"Let me help you with that." Taylor was back on her knees, a gorgeous flush sweeping up from her breasts to her cheeks, and with a smile, he handed her the condom and joined her on the bed. He watched as with long, slender fingers, she tore open the wrapper and rolled the condom down his cock. She kissed him, a slow, deep, lingering kiss, and stroked him. Tension gathered at the base of his spine and low in his stomach, and his cock jumped in her hands.

God, he normally had so much more control than this. It was as though Taylor had found his one loose thread and was pulling it every time she touched him, every time she fucking looked at him. He was coming undone. Because of her. And he needed to regain control. Go slow.

With what he hoped was a playful smile, he gently pushed her down onto her back, grabbed her legs and spread her wide before him. He lined the head of his eager cock up with her slick entrance, reminding himself to breathe. Again.

"Oh God, Colt. I want you inside me."

The word *me* was still on her lips as he pushed into her, and she let out a long, low moan, hooking her legs around his hips. He let out a strained half growl. She was glorious around him, hot and wet and tight. He groaned and starting pumping his hips, not going slow like he'd planned, but fucking her hard and deep.

So much for regaining control.

He eased his weight down on top of her, wanting more of her mouth, more of her skin against his, more of her scent. Just more.

And it hit him. One night was never going to be enough.

He kissed her, and she pushed up onto her elbows, as though trying to get closer to him, moaning into his mouth. He stroked in and out of her in sure, steady thrusts, pleasure skating up his spine and spreading across his body.

"Fuck, yes," she breathed, wrapping her arms around him and pulling him down for another hot, bone-melting kiss. "You feel incredible." He buried his face in her neck, dragging his mouth across her skin. "Oh God, so good. Don't stop. Don't stop. So fucking good!" she cried out especially loudly, as he thrust deep and scraped his teeth over her earlobe. She tightened around his cock, and he knew she was building toward another orgasm. Supporting himself on one arm, he slipped his free hand between their bodies and circled his fingers over her clit. She ground up into his touch and he lowered his mouth to hers again.

She started to come, and he kissed her through her orgasm, swallowing the delicious sounds she made, his entire world narrowing to the feeling of Taylor's body. Around him. Under him. She trembled against him, and he broke the kiss, needing to see her as he continued to stroke in and out, thanking the universe that he hadn't come yet. A faint sheen of sweat shone on her skin in the dim light, and he pushed a lock of her silky hair away from her face, basking in her soft textures. She pressed her cheek into his palm, the light highlighting her delicate, feminine features, and something in his chest tightened.

He wanted to keep her. He knew he couldn't, but he wanted to.

She pushed up onto her elbows again and bit at his bicep. "I want to ride you." He pulled out, grateful for the chance to regain a little more control, and rolled onto his back.

If he lived to be a hundred, he would never, ever, experience anything hotter than the sight of Taylor Ross, sex flush glowing on her skin, blond hair all disheveled, climbing onto him and lowering herself onto his cock. She bent forward and kissed him as she started to move her hips, and his hands went to her ass, helping her.

"I love how you feel inside me," she said, her voice slightly ragged as she moved up and down. Something about that statement made him want to gather her in his arms and keep her there, protecting her and sheltering her, giving her everything he had.

Clearly he hadn't been getting laid enough lately, because one good fuck and he was turning into a freaking girl.

But this was a hell of a lot more than just a good fuck, wasn't it? Usually, when he brought a woman home, he didn't want her to stay the night. Didn't want to deal with stilted, awkward morning-after conversation. Didn't want to expose anyone to his nightmares or answer any questions about them. But Taylor? He was willing to risk it just to see her sleepy morning eyes, all unguarded and vulnerable.

She fell forward, her breasts pressed against his chest, her hips undulating as she continued to ride him, and he felt the beat of her heart against his. She kissed his neck, biting and then soothing the skin with a sweep of her tongue. He let out a deep groan and pumped his hips up to meet her as his orgasm barreled down on him. He thrust up one last time and his hands went to her hips, stilling her and holding her tight against him as he came, emptying himself into her. All of his

strength, all of his energy, flowed into her, and he was happy
to let her take it.

She lifted her head, and their eyes met in the semidark.
Neither of them spoke for several seconds, their bodies still
connected, their hearts beating against each other. Taylor
raised a hand and wiped a bead of sweat away from his forehead, trailing her fingers through his hair and then down
over his arm, tracing the edges of his tattoo.

"Wow," she whispered, and something flickered across
her face, just for a second, but it was gone so quick he wasn't
even sure he'd seen it in the first place.

\* \* \*

On the quiet, dark street, Ronnie sat in his car with the windows rolled down and his hand in his pants.

He'd followed the cab from Sunset Boulevard up into the
Hollywood Hills and had been surprised when it had pulled
to a stop in front of a small, tidy house in Laurel Canyon.
He'd expected the brute to live downtown somewhere, in a
grungy loft, not in a little house in the Hills. Some kind of
classic car sat parked in the driveway, but Ronnie didn't give
a shit about cars. Only motorcycles, and even that was an interest with a purpose.

The house was dark like the street, so although the curtains weren't drawn, Ronnie couldn't see inside the house.

But he could hear.

The second-floor windows were open, and Taylor's
voice—that gorgeous, husky, unmistakable voice—flowed
out into the night.

"Oh God, so good. Don't stop. Don't stop. So fucking
good!"

He closed his eyes as he stroked himself, imagining he

was the one pulling those noises from Taylor, he was the one making her moan, making her scream, making her writhe with pleasure.

And someday—soon—he would be.

He pumped his fist up and down, absorbing Taylor's moans like the earth absorbs the sun, letting them sink into him, letting them nourish him. Her cries built to a crescendo, and he stroked himself faster. He bit his tongue hard enough to draw blood, and as he imagined having Taylor's blood on his tongue, of owning her so completely, he spurted his release.

He slumped down in his seat, a pleasant, heavy-limbed relaxation flowing over him. He cleaned himself up with a tissue, put his penis back into his pants, zipped up, and closed his eyes. They flew open at the sound of a deep male groan.

The brute. Colt. That was the name Taylor had been calling out just a few moments ago. Visions of punishing Taylor for her behavior danced through his mind, and he smiled.

And if she ever saw the brute—Colt—again, he'd punish him, too. And then Ronnie would take what was his.

* * *

Taylor's eyes flew open, and she was relieved to see that it was still dark out. She made a point of never staying over, and hadn't meant to fall asleep, but after the marathon sex she'd had with Colt, she hadn't been able to keep her eyes open.

He'd made her come six times. Six orgasms. No wonder she'd fallen asleep.

She blinked and lifted her head from the pillow, glancing at the clock on his side of the bed, glowing red in the dark. 3:58 A.M. The soft, crimson light filtered over his face, highlighting his chiseled jaw and sculpted cheekbones. She settled back down to the pillow and inhaled deeply, her stomach swirling pleasantly. Colt's arm, flung limply over her waist, tightened, pulling her into him. She wanted to turn around, stick her nose in his neck and inhale. He smelled so good, and it wasn't because of his cologne, or soap or anything. It was his skin. The simple, warm, masculine smell of *him*.

Over the past few hours, she'd never felt more beautiful, more worshipped, more desirable in her life. But it was time to go. He'd provided one hell of a distraction, but it was time to slink back to reality. As gingerly as possible, she started to move his hand from her hip, but his fingers flexed into her, and she knew he was awake.

Shit.

She rolled to face him and kissed him softly on the mouth. "Thank you so much for an awesome night, but I should go."

His eyes flew open and his arms came around her, pulling her against him. "No. Stay." He rolled onto her and kissed her, his mouth hot and gentle against hers. Immediately, her legs were around his waist, and she was kissing him back. She couldn't help it. He made her feel so damn good. *He* felt so damn good.

He moved against her, his hard cock rubbing over her thigh, and she knew she should go, that she was treading a dangerous line with him. She already liked him far more than was safe, and she had enough problems on her plate without adding another broken heart to the pile. She was still dealing with the last one.

And she knew, without a doubt, that Colt was a man who could break her heart if she let him get close enough. She wasn't sure how she knew it, but she did. It was like a truth in a dream, an undisputed, unwavering fact. She just knew it, as surely as she knew her own name.

He slipped a hand down between them and gently circled his fingers over her clit. She moaned and he deepened his kiss. His mouth was incredible, no matter where on her body he used it.

Oh, hell. She was going to stay. At least until he fell asleep again. After all, this was her last chance to enjoy that beautiful, talented mouth. Because no matter what, she couldn't see him again after tonight. No way.

He sat up and pulled her with him, guiding her into his lap. Between hot, deep kisses he grabbed a condom from his bedside table—their fourth of the night—and rolled it on.

He cupped her face as he kissed her, the head of his cock nudging against her clit. "I want you to stay, Taylor." His eyes met hers, and she felt the weight of his words; she squashed down the fear they stirred in her. She couldn't give him what he wanted, but she could give him this, right now. Without a word, she lifted her hips and eased herself down onto his cock. Colt's head fell back against the headboard as he let out a low, deep moan, almost a growl.

A hundred things to say flickered through her mind, but she couldn't say any of them. Wouldn't allow herself to say any of them. They were too open, too honest, and she'd already given him more than she should've tonight. More than she had to give, really.

So this had to be good-bye.

A dull ache took root right in the center of her chest, and as she rocked against him, his thick cock filling and stretching her, she brought her mouth to his shoulder, kissing a path across his collarbones and up his neck, wanting to memorize the taste of his skin. Wanting to imprint the scent of his skin on hers. Her core tightened, lust and need roaring through her like a fire.

"You are so goddamn beautiful, Taylor." His deep voice rumbled over her, and he pushed her hair off her neck, twining the strands around his strong fingers. With a sighing groan, he pressed his mouth to her neck, his arms tightening around her. "So goddamn beautiful." He repeated the words, his voice vibrating against her skin. Taylor bit her lip and continued to move her hips despite the thickness gathering in her throat and the mild stinging in her eyes. Everything was coiling her into tight little knots: his scent, the incredible feeling of his body inside hers, his big hands moving up and down her back, the sighs and groans coming from his mouth. She wanted to capture it all so she could keep it, like a memory in a snow globe.

His mouth blazed a trail across her breasts, and then he pushed away from the headboard, moving her onto her back and coming down on top of her. Even though she was nearly the same height as him, with his strong, muscled body surrounding her like this, she was keenly aware of how much bigger he was than her. And yet she didn't feel threatened by the strength and size difference. No, she felt protected. Safe, and cherished. More whole than she'd felt in months.

He picked up his rhythm, stroking hard and deep into her, and she started to unravel, pleasure snapping through her as she came again. "Colt! God, yes!" Propping his weight on one arm, he laced the fingers of his free hand with hers beside her head. Her heels dug into his ass as a tear slipped free, streaking down over her temple and into her hair. She blinked furiously, trying to prevent the rest from falling. "Colt." She moaned out his name again, her voice cracking slightly. He buried himself to the hilt and came, his deep, growling groans making her want to crawl inside him. His forehead pressed to hers, he sighed out her name and then kissed her, his mouth hot and sweet against hers.

Another tear fell free.

She couldn't do this. Mind-blowing, out-of-this-world sex or not, coming home with him had been a mistake.

* * *

Colt stirred and reached for Taylor, wanting to feel her warm body against his. Slowly opening his eyes, he rolled from his back to his side. Early-morning sunshine streamed in through his bedroom window, and he blinked against the pinkish-orange light bathing his bed.

Taylor's side of the bed was empty, and he pushed up onto one elbow, listening for the patter of the shower, water running in the sink, footsteps elsewhere in the house. But the house was silent, the only sounds coming from outside. Birds chirping. The distant rush of traffic. Leaves rustling. A chill worked its way over his skin, and he glanced at the open window. Even though it was April, the temperature was still dipping into the fifties at night. He hadn't meant to leave it open. He sat all the way up and surveyed the clothes and condom wrappers littering the floor.

Taylor's clothes were gone. As was his Led Zeppelin T-shirt.

"Fuck." He'd broken his own rule, had asked her to stay, and she'd still bailed. Bailed, and stolen his favorite T-shirt, too. He rubbed his hands over his face, anger and bitter disappointment curling through him as he tried to convince himself that her disappearing act was for the best. She'd cracked something open inside him last night, something that needed to stay firmly closed. He began to climb out of bed, but then froze when it hit him.

He hadn't had a nightmare last night. Granted, he'd only slept a few hours, but for once, his sleep had been deep and peaceful. He hadn't woken up, sweaty and shaking, guilt eating at him like a bad hangover.

He climbed out of bed and pulled on a pair of sweatpants, making his way to the kitchen. He flicked on the coffeemaker and braced his hands on the counter, watching as the liquid began to drip into the coffeepot. Taking a deep breath, he hung his head.

He'd brought Taylor home so he could spend the night fucking a gorgeous woman and forget about his baggage. But sex, for once, had failed him as a coping mechanism. And he knew it wasn't because of the what, but the who. Yeah, they'd had (a lot of) sex, but last night had been about more than that.

He'd asked her to stay, and he hadn't had a nightmare, and that had to mean something. Now he just had to figure out what to do about it.

# CHAPTER 3

Taylor flexed her fingers around the leather-wrapped steering wheel of her 1970 Corvette Stingray, the late-morning sunshine gleaming off of the pristine cherry-red paint as she drove south down North Fairfax. She squinted against the light despite the black-and-gold aviator-style sunglasses she'd shoved onto her face earlier. Her stomach dipped and swirled before knotting itself into a tiny little ball as she passed the turnoff for Sunset Boulevard, home of the Rainbow.

*Colt.*

Even the thought of his name sent a dizzying mix of lust, fear, and regret spiraling through her, which was ridiculous. It had been one night, and she didn't even know his last name. She'd never see him again.

That thought was supposed to be reassuring. Somehow, it wasn't.

All she'd wanted was a fun, hot distraction, but Colt had been more than that. It had become clear pretty quickly that he wasn't just a gorgeous bad boy. No. He'd been smart, and funny, and easy to be with. And then there was the sex. Holy hell, but he'd been incredible. Her traitorous brain immediately conjured up the sensation of Colt's tongue stroking into her mouth as his lips moved expertly against hers, the feeling of his hands on her body, the intense sensation of his cock inside her. Last night, her nerve endings had come to life, and it had felt as though every cell in her body had been yearning toward him, like plants following the sun.

God. One night and he'd turned her into a fucking Hallmark cheeseball.

No. It was for the best that she'd never see him again. They'd had a connection, yes, but she couldn't explore it. She couldn't afford to keep giving pieces of her heart away. Soon, she'd have nothing left for herself, and she already felt so empty.

She stopped at a red light and drummed her fingers against the steering wheel. Jeremy had called a few hours ago, insisting they meet for lunch. She knew she couldn't ignore him anymore, and he'd said it was important. Feeling guilty about the hell she'd put him through with her reckless behavior the past few months, she'd agreed. He'd always had her back, but she could sense that his patience was wearing thin, and she couldn't blame him. She knew she needed to rein it in, settle down, and actually write some damn music.

Trying to party away the pain wasn't the best tactic. It wasn't healthy, and it wasn't mature, and it certainly wasn't sustainable. But when she was chasing a high, whether it was from alcohol, or sex, or whatever, her heart didn't hurt. She'd forget, just for a little while, that she'd stupidly given it to someone who hadn't wanted it.

Finally, after this last shattering of her heart, she'd woken up. Finally, she got it. "Happily ever after" wasn't an attainable reality for messy, imperfect people like her, and she needed to stop chasing it. If she could just find the right chords, the right words, she could channel all of the hurt, the anger, the loneliness, the feeling of never being fucking *enough* into one hell of an album. It was as though she were trying to reach home, and she could see it, but she was stuck where she was, and didn't know how to get there.

She changed radio stations, landing on KROQ, and her stomach did a small somersault at the familiar chord progression of "Miss Your Misery," one of her biggest hits, now jamming through the speakers. Even though she'd been in the music industry for ten years now, it was still a thrill to hear herself on the radio. She sang along, harmonizing with herself. Her voice reverberated in the small space of the car, and she was glad she hadn't put the top down. It felt good to belt one out, to hear herself really sing. She needed to get back into the studio, to pick up a guitar again and experiment. For the first time in weeks, months even, she found herself wanting to play.

As the song ended on a punchy C-minor chord, she pulled into the parking lot behind the restaurant, easing the nose of the Corvette forward into an empty space. The DJ's voice came on the air before the final chord had faded away.

"That was Taylor Ross, 'Miss Your Misery,' on K-Rock. Man, I love that song."

The cohost chimed in as Taylor put the car in Park and leaned back against the headrest. "Did you see that video of her on the plane? I mean, she's great, but that girl's a mess. And wasn't she supposed to have a new album last year?"

Taylor cut the ignition, silencing the radio, and the buzzing of her phone was extraloud in the now-silent car. The engine ticked, a slow, off-kilter rhythm as it began to cool down, and she fished her phone out of her purse. The text was from an unknown number.

I need to see you. It's Frank. Dad.

Her vision narrowed for a second as a small wave of dizziness rocked her. She stared at the text, reading it several times, trying to believe what she was seeing. Trying to wrap her mind around the idea that somehow he'd found her. The thought sent her heart racing, and she forced herself to take a deep breath. She debated whether or not she should even reply, but in the end, her curiosity won out. Her fingers trembled slightly as she typed out her response.

How the hell did you get this number?

Her father replied almost instantly:

I got friends, sweetheart. Can we meet up?

She snorted, shaking her head and narrowing her eyes as her fingers flew across the screen, anger pushing out some of her fear. She'd let him bully her far too many times in the past, and while his text sent fear rippling through her, she also felt a surge of resentment. Resentment that he'd have the balls to contact her after everything he'd done, and resentment at the fact that even though she was angry, her hands were still shaking.

Go fuck yourself.

Without waiting for him to reply, she blocked the number and made a mental note to change her own ASAP. She didn't know how her father had tracked down her number, and the idea that he even could sent a slight chill crawling over her skin.

Given that the last time she'd seen him in person he'd broken her jaw, she wasn't giving him shit.

Swallowing against the tightness in her chest, she stepped out of the car, locking it behind her and making her way toward the restaurant, ignoring the handful of paparazzi on the sidewalk just outside the doors, just as she had last night at the Rainbow. They called her name, trying to get her to look their way. Whirs and clicks followed her as she kept her head down, not engaging with them. Instead, she took a deep breath, sucking warm, spring air into her lungs. In the past, she might've obliged them, giving them a smile and a wave, but things were different now. They weren't interested in her because of her music, but because of the money they could make off her mistakes, and she didn't want to add any more kindling to that fire.

Stepping inside the safety of the restaurant, she slipped her sunglasses from her face and tucked them into her purse just as Jeremy caught her eye and waved, his immaculately tailored suit clinging to his lean frame. In his midforties, he was handsome in a very elegant, debonair kind of way. Combined with his perfectly coiffed dark brown hair and designer wingtips, his look didn't exactly scream "rock and roll." But what he lacked in sartorial edge, he made up for with his extensive music industry knowledge and impressive contact list. Jeremy Nichols was the guy who knew everybody, and Taylor was glad to have him in her corner. By the time she reached Jeremy's table, he was standing and holding out her chair for her.

"You look like shit." His cultured British accent softened the blow of his words, but only slightly. "Did you just do a walk of shame or something?"

She slid into her chair and leveled a look at him, not in the mood for Jeremy's usual dry teasing. He took his own seat and smiled at her, unaware that his words had dug in a little deeper than he'd intended.

"Three things," she said, holding up three fingers. "First, thanks a lot. You really know how to sweet-talk a girl. Second, none of your damn business. And third, why is it called the 'walk of shame'?" She made air quotes around the words. "I mean, really. It should be called the 'walk of victory'." She sat back in her seat, her arms crossed over her chest. She rubbed her thighs together under the table, remembering just how *victorious* she'd been with Colt last night.

"Well. All right then." He folded his hands on the table in front of him, his long fingers interlocking as his left eyebrow crept up in an unspoken question.

She pressed a hand to her temple and closed her eyes, exhaling slowly through her nose as guilt ate at her. "Sorry. I'm just…" She shook her head and cleared her throat, knowing she needed to get it together. She'd tried to use sex to forget about everything last night, and it had failed. Spectacularly. Because now, she somehow felt worse. "What did you want to see me about?"

"Ah." He took a sip of his water and refolded his hands in front of him. "I've recently had a meeting with Ernie Glick."

"Ernie Glick as in the CEO of Pacific Records?" Her heart sunk into her stomach, joining the swirling contents there. She didn't know what was coming, but based on the tense line of Jeremy's shoulders, she wouldn't like it.

He nodded and took another sip of water. "The label is worried about…well, about you."

"You get booted off one plane." She pushed her menu away, no longer hungry.

"It's not just the incident on the plane. It's…they're worried about you actually making this album and fulfilling the contract you signed." He shrugged. "You're a bit of a loose cannon right now, and if you don't give them some new songs within the next week, they're threatening to drop you."

She shook her head, her hair swishing around her face. "I know I've been a bit crazy lately, but come on, Jer. You know I've been trying. And this whole 'ticking clock, we're running out of time' thing isn't really helping my creative mojo."

"I know you've been trying. But they're not willing to take any more chances on you."

Her mouth went dry, and she took a sip of her water, trying to brace herself for the shit that was surely about to hit the fan. "So what, then?"

"They're concerned about…" He paused, clearly searching for the right word. "Well, a lot of things, really. So they're going to hire a bodyguard for you, to make sure there are no further incidents like the one on the plane. They want you focused on writing your album."

She shook her head again and dug her fingernails into her palm, anger radiating through her. "Let me get this straight," she said, dropping her voice and trying unsuccessfully to unclench her jaw. "Because I've been less than perfect lately, the label's going to hire a bodyguard to babysit me? To somehow save me from myself?" She sucked in a deep breath, her face hot, her fists clenched in her lap. She looked down for a second, trying to focus on her white knuckles so that she didn't start flipping tables. "Do you have any fucking idea how insulting that is? 'Oh, let's save the poor, helpless, dumb woman from herself. If only she had a big strong man around keeping her in line, all of her problems would just go away.' Fuck that. Would they do this to me if I were a guy?" She stared at Jeremy, one eyebrow arched in challenge.

He simply looked at her, unable to disagree with anything she'd said, which somehow only made her angrier. She snorted out a breath.

"Go back to Glick and tell him it's not necessary. I promise to behave. Scout's honor." She held up three fingers. "I don't need a bodyguard to write my album. That's fucking ridiculous."

Jeremy gave her a look laced with something that almost looked like pity. "It's too late. You've run out of chances to behave. They want someone in place as soon as possible. Whoever they hire will be keeping an eye on you 24/7."

Her eyes went wide as a fresh wave of anger flashed through her. Anger tinged with helplessness and humiliation. "Twenty-four/seven? What am I? A fucking prisoner?"

He pursed his lips. "The alternative was that they drop you today. Luckily, they want that album enough to give you one more shot, Taylor."

A helpless sense of defeat weighed her limbs down, and from the serious line of Jeremy's mouth, the set of his shoulders, she knew there was no way out of this. Not if she didn't want to lose her record deal and what was left of her music career in the process. She sighed, leaning forward on her elbows and dropping her head into her hands.

"You get that this is meant to help you, right? We're all concerned about you, and we only want you to succeed."

"Because it's not like you make money off of me or anything."

"Taylor."

She glanced up and her stomach lurched at the genuine worry etched into Jeremy's features. Softening with guilt, she nodded. "Whatever. I mean, even if I hate this, I'm pretty much stuck, right?"

He twisted his mouth to the side and shrugged, tilting his head. "Pretty much. But maybe this is a good thing. We all need a kick in the pants every once in a while. It's good for us."

"Right." She sighed again, her shoulders heaving, her leather jacket suddenly feeling way too heavy. "So when does my freedom end?"

"You needn't be so dramatic. Really, you'll barely know he's there. Because you'll be so busy writing and recording songs." He arched an eyebrow, giving her a pointed look.

"Of course." She managed to shoot him a smile, hating that she now had to pretend to be grateful for this when all she really wanted was to smash things. "Thanks for talking them into not dropping me."

"I work hard for my fifteen percent."

She pushed up from the table, and he frowned. "Aren't you going to eat?"

"Nah. I'm not hungry. Thanks again, Jer." She gave him a quick kiss on the cheek and made for the door. As she pushed outside, the sunlight felt too bright and she squinted, shoving her sunglasses onto her face. Scowling at the photographers' cameras, she stalked back to her car, ignoring the baiting comments they hurled at her, trying to get a reaction. But she'd given them enough over the past few months, and she wasn't going to feed the vultures anymore.

\* \* \*

Taylor eased her Corvette up to the gated entry in front of her, rolled down her window and pressed a finger to the large white button on the intercom. She tipped her head back against the headrest and drummed her fingers on the door of the car, her hand hanging out the window. Frowning, she pressed the buzzer again. Sierra should be home. They'd been best friends for over a decade, and Taylor knew Sierra's day-to-day routine by heart.

Just as she was about to roll up the window and head home, the intercom crackled to life. "Yeah?" Sierra Blake's voice came through the speaker, high and slightly breathless.

Taylor leaned out the window. "Hey. It's me. Let me into your gated kingdom."

"Hey. Sure." The intercom went quiet and the sturdy gate began rolling back, allowing her to navigate up the curving drive lined with concrete planters filled with colorful hollyhock and lilac plants. The brand new Mediterranean-style house rose up in front of her, its yellow stucco walls radiating warmth. She parked her car and walked up to the heavy oak door, knocking twice with the wrought-iron ring in the center of it.

The door opened and there stood Sierra, tiny and beautiful, her hair dripping wet. A tag stuck up from the neck of her T-shirt, emphasizing the fact that it was on backward. Without a word, Sierra spun on her heel, silently inviting Taylor to follow her into the house. The heels of Taylor's boots clicked on the dark hardwood floors and echoed in the spacious two-story entryway. They passed the living room and headed for the kitchen, their usual hangout spot. A framed poster for Sierra's movie *Bodies* hung in the hallway, but the rest of the walls were bare. Cardboard boxes, some open, some still sealed, lined the hallway. After losing her home in a fire last year, Sierra and her boyfriend, Sean, had rebuilt on the same land, and they had just moved into the newly constructed house last week.

"Sorry. I was in the shower. Were you out there long?" Sierra asked.

"Nah. Sorry to barge in, but it's been a weird couple of

days, and I…just…needed to talk to you." Taylor slipped out of her jacket and slid onto a padded black stool, folding her legs under the lip of the counter and leaning her elbows on the island in the center of the kitchen, the off-white granite cool against her skin.

Sierra pulled an elastic band from her wrist and twisted her long, golden-brown hair into a bun on top of her head. It was messy, lopsided and off center, which she somehow managed to make look adorable.

Sitting with Sierra in her kitchen that still smelled vaguely of paint and sawdust, warm sunlight bathing the white walls, the rest of the house quiet and peaceful, Taylor felt whole. Safe. Happy. Truth be told, her friendship with Sierra was probably the most important relationship in her life. Sierra was family of the best kind: The kind she'd chosen for herself. The kind who loved her. Who never told her she was useless, or unwanted, or a mistake.

Sierra put a bottle of water down on the island in front of Taylor and hopped up on the stool across from her. "Weird couple of days, huh? Weird how?"

Taylor shrugged, suddenly not wanting to talk about her problems. She didn't want to rehash the conversation with Jeremy, and the anger and embarrassment that had come with it. Normally, she told Sierra everything, but this…she wanted to keep it to herself.

Sean Owens strode into the kitchen, water dripping from his thick, dark brown hair and onto his T-shirt. "Hey, Taylor." He gave her shoulder an affectionate squeeze on his way to the fridge, scrubbing his free hand over his closely cropped beard.

"Hi, Sean. Thought you'd be at work."

The big bodyguard shrugged, his impressive muscles bunching visibly through his T-shirt. "Working from home today." As if the wet hair and Sierra's backward T-shirt weren't enough of an indication, Sean winked at Sierra before heading into the living room, several containers of food in his large hands.

Taylor arched an eyebrow and smirked. "Still christening the new house?" she asked, jumping on the opportunity to tease Sierra despite the ache in her chest.

Sierra bit her lip and flushed slightly.

"Yeah. I should go." Something small and dark clutched at her ribs whenever she watched Sierra and Sean together, and right now that something was making it hard to breathe. She didn't begrudge Sierra her happiness, not at all. But it hurt because it was a reminder of everything she could never have. Everything she'd realized she wanted, only to find out she wasn't worthy of it.

"No. Taylor, don't do that." Sierra laid a hand on her arm, squeezing gently. "Tell me why you came over."

Taylor shrugged. "Same shit, different day." She twisted the top off the water bottle and took a long sip. "I'm fine. Just in a weird mood, I guess."

Sierra paused, biting her lip and lowering her voice. "You haven't been fine since Zack."

Taylor wrapped her fingers around her bottle of water, needing something to hold on to. Zack. The relationship that had changed everything. That had sent her into her current tailspin. That had forced her to tear down and then rebuild the walls around her heart, stronger than ever. She just shrugged, not really sure what to say. It seemed unfair to constantly dump her problems on Sierra. And yet Taylor knew that part of the reason she was holding back was because she wasn't sure what Sierra could even say. Sierra, who had her life together, with a great career, an amazing boyfriend, and a loving family.

Without a word, Sierra hopped down from her stool and wrapped her arms around Taylor. "I'm sorry you're so unhappy, babe. I'm sorry about Zack. I'm sorry you're lonely. I'm sorry for all the shit you've had to deal with."

To her horror, Taylor felt tears sting the corners of her eyes, and she blinked rapidly, trying to dispel them. God, she was lonely, but there was nothing she could do about it because she'd learned the hard way that it was much better to be on her own. Safer, and easier, and far less damaging. Because not being alone meant having to trust someone else—trust that they wouldn't hurt her, or leave her, or use her, or lie to her, or any combination of the above.

Trust, she'd learned, only opened the door to misery and heartbreak and betrayal. Trust was for suckers.

She'd let herself trust and fall too many times in the past. She didn't have the strength to keep doing it. To keep leaping off bridges only to find that the river below was frozen over, and when she fell, she ended up cold, broken, and alone.

Every. Damn. Time.

"I should go. I'm crashing your time with Sean."

"No, stay. I don't want you to leave like this. Hang out, just for a bit?"

"You don't have to leave on my account," said Sean, returning to the kitchen with the now-empty food containers. At six-five and well over two hundred pounds of impressive muscle, it was no surprise that he seemed to eat constantly. "I was gonna go out for a while, anyway. Hit the gym, check in at the office. But even if I weren't leaving, you know you're always welcome here, Taylor." He pressed a quick kiss to her cheek as he left the kitchen, and something warmed inside her. She really did love Sean. He was like this sweet, protective, older brother.

Once, she'd imagined that she could end up with a man like Sean. Strong, and smart, and kind. Gorgeous, and funny, and who made you feel safe and loved, every single day.

Once. She wouldn't make that mistake again.

# CHAPTER 4

Colt raised the shot glass to his lips and threw it back, swallowing the tequila and savoring the warm path it cut through his chest. He leaned back in his chair, the weathered wood and cracked red vinyl under his ass creaking against his weight. Guns N' Roses thumped through the speakers and vibrated against the scarred, wood-paneled walls, which were covered in a motley combination of neon liquor signs, sports memorabilia, and a few old Hollywood pictures in dusty frames. A jukebox glowed in the corner, fluorescent pink and blue, but a layer of grime dimmed its brightness. He rolled his shoulders and stretched his neck, waiting for the tequila to kick in and take the edge off his restlessness.

"Would you relax?" Roman Kekoa leaned his tattooed forearms on the table and angled his body toward Colt.

"What?" Colt eyed the big Hawaiian. And Roman wasn't fat big. No, Roman was more the "kick the shit out of you, make women drool" kind of big.

"You're glaring at that shot glass like it stole your car." Roman smiled darkly, his white teeth flashing against his dark beard and whiskey-hued skin.

Colt scrubbed a hand over his face. "Sorry." But he knew he was still glaring, could feel the tension stretching across his forehead and radiating down into his jaw.

"Fuck, man. I need to get laid tonight, and you keep looking like that, you're going to scare all the pretty ones away."

He nodded at Roman and chased his shot down with a swallow of beer.

Roman raised his eyebrows. "More tequila?" It was a question, but he was already standing, looking in the direction of the bar.

"Yeah. Sounds good."

As Roman made his way to the bar, Colt glanced around Frisky's—his favorite dive, even if it did share a name with cat food. No celebrities, and barely any tourists. Just good music, cheap drinks, and lots of locals. Cute ones, usually. Like the two brunettes, a blonde and a redhead at the booth in the corner. He caught the redhead's eye and smiled, tilting his chin at her slightly.

"She's hot." Roman set down a tray with a couple of shots and two more bottles of beer on the table as the redhead nudged the blonde beside her, who looked up and immediately started eyefucking Roman.

Colt picked up a shot glass and downed the tequila, no salt, no lime, closing his eyes briefly against the burn. As usual, turning off his brain was the main goal tonight, and right about now, drinking himself into oblivion felt like a damn good idea, seeing as how sex had completely failed him in that regard last night.

He nodded and leaned back in his chair, his beer bottle dangling from one hand. "Pretty cute."

Roman tossed his own shot back and set the empty glass down on the table with a loud clack. "Hell, yeah." He picked up his own beer and tapped it against Colt's. "Cheers, partner."

Colt smiled and tipped his bottle to his lips. He and Roman, both freelance bodyguards, had been working together for over a year now. While Roman had always been freelance, it was a fairly new world for Colt. He'd had a job as a bodyguard at one of the best security firms in California, and he'd managed to get his ass fired, naturally. He had a tendency to ruin anything good that came into his life—people, jobs, you name it. Getting fired from Virtus Security meant that no one else would touch him, and he'd been forced to strike out on his own. Working in the field, protecting people, implementing security plans—it was the only thing he was good at. But if he were honest, most days he missed working for a firm. He missed the job security, and he missed being part of a team. But he'd fucked it up, and he had to live with that. He'd misread a situation, had made a bad call, and because of Colt's mistake his boss, Sean Owens, had ended up injured. In the months following his firing, he'd tried several times to get his job back, but considering his mistake had almost led to Owens losing an eye, he hadn't been surprised when he wasn't given another chance.

Sometimes, he and Roman worked a job together if it called for two guys, and other times they each worked alone. Occasionally, they'd toss work to each other, depending on schedules and skill sets. Roman preferred the more laid-back gigs, while Colt liked the higher-risk stuff. They complimented each other well, and for the most part the partnership was working out.

He still missed the guys, though. Being part of a team.

Roman licked his lips and leaned forward again, his eyes flicking between the table of pretty women and Colt. "You give any more thought to what Lacey said?"

Colt set his beer bottle back down on the table, spinning it between his thumb and forefinger, and he shook his head.

"No. That door's closed for me. If Lacey wants to reconnect with Mom, that's her call, but I'm out. She's upset about it though, so of course, I feel like an asshole." He clenched his jaw and stared at his beer bottle.

"I'm sorry, man. Rough."

"Yeah." Colt's chest tightened as he thought of his sister and what she wanted to do: reconnect with their alcoholic mess of a mother, who'd blamed Colt every time a man left her. He'd simply been trying to protect his mom and his sister from creep after creep, but his mom hadn't wanted his protection. When he was seventeen, she'd kicked Colt out of the house after he'd put the biggest of the creeps in the hospital for trying to sexually assault Lacey, who'd been fifteen at the time. He was lucky he hadn't been charged, but at the time, he hadn't cared. All he cared about was protecting his sister and getting her the hell out of there. So they'd both left. Colt had dropped out of high school and gotten a job at a garage, finishing his diploma by correspondence. He'd waited for Lacey to finish high school, and then he'd enlisted in the United States Army. It had been the perfect solution for him. He could serve his country, protect others, get the fuck out of Los Angeles, and make a little money while doing it. Enough money to ensure Lacey had options.

And it had worked out, for the most part. He'd served his country for twelve years, and he never regretted enlisting. He'd helped Lacey through college, and now she was married with two young sons. The nightmares, the guilt, the knowledge that he'd come back from each deployment to the Sandpit a little more broken, a little more fucked-up, was worth it. For Lacey. For his country. To help and protect others.

Why she'd want to try and reconnect with their mother was beyond him, but he knew he couldn't stop her if she'd set her mind to it. He watched Roman ogle the blonde some more and swallowed against the hard knot in his chest.

"You ever get sick of it?"

"Of what?" asked Roman, taking a sip of his beer and not taking his eyes away from the blonde.

"All the different women. The lack of anything permanent. Don't you ever just want to find...I don't know. That one woman who makes you want to stop looking? Stop fucking around?"

Roman turned his head slowly from the blonde, his eyebrows raised. "Uh...no." He frowned. "God. One woman? Forever? I don't even want to think about how boring that would be." Roman shuddered before tipping his beer bottle to his lips.

"I don't know. With the right woman, I don't think it would be boring." Taylor sure as fuck hadn't been boring.

Roman looked at him, holding perfectly still. "I don't know if you're drunk or not drunk enough. Either way, you're talking crazy. How could you ever be satisfied with one woman? Why would you want to shackle yourself that way?"

"I'm not saying I want to. I'm saying with the right one, maybe it would all make sense." Meeting Roman's skeptical gaze, he waved a hand, brushing the topic away. "Never mind." It didn't matter. There was no right woman for him. Not in any kind of long-term sense. He would never do that to someone else. Would never expect a woman—especially one that he loved—to put up with him and his metric ton of baggage. Never ask her to. He just wouldn't. It didn't matter if he *wanted* a future with someone. A family. He couldn't have it. He couldn't have a family *and* protect those he loved, because there was only one way to protect people from himself.

Stay the fuck away.

And to numb the pain of wanting but not having, he used sex, drinking, and occasional bouts of cathartic violence. Yep. Super healthy. What woman wouldn't want that?

Roman ran a hand through his long hair, twisting it into a knot at the base of his skull before letting it fall around his shoulders. "So listen, I might have a job for us."

"Oh yeah? What is it?"

"You know I've worked with a few different clients from Pacific Records before, right?"

Colt nodded, picking at the label on his beer bottle. "Yeah."

"They called me this morning. They need two guys to start right away. Like, tomorrow. You in?"

Fuck, a job was just the distraction he needed to stop thinking about Taylor. "Yeah, I think so. Who's the client?" He raised his beer bottle to his lips.

"Taylor Ross."

Colt began choking on the mouthful of beer he'd just swallowed, coughing and sputtering as he hastily set the bottle down.

Roman stared at him, one eyebrow raised. "There a problem?"

Colt thumped himself on the chest, still coughing as he tried to pull air into his lungs. "Fuck. Wrong pipe," he managed to wheeze out. He wiped a hand over his watering eyes and kept coughing until his airway cleared. His throat burned as his lungs filled with air. Meanwhile, his brain, heart, and dick were engaged in a three-way battle over whether or not to take the job.

Swallowing with effort, he stared at Roman, trying to figure out if he somehow knew who'd been in Colt's bed last night and was playing a joke on him. Roman just stared right back, one eyebrow still raised.

If Roman wasn't playing a joke on him, maybe the universe was. He knew, given the way he'd responded to her, that he probably shouldn't see Taylor again. One night with her, and he'd started wanting things—with her, from her—that he had no right to want. Not to mention that she'd bailed before he'd even woken up.

And yet he had a hard time believing she'd been running *from* him, given that she'd stolen his T-shirt. He smiled, letting himself imagine—just for a second—Taylor wearing it, smelling it, sleeping in it. She'd taken it for a reason, and while he knew he should let it go, his mind kept circling back to the T-shirt.

Matter of fact, he wouldn't mind asking for that T-shirt back.

And this wouldn't just be seeing her again. It'd be spending hours and hours with her every single day. It would be protecting her. For a brief second, he contemplated not taking the job and leaving her protection up to someone else.

Yeah. Fuck that. Not gonna happen.

At the idea of protecting Taylor, of keeping her safe from anything and everything, his skin tightened, a possessive, excited energy vibrating through him. Heart and dick won out over brain, and he nodded. "Yeah. Let's take it."

Roman stared at him for another second before nodding slowly. "Great. It should be a pretty straightforward gig. I already did a preliminary background check, and there were no red flags. The way the guy from the label put it, we just need to make sure she stays out of trouble, and that trouble stays away from her while she works on her album."

"Sounds good." He rubbed a hand over his chest, an ache spreading like gnarled roots over his sternum. Whether it was a warning or anticipation, he had no fucking clue. For a brief second, he debated whether or not to tell Roman about his recent history with Taylor, but before he could make up his mind either way, Roman bit out a curse.

Colt followed Roman's gaze, tracking the movements of a pair of tatted-up bikers moving in their direction.

His muscles tensed, and Colt glanced at Roman. "What did you do?"

Before Roman could answer, the bikers were at their table, one of them leaning down, his hands splayed on the wood, his long, curly blond hair falling forward. "You must be Kekoa."

Roman pushed to his feet, pulling his shoulders back and standing to his full six-four height. Colt stood, too, his arms crossed in front of his chest. Excitement crackled over his skin. If these guys were angling for a fight, they'd come to the right table.

"I am." Roman met the blond dude's eyes, staring him down from a vantage point several inches above him.

He didn't seem deterred. "You fucked my girlfriend."

Colt quickly weighed the pros and cons of reaching for his beer, but decided against it, standing stock still next to Roman, who was a fucking idiot who couldn't keep his dick in his pants to save his life, but was a loyal friend. Colt couldn't even count the number of times Roman had had his back. No way would Colt bail on him now.

"Oh, yeah? Who's that?" Roman crossed his arms in front of his chest, a cocky smirk on his lips.

Tension coiled through Colt's muscles and a familiar tingle of anticipation worked its way down his spine.

"Lucy Han."

Roman frowned and looked up at the ceiling for a second before his eyes widened slightly and he smiled. "Oh, yeah. I remember her. Funny, she never mentioned you." Roman took a step toward him. "Then again, her mouth was otherwise occupied."

Colt's eyes darted between Roman and the Vince Neil wannabe, who lunged forward and shoved Roman hard. Roman kept his balance but stepped back into the table, tipping over a beer bottle and sending it crashing to the floor. Every head in the place swiveled in their direction.

Before he could right himself, the blond biker was already taking a swing at Roman. Colt locked eyes with the guy standing in front of him, tall and bald and built like Mr. Clean, and the second he made a move to jump on Roman—who was already making the jealous boyfriend sorry for picking a fight—Colt took a swing with his right fist, connecting with the guy's jaw, and quickly followed it up with a second punch, his knuckles cracking against cheekbone. He shoved him into his buddy, sending them both off balance and giving Roman a chance to get his knee into the blond guy's stomach. Colt's blood pumped hot and fast through his veins, and he felt alive. Alive and worth something.

Wiping blood from his mouth with his thumb, Baldy lunged for him, and Colt took another swing but missed this time. He swung again, only to have his punch blocked. Baldy shoved him and used the bit of space between them to connect his fist with Colt's face. Pain shot across his cheekbone and then exploded against his nose as Baldy landed a second punch. Blood trickled into Colt's mouth as adrenaline surged through him, numbing the pain. Numbing everything. Out of the corner of his eye, he saw Roman slam his biker into the table, a grim smile on his face. The bar's bouncers were now swarming toward them, and Colt seized the opportunity to crunch his fist against Mr. Clean's nose, landing one final punch.

"That's enough!" roared the head bouncer, a vein throbbing ominously on his forehead as the others surged forward to separate Colt, Roman, and the bikers. "Get the hell out, all of you, before I call the cops."

Colt held his hands up in front of his chest, fingers pointing to the ceiling in a placating gesture. "We're leaving, Donny. For the record, we didn't start it."

"Sure as fuck finished it, though," said Roman, his split upper lip his only injury. With blood trickling from noses, lips, and other cuts, the two bikers were in much worse shape.

Colt started to smile, but it quickly turned into a wince. Raising his fingers to his cheek, they came away smeared with blood. Already, he could feel his eye swelling.

He reached into his pocket for his wallet, tossed a few bills down on the table, and clapped Roman on the shoulder. "Let's go."

His heart still beat furiously against his ribs, the high from the fight giving everything a euphoric tint. The physical release, the satisfaction of having his friend's back, the pride at holding his own and taking a few punches, all of it swirled together inside him, cresting in a wave he was more than happy to ride. Right before they reached the door, Roman spun around, facing the bikers who were being restrained by the bouncers.

"You see Lucy, you tell her to give me a call. Now that she's had a taste of a real man, I doubt she'll want anything to do with you." Shooting them a cocky grin, he pushed the door open and Colt followed him outside, ready to spend the rest of the night savoring this high.

And tomorrow he'd see Taylor again.

# CHAPTER 5

Taylor turned her Corvette into the parking lot of what she affectionately referred to as the Sanctuary. It was an old church on the edge of the trendy Silver Lake neighborhood that she'd bought a few years ago. She'd spent months renovating it, turning it into exactly what she wanted. The high ceilings were fitted with sound panels in between the exposed wood beams, and large windows filled the space with natural light. The hardwood floors were draped with Oriental rugs, and comfy, broken-in leather furniture, all in shades of brown and tan, was spaced throughout. Stocked with top-end gear, including her ever-growing collection of guitars, it was definitely one of her happy places. Usually. When the specter of unwritten songs wasn't following her around.

She hadn't actually been to the space in months, too afraid to face the physical representation of everything she used to be able to do—sing, jam, perform, write—while in the biggest writing funk of her career. But this morning, she'd woken up with chords running through her head for the first time in ages. Chords and lyrics, too, and so she'd called Jeremy to let him know she'd be spending the day actually working on music. He'd been overjoyed.

He'd also told her that her new shadows had been hired, two freelance bodyguards. The first one on duty would be meeting her at the Sanctuary, and then he and his partner would trade off, keeping tabs on her round the clock. They'd be in her space—the Sanctuary, her house—babysitting her.

She blew out an angry breath and rolled her shoulders, trying to work out some of the tension gathered there. Fine. Whatever. She'd just ignore them and do her thing. They could treat her like a prisoner, but she would try to focus on the music, on trying to find the joy in creating something. Of pulling sounds from her brain and translating them into music with her hands on a guitar or a piano, and her voice. When the writing went well, there was a high that came with it, a creative buzz that only seemed to feed more creativity. But when it wasn't? Her brain didn't know what to do with itself.

She put the car in Park and switched off the ignition, gathering up her purse and iPad before making her way toward the solid oak double doors at the front of the Sanctuary. She paused midstep, let out a low whistle, and made a beeline for the car parked on the other side of the small lot. If she wasn't mistaken, the car drawing her like a bee to a flower was a 1968 Dodge Charger in beautiful condition. Shiny and black, it sat gleaming in the sun, calling to her like a beacon. Unable to resist, she ducked down and peered inside, trying not to drool over the custom leather interior and the upgraded chrome finishes shining in the morning light. The Charger's interior was pristine, the only disturbance an empty water bottle on the passenger seat. She walked around the car in a slow, appreciative circle. God, would she love to wrap her hands around that steering wheel.

Then she stood up straight when she realized that it must be the bodyguard's car. It didn't belong to any of the studio's staff or musicians, whose cars were parked throughout the lot, and she could see Jeremy's Bentley SUV parked several spaces away. So unless someone had illegally parked on private property, process of elimination pointed to him. And she had a feeling that whoever drove this car would never risk parking it illegally.

"Huh," she said out loud, tearing herself away from the car and heading into the studio, a rush of cool, quiet air greeting her, and it hit her just how much she'd missed this place. Maybe avoiding it during her dry spell had been a mistake, because as she pulled the scent of it into her, she was suddenly eager to have a guitar in her hands. She pulled her sunglasses off and dropped them into her purse. Her black boots clicked against the floor as she entered the main rehearsal space, and a tension she'd been carrying for months now began to lift.

"Taylor?" Jeremy poked his head around the corner, a relieved smile turning up the corners of his lips.

"What? You thought I wouldn't come?" She quirked her mouth up in a teasing smile.

"It crossed my mind, yes. Can't imagine why."

Rolling her eyes, she strode forward into the large, open space and dropped her purse on one of the leather couches, peeled off her jacket and tossed it down beside her bag. Reaching over the couch to the guitar rack nestled against its back, she pulled out her Gibson Western Classic, a large acoustic guitar that she loved for its rich, full sound. She hadn't held it in months, and the feel of the polished wood against her fingers was like coming home. Something inside her was waking up after a long hibernation. Finally.

She turned, and her heart dropped into her stomach at

the sight of Colt, sitting on a stool at the back and chatting
with Mike, her studio manager. Totally relaxed and at home.
Drinking a cup of fucking coffee. Looking sexy as hell.

Looking as if he had every right to be here.

"Taylor, this is Colt Priestley." Jeremy waved a hand in
Colt's direction, who stood from his perch on the stool and
strode toward her. A flash of metal at his hip caught her
attention, a holster peeking out from under the hem of his T-
shirt.

Oh God. Colt was a bodyguard. He was *her* bodyguard.
Everything clicked into place—his protectiveness at the bar
the other night, the military tattoo she'd seen in the dark, the
scars she'd noticed on his body, but hadn't asked him about.

*No. No, no, no.* She couldn't do this.

A dizzying swirl of emotions crashed into her, and for a
second, she forgot how to breathe. Anger, fear, disappointment, lust, and anxiety all wove together into a fucked-up
tapestry, wrapping her in its unwelcome fabric. She suddenly felt cold, despite the trickle of sweat working its way
between her breasts at the sight of him. Glancing over her
shoulder at the door, she wondered what they'd all do if she
bolted, just got in the Corvette and drove away. But instead,
she stood where she was, pinned by the weight of it all.

"What the fuck?" She didn't realize she'd spoken the
words out loud until Jeremy shot her a puzzled glance. Her
skin tingled uncomfortably, a cold wave of dread crashing
into her. She recovered quickly as Colt's eyes met hers.

He wore beat-up jeans and a gray Henley shirt, his
sleeves pushed up around his elbows, leaving a swath of
those tantalizing feathers exposed. His jeans emphasized his
muscled thighs, and suddenly she was looking at his pack-
age and remembering how freaking fantastic he'd felt inside
her.

She snapped her eyes back up, and the confusing turmoil of emotions continued to churn through her, disorienting her. She hadn't wanted to see him again, and now here he stood, staring at her with those gorgeous green eyes, and she knew she was in trouble. Because even though she'd had the sense to run after the intensity they'd shared, she still wanted him. Wanted his mouth on hers, his big hands on her hips, and everything that came after.

He rubbed a hand over the back of his neck and she noticed his knuckles, bruised and scraped. Her eyes darted back to his face, and she saw the black eye and the cut across his cheekbone that she'd been too stunned to notice at first. The obvious signs that he'd been in a fight sent another completely unwelcome ripple of arousal pulsing through her. He looked so damn sexy all scuffed up. She wanted to reach out and skim her fingers over the cut on his cheek, but instead, she curled her fingers into her palms, trying to shrink into herself and away from him. She wanted very much to pick up right where they'd left off, and that simply couldn't happen. For her own sake, she had to fight this pull she felt toward him.

Her breath caught in her throat as she remembered the intensity in his green eyes as he'd asked her to come home with him. Being with Colt had been so much more than a simple distraction, and she knew that he'd consume her if she let him. Consume her like fire, and considering she was already ashes, she couldn't let that happen.

She paused for a second, wondering why the hell she was so convinced that he'd hurt her if she gave him the chance. And then it hit her.

It was because he seemed too good to be true, and so had Zack. Colt was hot as hell, funny, kind, tough, and amazing in bed. But thanks to that experience with Zack, now she knew that if something seemed too good to be true, she needed to run.

She met his eyes again, and she felt pinned in place, naked and exposed. She opened her mouth, but then promptly closed it. What the hell was she supposed to say to him? Nice to see you again? *Shit*.

So instead, she caught Jeremy's eye and cocked her head toward the door that led to the small office. She fought against the urge to keep staring at Colt, to keep drinking him in with her thirsty eyes.

"Can I talk to you?" she asked. Without waiting for Jeremy to respond, she grabbed him by the elbow, strode to the office and flung the door open, hoping no one would notice the slight tremble in her fingers.

"What?" he asked, leaning back against the desk, a puzzled look on his face.

"This isn't going to work out." She bit her lip and looked down at the floor.

"Why on earth not? You haven't even spoken to him. Don't you think you're judging awfully fast?"

She resisted the urge to scuff her foot against the floor as hot tears pooled in her eyes. She let out a panicked laugh, and anger began to push out the initial shock at seeing Colt again. She clung to that anger, feeding off of it, letting it strengthen her.

"Because I don't need a bodyguard. This is ridiculous. I'm exactly where I said I was going to be today, aren't I? Give me one more chance, and I promise I won't let you down."

He laid a hand on her shoulder. "He's here to stay. I'm sorry you don't like it, but he and his partner have been contracted by the label. It's done. There's nothing I can do." Jeremy arched an eyebrow, waiting for her to respond.

Not keen to share her one-night stand with Colt and further emphasize her recent track record of less-than-stellar behavior, she simply shook her head.

"Good. I have to go; I have a meeting. Play nice."

She closed her eyes and took a breath, pulling herself together. She could do this. Somehow, she'd find a way to cope being around him. She'd focus on her music. She'd ignore him. She'd pretend that night had never happened.

And then, like a bolt of lightning, an idea charged through her, hot and searing. She could drive him to quit. Push him away and make him regret ever signing up for this job. She'd kill two birds with one stone: she'd protect herself, and get rid of the studio's insulting bodyguard in one fell swoop. She'd keep her heart to herself and channel her anger. It was win-win.

She took another deep breath, walked back into the studio's main area and picked her guitar back up. She sank down onto one of the leather sofas and began fiddling with the tuning keys.

"Hey. Are you okay?" It was the first time Colt had spoken to her.

Unable to help herself, her head snapped up, and she asked the question that had been spinning through her mind for several minutes now. "Is this some kind of joke? Had you already taken this job before we...the other night?"

His eyes widened for a second, and then he shook his head slowly, watching her with a wariness that hadn't been there before. "No. I didn't. I wouldn't have kept this from you. I learned about the job after." He sat down on the sofa opposite her. "And I took it because I wanted to see you again."

Her stupid, traitorous heart fluttered in her chest at his words, but she stomped down the flutters, still clinging to that anger. To the idea that he couldn't be here. "Well I didn't want to see you." Her mouth moved before she could stop it, and at the fleeting flash of pain in his eyes, she wished she could call the words back.

He cleared his throat and leaned forward, his forearms braced on his thighs, his green eyes flashing with an undercurrent of danger. "That why you stole my T-shirt? Because what happened meant nothing to you?"

"I just really like Led Zeppelin," she said, struggling to keep her tone flat and her face neutral.

Colt rubbed a hand over his mouth—a mouth that she knew could make her moan, could make her wet, could make her ache with need—and exhaled loudly. "Why are you being like this? I thought we…"

"We what?" She blinked at him. "It was one night, Colt. That's all." She paused for a second. "Did you take this job thinking you'd get another chance to…" She swallowed, struggling to maintain focus with all of the tiny, fleeting thoughts flickering through her brain, each one bouncing up against the other, but nothing joining together to make a cohesive picture.

He closed his eyes for a second. "Of course not. I'm here to help you."

She didn't say anything, unable to make her mouth work, and just kept fiddling with the tuner keys, needing something to do with her hands, otherwise she'd grab him and kiss him, and completely ruin the progress she'd already made at shoving some distance between them.

He sat back on the couch, and she tried not to pay attention to the way his forearms flexed when he crossed his arms, or to the way his low voice sent dangerous ripples of lust chasing one another over her skin. Tried to ignore the way his face attracted her eyes like a magnet. She'd only seen him in dim light the night before, and she hadn't noticed the faint dusting of freckles across his nose. Paired with the slight scruff highlighting his perfectly formed jaw, he looked rugged and sexy, with the tiniest hint of pretty. With his wide shoulders, strong arms and sturdy frame (not to mention the black eye and the tattoo), he didn't look like someone you'd want to mess with.

He was strong, and sturdy, and completely off-limits.

* * *

"Taylor," Colt started again, trying to figure out what the hell was going on. He'd known just showing up was a risk, but he hadn't expected her to react like this. She didn't look at him when he said her name, just propped the guitar on her knee and started playing easy, slow scales, gradually speeding up. She didn't watch her hands as she plucked gracefully at the strings.

"Hey, hand me that capo."

"What?" He frowned. Those were *not* the words he'd been expecting to come out of that pretty mouth.

"That black thing on the table. Toss it."

Doing as he was told, he picked up the small black clamp and lobbed it to her. She caught it easily in one hand. He watched with a mixture of curiosity and lust as she shoved her guitar pick between her lips and began fastening the capo over the guitar's neck, securing it behind the second fret. She swung the guitar back down over her knee and began strumming the opening riff of "Smoke on the Water." Strumming her gleaming acoustic guitar and ignoring him. Trying and almost succeeding at looking as though seeing him meant nothing to her. Her eyes darted up and caught his, and there was a guardedness that hadn't been there the night before.

The certainty that someone had hurt her—badly—settled

over him like a blanket. He studied her intently. He could see
the tension coiled her shoulders, the stiff tilt of her neck.

She chewed on her lip as she strummed, and he clenched
his jaw at the intense urge to trace his tongue over the in-
dents left by her teeth, to soothe the bite before maybe
replacing those marks with some of his own. He stirred in
his jeans at the thought and clenched his jaw even harder, his
back molars squeaking under the pressure.

For whatever reason, she was throwing up walls around
herself, trying to keep him out. And if that was what she
wanted to do—what she *needed* to do, for whatever reason—he'd let her. But he also wasn't going anywhere. He
knew, without a doubt, that he'd done the right thing taking
this job. He'd been carrying around an uneasiness since he'd
woken up alone, her side of the bed cold, and it had only
lifted when he'd set eyes on her again. So she could keep
him out, but meanwhile, he'd keep her safe.

Long moments went by and she just kept strumming. Not
looking at him. Not talking to him. Not giving him anything.
She sighed and her shoulders slumped a little. Finally, she
spoke. "So. Just how short is my leash?"

"Your leash?"

She set the guitar down beside her. "How does this work?
What are the rules?"

"Pretty simple, really. Your label's hired me and Roman—
who you'll meet later—to be your bodyguards, so wherever
you go, so do we. I'm sure you've had a bodyguard before."

"Uh huh. And how is this 24/7 thing going to work?
You'll be in my house?" She pushed up off the couch and
walked to the stainless-steel fridge near the office door.
Reaching inside, she pulled out two bottles of water. Striding
toward him, she tossed one to him.

"Yeah. We'll be in your house."

Her delicate features tightened. "So I guess I should just call you warden, then." She blew out a breath and twisted the cap off of her water.

"It doesn't have to be that way. Roman and I are here to help you. We can deal with the paparazzi and make sure there are no other threats to your safety while you're working on this album. You asked me why I took this job, and I told you it was because I wanted to see you again. That's the truth. I also took it because when I heard your label was hiring security for you, I didn't want to leave it up to anyone else."

Raising her eyebrows, she plopped back down in the chair, letting his words hang between them. Setting her water on the floor, she picked up the guitar again, removed the capo, and tossed it down beside the water. She began playing "Blackbird," this time singing as well as playing, seeming to forget that he was sitting right in front of her. Soon, he found himself leaning forward, as if under a spell, as she sang. Her voice was beautiful, rich and strong, with a feminine rasp to it. He'd heard her music before—on the radio, on TV—but hearing her sing from only a few feet away was an entirely different experience. Her fingers moved easily over the frets, moving seamlessly from chord to chord. She leaned over the guitar, and her blond hair spilled over her slender shoulders, catching the sunlight that streamed in through the large windows and taking on a sheen like spun gold.

For the first time in his life, he understood why women threw their panties at rock stars. Watching her play and listening to her sing in person was a much bigger turn-on than he ever would've anticipated. He took a sip of his water, trying to taper the edge of his arousal.

She played the whole song through, and he sat and listened as he mentally replayed their night together for what had to be the five hundredth time. When she was finished, she looked up at him, her lips turned up in a sexy half smile, as though the music had somehow relaxed her. "How'd you get the black eye?"

"Just a little misunderstanding in a bar."

"Looks like more than just a little misunderstanding."

He returned her smile. "You should see the other guy."

She picked her bottle of water up off the floor, peering down and hiding her smile. But he saw it anyway, and it caught him right in the chest. She stood again, and walked to the guitar rack behind him, her loose Guns N' Roses T-shirt hanging from her shoulders and gathering around her hips. As she paced by him, he watched her legs, once again clad in black denim, and he was hit with the memory of just how fantastic they'd felt wrapped around his hips.

"I saw your Charger out there. It's…pretty nice," she said from behind him.

He nodded. "Thanks. Restored it myself." He looked up at her as she resumed her seat opposite him, resting a white-and-gold electric guitar across her lap. "You're into cars?"

"Fast ones, yeah."

"What do you drive?"

"I have a 'seventy Stingray."

He let out a low whistle. "Nice. Automatic?"

She looked at him like he was crazy. "Course not."

He smiled and then swallowed thickly. Damn. Just when he couldn't be more attracted to her. She was gorgeous, and talented, and a hundred other things.

She was everything he had no fucking right to want, and he'd do them both a favor if he remembered that.

* * *

Ronnie sat on the floor of his apartment, the parquet squares hard and cool against his naked flesh. The door to the linen closet sat open in front of him and he stared blankly ahead, trying to sift through the emotions tugging at him. He didn't know what to do with those emotions. They crawled over his skin like bugs, skittering over him in different directions. Tiny and ugly and worthless. He closed his eyes and took a deep breath, and one by one, he picked up the bugs and crushed them between his fingers, savoring the crisp crunch of shell and legs.

The power to destroy something was a beautiful thing. Destruction was control. It was ownership. There was a succulent completeness to ending something's existence, to witnessing the moment something ceased to be. To own that last moment…there was nothing more intimate. More divine.

He opened his eyes and focused on what was in front of him. Over a year ago, it had started with pictures from websites he'd printed off, or cut out of old magazines he'd stolen from the library, and it had grown into something special. A symbol of his devotion. A shrine to the woman he loved. He'd covered the inside of the linen closet with pictures of Taylor, both professionally taken ones and ones he'd taken himself starting several months back once he'd found her. She'd been surprisingly easy to find—there was information on fan websites about her studio, and by searching real estate records at the library, he'd quickly figured out which building it was. He'd only had to stake it out for a couple of days before she made an appearance, and he'd followed her home that night.

He'd been following her ever since, and the other night at the Rainbow, he'd finally worked up the courage to talk to her, only to have that fucking brute ruin everything. If it hadn't been for him, Taylor would've been his that night, and she never would've left. He would've kept her. Forever.

And then the brute had shown up again this morning at her studio.

He was a problem. One Ronnie knew Taylor needed his help with.

With a frustrated snarl, he returned his attention to his shrine. He'd scoured eBay for Taylor Ross paraphernalia—T-shirts she'd worn in concert, guitar picks, signed CDs. The items lined the shelves, and he reached out a hand, running his fingers over the cool glass of a signed, framed concert picture of Taylor.

He took a deep breath and soaked it all in, waiting for it to replenish him as it always did.

But this time, it wasn't enough. Not after he'd had his hands on her. Not after he'd smelled her hair, felt the warmth of her skin.

He needed more. He needed to be closer to her.

He would continue to watch, but he knew he needed to figure out how to take what belonged to him. To win her over and get rid of the brute, as he knew she wanted him to.

To take her and keep her and love her and own her.

# CHAPTER 6

The scent of grilling meat and fresh-cut grass filled Colt's nostrils as he walked through the open gate and into his sister's backyard. His eyes scanned the space, darting over the patio table and chairs, the play set, and the bench nestled under the ash tree in the corner. Lacey had sworn up and down she hadn't invited her, but it wouldn't be beyond her to trap Colt and their mother into spending time together. He let out the breath he hadn't realized he'd been holding.

"Uncle Colt!" A small body barreled into him, wrapping skinny arms around Colt's legs.

Smiling, Colt ruffled his five-year-old nephew's hair. "Hey, Ben. Good to see you buddy."

"Benjamin Thomas Abbot! Did you hit your brother?" His sister Lacey's voice came from several feet away, stern and annoyed. Colt hoisted the kid up and hung him upside down by his ankles. Ben squealed with laugher and tried to wriggle free.

"Are you being good? Or are you a troublemaker?"

"Mom says I'm a troublemaker like you," he said, smiling upside down and revealing a missing front tooth.

"You know what they do to troublemakers like us?" Colt asked, struggling to keep his expression serious. Ben shook his head, his light brown hair fanning out around him. "Tickle torture!" He laid Ben down on the ground and went to town, eliciting shrieks and giggles from him.

"I'll be good! I promise!" he gasped out between fits of giggles.

"Dude, you caved *so* fast. You're such a baby." Ben's eight-year-old brother, Nick, stood over them, his arms crossed.

"No one can withstand my tickle torture." Colt wiggled his eyebrows and let Ben up before he peed his pants.

Lacey crouched down in front of Ben. "No hitting. You know the rules. If you're upset, use your words. Next time, you're in time-out. Got it?"

Ben nodded. Nick smirked.

"And you." She wheeled on Nick. "Enough with the tattling. Now please, go play without killing each other." She waved them away and they took off for the play set on the other side of the backyard. By the time they got there, Nick had Ben in a headlock. Almost immediately, they were wrestling.

Lacey let out a long breath. "Boys. Only so much you can do, right?"

Colt smiled and gave her a peck on the cheek. "Pretty much. But they're good kids, Lace." She nodded and headed back into the house, a kitchen towel slung over her shoulder.

And they were good kids, most of the time. He loved his nephews. Loved roughhousing with them, tossing a ball around, playing Legos, watching *Star Wars* and *The Avengers* with them, over and over again. He rubbed a hand over his chest, and reminded himself to be happy with what he had. To stop wasting time and energy pining over something that could never happen.

Immediately, he thought of Taylor.

She'd spent several hours at her studio yesterday, ignoring him while she worked on a new song. While she'd been working, her manager, Jeremy, had reappeared, and he and Colt had had a serious conversation about making sure Taylor behaved. No more trouble. Her focus needed to be on writing new music.

At the end of the day yesterday, she'd tossed a casual "See ya, Priestley" over her shoulder and made for the door. Roman had come to pick her up and escort her home, where Colt would be joining them later. For the next few weeks, Colt and Roman would trade off on Taylor duty, never leaving her unattended. Thinking about it, he understood why she felt like a prisoner. Why she'd been so angry yesterday. He'd seen it—in her eyes, in the stiff set of her shoulders, in the jerkiness of her movements—but he hadn't fully got it until he'd transferred her over to Roman's care. They'd each set up in one of the guest rooms, trying to give Taylor as much space and privacy as possible while still making sure she was safe. Although considering she was her own biggest threat, the fact that her label had hired two professional bodyguards to babysit her was pretty damn insulting. But he was happy to be under the same roof, less than a hundred feet away.

Roman was with her now, giving Colt the afternoon off so he could go to Lacey's for a barbecue and some time with his nephews. Reaching into his back pocket, Colt fished his phone out, knowing that Roman would call if anything came up. A couple of texts, but no missed calls. He opened the texts and frowned. Both were from unknown numbers.

What's your favorite animal for playing?

He swiped to the second message.

Do you have more than one costume?

Weird. Wrong numbers, maybe. At least there was nothing work related. He was free to enjoy his afternoon.

"Hey, Colt. How are you?" His brother-in-law, Paul, wandered over from his position in front of the barbecue, a can of soda in each hand. He extended one toward Colt, who accepted it with a smile and cracked it open.

"I'm good. You?"

"Yeah. Good. Lacey tells me you're working for Taylor Ross?" He arched an eyebrow and leaned in. "That true?"

Colt took a long swallow of his Coke. "Yep."

Paul whistled. "Man. She's on my list."

"Your list?"

"You know, the freebie five? Five celebrities that, if given the opportunity, I can sleep with and get a pass."

Colt almost snorted soda through his nose. "I see." Not one to kiss and tell, Colt let the comment slide, and his phone buzzed again from his back pocket.

You make my tail wag back and forth really fast, cutie.
What's your favorite animal?

"The hell?" Colt muttered. Another unknown number.

"Something wrong?" asked Paul, trying to peer at Colt's screen. Colt knew Paul liked to live vicariously through him—being a bodyguard to celebrities and other high-profile clients was a lot more exciting than being an accountant for a chain of sushi restaurants—and he was usually

happy to humor him with what details he could without vio-
lating a client's confidentiality. He knew Paul wasn't trying
to be nosy. In fact, he really liked Paul. He was the only one
of Lacey's boyfriends he hadn't wanted to punch in the face.
Hell, he *had* punched a couple. But they'd deserved it. No
one hurt Lace and didn't answer to him for it.

"Nah." He tucked his phone back in his pocket just as
it buzzed. Again. This time the text message was accom-
panied by a picture of a person wearing a head-to-toe fox
costume, like the kind you'd see an entertainer wearing at
Disneyland.

This foxy lady wants to play! What do you say, sexy?

"The fuck?" He muttered again.

"Watch your mouth," chimed in Lacey, who'd just reappeared from the kitchen carrying a tray laden with water-
melon slices, potato chips, sliced-up veggies, and a bowl of
dip.

"Sorry," he said, taking the tray from Lacey's hands and
setting it down on the nearby table.

"Can I talk to you?" she asked, and turned back toward
the house without waiting for his answer. It was sweet, the
way she pretended he had a choice. He followed her, and
as he stepped inside the small but warm and welcoming
Spanish-style bungalow, his phone buzzed again. He quickly
checked it again to make sure it wasn't Taylor or Roman. It
wasn't. With a grunt, he shoved it back in his pocket. But it
buzzed. Again. And again. More texts came in, some featuring pictures of people dressed up as various animals.

A woman dressed as a life-sized bunny: Like what you
see, your highness?

A man dressed as a bull: You make me horny.

His jaw tightened as he changed his phone from vibrate mode to ring, and assigned both Taylor's and Roman's numbers a unique ringtone, ignoring the rest for now. He needed either of them to be able to get in touch, but everyone else could fuck off. He tossed his phone, screen down, on the table, and sat down across from Lacey. A pair of green eyes that he knew were identical to his own stared at him, tension etched across her brow. She tucked a strand of her auburn hair behind her ear.

"She really wants to see you, you know."

He knew exactly the "she" Lacey was talking about. Their mother, who'd blamed him for her first husband—and Colt and Lacey's father—leaving. Who'd been nasty, and cold, and a shitty excuse for a mother. Who'd dragged him and Lace from one bad relationship to another. He'd spent most of his life looking after Lacey, keeping her safe and making sure everything turned out okay for her. Making sure that if anything bad was coming their way—and with their childhood, there'd *always* been something bad coming—he would be the one standing in front of her, ready to take the brunt of it. As far as their mother was concerned, anything that ever went wrong was somehow his fault, given his propensity for driving away her scuzzy boyfriends, and after he'd beat the snot out of that creep for touching Lacey, his mother had given him the boot.

He'd come home from his job at the Shell gas station up the road to find his stuff in a beat-up box on the porch. Lacey had sat on the stoop, her eyes red from crying. He'd never forget the feeling of disgust that had nearly choked him because all he'd ever wanted was to shelter her from as much shittiness as possible, and he'd failed. He'd spent his entire life protecting her, and ultimately, it had blown up in his face because their mother had repeatedly chosen her latest boyfriend over her own children.

*This* was the woman Lacey wanted to build a relationship with.

Colt sighed and leaned back in his chair. "Yeah, well. I don't want to see her, and frankly, I'm surprised you do. You don't remember what she put us through?"

"Of course I remember," she said softly, looking down at her lap. "But she's still our mother. And she's better, Colt. Better than I've ever seen her. She's sober, and she's got a job. A nice apartment. No man in her life. She's really trying."

"I can't, Lace. I can't open that door."

"Why not?" She leaned forward, challenging him.

"Because *I'm* trying, too, and I'm finally in a good place with everything. Seeing her, talking to her, whatever…it'll just undo it all." He watched the storm clouds gather in his sister's eyes.

"Bullshit. You're not in a good place, Colt." She reached out a hand and laid it on his forearm, her hand pale against the black feathers marking his skin. "I worry about you."

He laid his hand over hers and gave it a squeeze. "Don't. I'm good."

She narrowed her eyes at him. "You are not. You're lonely, and I'd bet you still have nightmares."

Lacey had always had a knack for making him feel as if she could see right through him. She was right; he did still have nightmares.

Except for the night with Taylor. He'd slept more peacefully that night than he had in years, and he knew it wasn't just because of the fantastic sex. There'd been something about her, the peace that had settled over him with her in his arms. Something he needed to chase. Something he couldn't just let go.

"I'm fine. I'm not lonely, or unhappy, so please don't worry about me, okay?" He rolled his tight shoulders as he lied to his sister. He stood and paced to the window, his chest tightening as he watched Ben and Nick play pirates on the play set. She came and stood beside him, leaning her head against his shoulder. They stood in silence for a moment, watching the boys play, and then watching Paul chase them around the yard, each holding a foam sword.

"You said that you're not lonely or unhappy, but you didn't deny that you still have nightmares." She looked up at him.

He didn't say anything, just kept his gaze straight ahead, watching his nephews play.

She waited several moments before saying quietly, "You could tell me about what happened over there. It might help."

He pressed his lips into a firm line and a wave of nausea rolled through him.

"Nothing to tell, Lace." Even to him, his voice sounded strained, rough. He hated lying to her.

She wrapped her arms around his waist and gave him a sideways hug. "People don't have nightmares about nothing."

No. They didn't.

* * *

Fuck. He was so fucking fucked. Frank Ross curled his hand into a fist and slammed it down onto the table, making its contents jump.

He hadn't been surprised when Taylor had told him to go fuck himself. But the bitch had changed her number, and now his only connection to her was gone. He listened as the prerecorded message played over again in a robotic female voice.

"Welcome to Verizon Wireless. The number you dialed has been changed, disconnected, or is no longer in service. If you feel you have reached this recording in error, please check the number and try your call again."

With a forceful jab of his thumb on the screen, he ended the call, then threw his phone onto the table and jammed his hands onto his hips as his pulse hammered away wildly in his throat. He paced the small room at the back of the bar. A loud shout erupted from the front room, followed by the thud of boots scraping over the worn wood floor as a couple of bikers from the gang came to blows. Just another Thursday night.

Frank stared at the table in front of him, at the neat pile of white bricks wrapped in plastic. Eight kilos of cocaine.

There were supposed to be twelve. And at $30,000 each, that meant he was in the hole $120,000. It was money he didn't have. And if the rest of the gang found out about this, he'd have a mutiny on his hands. If they found out he'd started dipping into the supply, they'd kill him for bringing the Golden Brotherhood heavies down on them. And that was if the Golden Brotherhood didn't kill Frank first for stealing from them.

The Golden Brotherhood, the biggest, most powerful organized crime group in Los Angeles, had contracted the Grim Weavers to move the cocaine the Brotherhood was bringing in from Colombia. According to the books, the Brotherhood had given them twenty kilos to move a month ago. They'd dealt eight, and they should have had twelve kilos left. Frank had no reasonable way to account for the four missing kilos. It had started out so small; he'd taken a little—such a fucking small amount, really—for himself. No harm in a little skimming off the top. But he'd done more than skim, and he'd quickly developed a ten-gram-a-day habit. So he'd taken a little more of the supply, selling it for a little extra on the side, trying to make enough to make up the difference. He hadn't. So he'd sold a whole kilo to another gang, inflating the margins.

It still hadn't been enough, and now he needed that $120,000 so that the Brotherhood wouldn't know he'd stolen their powder. And the only person he knew who had that kind of money had changed her number. He rubbed a hand over his chest, acid burning a path up its center, and he forced several deep breaths down his throat. He raised a hand to wipe away the sweat dotting his forehead, his hand trembling. The tremble turned into a full-blown shake as his panic poured out of him like lava from a volcano. He spun, grabbed the desk chair, and tossed it against the wall, watching numbly as one of the little wheels popped off and rolled across the floor. Slumping against the wall, he pressed a hand to his face, cursing Taylor, cursing the Brotherhood, cursing himself.

He was running out of options, and running out of time.

* * *

Taylor sat on her couch, her acoustic guitar in her lap and her notebook open beside her, the page filled with her third new song in as many days. She strummed through the up-tempo, slightly grungy E-minor-A-D chord progression again, feeling more like herself than she had in weeks, despite the sex god camped out in one of the guest rooms upstairs. God, it felt good to write, to create something that was entirely hers. Writing music always made her feel like Rumpelstiltskin, taking something coarse and unrefined and turning it into gold. There was an alchemy to it she tried not to question. She ran through the chords again, her mouth quirking up in a smile as lyrics began to take shape.

*You only get one night*
*So give it your all*
*Give me all you've got*
*Until the cops are called*
*Make me scream, make me beg*
*Try to make me fall*
*Make me wanna miss you*
*Let's shake the walls*

Realization crashed into her and she threw the pen down as though it had burned her. "Holy shit," she whispered, her hand clasping the guitar a bit tighter.

She was writing about Colt.

*Well, fuck.*

And not only was she writing about him, but she'd written three new songs since he'd burst into her life.

*Double fuck.*

She pried her white-knuckled hand from the guitar and set it aside, swallowing thickly, her mouth suddenly dry. Pushing up off the couch, she walked into the kitchen, switching on lights in the dark house as she went, grabbing her phone from where it sat charging on the counter.

Colt. She couldn't get his name out of her brain. His name, his face, his scent, the way he'd felt inside her...all of it was always there, simmering in her mind. And when she wasn't thinking about him, she was *with* him. It was a fucking nightmare. All she wanted was to stop thinking about him, and even when she pushed him down, away, he was still there, making his presence in her subconscious known through her songs.

Which was why she had to push him away. She opened the browser on her phone and navigated to the online dating site where she'd created a profile for Colt.

It was an online dating site that catered exclusively to furries. She smiled, biting her lip as she reveled in her own joke. She'd used his real cell number for the profile, and based on the number of views the profile had received—she *had* paid for the premium membership, after all—he was probably getting inundated with texts.

She studied the profile she'd created for him. Yes, it was childish and bratty, but she was so goddamn angry about the situation that she needed an outlet, and if she could channel that anger into an outlet that pissed Colt off, all the better.

At the top of the profile was his title: Prince Sparklepants, heir to the unicorn kingdom. She'd used some random pictures of a man dressed up in a full-body unicorn costume, complete with purple mane and tail, and a large glittery horn. She hadn't used his real picture, but the texts alone were probably driving him crazy. She'd nearly cracked and asked him about it when he'd come home earlier, trading off babysitting duty with Roman, but she'd restrained herself. Instead, she'd shut herself away, working on her new songs, and trying not to think about the man under her roof she was doing her best to ignore. She'd avoided him as much as possible since he'd come back around seven o'clock, and she'd stayed in her room until he'd knocked on her door at eleven and told her he was going to bed and that he'd already set the alarm. She'd thought he and Roman—the pile of muscle and hair of whom she'd already grown quite fond—would trade off, but it seemed as though Colt intended to be around as much as possible, with Roman providing relief when necessary.

*Fan-fucking-tastic.*

She navigated away from the dating site and to Colt's LinkedIn profile, and her stomach dipped in appreciation. God, the man was gorgeous. And fucking fantastic in bed. And he made her feel…She glanced in the direction of the stairs. God. He was under the same roof. Probably half naked. In a bed.

"No," she whispered, dropping her phone onto the counter and scrubbing her hands over her face, her eyes dry and tired. Yawning, she glanced at the clock on her stove, which told her it was after midnight and time to call it a night. She rolled her stiff neck, trying to work out the kinks left behind after spending hours hunched over her guitar. She grabbed her phone and shoved it into her back pocket. As she extended a hand to turn off the kitchen lights, she saw it.

A shadow moved quickly across the large window over the sink. She froze, her heart picking up its tempo in her chest, and she flicked the lights off, plunging the kitchen into darkness. At least if there *was* someone outside, they could no longer see in. Moving out of sight of the window, she listened, straining her ears as the quiet of the house hummed like static in her ears. It would be so easy to simply go upstairs and get Colt. But she didn't want to need him. Didn't want to seek him out in any way at all. After several moments of staring, waiting, listening, she relaxed slightly, her shoulders dropping from down around her ears.

Shaking her head at herself and glad she hadn't gone upstairs and got Colt for nothing, she checked to make sure all the doors were locked and the alarm set. She trailed her fingers over the smooth, cool metal of her front door handle and began to turn away when another shadow moved, this time on her front porch. The shadow ghosted from left to right, visible through the frosted glass panes on either side of the large, heavy front door. Ice trickled down Taylor's spine, and she pressed a hand to her mouth, backing slowly away from the door as her skin prickled, her pulse throbbing in her throat.

She backed into the entryway, her eyes still glued to the doorknob, waiting for it to twitch, for the scrape of metal in the lock. Getting ready to scream for Colt.

A dull, soft thump near the kitchen window made her jump, and she froze in the entryway. Yanking her phone from her pocket, she used the screen to light a path, sweeping the phone back and forth with a trembling hand. Another thump sounded, this time from the other side of the house.

She ran for the stairs, taking them two at a time.

# CHAPTER 7

Colt rolled over in bed and reached for his phone on the bedside table. The display read 12:52 A.M. He groaned softly and rubbed a hand over his eyes, pissed that he'd barely fallen asleep before waking up again. He knew he hadn't had another nightmare—he wasn't drenched in sweat and shaking. Even when he woke up without remembering the dream, he knew he'd had a combat nightmare by the way his entire body practically vibrated with it. He pulled the covers up around himself and closed his eyes, settling back into the pillow, when a firm knocking at his bedroom door had his eyes snapping back open. He threw the covers off and crossed the space to the door, pulling it open to find Taylor on the other side.

He opened his mouth to ask her if she was all right, but couldn't seem to find any words once his eyes landed on her, and he took in what she was wearing.

Nothing but his Led Zeppelin T-shirt. No makeup. Hair in a thick ponytail, flung over one shoulder. Before he could stop himself, his eyes wandered from her face to her breasts, then down her torso and over her long, slender legs and bare feet. Everything from the other night came rushing back, sending blood flowing to his dick. The feel of her mouth on his. His arms around her. The sounds she'd made as he'd fucked her. The glory that was his name on her lips as he'd made her come, over and over.

"Everything okay?" he asked, his voice low and hoarse with sleep.

"Um." She stared at him, seemingly surprised to see him standing there, even though she'd been the one to come and knock on his door. Her eyes skimmed down his chest and straight to the bulge in his boxers, which he knew hid nothing, and she bit her lip. He could've sworn she made a soft whimpering noise, and butterflies crashed into each other in his stomach.

Jesus. What the fuck was wrong with him? Just standing here with her gave him butterflies? But not butterflies, because he'd probably lose his man card if he ever admitted that to anyone. So, not butterflies. No. She gave him… scorpions. Yeah, that was better.

Man card intact, he cleared his throat. "Something wrong?"

She paused, and when she spoke again, there was the slightest tremble to her voice. "I…don't know. This sounds so stupid."

He rubbed a hand over his face, fighting the urge to wrap his arms around her. Fighting the urge to kiss her and pull her onto the bed less than ten feet away. "What's wrong?"

She frowned, hugging herself, and his muscles stiffened, tension rolling through him as he waited for her to answer.

"I thought maybe someone was here. I saw shadows, outside my kitchen window and on the front porch. Or, at least, I thought I did. And for a second, it sounded like someone was trying to open the kitchen window."

By the time she'd finished speaking, he'd already stepped back into the bedroom and yanked on his jeans.

"You have your phone with you?" A surge of anger that someone had tried to mess with her merged with the adrenaline coursing through him. He jammed his feet into his boots and pulled a T-shirt over his head before grabbing his SIG Sauer P226 from the nightstand.

She nodded, holding out one hand and showing it to him.

"Good. Stay in here with the door closed. I'll do a sweep."

"No, but…"

He paused in the doorway, his breath sticking to his ribs at the sight of her in nothing but her underwear and his T-shirt. *God damn.* "But what?"

Her eyes flicked between him, the gun in his hand, and the bed with its disheveled sheets. "Be careful," she said softly, and crossed the room to sit on the bed. The bed he'd been in just a few minutes ago. She crossed her long, bare legs and something charged through him. Lust, but something more. Something hot and protective. Something maybe even a little possessive.

She was his to protect. She might be pissed that he was here, and he understood why, but he couldn't deny that right here, right now, he was fucking glad he was here to keep her safe.

"I will. I'll be right back."

Quickly, Colt moved through the house, clearing each room as he went, but nothing was out of place. The house was silent and mostly dark, and as he went, he checked all of the windows and doors on the lower level for any signs of forced entry, but everything looked secure. With his SIG clasped in his right hand, a small flashlight in his left, he stepped outside and did a perimeter check, looking for anything suspicious—footprints, damaged shrubs, litter, damage around the windows. He circled around to the other side of the house, still on high alert for anything suspicious, but not finding anything. He slipped the flashlight back into his pocket and walked back into the house, locking the door and resetting the alarm behind him. He flipped on a few lights as he went back through the house this time, his eyes still scanning each room as he passed, darting into the corners, watching for movement, for anything out of place. He grabbed the iPad from the kitchen and quickly pulled up the security camera app.

When he and Roman had scoped out her place, he'd been mainly happy with the security she already had in place for the house. But he had updated a few things, including syncing her cameras with an app that fed the footage directly to her iPad. She'd pretended to ignore him the entire time he'd been explaining it, but he'd known she was listening from the way her eyes had tracked his hands as he'd showed her how to access the information in the app.

He pulled up the camera feeds from the front door, backyard, and garage for the past hour and quickly scrolled through them, dragging his finger across the screen, but he didn't see anything. No mysterious intruder, no one near the house.

He'd been about to close the app when something caught his eye, a flicker almost off camera. Frowning, he rewound the footage from the front door and played it back at regular speed. A shadow flickered, headlights flared from the street, and then the shadow was gone. The cameras were good, but not high-res, and if he zoomed in, he knew the image would only get pixelated and fuzzy. It was almost impossible to tell if there'd actually been someone at her front door, or if it was a trick of the light. Even if there had been someone—a thrill-seeking fan, maybe—they were long gone now.

Colt made a mental note to adjust the camera angles in the morning, and headed back upstairs. He strode down the hallway and opened his bedroom door, practically crashing into Taylor, who'd been crouched on the other side of the door. Instinctively, he held out his hands out to steady her, and she swayed into him, just for a second, before taking a step back.

"Did you find anyone?" she asked, leaning her shoulder against the wall just inside the doorway. There was a hollowness around her eyes, and it made him want to push her up against the wall and kiss her until neither of them could breathe.

"No. No sign of anyone." For a brief second, he debated whether or not he should tell her about the shadow on the security camera, but decided it was a worry (and probably a worry over nothing) that she didn't need right now. She had enough to deal with, with her record label breathing down her neck, and he and Roman encroaching on her personal space.

"I let my imagination get the better of me. I shouldn't have woken you." She yawned and stretched her arms above her head, and the shirt—*his* shirt—rode up her thighs, a scrap of black lace barely visible between her legs before the cotton dropped back down. Her eyes met his, and she hugged her arms around her waist, closing herself off from him, and he couldn't take it anymore.

She frowned when he leaned against the wall a few feet away from her, facing her and mirroring her posture. "What the hell are you running from?"

She cocked her head to the side and narrowed her pretty blue eyes. "I'm not running from anything. I thought I saw something, and I panicked, which I shouldn't have done. What does that have to do with running?"

He pursed his lips and nodded. "You know what I think?"

She shook her head, her bottom lip caught between her teeth.

"I think I scare you." Maybe it was because he was looking for an excuse to get close to her, but he suddenly took a step toward her, backing her against the wall. "I think you want me just as much as I want you, and that freaks you out. It's why you bailed before I woke up. It's why you're trying to keep your distance from me now." He dipped his head so that his mouth was nearly touching her ear. "But you don't have to be scared, gorgeous. Not with me." And despite his reservations, he knew he was telling the truth.

Paying attention to her cues, he didn't miss the way she arched toward him, the way her breathing hitched slightly. Bracing one hand on the wall by her head, he leaned in farther. He moved her ponytail off her shoulder with his free hand and caressed down the length of her arm. "I think someone hurt you, and you're trying to protect yourself." Unable to stop himself, he pressed a kiss to her neck and she moaned softly, her fingers curling into the fabric of his T-shirt.

"I think there's a part of you that wants me to fuck you up against this wall. Right here, right now." He pressed another kiss to her collarbone. "I bet you're wet just thinking about it. How good I would feel inside you. How hard I could make you come." He pressed his face into her neck and she moaned again, her body arching into him.

He spoke, his lips and teeth trailing over the skin of her neck as he did. "The other night—" unable to help himself, he brushed his lips over hers "—you were mine. And I take care of what's mine."

Her eyes locked with his for a brief second, and then she shoved him away. Her shove wasn't hard enough to move him, but he took a step back anyway.

"I'm not yours, Colt. It was a one-night stand, and it's not gonna happen again."

He took another step back, and she spun and left the room, pulling the door closed hard behind her. He stood completely still for a moment, hands clenched into fists, tension radiating up his jaw.

Son of a bitch, but she was maddening.

Adjusting his aching cock, he yanked open the door and did another sweep through the house, trying to ignore the confusing mixture of possessiveness, arousal, and frustration swirling through him. He wanted her, and regardless of the walls she was throwing up whenever he was around her, she wanted him, too. With just the brush of his fingers and a few small kisses, he'd had her arching into him, trembling for more.

Fine. If she wanted to push him away and practically wrap herself in barbed wire, he'd let her. He could sit back and let her play her games. Because every time he thought about the night they'd shared, every time his eyes landed on her, even though he knew he should let her go, he just couldn't.

* * *

Taylor strode into the Sanctuary early the next morning ahead of Colt, who was parking the car and doing a quick perimeter check. She liked working in the morning, with the promise of a fresh day ahead of her, and she was eager to work on the new songs sprouting from her like saplings. She sat down at the piano just as her drummer, Zephira, walked in, a tray of coffees in her hands.

"Morning, sunshine," she said, setting the tray down on a coffee table near one of the leather sofas and shrugging out of her leather jacket. Taylor had always thought Zephira, with her Afro and gorgeous medium-brown skin, was the epitome of badass cool. And on top of that, the chick could really drum. They'd worked together on Taylor's last album and tour, and had become friends. The road had a way of bonding people, but Taylor had a feeling she and Zephira would've become pals in just about any circumstance. Zephira tossed her jacket over the back of the sofa.

"Who's the hottie in the parking lot?" she asked, stretching her long, elegant neck from side to side.

"The bodyguard the label hired for me."

"What do you mean, bodyguard? You in some kind of trouble?"

Taylor snorted and played a few chords, the keys cool under her fingers. "I'm not in trouble. I *am* trouble. Which I guess means I'm *in* trouble, but in a different way." As she played lazy chords, she told Zephira the story—leaving out the part about the one-night stand—of her new warden.

"Oh, girl. That is some stone-cold bullshit right there. You *know* if your name was *Tyler* Ross, they wouldn't be pulling this shit on you."

Taylor sighed, rising from the piano bench and crossing the space to scoop up one of the green-and-white paper cups. Shaking her head, she raised the lid to her lips. "Oh believe me, I know."

"Good morning," Jeremy called as he walked through the door. "You're here early. Glad to see our new arrangement is working out." As he helped himself to one of the coffees, Taylor and Zephira exchanged a pointed glance, both rolling their eyes behind Jeremy's back.

"So," he said, clapping his hands together, "I had a call from Walker Stone's agent this morning."

"Oh yeah?" She ran her fingers over the piano's keys and

started to play again. She'd let Walker Stone, an up-and-coming country singer, record his album at the Sanctuary last year, and they'd developed a friendship. Truth be told, she'd had a bit of a crush on him, but she knew he was hung up on his ex, country singer Monroe Bell, who was both gorgeous and a little crazy. Taylor felt like a Girl Scout around Monroe, who was way wilder than Taylor had ever been. Taylor and Walker spending time together hadn't put Taylor in Monroe's good graces, either, and more than once, Taylor had gone out of her way to avoid Monroe at parties and various events.

"Yeah. He wants to know if you'll play with him at the CMT Music Awards in a few days. They're doing this whole genre mash-up thing, so everyone who's performing is playing with a noncountry artist. Stone requested you."

"Yeah, totally. I'd love to."

"Great, I'll let them know. He'll come by tomorrow to rehearse with you."

Excitement pinged through her. Onstage, a guitar in her hands, rocking out with thousands of fans—that was where she felt most alive.

Colt strode through the Sanctuary's door, pulling his sunglasses off his face as he walked. He nodded at the others as he passed, and everyone dispersed, the impromptu meeting adjourned. He came to a stop directly beside the piano, his phone in his hand. He showed her the screen, and her stomach dropped when she saw the Prince Sparklepants profile she'd created for him.

"You do this?"

She held her breath, waiting for his anger. Instead, after a brief second, humor lit up his face, his green eyes crinkling in that way that made her stomach flip and bounce.

"Because it's pretty freaking hilarious."

"How…how did you find it?" she asked, unsure how to read him.

"Gorgeous, I'm ex-military and a security expert. You can bet that if I'm getting weird-ass text messages, I'm going to figure out where they're coming from."

"Uh, well, I—"

"As far as pranks go, this is pretty good. Really. Shows creativity." He leaned his forearms on the piano, smiling down at her. Challenging her. "Just be warned. You're throwing the glove down on a prank war with someone who was in the Army for twelve years."

She tried and failed to suppress her wide grin. A thrill zapped through her, hot and electric.

*Game fucking on.*

* * *

Frank stepped into the private room at Brillare, one of the most expensive restaurants in Los Angeles, feeling completely out of place in his scuffed boots, black jeans, leather vest, and gray T-shirt. A narrow stream of sweat trickled between his shoulder blades, and despite the fact that he was flanked on either side by members of the Grim Weavers, he was extremely aware of just how exposed he was, walking into Golden Brotherhood territory. The jazz piped through the restaurant's speakers grated on him and he ground his teeth together, determined not to show any fear.

As he approached, the man who'd summoned him didn't stand from his spot in the center of a cushy, red-leather covered booth. With his fingers wrapped around a tumbler of amber liquid, his designer suit impeccably tailored and spotless, he emanated power and control. Two things Frank was used to commanding himself, and the fact that he could feel them slipping through his fingers scared the fuck out of him.

Without a word, Jonathan Fairfax motioned for Frank to sit on one of the wooden chairs facing the booth. Frank sat, and his men, Roadrunner and Drifter, stood behind him. He'd specifically chosen them because he knew they'd have his back. He and Drifter went back almost thirty years, and while Roadrunner was a newer addition to the crew, he was devoted to Frank and the Weavers. They hadn't been relieved of their weapons as they'd entered, and Fairfax had to know they were packing. That he wasn't intimidated at all set Frank's teeth on edge. Everywhere the Grim Weavers went, people scrambled to either accommodate them or get the fuck out of their way. But this pretending not to care shit? Fuck, but it was unnerving. Frank's heart hammered in his ears as he swallowed thickly, trying and failing to get a read on how to play the situation.

"You know, I don't normally concern myself with people like you," said Fairfax, tracing his pinky around the rim of his glass and not making eye contact. Fairfax was the head of the Golden Brotherhood and not someone to be fucked with. He was Hollywood's Oscar-winning golden boy, but most people, including his beautiful daughter, Alexa, had no idea who the actor *really* was.

Fairfax rubbed a hand over his thinning dark brown hair and finally looked up, his eyes cold and hard. "But when one of my lieutenants tells me there's a six-figure shortfall on the books, I get interested pretty damn fast."

Frank didn't say anything, just rubbed his sweaty palms over his thighs.

Fairfax looked down, consulting a single slip of paper in front of him. "You—the Grim Weavers—were given twenty kilos of coke to move for us. Each of those kilos has a street value of $30,000. Now—and correct me if I'm wrong," he said in a tone that didn't seem open to correction at all, "you claim to have dealt twelve kilos. Even after your twenty-five percent cut, and again, stop me if I'm wrong, I should see $270,000." Fairfax leaned forward slightly. "Is my math right?"

He held Frank's eyes, waiting for a response. Frank nodded gruffly.

Fairfaix nodded, rubbing his chin. "You see, that's what I thought. But I only see $172,000 in the books, meaning you're short almost $100,000." Fairfax cocked his head, studying Frank. "Where the fuck is the money, Ross? You wouldn't be stupid enough to steal from us, would you? To sell coke on the side that doesn't belong to you?"

Frank mustered every ounce of bravado he could. "You be careful who you call stupid. We're on your turf, so as a sign of respect, I'll let that slide, but you'd better remember who the fuck you're talking to."

Fairfax nodded at someone behind him, and the cold press of metal against Frank's temple sent his stomach churning. He strained his eyes as he glanced to the side as far as he could without moving his head, catching a glimpse of suited men with guns trained on his men, muzzles pressed against the backs of their skulls.

Fairfax sipped his drink and studied the tumbler for a moment, his calm, slow movements making Frank want to flip a fucking table.

"Listen. I don't want your brains decorating my wall. I've already got plenty of artwork." Fairfax waved his hand, as though he were making casual conversation and not threatening murder. "I know, I know, it's only $100,000. Not a lot of money in the grand scheme of things." He *tsk*ed and let out a frustrated sigh. "But it's the principle of the thing, Frank. If I let you steal from the Brotherhood and walk away, what kind of message am I sending to everyone else?" He shook his head sadly. "So here's what's going to happen." The gun held at Frank's temple pressed more firmly against him. "I will get my money, Frank. It's not a matter of if. It's only a matter of how. So you figure it the fuck out." He looked at the man behind him. "Break his toes."

# CHAPTER 8

Ronnie gripped the knife firmly in one hand, scraping it rapidly back and forth over the sharpening steel, and the metallic sound hummed through him. Setting it aside, he turned to the carcass hanging in front of him, swaying ever so slightly in the chilled air of the walk-in freezer. Without hesitating, he slipped his knife beneath the fat and, with a series of sure, quick strokes, began pulling the muscle away from the bone. He pulled the pork loin free and set it on the butcher block counter. Even though the meat was cold against his hands, he chose not to wear gloves. He liked the feel of flesh under his fingers, raw and exposed.

Picking up a rag, he wiped at the pinkish water sitting on top of the counter, and as he cleaned, he wondered what Taylor's flesh would feel like beneath his fingers. Would it be firm and supple, or softer, more yielding? Which part of her would feel the best? Would he like her best warm or cold?

Would she scream as he peeled her skin back? His dick stiffened, and he fought back a groan. The idea of being inside her and seeing inside her at the same time was almost too much. He needed to get control of himself so that when the time came, he wouldn't waste his time with her.

Maybe, when she was big and round with his child, she'd let him pull the baby from her. Let him slice into her womb to touch their child, to touch her. A baby they'd made, covered in Taylor's blood.

The idea brought tears to his eyes.

Ronnie's phone buzzed, and after washing his hands, he retrieved it from his back pocket.

I'm here. Back door.

A surge of excitement charged through him, and he glanced over his shoulder, making sure no one was coming into the back room. He pushed open the rear exit door and let the man in.

"You got my money?"

Ronnie pulled a roll of bills out of his pocket and pressed it into the man's hand, taking the box of black-market spy equipment in return. With a curt nod, the man turned on his heel and left, leaving Ronnie to explore his treasures.

\* \* \*

Taylor ran her brush through her hair, letting the strands trail over her shoulders. Pursing her lips, she leaned forward and scrutinized herself in the bathroom mirror. With her pinky, she wiped at a tiny smudge of mascara under one eye.

"Your ride's here," called Roman from out in the hallway before heading down the stairs. Over the past couple of days, he and Colt had made themselves at home, encroaching on her space and tracking her every move. She'd avoided Colt as much as possible since the night of the imaginary intruder. He'd had the past day off, leaving her under Roman's supervision.

And goddammit, she liked Roman. She didn't want to like Roman. She didn't want to…whatever the hell it was she felt about Colt. And she especially didn't need or want them in her space.

Taylor stomped to her front hallway, hating the excitement that shot through her when she drank in the sight of Colt standing there.

"You ready to head out?" His hands were tucked into the front pockets of his jeans, and before she could stop herself, her eyes skated down his body and back up again, taking in the perfectly mussed light brown hair, dark gray T-shirt, jeans, and boots that all seemed to fit him perfectly, hinting at what she knew was a killer body under that cotton.

"Yeah. We'll take my car, though," she said, wanting to claim back even just a tiny slice of her freedom.

"No. We're taking mine."

"You saying you don't want to go for a ride in my 'Vette?" She closed her eyes for a second, wondering how the hell she'd gone from being pissed at the situation to flirting with him. *Again.*

He crossed his arms and studied her with a half smile that crinkled his eyes and sent her heart scrambling into her stomach. "No, I do. Just not today. I'm driving, and we're taking my car. If you behave, maybe I'll even let you drive it."

She frowned, anything good she'd been feeling evaporating. "I'm not some ill-behaved toddler that you can bribe with treats, you know."

His expression softened, and he held her gaze for a second before nodding slowly. "You're right. I'm sorry. I shouldn't have said that."

She ignored his apology and kept talking, unsure how

that easy yet sincere apology made her feel. It seemed al-most unfair the way he could toss something like that at her and expect her to know what to do with it. "Besides," she continued, "my Layla's got more style, torque, and horse-power than that thing." She leaned around him and eyed the Charger sitting in her driveway, itching to wrap her fingers around the steering wheel despite the way she was teasing him.

He scoffed. "You named your car? Really?" Arching an eyebrow, he smirked. "And don't think I haven't noticed you stare at my Charger the way a fat kid stares at cake."

She raised an eyebrow, unwilling to give him the satisfac-tion of knowing just how right he was. "It's got a certain rough charm." She shrugged and frowned. "But it's no 'Vette."

"Oh yeah? What's so freaking great about that?" He stabbed a finger in Layla's direction.

She began counting off on her fingers. "Number one: Corvettes are the most popular all-American high-performance car of all time, outselling all others since their introduction in 1963. Number two: Four thirty-five horsepower. You've got…what?" She eyed the Charger again. "Three fifty? *Maybe* four twenty? And that's if you've got a HEMI in there, which I don't think you do. Number three: Even with a smaller engine, the Corvettes have better performance than pretty much any-thing comparable. Number four: It's a fucking tank. Good luck trying to dent it. Number five: It—"

"I think I love you." Colt studied her with an amused smirk, rubbing a hand over his mouth.

Suppressing the tiny thrill that shot through her, she rolled her eyes. "Shut up, Colt." He chuckled, the sound low and warm, as she turned back into the house to grab her purse and keys.

She was pleasantly surprised when, as she walked toward

his car, he stepped in front of her, opening the passenger door for her. Trying to ignore the electrical tingle that worked its way across her skin at the nearness of his wide, muscled body, she slipped into the passenger seat. He walked around the front of the car to the other side and dropped into the driver's seat with an easy, masculine grace. The engine roared to life, and she had to suppress a smile. It was no Stingray, but it was a pretty awesome car all the same. Pristine black leather seats, fully restored dash, gleaming chrome and faux-wood finishes. Upgraded stereo system that she couldn't help but notice was tuned to her favorite classic rock station. The Charger was sexy and rough and masculine. Kinda like its owner. And that was exactly the way she shouldn't be thinking.

"Definitely no HEMI in this," she said, propping her elbow on the window's ledge.

"It's not all about the size of the engine, you know." His eyebrow arched up over the aviator sunglasses he'd just slipped on, and she watched his large hands as he wrapped one around the steering wheel, the other over the gear shift. Heat prickled over her skin as she remembered how good those hands had felt on her.

"Spoken like someone with a small engine."

"Oh, honey. We both know there's *nothing* wrong with the size of my engine." He glanced over at her, that smug, cocky grin tilting his lips up in a way that made her insides feel like melted butter, all hot and sweet and heart stopping. Her stomach did a flip and she cleared her throat, shifting in her seat.

Switching gears and the subject at the same time, he glanced over his shoulder as he pulled out onto her street. "So, listen. I'm having some guys over for poker tonight, so I'm trading off with Roman. I know it's supposed to be my night on, but I didn't see anything in your schedule. That okay with you?"

"Whatever. I don't care." But she tucked away that little piece of information, wondering if she could do something with it.

"Okay. But if anything comes up, if you need anything, I'm around."

As he shifted into gear and forward into traffic, a strange warmth settled over her chest. She liked that he was in her corner, that he was…around. And goddammit, she wasn't supposed to like it. She was supposed to be angry. Supposed to be keeping her distance. And she was struggling and failing on both counts.

They rode the rest of the way in silence, Taylor not daring to open her mouth for fear of what horrifyingly honest thing might fall out.

Colt turned into the Sanctuary's parking lot and pulled into a spot near the entrance. Once again surprising her, he came around and opened her door for her, and once again, she tried to ignore the sparks shooting through her at being so close to him. She could feel the warmth coming off his skin, smell the faint, woodsy-fresh scent of his aftershave. Before she lost control of every single brain cell, he moved to the back of the car, opening the trunk and lifting out a small cooler. She shot him a questioning glance and he shrugged.

"I get hungry."

Something about the cocky pull of his lips sent a thrill up her spine. He brushed by her as she closed her door and lowered his head, just slightly. He was only a couple of inches taller than her and didn't have far to go to bring his mouth a whisper away from her ear. "I've got a big appetite. As I'm sure you remember."

He was halfway to the front door before she was able to move. Her pulse fluttered in her throat, and heat pooled between her legs as memories of that night flashed through her mind for what had to be the thousandth time.

Thankfully, Walker's SUV pulling up was enough to jolt her out of her haze, and she put her legs in motion. In a plaid shirt and jeans, with his short, blond hair catching the morning sun and a couple days' worth of stubble clinging to his square jaw and cleft chin, he looked every inch the country hunk his legions of female fans worshiped. After a quick greeting, she sat down with Walker in the rehearsal space, bottles of water at the ready, lyrics and chords printed out and propped on stands. She greeted Zephira and Jeremy, along with a few other musicians and people from Walker's entourage. The space hummed with activity, and she took a deep, cleansing breath, settling into herself.

Shouldering her favorite Gibson Explorer, she reached for the guitar pick case on the nearby table. She frowned when she found it empty.

"Sorry, just need to find a pick. Hang on."

"Sure thing, darlin'." Walker sent her an easy smile and picked up a guitar, strumming softly.

She rummaged around, searching for a pick as Walker filled her in on the details of their upcoming performance at the awards show. She suppressed a frustrated growl as she continued her search. Walker strummed idly on his guitar as she hunted from table to table, drawer to drawer, even digging into the couch cushions. Nothing. She came up empty-handed and thrust a hand into her hair, several people watching her with arched eyebrows and puzzled frowns.

"Taylor, I've got a spare pick if you need one," called Walker, sitting back on a stool.

"What the hell? Where did they all go?"

Her eyes landed on Colt as he walked back into the main area from the kitchenette, focused intently on his phone and trying very hard to look innocent. Trying and not quite succeeding.

"By the way," he said, not looking up from his phone. "I made you a snack. It's in the fridge."

Exhaling a hard, sharp, breath, she strode to the kitchenette off to one side of the studio and flung the refrigerator door open. She felt something give as she tugged, and a springy pop sounded just before what had to be a pound of multicolored glitter exploded in her face. She stood completely still in front of the fridge, eyes screwed shut against the tiny, sparkly pieces of plastic as laughter erupted around her.

She spit out a small mouthful of glitter. "Pah. Fuck!" She wiped at her eyes and pried first one, then the other open cautiously. Glancing down, she groaned as she surveyed the damage. Her black leather pants and white tank top were covered in glitter. With a disgusted *tsk*, she wiped at her clothes, but that only seemed to spread the glitter around.

"Nice sparkle pants," said Colt, an evil grin on his face. He tipped his chin toward the fridge. "You never found your snack."

Her head snapped back around and her muscles tensed as she braced for another onslaught of craft supplies. In amongst the beer, water bottles, take-out containers, and a lone bottle of half-used ranch dressing sat a bright red Jell-O mold, and in it was every single guitar pick from the studio. They all sat suspended in red goo, wiggling at her in some kind of processed food taunt.

"Colt!" She ground out his name through clenched teeth.

He laughed, cocky and proud of himself, sending irritation and lust sparking through her system. "Hey, I warned you."

For some reason, she hadn't thought he'd actually prank her. That maybe he talked a big game but was full of shit and was trying to intimidate her into backing down. That maybe he wouldn't get her back for the Prince Sparklepants thing.

"It's real sweet that you cooked for me," she said, her voice dripping in sarcasm.

He stepped closer, and once again every nerve ending in her body came to life. "You looked hungry." His green eyes darkened to a deep emerald, just for a second, as he studied her, and his low, rough voice sent heat rippling up her spine and straight to her core.

"Is that how I look to you? Hungry?" She stepped closer, so close she could smell the fresh, clean-laundry scent of his T-shirt. She was tempted to rub herself all over him. To transfer some of the glitter. Not because he looked like some kind of sex god, all muscled and cocky and laughing. Nope. Solely for glitter transfer purposes.

"We still talking about food?" His voice dropped even further, and she fought the urge to squirm against the throb starting between her legs. He leaned toward her and reached for the Jell-O mold, taking it from its spot in the center of the fridge. He was so close that his chest brushed against hers, and her nipples tightened.

"That's just a small sample of what's to come if you want to continue this little prank war. Have fun digging those out, Prin*cess* Sparklepants. Oh, and I've been told that glitter sticks to everything, so it might take a few days to come off." He shrugged and placed the plate containing the gelatinous red glob in her hands, dusting his hands off as he walked away. She watched him, transfixed by the way his Levi's hugged his perfect, muscular ass. He stretched and his T-shirt rode up, exposing a flash of metal tucked into the waistband of his jeans.

"What the hell is going on?" asked Walker, who was standing on the other side of the kitchenette, an amused smirk on his face as he studied her. God, she must look ridiculous, covered in glitter and holding a Jell-O mold filled with guitar picks.

Well. Score one for Colt.

"Just a stupid prank. Give me five minutes to run this under hot water and clean myself up and we'll be good to go."

Walker chuckled as he walked away. "It might be a prank, but from over here, it looked a lot more like foreplay."

With the growing ache between her thighs, she couldn't help but silently agree. Foreplay, and something more. Something deeper. Something real, and fun, and…happy.

And she knew exactly how she'd pay him back.

# CHAPTER 9

Colt popped a potato chip in his mouth and wiped his greasy fingers on his jeans, setting the bowl of chips down on the kitchen counter.

"So how's working for Taylor Ross?" Clay Michaels sat back in his chair at Colt's kitchen table, a bottle of beer clasped lazily in his hand.

"It's all right," Colt mumbled around a mouthful of chips.

"Must be good money." Clay ran a hand through his shaggy blond hair. He was a private investigator Colt had worked with at Virtus, and despite the fact that Colt had been canned, the two had remained friends. Sometimes, when a job called for it, Clay did a little freelance work for Colt and Roman as well.

"It is. And it doesn't need a PI. Find your own gig, Michaels."

Clay laughed as a burst of staccato raps erupted from the front door. Still crunching and enjoying the carbs and saturated fat—two things he usually didn't allow much of in his diet—Colt strode to the front door and flung it open, interrupting the rhythmic knocking. Jamie Anderson, another bodyguard he'd worked with at Virtus, stood on the other side of the door. It was another friendship Colt had managed to retain despite everything that had gone down.

"Hey." Colt stepped back and gave Jamie space to enter, accepting the six-pack Jamie thrust into his hands. Jamie tipped his chin at him and clapped him on the shoulder. Before he could close the door, he saw Paul's car pull up in front of his house, so he left the door open and headed back into the kitchen to stash the beer in the fridge. He pulled four cold ones out and turned just as Paul entered.

"So I heard that you're working for Taylor Ross now," said Jamie as he began divvying up the poker chips piled in the center of Colt's kitchen table. Something flashed in his light blue eyes, and he rubbed a hand over his blond buzz cut and then over his mouth, as though he were suppressing a smile. Colt flipped the stereo on before taking his place between Jamie and Clay. Stevie Ray Vaughan started coming through the speakers.

Colt took a sip of his beer. "You did, did you?"

"Yeah. I guess you don't know the, uh, connection there, huh?"

Colt glanced at his cards and frowned, and not just because of the shit hand Jamie had just dealt him. "What connection?"

"Taylor's best friend is Sierra Blake. They're like sisters."

"And?"

"Sierra's also Sean's girlfriend. They just moved in together."

Colt took another swallow of beer. "Sean Owens?" As in the guy who ran Virtus, the guy who'd fired Colt? At the mention of Owens, the night he'd lost his job began playing through his mind. The noisy club, filled with writhing bodies, flashing lights and throbbing bass. The fight that had broken out between their client—hip-hop star Tha Thrill—and another clubber. Owens had stepped in to break it up. Colt had backed him up, charging in when he saw the metallic glint of what he'd thought was a knife. He'd shoved Owens aside, and right into the path of another member of the other guy's posse. Owens had taken a beer bottle in the face because of Colt's mistake. The other guy hadn't had a knife, and Colt wasn't sure if it was a trick of the flashing lights, or his own combat memories surfacing at an inopportune time, but he'd misread the situation and fucked up huge. Owens had fired him that night.

And he was dating Taylor's best friend. He turned over that piece of information in his mind, and he knew it was only a matter of time before Owens found out he was working for Taylor, if he hadn't already.

Not a conversation he was looking forward to.

"Anyway, just thought I'd give you a heads up on that. Job's going well?" Jamie glanced briefly at Clay before tossing a few chips into the center of the table.

"Yeah, it's fine. She's a bit of a handful, but it's nothing Roman and I can't handle. Call." He tossed a couple of chips on top of Clay's.

The doorbell rang, and all three turned to look at Colt, who frowned and shrugged before laying his cards down and pushing up out of his seat. As he left, Jamie leaned forward, whispering something to Clay and Paul. A quick glance through the peephole had adrenaline surging through him. He opened the door to three uniformed LAPD officers, all with stern expressions on their faces.

"Are you Colt Priestley?"

Tension shooting through his neck and up into his jaw, he

nodded once as he furiously racked his brain, trying to think of what he'd done to bring not one but three cops to his front door.

"Sir, if you could step back into your house, please." The three cops surged forward, and Colt froze, noticing that they didn't have bulletproof vests on, and that the badges and guns looked decidedly plastic.

"Is there a problem here?" he asked, shutting the front door behind them but leaving it unlocked. He narrowed his eyes at the boys in blue as a knot coiled in his stomach. If this was some kind of home invasion, they'd picked the wrong fucking house.

"Have a seat please." The three cops surrounded him and guided him back to his seat in the kitchen. Just as his ass hit the chair, he noticed that it was now facing outward instead of toward the table, and that the stereo had been shut off. The knot in his stomach tightened. These guys weren't cops, but they didn't seem hostile at all either. What the hell was going on?

"You have the right to remain—"

The strains of Foreigner's "Feels Like the First Time" began playing from one of the cops' radios and Colt tried to stand, but was pushed back into his seat by one of the cops.

"—sexy!"

*Oh, fuck.*

They weren't cops.

They were strippers.

And three guesses who'd sent them.

Suddenly, all three of them had their shirts open, waxed chests glistening as they began gyrating toward him.

As Jamie, Clay, and Paul nearly doubled over with laughter, the three strippers tossed their shirts to the floor, their tight buns wiggling dangerously close to him. A blinking red light caught Colt's attention and he groaned. *Of course* Jamie was recording this. Bastard.

He began to stand again, but was once again pushed down as two very toned, muscular butts wiggled in his face. His head swiveled from left to right as he glanced at his friends, unsure what to do.

And then he felt the cold scrape of metal against his wrist, followed by a sharp click. He jerked his hands away from the chair, only to find his right hand was now fastened securely to it. They might be fake cops, but their handcuffs were very real. Colt bit back a laugh.

"Son of a bitch," he managed, fighting halfheartedly against the handcuffs as the three police officers each tore away their pants, one after the other, revealing what could only be described as banana hammocks, one in red, one in white, and one in blue. They left nothing to the imagination, and Colt couldn't stop the laugh pressing up into his throat, a blush crawling up his neck and over his face.

A pair of very large, very masculine hands landed on his knees, and he looked up into the face of the stripper directly in front of him, frozen to his seat. The stripper's hands began to move upward over Colt's thighs, and he nearly leaped out of his chair despite the handcuffs.

"Whoa! Hey, now," he yelped, his eyes starting to water with laughter.

Taylor was going to pay for this.

* * *

The inside of the Staples Center was Taylor's favorite kind of chaos as crew members scurried back and forth, some carrying large coils of cable, while others spoke into headsets. The arena had been transformed from a sports venue to a concert venue; a massive stage stood at the far end, illuminated stairs crawling up its sides. The lights flashed from blue to red to white and back again as the technicians tested them. Three huge screens hung behind the stage. More technicians worked on the lighting rigs suspended from the ceiling, aiming spot-lights and speaking into buzzing walkie-talkies.

The stage itself was covered with various instruments, cables, microphones, and tools, and was marked up with crisscross patterns of masking and electrical tape. Taylor took a deep breath as a sense of contentment settled over her. Places like this, filled with the promise of great music and entertainment, made her feel more alive than just about any-thing. She spotted Jeremy chatting with Walker and started toward them, picking her way over wires and equipment, Colt at her back. Surprising her again, he'd insisted on car-rying her heavy guitar case and purse for her.

"Morning, beautiful. Looks like you got most of the sparkles off," Walker said by way of greeting.

She nodded. "Yeah. Most of them." She'd spent the better part of yesterday evening de-glittering herself. Colt had been right; that shit stuck to everything. Especially skin. And leather pants.

"I'll meet you backstage in a few," said Walker, tipping his hat and heading off in the direction of the stage.

"I think he's got a little crush on you."

Liquid heat pooled in her belly at the sound of Colt's low rumble.

"How was your poker game?" she asked, ignoring Colt's comment and the accompanying thrill that he might be jealous.

He smiled as he set down her guitar case and the skin around his eyes crinkled. Her stomach did a slow turn in re-sponse. "Arresting."

She snorted before tossing her head back and laughing. "Glad you enjoyed it."

"Hey, now. Didn't say that."

Just when she thought she couldn't have been more attracted to him, he blushed. This guy, who might as well have had ALPHA MALE tattooed on his forehead, *fucking blushed*, and alarm bells rang, shrill and clear, through Taylor's mind. She couldn't remember the last time she'd been so attracted to someone. She hadn't even felt this way with Zack.

And that was dangerous. After everything that had happened with Zack, and the crazy-hot night she'd shared with Colt, she knew better than to let herself feel anything for him. But she knew better about a lot of the stupid shit she did.

"Hey, you've got a little something…" He reached out his free hand and rubbed his thumb over her jaw, skimming his warm hand against her ear. "Sparkles." He smiled again and pulled his hand away, rubbing his thumb rapidly against his fingers, and sure enough, a few silvery fragments fell from his hand like fairy dust.

For a second, she froze, watching the glitter fall and catch the light while her insides melted.

*Fuck.*

Needing to escape, she snatched up her guitar case, spun on her heel, and hurried backstage without a word.

\* \* \*

Colt watched as Taylor walked away, frustration warring with lust. One second they'd been flirting, and the next she'd thrown her shields back up and was practically running in the opposite direction. Again.

A vibration from his left hand startled him out of his lust-

ful staring and when he looked down, he realized that he
was still holding Taylor's purse. He glanced around before
peeking inside, and a smile broke across his face when he
confirmed that the vibration had come from her phone.

Time for a little revenge.

He settled himself in one of the seats to the side of the
stage, keeping an eye on Taylor as she tested her guitar,
popped in an earpiece, and asked a question about her amp
through the live mic. Colt was doing his best to stay out of
everyone's way, and he figured his seat up and away from
the action was the best spot to watch and work on his next
prank.

He glanced around again before pulling her phone out
and tucking her purse beneath his seat. Feeling only slightly
guilty that he'd observed the pattern she used to unlock her
phone, he swiped his finger in a zigzag across the screen.
Opening up her texting app, he went to work.

A while later, he looked up when the overhead lights
dimmed and the stage lights came to life. Musicians took
their places onstage, and his eyes immediately jumped to
Taylor, who had her white guitar slung around her neck.
The opening drum roll and bass line of Walker's hit, "Damn
Shame," echoed out across the stage as Walker entered, guitar in hand, cowboy hat on head, striding confidently to the
mic at center stage.

But Colt wasn't watching Walker, because he couldn't
have torn his eyes away from Taylor if his life had depended
on it. Sure, he'd spent the past few days with her in her
studio, listening to her rehearse, but seeing her up onstage
was something else entirely. Watching her strut around the
stage, all sexy confidence and bad-girl swagger, playing
crisp, strong chords on her guitar, was one hell of an aphro-
disiac. She flung her head back, her blond hair falling around

her slender shoulders like a gold curtain and she smiled, seductive and sure. He shifted in his seat, making room in his jeans for his quickly rising cock.

And then she worked her way to the mic beside Walker's, opened her mouth and joined him on the chorus. Rich and feminine with that crazy-hot rasp to it, she added a sexy little rock-n-roll growl every time she sang the words "damn shame," and for a second, Colt didn't understand why Walker would want to play with Taylor, because she was upstaging him and completely stealing the show. Even Walker couldn't seem to take his eyes off her as she sang and played; there was no denying the presence she had onstage.

She broke into a guitar solo, her long, slender fingers moving easily as she picked out notes, twisted them and wrung them out, stage lights strobing and pulsing, seemingly in time with Colt's blood. They finished the song, and the director hopped onstage to give them some pointers about camera angles.

Between takes of the song, as if sensing his eyes on her, she looked up and searched for him in the stands. His heart lurched against his ribs when her eyes landed on him. Even with the stage lights casting shadows and the distance separating them, he could see an intensity there as she stared at him, her tongue poking against the inside of her lip, her brows drawn in a contemplative frown.

As if she were puzzling something out, unsure of the answer.

He raised his hand in a wave, smiling, and she returned his smile, slow and sure, erasing the frown.

Maintaining eye contact, she bit her lip and played the opening riff of "Feels Like the First Time," shaking her hips a little in time with the chords, and he laughed, leaning his cheek against his fist. He wondered if Jamie had somehow sent her the video, and right now, she was just so fucking cute as she teased him that he didn't even care.

\* \* \*

Ronnie glanced around Taylor's street, watching for nosy neighbors, traffic, anything that could derail his plans. But he knew she wasn't home, and there was no sign of the brute or the other one, the one with all the hair, either, so he knew the house was empty. The housekeeper came once a week, and she wasn't due to show for another few days.

Something cold and dark tightened in his stomach as he thought of the brute. He knew he'd have to do something about him. He couldn't let him keep hanging around Taylor indefinitely. Not only was it bad for Taylor, but it was bad for *them*.

He forced himself to take a deep breath. One thing at a time. With a final glance around, he pulled the straightened wire clothes hanger out of his duffel bag and slid it into the gap where the garage door met the door frame, right at the top center edge of the door. After a few tries, he was able to successfully hook the garage door opener release cable, pulling it hard enough to disengage the garage door opener.

Tucking the hanger back into his bag, he crouched down, and with another glance around, he lifted the door enough to roll underneath, pulling it closed behind him. Quickly, he reattached the garage door opener release cable, not wanting to arouse suspicion when Taylor arrived home and her garage door wouldn't open. He crossed the space to the door leading to the house and pulled the radio frequency jammer from his bag. Holding his breath, he switched it on and tried the doorknob. It turned all the way, and the door into Taylor's house swung open. Smiling to himself, he left the jammer by the alarm's console and made his way into the house, scoping out the best spots for the tiny, wireless cameras and microphones in his bag. Ultimately, he picked the living room, her bedroom, and her bathroom, hiding the cameras and microphones as best he could while still giving himself the best vantage point. He stashed the living room camera in a potted plant, which was the easiest task. Next, he moved into the bedroom, where he unscrewed the top of the DVR and slipped the camera inside, aligning it with the grill. Finally, in the bathroom, he unscrewed the vent cover, positioned the camera inside, aimed it at the shower, and replaced the cover.

Once they were set up, he sat down on her unmade bed and pulled his iPad from the bag. He linked it to the camera feeds and made sure each of them was broadcasting, and that the angle was what he wanted. Satisfied, he laid down on Taylor's bed and inhaled deeply, rubbing her sheets against his skin. Soon, that scent would belong to him.

# CHAPTER 10

Taylor flopped down on her couch, pajamas on, hair up, a glass of wine in one hand and her phone in the other. She was out of gas for the day, even though it was only nine. After the sound check with Walker, she'd had lunch with Jeremy and several label executives. She'd assured them that she was hard at work on the new album.

While at lunch, someone at the restaurant had tipped off the paparazzi, and the sidewalk had been crowded with photographers as she exited. Her stomach fluttered as she remembered how Colt had handled the situation. He'd sheltered her from the lenses as they'd shouted at her, asking her rude questions about the plane incident, trying to get a reaction, and thus get better pictures that would fetch more money from the photo agencies. She was used to dealing with the paparazzi, and they usually didn't bother her much. But today, they'd gotten closer than usual, screaming at her, asking her how many times she'd joined the mile-high club, if she thought her slutty behavior was a bad example to her young fans, if she minded America having a laugh at her expense. She must've looked angry, or scared, or panicked (and she had been), because Colt had leaned in close and spoken directly into her ear, saying "Hey, you're okay. I'm not gonna let anything happen to you." His words—spoken in his deep, rumbly voice—had washed over her, calming and settling her. Then he'd turned around and barked at the photographers to "back the fuck up," his green eyes flashing in a way that had her entire body pulsing with heat.

After the sound check with Walker, lunch, and dealing with paparazzi, she'd headed back to the Sanctuary to work some more. It was as though something—or *someone*—had fixed whatever had broken inside of her, and the music was flowing out of her at an almost alarming rate. She'd come home wiped and had barely had the energy to eat a salad and take a quick shower.

She stretched, took a sip of wine and settled in to the couch, knowing she had several unanswered texts and e-mails to deal with. But instead of opening them, she found herself glancing at the stairs, her body practically vibrating with the knowledge that she and Colt were alone in her house together.

Rolling her eyes at herself, she texted Sierra.

Taylor: Colt is a sexy beast, you busy?

Her eyes widened in shock as she saw what she'd sent. She'd typed "hey," *not* "Colt is a sexy beast." God. She must really be exhausted. Giving her head a shake to clear the cobwebs, she tried again.

Taylor: Sorry, I don't know wtf that was. Didn't mean to type that, obvi. Was only trying to type Colt is a sexy beast.

In that moment, she remembered that she'd left her purse—and in it, her phone—with Colt at the sound check. Clearly, he'd done something to it as payback for the strippers.

Sierra: Um…are you ok?
Taylor: I'm Harry Potter.

She grunted in frustration. She'd simply tried to type "yes."

Taylor: For fuck's sake.
Taylor: I'm Harry Potter.

She snarled at her phone. Apparently "yes" was out as well.

Sierra: Ok…? I'm not busy. What's up, boy wizard?

Reading Sierra's text, Taylor almost choked on her wine, sputtering with laughter.

Taylor: I have an extra ticket to the thing tomorrow night, if you want to come.
Sierra: I can't, I have a photoshoot thing in Malibu all day.
Taylor: Have you seen my vibrator?
Taylor: Jesus! I can't even type Have you seen my vibrator?

"Goddammit, Colt!" She swore through gritted teeth. She'd tried to type "ok." And he'd programmed her phone to change "ok" to "Have you seen my vibrator?"

Sierra: I'm laughing so hard right now.
Taylor: I'm going to kill Colt, King of all that is awesome, who has a large and aesthetically pleasing penis.

Taylor closed her eyes and exhaled slowly through her nose as it became crystal clear what Colt had done. He'd changed the shortcuts for various words, so that if she typed something, the texting app automatically inserted the shortcut he'd created. If she weren't so tired, she probably would've figured it out faster.

Sierra: Tears. I have tears.
Taylor: I give up. He who shall not be named fucked around with my phone.
Sierra: Who's Colt?
Taylor: My stupid bodyguard.
Sierra: Since when do you have a bodyguard?

Taylor stared at her phone, running an index finger over her bottom lip as she thought. She didn't normally keep things from Sierra, but she didn't want to get into the whole story right now.

Taylor: It's kind of a long story, but it's not because I'm in any danger or anything like that. It's just the label being overcautious dicks. Talk to you later P.S. I have a huge crush on Justin Bieber.

Taylor closed her eyes and pressed her hand to her forehead. Oh, she would get him for this. When her brain was fully alert, she'd think of something.

Sierra: I'm never deleting this conversation. Ever. We still on for Karaoke on Wednesday? Chloe's back!

She'd been about to type "yes," but remembered that it was out of commission.

Taylor: For sure. I'm going to spend the night at the STD clinic and plot my revenge.
Taylor: FUCK

And he'd changed "home" to "the STD clinic." Classy. But try as she might, she couldn't suppress the laughter spilling out of her.

Sierra: Good thing it's only me you're texting. God, I can't breathe. My stomach hurts.
Taylor: I'm Harry Potter. It's hilarious.

Crap. She navigated to her shortcuts and reset everything, clearing all of the ridiculous (but admittedly hilarious) short-cuts Colt had put in. After a second, Taylor's phone buzzed again with another text.

Sierra: Wait. Is Colt's last name Priestley?
Taylor: Uh, yeah. Why?
Sierra: He used to work for Virtus, before I started dating Sean. He's the reason Sean has that scar on his cheek. Sean fired him, and doesn't think much of him. Be careful, Taylor.

Taylor frowned as she absorbed that piece of information. Colt had never mentioned working for Virtus, but then again, why would he? She felt guilty for keeping Sierra out of the loop, but now that she knew Colt was a former Virtus bodyguard, she was glad she hadn't told Sierra about the one-night stand. Taylor was still trying to sort through how she felt about him, and she didn't need any extra complications right now, like tension between her and Sierra because of any involvement Taylor might have with Colt.

Taylor: I will. Do me a favor?
Sierra: Anything.
Taylor: Maybe don't mention this to Sean? He'll swoop in
and be all overprotective, and I don't want Virtus involved.

There was a long pause between messages, and Taylor
hated that she was asking Sierra to deliberately keep information from her boyfriend.

Sierra: Because of Zack?
Taylor: Yeah. Exactly.
Sierra: I understand. I won't say anything to him. For now.
Night, T.

After responding to a couple of e-mails and proofreading
everything twice to make sure there were no surprises, she
glanced in the direction of the stairs again. Chewing her lip,
she pushed up off the couch and took the stairs two at a time,
unsure what she was even doing. Unsure if talking to him
was a good idea.

Although when it came to Colt, her sense of good idea / bad
idea was skewed, because he made her forget all of the shit, all
of the pain, of the past few months. He made her laugh, made
her feel good. She could be herself around him, and there was
something so freeing about that. She could swear and drink
and play stupid pranks, and he *liked* it. Being around him made
her forget that her heart wasn't only damaged but unwanted.

Which was an incredibly dangerous thing for her to forget.
And yet here she was, knocking on his bedroom door. She
heard movement on the other side, and she nearly swallowed
her tongue when he pulled it open. He stood there in nothing
but a white towel, knotted dangerously low around his hips,
and looking like the sex god she knew he was. Water dripped

from his mussed hair and onto his gorgeously sculpted chest, his skin fresh and damp. She watched as a drop fell onto the Ranger tattoo covering his left pec, and she curled her fingers into her palms, stifling the urge to trace the drop's path, to trail her fingers along the edges of the tattoo. He took a breath, his abs contracting with the motion, and she clenched her thighs. For a second, they just stared at each other, and she could feel the weight of his green eyes as they dragged over her body. He smiled that cocky half smile and moved his big hands from the door frame to his hips, drawing attention to the muscular V that disappeared under the towel. It was slung so low that she could see where the faint happy trail of light brown hair started to become thicker.

"You're an ass," she said before her brain stopped working entirely and she forgot why she'd knocked on his door in the first place. "Don't fuck with my phone."

"I didn't. I improved it."

She bit her lip, chomping down the smile that so desperately wanted to break free. "I'm surprised you didn't take a picture of your dick and set it as my wallpaper."

Humor and something darker and hotter flashed in his eyes. "Damn. Didn't think of that." He moved his hands slightly lower, his fingertips on the edge of the towel. "Guess that means you want to see it again, huh?"

She wasn't sure if that was a challenge, a threat, or an invitation, and she bit down on her lip harder, this time suppressing the whimper rising up in her throat. God. She never fucking learned.

"You wish," she said, the slight tremble in her voice giving away just how turned on she was.

He studied her intently, his eyes doing a slow sweep down and then back up her body. The towel twitched as his growing erection tented the cotton. "You're right. I do."

Her stomach did a somersault, and she took a deep breath, unsure what to say next. Before she could formulate a response, he'd backed her up against the wall, one hand on either side of her, caging her in. The towel slipped a fraction of an inch, and she couldn't help but glance down.

"Taylor." Colt's voice was low and rough, and she tore her eyes away from his now fully erect cock beneath the towel and back to his face, her breath catching in her throat at the heat there. "You can run, and you can push me away, and you can put up wall after wall. But I'm not going anywhere, gorgeous."

"Of course you're not. It's your job to—"

He cut her off by inching closer, his cock pressing against her hip. "*This* has nothing to do with my job, and everything to do with *us.*"

"*That* has everything to do with you getting me in bed again, and nothing to do with *us* because there is no us."

"There could be, if you'd let me in. We would be so fucking great together, Taylor. In and out of bed."

With his strong, masculine body surrounding her, his scent filling her, his eyes practically devouring her, she found herself wanting to give in, to take what he was offering. He wasn't wrong. They were like fire between the sheets, but there was more to it than that. She liked how she felt when she was with him. Liked that she could laugh with him and be herself. But to have all of that meant opening herself up in a way she wasn't sure she could handle. With Sierra's warning echoing through her mind, she ducked under his arm and stepped away from him.

"Don't touch my phone again." It was the only thing she could think to say before she practically ran down the hall, locking her bedroom door behind her.

# CHAPTER 11

Taylor opened her eyes slowly and rolled over in bed, pulling the covers tighter around her shoulders and burrowing her head into the pillow. After an hour of restless tossing and turning, her mind spinning with anything and everything to do with Colt, she'd finally drifted off into a light, uneasy sleep. She let her eyelids fall again and had just started to sink back into sleep when a steady, sharp knocking pulled her back to the surface. Tension snapping through her, she pushed herself up to sitting and rubbed a hand over her face, listening to the knocking echo through her silent house. She grabbed her phone to check the time: 1:04 A.M.

The knocking stopped for a second, and she curled her fingers around her phone, holding it against her chest. She forced herself to take a shaky breath and then threw back the covers. Her bedroom was at the back of the house, and before she reached the guest room at the front of the house, the knocking started again, louder and more insistent this time. She jumped and her phone fell out of her hand, clattering on the hardwood floor. Scooping it up, she hurried to the guest room just as Colt flung open the door, his gun clutched in one hand, wearing nothing but a pair of snug, black boxer briefs. His hair was mussed and a faint crease line adorned one cheek.

Pushing past him and into the room, Taylor peeked cautiously through the curtains. A Harley sat in her driveway, and her chest constricted almost painfully. Even now, all these years later, the sight of that black-and-orange logo churned her stomach, making her want to heave.

"Do you know who that is?" Colt's voice rumbled from behind her, low and rough with sleep. He peered over her shoulder, his breath fanning against her shoulder.

"My…my dad." She held completely still, barely even breathing, her skin both too hot and too cold at the same time. She watched as her father paced from her front door into her driveway, peering up at the house, and with a gasp, she ducked down under the window. Colt turned to head down the stairs, but she reached out, her hand brushing his bare calf. "Don't. Please. Just wait for him to go."

Somehow, he'd found her, and was now intent on banging down her door in the middle of the night. All the strength slid out of her muscles, and she sank to the floor, pulling her knees to her chest as her heart pushed up into her throat. Fear and anger coiled into tight little knots in her chest, making it hard to breathe. She hated that after all these years, he still had this kind of power over her.

"I know you're in there! Taylor!" Something crashed against the door, rattling it. "I need to talk to you. Get out here!"

"I'm not just going to stand here while he tries to break your goddamn door down." Colt checked the clip on his gun and again moved toward the bedroom door.

"No! Colt, he's dangerous. Please, just wait with me. Please don't leave me alone."

His nostrils flared as he looked out the window, toward the door, and back down at where Taylor was crouched on the floor. She looked up at him, and she felt as though flames were licking at her skin. The sight of him above her—muscles tensed, gun clutched in one big hand, practically naked—seared through her, and the tiniest whimper pushed its way past her lips. In the semidark, their eyes met, and something in his expression softened. After a second, he sank onto the floor beside her and slipped his arms around her, pulling her into his chest. She closed her eyes and pressed her face into him, using the steady beat of his heart against her cheek to anchor herself against the fear until after several minutes, the knocking stopped, and the roar of a motorcycle ripped through the night.

* * *

Colt stroked a hand over Taylor's messy blond hair as tension radiated across his jaw. He clamped his teeth together, fighting the urge to go out there and confront the man who'd made the blood drain from Taylor's face. Whatever the bastard had done to make Taylor so afraid of him, Colt wanted to make him pay for it. "You okay?"

She eased away from him, twisting her fingers together, and an almost overwhelming sense of protectiveness rocked into him, tilting his world for a second. "I'm sorry."

"Hey." He slipped a hand under her chin and tipped her face up. "Nothing to be sorry for. I'm here to protect you, no matter what. Keep your sorries, gorgeous."

Her breathing hitched and her lip trembled. With a gasping sigh, a tear slid down her cheek, and Colt pulled her back into his arms. She tensed, but as he ran a hand down her back, she relaxed into him, her face pressed against his neck.

For several moments, he just held her, not saying anything, not asking all of the questions he wanted to ask.

All too soon, she pulled away, wiping hastily at her eyes, and he saw the shields go back up as she stood up and moved away from him.

"Thank you," she said, wrapping her arms around herself.

"I didn't do anything, but you're welcome." He stood, studying her. "So your dad's bad news, huh?"

"Yeah. He…" She shrugged. "He was pretty rough with me when I was a kid."

Something in Colt's chest tightened, and he wanted to pull her back into his arms. Based on how scared she'd been, there was more to it than that. "You want to talk about it?"

She shook her head. "Nope."

"Does he do this a lot?"

She shook her head again. "I haven't seen him in years. But he…he texted me a few days ago." She turned and sat on Colt's unmade bed, and he didn't miss the way her eyes lingered on the rumpled sheets before darting back to him. He crossed his arms over his chest, steeling himself against how badly he wanted to join her on that bed and make her forget about everything except how good he could make her feel.

"What did he want? When he texted you, I mean."

She fisted her hands in the sheets. "Just said he wanted to see me. I told him to fuck off, and I changed my number." She looked down at the floor, dragging her toes across the hardwood. "I didn't know he knew where I lived."

"What did you mean when you warned me he was dangerous?"

She swallowed, and he could've sworn he saw her shiver. "When I was a kid, he was a member of the Grim Weavers. I'm pretty sure he still is. Still had the Harley and the vest tonight."

Shit. The Grim Weavers were one of the most notorious outlaw biker gangs in California. Roman had done a cursory background check on Taylor, standard operating procedure for any new client they took on, but this hadn't popped up. Probably because her father wasn't in her life, and she likely hid the connection as much as she could. He knew he would have, in her shoes. His heart ached for Taylor, growing up with a nasty biker for a dad. Again, he wanted to reach for her, but he knew she'd just pull away again, so he stayed right where he was, arms still crossed.

"What's his name?"

"Frank Ross."

"I have a buddy who's an investigator. I want to see what we can dig up on him, find out why he's suddenly popping back up."

She nodded and stood from the bed, and he couldn't take it anymore. He slowly crossed the room and pulled her into his arms again, slipping his arms around her waist. "I'm glad I'm here, Taylor, regardless of the circumstances."

"Me too." She laid her head on his shoulder and sighed softly.

"I'm not going to let anything happen to you, gorgeous. You're safe with me."

She trembled slightly and then lifted her head from his shoulder, her lips parted slightly and only inches from his. A tension hung between them, shimmering in the air like heat. He inched his face closer to hers, waiting for her to pull away. Her eyes flicked down to his mouth and she dipped her head slightly, grazing her nose against his cheek.

Steeling himself against the excitement shooting through him and stiffening his dick, he took a steadying breath— which was a mistake, because that deep inhale brought with it the sweet, warm scent of her skin. It made him want to bury his face in her neck and taste the skin where her pulse beat.

She pressed her hips against him, and he knew she could feel how hard he was. She leaned forward until her lips were millimeters from his ear. "Thank you."

His hands splayed across her back as he pulled her tighter against him; her nipples were tight little buds under the thin cotton of her T-shirt. He tucked a strand of hair behind her ear, tracing her delicate jaw with the tips of his fingers.

"You're welcome." He pressed a kiss to the center of her throat, and her eyes fluttered closed.

"Fuck," she breathed, as he trailed his mouth over her collarbone, leaving goose bumps in his wake.

His hands skated up her back and into her hair, and he gave the locks tangled around his fingers a gentle tug, forcing her to meet his gaze. "I want you so fucking much, Taylor."

"Colt." His name was a strangled sigh on her lips, and he dipped his head, his lips teasing the shell of her ear as he spoke.

"Tell me that night didn't mean anything to you."

She pulled back and met his gaze, not saying anything. She didn't need to, because everything he needed was right there in those beautiful blue eyes. Every single cell in his body roared to life as he closed his mouth over hers in a tender, gentle kiss. She moaned, and then pulled back almost immediately. Shaking her head, she pressed her fingers to her mouth.

"I'm going to bed. Alone." She turned and left without a backward glance.

* * *

The limo ride from the Staples Center to the Standard Bar after the awards show took nearly twenty minutes, despite the fact that the two locations were less than a mile and a half apart. Colt shifted in his seat next to the driver and stared at the rows of red taillights on either side of the street. It didn't matter that it was well past rush hour; shitty traffic was a fact of life in Los Angeles.

Taylor's laugh echoed from the back, even though the divider was up. She was back there with some suits from Walker's label, and Walker, who, Colt had noticed, had been eyeing Taylor all night the way a starving man eyes a steak. It sent tension radiating up his neck, into his jaw and over his scalp.

But Colt had been the one to kiss her last night. He shifted in his seat, trying to ignore the tightening pull low in his stomach as he replayed that night again, remembering how she'd felt underneath him, her mouth on his, her legs wound around his eager hips. He lost himself in the memory of all the different ways he'd made her moan and beg. Of how good it had felt to hear his name in that raspy voice as he'd discovered exactly how she liked to be touched, where she liked to be kissed.

Pushing it aside, he gave his head a subtle shake, knowing he was in over his head with this woman. He shouldn't be chasing her the way he was. She was running, and he should let her. He knew he was fucked up because of the terrible shit he'd seen. The truth was, he cared about Taylor, and if he wasn't a selfish asshole, he'd want something better for her than anything he could offer. And yet he wanted Taylor. Wanted to protect her, and comfort her, and feel the slide of her skin against his again.

The limo pulled to a stop in front of the Standard, where a red carpet and a black-and-gold backdrop featuring the logo

of Metro Music Nashville—Walker's label and the spon-
sors of the post-awards party—lined the walkway in front
of the entrance. In a cordoned-off area behind velvet ropes,
rows of photographers waited, cameras poised. Walker and
Taylor hit the carpet together, Colt following a few feet behind, his eyes scanning the crowd for any potential threats.
Walker slid his arm around Taylor, his fingers curling over
her slender waist. She smiled at him and then leaned in
and whispered something in his ear, which earned her a
smoldering look from Walker. Swallowing, Colt worked his
jaw loose, fearing he'd crack a tooth with the pressure he
was putting on his back molars. Tamping down the jealousy
churning his gut, he returned his attention to the crowd and
tried to focus on simply doing his job.

Inside, the party was already in full swing, rowdy country
music thumping from the speakers. The walls were awash in
gold and red lights that served to illuminate the space while
casting the buttery-yellow leather booths lining the walls
into shadow. Waitresses in tight red cocktail dresses circu-
lated through the crowd carrying trays laden with beer, shots
of tequila, shakers of salt, and bowls of lime wedges. The far
wall glittered with lights that were flashing and pulsing in
time with the music. At one of the booths, a tray with several
lines of white powder was being passed around, along with
a rolled up hundred-dollar bill. Dread dropped into Colt's
stomach like a weight. He must've been wearing his appre-
hension plain as day, because Taylor turned toward him and
touched his arm.

"Relax. I don't do drugs." She shot him a reassuring
smile, walking past the booth with the cocaine.

"I'm glad to hear it." And he meant it.

She shook her head and snorted out a laugh. "Yeah, well,
hold the parade. I'm just scared I'd like them too much."

Something angry and raw flashed in her eyes. "God knows my mom did." She stilled and the light in her eyes changed. "She OD'd when I was fourteen."

"I'm sorry." He'd known from the background report that her mother had died over fifteen years ago. Out of respect for her privacy, given the nature of the job, he hadn't dug any further than that. But now an empathetic ache bloomed in his chest, along with a sudden, intense, almost overwhelming need to comfort her. He wanted to know more, to take some of that pain he'd glimpsed and carry it for her. Before he could open his mouth, one of the waitresses circled close by, making eye contact with Colt and smiling, winking and tossing her hair over her shoulder as she sashayed away.

"Go on and get you some, cowboy," said Taylor in his ear before giving him a smack on the ass, grabbing Walker's hand and leading him toward the bar. Following several feet behind, Colt watched as Taylor laughed at something Walker said and then lifted his cowboy hat off his head and plunked it down on her own, tilting it at a flirty angle. Sidling up to the bar, Walker grabbed two shots of tequila and slid one to Taylor, who downed hers like a champ.

A commotion near the door caught his attention before he could find an inconspicuous spot along the wall, and he set himself between Taylor, who was several feet away at the bar, and the disturbance, his shoulders tensed, bracing himself for whatever was coming.

"Y'all gonna let me in, or what?" A tiny blonde emerged from the crowd, and Colt recognized her instantly. Monroe Bell had just walked in.

# CHAPTER 12

Is it working?" Taylor asked, leaning in to shout in Walker's ear over the loud music. Lifting his head, he looked in Colt's direction before trailing a hand up her arm.

"Oh, yeah. Dude's jealous as hell."

She smiled, satisfaction shooting through her. "Thanks for helping me with this, Walk."

He glanced at Colt again, smiling skeptically. "I get punched, you owe me."

"I owe you regardless." She laid a hand on his thick forearm and gave him a friendly squeeze.

He took a sip of his beer, his tongue swiping away a stray drop that clung to his full lower lip. Taylor watched, and she found herself wondering if kissing Walker would be going too far in her mission to piss Colt off and push him away. Before she'd made up her mind, Walker leaned in and shouted a question in her ear.

"So why you doing this, sweetheart? If you want him, just go get him. You're torturing the guy."

Taylor brought her beer to her lips, trying to find a way to explain. She wasn't torturing Colt because she was pissed at him, but pissed at herself. She'd come so close to letting him back into her bed last night—*twice*—and it was such a terrible idea. And yet...she'd been so relieved he was there last night. She'd felt safe, just knowing that he was in the house.

She couldn't help but wonder if she was letting what had happened with Zack scare her away from something potentially awesome. Which would be a terrible waste, now wouldn't it?

She swallowed thickly and looked over her shoulder at where Colt stood several feet away, but his attention was focused on the bar's entrance, where a five-foot-two blond hurricane was pushing her way in.

"Uh-oh," she said, turning back to Walker, who'd also just noticed Monroe's presence.

"Shi-it," he said, drawing it out into two syllables.

"You stupid, two-timing motherfucker!" yelled Monroe, spotting Taylor and Walker and making a beeline for them. "And you! You dumb bitch! I'm gonna kick your a—" The last word turned into a shriek as Colt scooped her up and tossed her over his wide shoulder like a sack of potatoes. Everyone in the party was now watching. The DJ cut the music, giving everyone the opportunity to listen to the confrontation.

Taylor pressed a fist to her mouth, hiding her laughter. One second, Monroe had been hell on high heels, steamrolling her way toward them, and the next, Colt was there, calm and sure. Sturdy, as always. She never would've thought she'd be so turned on by sturdy, but damn, was his dependability appealing.

Monroe struggled against Colt, who held her in place as

though she were made of feathers. He didn't even look like he was trying. "Put me down! You have no right to touch me. I'll—"

"It's for your own safety, sweetheart. Because if I put you down, I'm pretty sure someone's gonna get her ass kicked, and my money's on that someone being you." He met Taylor's eyes and winked and something inside her softened. The situation with Monroe could've been very bad if Colt hadn't stepped in, because anything between her and Monroe wouldn't have ended well, especially given all the shit Monroe had talked about Taylor in the tabloids.

"Roe, settle down. Let's go talk somewhere. All right?" Walker bent over to meet her eyes, her blond hair fanning out around her in a platinum curtain. "Taylor's got nothing to do with this. She and I are just friends. Honest."

"Y'all were all over each other. I saw. You been fucking her, Walk?"

Colt glanced over his shoulder at Walker, clearly interested in the answer to Monroe's question.

"No. Taylor and I have only ever been friends."

"Yeah, y'all sure looked friendly." But Monroe had lost some steam and was calming down. Being helplessly pinned halfway upside down could have that effect on a girl.

"We were just joking around. Roe, she *asked* me to flirt with her, to…" Walker glanced up at Colt and shrugged.

Colt met Taylor's eyes and smiled that cocky smile, the one that crinkled the skin around his eyes and had her toes curling and thighs clenching.

"I put you down, you gonna behave?" Colt asked over his shoulder.

She waited a second before nodding, which looked more like head-banging since she was still suspended upside down. Bending his knees, Colt gently lowered her to the ground, watching her warily. Walker took her by the arm and led her out, everyone watching as they left.

Taylor turned back to the bar and picked up her beer, taking a long sip. What a mess. And yet based on the heat and intensity arcing between Walker and Monroe as they left the bar, Taylor would've bet good money that they'd be tearing each other's clothes off at the first opportunity.

"You know, if you'd told me I'd be picking up women tonight, that's *not* what I would've had in mind." Colt leaned against the bar beside her, humor dancing in his eyes. He rubbed a hand over his hair.

Unable to help herself, she bit her lip and laughed. God, it felt good just to be around him. And not just because he was so gorgeous she sometimes didn't feel like she could think straight when she looked at him. It was his sense of humor, his intelligence, his ability to keep her safe. Just *him*. Colt.

"Thanks for stepping in. I appreciate it."

"That's what I'm here for. I've got your back." He tapped the brim of her hat and leaned in closer. "I like this on you. It's cute."

She felt her cheeks heat, his deep voice rumbling down her spine and making her want to arch into him. Laughing, she pulled the hat off and settled it on Colt's head. He adjusted it before giving her a fake-model-type stare, intense eyes and pursed lips, like Derek Zoolander's patented "blue steel" look. She laughed so hard she snorted and he broke, laughing along with her.

"I should get back to my post. Ma'am." He touched the brim of his hat before stepping away from the bar.

Her heart thumped happily in her chest as she watched him. *Well, shit.*

* * *

The scent of smoke filled Colt's nostrils, and he blinked rapidly against the harsh sunlight, his eyelids gritty with sand. The metallic rattle and pop of gunfire echoed around him, spraying up sand around his feet. Chunks of mortar rained down on him and knocked against his thick helmet. A bright flash in the distance cut the air and he ran forward, sweat pouring down his back, his rifle clutched in his hands.

"Benson, Gomez, get down!" He dived on the two soldiers just as a large blast rocked the ground underneath them. Colt set his M4 in front of him and reloaded it, then crouched on the ground, surrounded by men, sand and rock. He took aim and opened fire; the staccato burst of gunfire vibrated through him as he braced and squeezed the trigger again. "You get them in your sights, you fucking fire!" he shouted over his shoulder to his men.

For several long, tense minutes, the Third Ranger Battalion traded gunfire with the Taliban militia. They'd managed to push the militia out of the valley, finally, but they'd been fighting over the area for weeks.

The bullets suddenly stopped, and Benson looked over his shoulder at Colt. "Where they at, Sarge?" he asked, his voice loud in the sudden quiet.

A flash of something shiny caught Colt's eye. "East!" Bullets rained down like hail, followed by a deep, booming explosion that knocked him flat on his back, crushing the breath out of him. Sweat ran into his eyes as he struggled to get up and check on his men. His pulse pounded like a drum in his temples, and his vision swam. His ears rang, high-pitched and discordant, as he pushed to his feet. He spat out equal parts saliva, blood, and sand. Staggering forward, his feet tangled in something, and he fell. Glancing back, he saw what he'd tripped on and ground his teeth against the nausea rising up. It was a nausea he'd felt many times over the past ten years, but he'd never given into it. Not once.

Pushing the bloody, severed leg to the side, he wiped the sweat out of his eyes and moved forward on shaky legs, taking stock of the soldiers lying on the ground, some moving, some not. Heat pressed down on him, heavy and oppressive, and bullets began flying anew. He tripped again, and when he landed facedown in the dirt, his eyes came level with Benson's glassy, vacant stare. Another blast rocked the ground, and a searing pain bit into his shoulder. He struggled to push himself up, gritting his teeth against the pain, surrounded by the lifeless bodies of the men he'd led into this valley and—

Colt bolted upright in bed, his heart pounding and sweat pouring down his face and chest in narrow streams. He sucked in several deep breaths and pressed his hands to his face as he tried to slow his racing pulse.

"Fuck," he whispered aloud, bringing his legs toward his chest under the sweat-drenched sheet and resting his elbows on his knees. He rubbed his hands over his face, concentrating on his breathing. His temples throbbed, the familiar adrenaline-hangover headache setting in. Reaching his right arm across his body, he ran his fingers over his left shoulder, tracing the puckered scar left by the shrapnel, trying to feel lucky instead of guilty that he'd made it through. He took several deep breaths before swinging his legs over the side of the bed and clicking on the bedside light. He picked up his phone and checked the time: 3:13 A.M. *Fucking great.*

Bracing his hands on his thighs, he pushed off the bed and padded to Taylor's kitchen in his bare feet and boxers. Opening the cabinet where he knew she kept her liquor, he pulled down the half-empty bottle of Johnnie Walker. Its am-

ber liquid gleamed with the promise of numbing the guilt,
the anxiety, and the anger squeezing the air out of his lungs
and making him want to hit something. He'd gone weeks
without a nightmare, but this one had been bad. When they
happened, they felt so real, so fucking visceral, that he might
as well have been back in the Sandpit, staring into the dead
eyes of a soldier whose death was Colt's fault.

Pouring a healthy amount of scotch into a tumbler, he
put the bottle back into the cabinet before shuffling into the
dark living room. The hardwood floor creaked softly under
his feet as he settled into the black leather armchair looking
out onto the terrace. The not-so-distant lights of Hollywood
shone in the night, glimmering against the darkness. As he
stared at the lights, white and yellow against the velvet purple of the sky, he raised his glass to his lips, closing his eyes
against the welcome burn.

He slid down lower and rested his head against the back
of the chair, trying not to think. Trying not to remember.
Trying not to feel as though he had a giant hole in his sternum, sucking everything he had out of him and leaving him
empty. He took another swallow of scotch and rubbed a hand
over his chest. With slow, steady breaths he began to conjure
up his safe place, where he was happy, whole, and home. He
hadn't had a lot of happy, whole places to call home growing up, so he usually thought of Lacey and his nephews, but
a new series of images pushed into his brain this time, each
different, but each featuring the same person.

Taylor. Laughing and plopping a cowboy hat on his head.
Sitting in the passenger seat of his car, making fun of his
engine. Trembling against him in her doorway. Rocking out
onstage, sending him flirty looks. The feel of the soft skin of
her throat against his mouth.

That incredible night they'd spent together.

Her. She was beautiful, and funny, and made him feel good. Alive, but without all of the usual shit he felt when he wasn't numb.

He tossed back the rest of his drink, and he felt something broken deep inside him shift, and even though he *didn't* deserve her, he wanted to try to be worthy. The realization that she was the first woman who'd made him want to try to live again caught him right in the chest. Something about her called to him, not as the man he was, but the man he wanted to be.

The man he hoped he could be.

* * *

Taylor felt like an idiot, tiptoeing around her own house, sneaking down the stairs and avoiding the creaky spots like a teenager slipping out to meet her boyfriend for a make-out session. She yawned and paused with her hand on the doorknob to the garage, listening for any sounds of life in her house. Only silence greeted her. Colt was probably still sleeping. In a bed. In her house. Probably wearing nothing except those stupidly tight black boxer shorts.

Grinning, she grabbed the old metal Slim Jim her foster brother had given her years ago, along with several massive bags filled with the Ping-Pong balls left over from a music video shoot. They'd been taking up space in her garage for years now, and as she'd lain awake the night before—unable to sleep because every time she closed her eyes, she only saw Colt—she'd remembered them. She'd been sifting through prank ideas, wanting to get him back. Funny how the prank war had started as a way to push him away, but it was only pulling them closer together. And yet despite that, she wanted to keep playing. Wanted to keep inching closer to him, needing more of how good she felt around him.

Hefting the bags over her shoulder, she slipped out the side door of the garage and set them down next to the Charger, glancing around to make sure no one was watching. The last thing she needed was a nosy neighbor calling the police on her for breaking into a car parked in her own driveway. But the street was quiet, the only sound the distant rush of early-morning traffic and the wet whir of a sprinkler from a few houses away. At six thirty in the morning, the sun was stretching up over the horizon, casting a pinkish orange glow over the neighborhood. The cloudless sky above was an airy, misty azure that hinted at the warm, sunny day to come. The palms in her yard rustled softly in the light breeze.

Looking once more over her shoulder, she set the bags down in the driveway, peering up at her house for any signs of life, but it was dark and silent. Careful not to scratch the paint, she slipped the Slim Jim in between the weather strip and the glass of the driver's-side window and carefully slid it down, moving the tool back and forth until she saw the lock start to wiggle a little bit on the other side of the window. Biting her lip and concentrating, she gingerly hooked the door lock mechanism and gently pulled up, unlocking the Charger. She eased the Slim Jim free and slipped it into her back pocket. Tearing open one of the bags of Ping-Pong balls, she dumped its contents across Colt's front seat. She suppressed a giggle as she imagined his reaction when he went to open his car later this morning. Then maybe at least they'd be able to take the Corvette. She was so caught up in her work that she didn't realize Colt was right behind her until he spoke.

"What the hell do you think you're doing to my car?"

The bag still in her hands, she spun around abruptly,

sending little white balls bouncing across the driveway. Her mouth went dry at what she saw.

Colt stood in front of her, impressively muscled arms crossed over his equally impressive bare and sweaty chest. The faintest dusting of light brown hair covered his defined pecs and trailed in a straight line down the middle of his six-pack, disappearing into his black shorts. His cheeks were flushed with exertion, and a pair of earbuds dangled around his neck. His light brown hair was dark with sweat, clinging to his temples.

"I...it was just a prank. I promise, I didn't do any damage," she said once she found her voice, setting the bag down in front of her and raising her hands in a placating gesture. She hadn't counted on getting busted in the act, especially by a sweaty and bare-chested Colt, who, she had to admit, looked sexy as hell when he was pissed.

He arched an eyebrow, eyes darting between her, his car, and the bags of Ping-Pong balls. "Why am I not surprised that you know how to break into a car?" The corner of his mouth tipped up in a half smile, that, when paired with his shirtlessness, made her stomach dip and swirl in a very appealing way.

"Hey, I'm a poster child for the foster care system."

The smile dropped off his face and his brow creased. "You were a foster kid?" He brushed a drop of sweat from his brow, muscles rippling below his taut skin.

God. She wanted to lick him. Every. Damn. Inch.

She shrugged. "For a few years, yeah. So?"

He mirrored her shrug. "Nothing. Just...I bet that was rough."

"Yeah, well. It was better than staying with my dad." A chill ran through her at the memory of how awful things had been right before she'd been put into the foster care system.

The verbal abuse. The beatings. The lack of food. The general fucked-up-ness of every day that had only gotten worse after her mom's death.

Colt exhaled a sharp breath through his nose and nodded. "I hear that."

"Really?" Her eyebrows shot up, her voice flat and disbelieving.

He nodded slowly. "Really. I was never in foster care, but…" He trailed off, shrugging his broad shoulders again. "Let's just say that my home life wasn't the greatest." He shot her a sympathetic smile before clearing his throat, a faux-serious expression dropping into place over his features. "Clean this shit up. I'll be in the shower."

Something hot and delicious pulsed low in her stomach at the thought of Colt in the shower. The water sluicing across that gorgeously masculine torso, rivulets running over the peaks and valleys created by his strong, muscular physique. Foamy lines of soap dripping off his skin, his eyes closed as he tipped his head back under the hot spray.

*Holy hell.*

She licked her lips and swallowed, her eyes darting up to his. Her heart felt as though it had literally skipped a beat, stopping just for a second and then restarting at double time when she saw her lust mirrored in his eyes.

"Yeah, sure. I'll get right on that." She snorted out a laugh, and almost choked when he took a step toward her, backing her into the body of the Charger.

"You'll get right on what? Cleaning up your mess?" He leaned one hand on the roof of the car, and her insides turned to molten lava, pooling between her thighs. "Or me, in the shower?" He leaned in even closer and circled one hand around her waist. She tried, but she couldn't suppress the tremble that worked its way through her. Lust. Anticipation.

Need. Hunger. Fuck, yes. This was happening, and no way was she going to be able to fight it this time.

And then he yanked the Slim Jim out of her back pocket and stepped away.

He held it up and wiggled it. "I think I'll hang on to this."

"Hey!" She took a step forward, and he backed away, laughing. Shooting her that cocky smile, he turned around and headed for the front door. "Just *wait* until I tell Jeremy that you abandoned your post!" she called, but he just laughed and headed into the house.

# CHAPTER 13

Colt sat on a couch in the Sanctuary, watching Taylor rehearse another new song with her band. While rehearsing, the band, including Taylor, configured themselves into a circle, all facing each other as they played, so her back was to him. It meant that he couldn't see her face, but he *could* see her cute little ass in her tight jeans, so overall, it was a pretty nice compromise.

After his combat nightmare, he'd fallen asleep and dreamed of her. In his dream, they'd been in a hotel room, completely alone and sheltered from the outside world as rain pounded the windows. They'd kissed, slowly at first, tasting and exploring, but eager lust had quickly spread between them like wildfire. He'd gathered her up in his arms and carried her to the bed, where, between hot, intense kisses, they'd shed their clothing in record time. Naked beneath him, her long, slender body had lined up perfectly with his. Skin to skin, her legs intertwined with his, he'd just closed his mouth over hers again when he'd jolted awake, drooling and hard as concrete. He'd had to take a minute before easing out of bed, so painfully aroused he feared he'd snap his dick right off if he moved.

Already, he knew, he could get lost in her. And if she'd have him, he'd let himself, despite his growing suspicion that she had often been given far less than she deserved, and his guilt over possibly adding himself to that category.

He'd gone for his morning run as though he weren't on the verge of completely losing control. At first, he'd been pissed to find Taylor messing with his car, but once he'd realized no actual harm had been done, the humor hadn't been lost on him.

He'd still confiscated the Slim Jim, though. Just to be on the safe side.

In between takes of the song, one of the studio assistants waved him over, signaling toward the Sanctuary's front door. A flower delivery van sat parked outside, and before he could even speak, a young, lanky guy shoved a large bouquet of white roses into Colt's arms, spinning on his heel and heading back toward his van without a word. Frowning, Colt glanced down at the card poking out from among the petals, Taylor's name printed neatly on the envelope. He swallowed against the knot of jealousy sitting low in his throat. Maybe they were from Jeremy, congratulating her on her kick-ass performance the night before. Or an apology bouquet from Walker, since he'd ditched her at the after party.

"These are for you," he said, extending the bouquet toward her as he walked back into the rehearsal area of the space. She studied him for a second before reaching out and taking the flowers.

"You got me flowers?" she asked, and a smile bloomed across her face. His chest tightened, because someone else had earned that smile. Not him. She was so beautiful when she smiled like that. When she smiled like she was genuinely happy.

He rubbed a hand over the back of his neck, his skin hot and itchy. "No. A delivery guy just dropped them off."

"Oh. Cool. Thanks." She bit her lip, something that looked a hell of a lot like disappointment flashing in her eyes, and turned away from him, pulling the card from the bouquet.

He watched as she read the card, trying to read the slender lines of her back for clues, his jaw clenched. Suddenly, she spun and stalked toward him, hitting him in the chest with the bouquet and sending white petals fluttering to the floor. She released the bouquet and he gathered it awkwardly to his chest to prevent it from falling.

"Not funny," she said, her brows drawn.

He frowned, set the bouquet aside and held up his hands in innocence. "I told you, they're not from me."

"So this isn't a prank?"

"Sending you roses isn't much of a prank."

"Here." She thrust the card at him and he noticed the slight tremble in her fingers as he took it from her.

*It's time to stop hiding our relationship from everyone. I want to scream from the rooftops that I love you and that you're mine. I want to burn your name across my skin. I need the world to know who you belong to.*

*I will mark your body the way you've marked my soul.*

*See you soon, my darling, my true love, my bride.*

*Love, your devoted husband.*

Colt clamped his lips together and rubbed a hand over his mouth as he read the card a second time. He laid a hand on Taylor's shoulder, and her wide blue eyes met his, bright with worry.

"Do you have any idea who might've sent these?"

She shook her head, her teeth digging into her bottom lip. "There were no red flags in your file."

She opened her mouth to speak but then paused, frowning. Two little lines dug in between her eyebrows. "You have a file on me?"

"When we took this job, Roman did a background check. It's standard operating procedure." He took a step closer to her. "I had him do it instead of doing it myself. It felt wrong to dig into your past after we…" He cleared his throat. "Anything I should know about?"

She shook her head. "No." Her voice was barely above a whisper, and she shivered and hugged herself. "This is really fucking creepy. The flowers were delivered here, so whoever this guy is, he knows that this is my space." She rubbed her hands over her upper arms as she spoke. "And the card…" She shuddered. "Who says shit like that?" Frowning, she bit her lip again.

He gave her shoulder a light squeeze and her eyes snapped back to his. "Hey. As long as I'm around, nothing bad will happen to you. You're safe." He gave her shoulder another squeeze, although what he really wanted to do was pull her into his arms. "I'll take care of you. I promise."

She met his gaze and nodded.

"I'm going to call Roman to come take over here. I need to hit up the flower shop, see if I can get an ID on whoever sent these."

She nodded again, her brows drawn tightly together. She gave her head a shake and then turned back to her band, doing a hell of a job at hiding her fear.

When Colt got his hands on whoever was messing with his girl, he'd make them hurt.

* * *

Less than half an hour later, Colt pushed open the door of Petal Pushers Flowers, cool air and the heady scent of hundreds of flowers greeting him. He scanned the shop, but it was empty except for an older lady agonizing over two different bouquets of lilies. Glancing up into the corners of the ceiling, he saw the small, black domes—housings for security cameras—he'd been hoping to find. He just hoped they weren't dummies, fake cameras meant to deter but that didn't actually record anything. At the sound of the door chime, a young woman came out to the front counter from the workroom in the back, thick gloves on her hands and a green apron draped over her neck. When she spied Colt, she smiled, and he put his hastily devised plan into action.

A flicker of heat flared up his spine as he reached a hand into his pocket. Fuck, this was a dumb, potentially dangerous plan, but he needed access to that security footage, and this was the fastest way to get it.

If it worked.

Keeping his expression serious, he approached the counter and pulled out the fake LAPD badge he'd bought online and flashed it quickly before tucking it away. "I'm Detective Thompson, LAPD. You have a minute?"

The young woman's eyes widened at the flash of his badge, and she stood up a little straighter. "Is...is there a problem?"

Colt smiled, trying to put the girl at ease. "No, no. But we have reason to believe someone we've been tracking was in your shop earlier today." He pointed up at one of the security cameras. "Those live?"

She nodded, swallowing thickly. "Yeah, but my boss isn't here, and..."

"I just need to take a quick peek to see if the guy we're looking for was here. That's all," Colt bluffed. He wasn't sure who he was looking for. He did know that the shop was small enough that they didn't take online orders, and the writing on the card had been decidedly masculine—the asshole had likely written it out himself, which meant he'd been here.

The girl pulled off her gloves and ran her hands down the front of her apron, smoothing away invisible wrinkles.

"I just need a few minutes and then I'll be out of your hair. You can call my LT if it'll make you feel better." He pulled out one of the fake business cards he'd had made up and slid it over the counter to her. If she actually called the number on the card, she'd get Roman's cell phone. She stared at the card for a second, and then looked up at Colt, who smiled again. She toyed with the card, thinking.

"You'd be doing us a big favor, here, miss."

"I don't really know how to use the security software," she said, chewing on her bottom lip, and Colt knew she was about to give in.

"You leave that to me. Your computer's round back?"

She hesitated for another moment and then nodded, motioning for him to follow her back. She led him into a small, cramped office and pointed at the computer stationed on the old metal desk. She shut the door behind her as she left, and with a few clicks, Colt accessed the security camera software. Thankfully, it was a program he was familiar with. He settled himself behind the desk and pulled up the camera feeds, rewinding to thirty minutes before Taylor's flowers had been delivered, then worked backward in half-hour chunks, scanning through and looking for anything that jumped out at him. He knew he was likely looking for a man who'd come in alone, had quickly ordered and left without browsing the shop, and had written the message on the card himself.

Suddenly, an image popped up on the screen, and Colt

leaned forward in his seat and rewound a few minutes, playing the video feed back at normal speed. With a few taps on the keyboard, he zoomed in the camera as much as he could before the picture quality deteriorated. A white guy in his late twenties, wearing a plain white T-shirt and jeans, had stepped into the shop. His hair was closely cropped on the sides and a little longer on top, and he wore a pair of horn-rimmed glasses. Something about him was familiar. Really familiar. Fingers pressed to his mouth, Colt watched the video as the man selected a bouquet of white roses, wrote out a card, paid cash, and left. He turned toward the door, and his face came fully into focus.

It was the guy who'd grabbed Taylor at the Rainbow. Colt pulled his keys from his pocket and snapped the USB stick free, jamming it into the computer and downloading the section of footage he needed. He glanced at the clock in the bottom right-hand corner of the computer. The Rainbow would be open, the last of the lunch crowd finishing up. He pushed up out of his seat and strode back to the front of the shop, calling "thank you" over his shoulder as he headed outside.

His mind spun as he drove the short distance to the Rainbow. They were potentially dealing with a stalker situation, and the sooner Colt could get a positive ID on this guy so they could slap him with a restraining order, the better.

The interior of the Rainbow was more brightly lit than the last time he'd been here. Come to think of it, he'd never been during daylight hours. A few steps in, he spied one of the longtime waitresses, and approached her with a smile.

"Hey, Cindy, how's it going?"

She shot him a questioning glance before returning the smile. "Colt, right? You're here kinda early, aren't you? Get you a drink?"

"Actually, I'm working," he said, hefting the laptop he'd

grabbed from the Charger's trunk under his arm, "And I was wondering if you could help me out with something. You got five minutes?"

"For you? Sure. Just give me a sec." She zipped behind the bar and dumped her tray and the rag she'd had over her shoulder. She poured herself a glass of water and gestured toward a booth. Colt settled himself in the booth and opened up his laptop, jamming the USB stick in.

"So what kinda work you do?" asked Cindy, sliding in beside him, her long, brown ponytail swishing.

"Private security. I've got some footage here I'd like you to take a look at. This guy was here the other week, and I'm trying to get an ID on him."

She nodded and he queued up the footage, sitting back and hitting Play. Cindy watched, frowning, her mouth twisted to the side as she studied the screen. Finally, when the man turned, she let out a little gasp.

"That's Ronnie."

"You know him?"

"Just his first name. He comes in here maybe once a week. Real quiet. Only ever orders soda. Always pays cash. Keeps to himself. I always thought maybe he was lonely. Seemed to do a lot of people watching."

"You ever talk to him?"

"Not much. I only know his name because I overheard someone else call him that."

"Someone else knew him?"

"Yeah, this other guy, a biker type. Ronnie left right away after that."

It was a picture and a first name, but it was a start. Time to let Clay work his magic.

* * *

Taylor sat on the leather couch in her studio, late-afternoon sunshine filtering in through the stained-glass windows and tinging the room with moody purples and blues. The rest of the studio musicians had left, and Roman had locked up behind them. Colt had been gone for a couple of hours, but she was content to wait, enjoying having the space practically to herself for a little while. It was challenging to work on the more personal songs with everyone around. They needed a little more room to grow before she'd be ready to share them with anyone.

Roman sat on the couch on the other side of the room, keeping both her and the door in his sights. He glanced up from his phone and shot her a smile. "Colt's on his way back. Sounds like he found some information about your admirer."

"He's not an admirer—he's a sick freak."

The smile dropped from Roman's face, and he nodded. "You're right. Sorry. Didn't mean to be a dick about that."

She studied him, taking in the long hair, the tattoos, the big, muscled body, the beard, and she saw it all for what it was. Armor. She knew, because she did the same thing, with eye makeup, and leather, and the way she felt most comfortable when there was a guitar between her and whoever else.

Roman's phone buzzed and he glanced down at it, a half smile on his face as he swiped his finger across the screen.

"Colt?" she asked, toying with the tuner keys of her guitar.

He shook his head. "Nah. Woman from Tinder."

She scoffed out a laugh. "Tinder? Come on, big guy. I think you can do better than that." She shot him a meaningful look. "You're not going to find what you're looking for on Tinder."

"Oh, yeah? And just what am I looking for?"

"Something real."

"You don't know the first thing about me, sweetheart." A darkness had crept into his eyes, but it didn't deter her.

"You and I are a lot more alike than you might think."

He barked out a laugh. "I doubt that."

"Just hazarding a guess here, but I'd be willing to bet my favorite guitar that you like to be in control, but being in control means keeping a tight leash on all those pesky emotions." She arched an eyebrow at him. "Am I close?"

Roman shifted in his seat, but didn't say anything, just met her gaze with his.

"I think you're scared to let people in. So you keep everyone at arm's length with the jokes and the screwing around. You want everyone to think you're having fun, but under it all, you're unhappy."

He sat back and extended his arms over the back of the sofa. Making himself bigger. His smile didn't reach his eyes. "Like I said. You don't know the first thing about me." He pushed up off the couch and headed for the bathrooms at the front of the studio. She hadn't meant to strike a nerve, but she also couldn't help but wonder if she would've spun so far out of control if someone had called her on her shit sooner.

She picked at the acoustic guitar in her lap, her notebook open on the seat beside her. She strummed gently through the E-A-B chord progression she'd been working on, fine tuning the rhythm and setting it to the lyrics she'd had spinning through her mind for a few days now.

> *I wanna let you in*
> *I wanna let you see*
> *I wanna start where we stopped and begin*
> *I wanna ask for more*
> *So I'm opening the door*

She took a breath and launched into the chorus, strumming harder, her eyes closed, eyelids glowing a soft orange in the tinted light.

> *Let's forget about the past*
> *Let's make something that will last*
> *Take my heart and hold it in your hands*
> *I wanna give it to you*
> *I hope you want it too*

"That's really pretty," said Colt from several feet behind her, and she jumped, dropping the guitar into her lap. The strings squealed as they scraped against her fingers, and she swallowed around her heart, which had leaped up into her throat at the surprise of hearing Colt's voice.

She blew out a breath as blood rushed to her cheeks, and she wondered if he'd heard the lyrics and, if he had, if he knew they were about him. She pushed her hair out of her face and turned to look at him.

For a long, shimmering second, their eyes connected, and the rest of the room dropped away. Her body tingled with awareness, and everything slammed into her like a rapid-fire montage, not of scenes, but of snippets of image and sound, smell and taste. Colt's naked body against hers, his hands roving over her skin. The fluttering of her heart in her chest. His scent. The way his eyes crinkled when he smiled. The way her skin warmed at his touch. All of it melded together in a kind of cinematic bang, and she swallowed thickly.

Colt rubbed a hand over the back of his neck. "I need to talk to you."

She gestured for him to sit down on the couch beside her, pulling her guitar back into her lap.

"I think you have a stalker."

Her heart dropped from where it had set up camp in her throat to her stomach. "Really?"

Colt nodded. "I went to the flower shop, and I convinced them to let me take a look at the security cameras." He paused, shaking his head slightly. "You remember the guy from the Rainbow, the night we...met? He's the one who sent you the flowers."

"Shit," she whispered, her stomach churning, its contents feeling like concrete.

"His first name is Ronnie. I've got my PI buddy Clay on it. He's seeing if he can use the image from the security camera footage and the first name to track down who this guy is."

"So that's it? We just wait?"

"Nothing much else we can do right now, gorgeous." He moved closer on the couch and pulled the guitar gently away from her. "But I can promise you this. I won't let that creep get anywhere near you."

She wrapped her arms around herself, trying to hold everything together. After a second, she let out a shaky laugh. "When it rains, it pours, eh?"

"You talking about your dad?"

She nodded, chewing her lip.

"I'm having Clay look into him, too. We'll figure out what's going on. Come on. You wanna go home?" He stood and offered her his hand. She stared at it for a moment, absorbing the strong, thick fingers and wide palms, the slightly rough texture of his skin and shivering at the memory of how fucking fantastic those hands had felt on her skin. In her hair. In her.

Her eyes once again met his, and in a gesture that felt much bigger than it looked, she put her hand in his and let him help her off the couch. She quickly gathered her things and watched as Colt briefed Roman, who was going to lock up behind them. Something tightened and then instantly melted in her chest at the easy familiarity with which Colt moved through her space. He took her hand again, slipping his fingers between hers as he led her toward the Charger, his eyes scanning the empty parking lot and the street. His grip tightened on her hand almost imperceptibly, but he kept his stride steady. He opened the passenger door for her, and once she was tucked safely inside, he strode around the car, dropping into the driver's seat and hitting the door locks.

"We're being watched."

She looked around the parking lot and out at the street. "What makes you say that?"

"That exact same van was parked near your house this morning. The studio's in a completely different neighborhood than your house. What are the odds that the exact same van would be both in front of your house this morning and in front of your studio right now?"

Taylor's pulse sped up slightly. "How do you know it's the same van?"

"Same plates."

He turned his key in the ignition, the Charger's engine roaring to life. "Let's see if they follow us." Surprising her, Colt pulled smoothly out of the parking lot and onto the road.

"I thought you would've gunned it," she said, staring into the side-view mirror.

"If he is following us, I don't want him to know that I know." He glanced over at her. "Countersurveillance one-oh-one. Besides, the last thing we want is to get involved in some kind of car chase. That's pretty much the opposite of keeping you safe." Instead of heading for the freeway, Colt took a winding route through the city, through dense traffic and a seemingly endless stream of traffic lights. "He's definitely following us, but he's at least two lights back now. I'm going to make a sudden right, and then accordion my way up to the freeway. He'll think he lost us, and not the other way around."

True to his word, with a glance in the rearview mirror, Colt swung the Charger into the far right lane and made a sharp right, accelerating as he zipped through turn after turn. His fingers flexed on the steering wheel, and Taylor watched through the side-view mirror for any sign of the van as her heart hammered in her ears.

"I...I think you lost him," she said, settling back into her seat and trying to wrestle her thoughts into some kind of coherent order. First her dad had texted her out of the blue, then had shown up at her door, maybe more than once. And now there was the additional threat of the stalker. Had *he* been the one to sneak around the outside of her house? Was he the one who'd been following them just now? Or was the tail related to her dad and whatever fucking mess he'd gotten himself into?

Questions without answers. And the only certainty she had in all of it was that Colt would keep her safe.

# CHAPTER 14

Karaoke at the Brass Monkey was exactly the distraction Taylor needed after the day she'd had. At first, Colt had tried to talk her out of coming tonight, but she'd been looking forward to seeing her friends, and she needed the stress relief of a night out. Eventually, he'd agreed but had insisted on bringing Roman along to keep things under control, if need be. Although it wasn't impossible, it was very unlikely that her creepy admirer would try anything in public with security around.

"You okay?" Sierra hooked an arm around Taylor's waist and gave her a side hug as Colt scouted the place out and Roman secured them a table. "You've been quiet."

"I'm just tired. It's been a long day, but don't worry. I'll rally." She didn't want to talk about everything weighing on her: the album deadline, her unsettling attraction to Colt, the news of a potential stalker, and her dad's sudden reappearance. Normally, she'd tell Sierra everything, but she didn't have the energy. Not tonight.

Her eyes roamed over the bar, taking in the upbeat atmosphere, and a warmth spread over her when her eyes found Colt, several feet away, his eyes on her. Wearing a khaki-green Henley shirt, worn jeans, and beat-up boots, he looked rugged, sexy, and perfect. His five-o'clock shadow was starting to come in, highlighting his strong jaw and full lips. He smiled and displayed his perfect white teeth, the skin around his eyes crinkling.

"Oh, shit." Sierra smacked Taylor's arm, jolting her. "You have a *thing* for him."

"I…we…" Taylor scuffed her toe on the floor, avoiding Sierra's gaze.

Sierra's eyes widened. "Ladies' room. Now." She took Taylor by the elbow and began leading her through the bar. Meeting Colt's eyes, Taylor tipped her head in the direction of the bathrooms, and he nodded. Taylor silently prayed that Sierra wasn't mad at her, or hurt that she'd shut her out.

The second the door whooshed closed behind them, Sierra turned on her, her arms crossed. "You. Spill. Everything." Her green eyes blazed, and Taylor knew she was at least a little pissed.

Taylor opened her mouth and the entire story came spilling out. The one-night stand, and then Colt turning up as the bodyguard hired by the label. Her dad. The stalker. Her undeniable attraction to Colt and her jumble of feelings for him. She let out a long breath once she finally finished talking. "So…yeah. That's what's been going on with me."

"Wow." Sierra gave Taylor's shoulder a squeeze; any anger she may have felt seemed to have disappeared. "That's…wow. How are you feeling?"

Taylor shrugged, lowering her voice as another woman entered the bathroom and headed for a stall. "I don't even know. It seems to change from hour to hour."

"What do you want?"

"That's the thing. I know what I want. I just don't know if I have any right to think I could…" She sighed heavily. "I thought Zack was that guy, you know? At first it was just fun, but it turned into something a lot more than that. At least, it did for me. I'm scared of putting myself in that position again, of thinking I've found this great guy, giving him everything I have, and letting him rip my heart out."

Sierra squeezed her hand. "Zack led you on, and that wasn't fair of him—"

Taylor didn't let her finish. "But I'm the one who broke the rules. We agreed, upfront, that we were casual, no strings. I'm the idiot who fell in love with her fuck buddy. And I can't go down that road again. I can't leave myself open and exposed and stay whole when it doesn't work out."

Sierra leaned against the tiled wall. "I don't know him. I only know what Sean thinks of him, and what you think of him."

"And Sean thinks he's an asshole."

Sierra shrugged. "Pretty much. But there are two sides to every story. Have you asked Colt about it? About his side?"

Taylor shook her head. "No. It hasn't come up."

"You should ask him. I…I don't think you should ignore your feelings for him."

"Why not?"

Sierra laid a hand on Taylor's cheek. "Because you light up like Christmas when you look at him. How do you think I picked up on the fact that something's going on between you two?" Sierra took her arm and began leading her out of the bathroom. "For what it's worth, Zack didn't make you light up that way. So regardless of Colt's bad history with Sean, there's something there."

As they made their way through the bar, a group of obviously tipsy girls took the stage and began half-shouting, half-mumbling their way through TLC's "No Scrubs," and Taylor smiled. This was the Brass Monkey at its best. Unpretentious and welcoming, with awesome drinks, greasy food, and a huge songbook. Even though it was relatively early, the bar was nearly full, with people crowded around the small wooden tables. Most of the walls were exposed brick, with a few sections of wood paneling, including the makeshift stage adjacent to the bar.

"Hey guys!" Taylor and Sierra both spun just as Chloe Carmichael ran up to them, her arms open, a huge smile on her face. Her gorgeous light brown skin glowed, her thick cinnamon-colored hair bouncing in loose waves around her shoulders. She flung her arms around her friends just as the final member of their group, Alexa Fairfax, appeared in the doorway, another bodyguard accompanying her. Alexa was adorable, with her tiny frame, blond curls, and perfect nose. She was also by far the biggest celebrity in their group. Her family, the Fairfaxes, were one of the most famous families in Hollywood, on par with the Barrymores or the Fondas. But even though she was the most famous, she was also a sweetheart, always wanting to make her friends happy and, as far as Taylor was concerned, putting others before herself far too often.

Roman waved them over to a table near the back, and several heads turned toward them as they wove their way through the crowd. However, the Brass Monkey was known for its star sightings, and they weren't the only celebrities in the bar. On the way to their table, Taylor noticed a very famous comedian, a world-champion boxer, and a former *Friend*.

The waitress came by and took their drink orders, and as Chloe filled them all in on the details of writing and producing her first movie, Taylor found her eyes scanning the crowd until she picked out Colt. He stood against the wall several feet away, chatting with someone else who was clearly a bodyguard, with his suit and no-nonsense expression. She watched Colt's hands as he talked, gesturing animatedly, telling a story. He talked with his hands a lot, she'd noticed. It was cute.

Chloe elbowed her, drawing Taylor's attention back to her.

"Are you gonna sing?" she asked, flipping through the songbook, a stack of song request slips beside her, and a pencil poised between her fingers.

Taylor had been about to reply that she just wanted to watch when the idea of showing off for Colt snapped through her, actually making her sit up a little straighter.

Looking at him, she knew she couldn't turn off how she felt about him. The attraction was a big part of it, sure, but there was also the sense of safety she felt whenever he was around. The sense that someone had her back and was looking out for her. She liked how she felt around him, both in the wanting to "shove him onto a bed and have her way with him" way, and the...other way. The "can't stop writing songs about him" way.

She peered down at the songbook, but before she could make a decision, Sierra cleared her throat, her green eyes bright. "So, uh, I have some news to share," she said, licking her lips. Taylor, Chloe, and Alexa all looked at her expectantly. Slowly, Sierra pulled her hands from her lap and held her left one up in front of her, wiggling her fingers. An antique-style diamond ring glittered on her ring finger. Chloe and Alexa both gasped, and Taylor grabbed Sierra's hand.

"Uh, excuse me, but is this what I think it is?" she asked,

studying the ring and pushing down the tiny surge of jealousy tightening her chest. God, she'd been so caught up in her own drama earlier that she hadn't even noticed it.

A huge smile sprung up on Sierra's face, and she nodded quickly. "If you think it's an engagement ring, then yes!"

Chloe squealed and pushed up out of her chair, gathering Sierra in a hug.

"When did he propose?" asked Alexa, just as the waitress returned with their drinks.

"Last night. I knew we were headed down that path, but I wasn't expecting it this soon." Sierra and Sean had been together for nearly a year, and Taylor was willing to bet no one was surprised. Sierra and Sean were crazy about each other.

"Okay, so tell us the story. How did he propose?" Alexa leaned forward expectantly, her eyes bright.

Sierra's face reddened and Taylor slipped an arm around her, pulling her in close. "Aw, you guys. I think they were naked."

Sierra laughed, pressing a hand to her cheek. "Maybe."

"You don't have to give details. We just want the broad picture." Alexa smiled reassuringly, and Taylor wondered if Alexa and Chloe were as weirdly happy-jealous as Taylor was, or if it was just her own messed-up reaction.

"Uh, well. We've been, um…working on christening the new house. And we were in the, um—" she cleared her throat and took a sip of her drink "—kitchen. On the island." She took another sip of her drink and rushed through the rest of her story, not pausing for breath. "So, we, um, did, you know, our thing, and then he said a bunch of romantic stuff and asked me to marry him and I said yes, and he pulled the ring out of a drawer in the kitchen."

Chloe clutched her hands to her chest. "Aw! I love that. What romantic stuff did he say?"

"You don't have to tell us if you don't want to," said Alexa, giving Sierra's arm a squeeze.

Taylor snorted. "Yes, you do. Spill it."

"He...he told me I was the most incredible, beautiful, amazing woman he'd ever met, and that not a day goes by where I don't make him feel like the luckiest man alive. That he loves me, more than he ever thought he'd love someone." Sierra sighed, looking down at the ring. "Then he said he wanted to spend every single day of his life by my side, loving me. And he asked me to marry him."

Alexa's eyes shone and she sniffled. "I hope I find that someday."

Chloe pulled her in for a hug. "You will, babe. You're still young. Tons and tons of time."

After a few more minutes of mushiness, they moved on, and thank goodness, because Taylor wasn't sure she could've handled much more. She was already in a weird, off-kilter mood, and while she was happy for Sierra, the news of her engagement was only adding to Taylor's funk. Which was messed up and selfish, but true nonetheless.

"Sean's not coming later?" asked Chloe, standing to go hand in her song-request slips.

"No, he's working tonight. Virtus just landed a contract with the Dodgers, so he's in heaven. Don't feel too bad for him." The dopey smile she got every time she talked about him stretched across her lips. Sierra was called to the stage, and the crowd cheered her on as she wove her way between the tables.

The opening strains of "Ice Ice Baby" pumped out of the speakers, and Sierra picked up the mic, smiling sweetly. The girl couldn't sing to save her life, but she had surprisingly good flow. From her spot at the table, she saw Colt watching as Sierra rapped, mustering up as much swagger as a white girl from Pasadena could. He smiled, and Taylor had to admit that Sierra was pretty adorable up there, nailing the lyrics.

Glancing again at Colt, Taylor began flipping through the pages of the songbook. Normally, she let her friends have the fun, not wanting to hog the spotlight or steal anyone's thunder. But not tonight. No, she felt like showing off tonight.

After agonizing over her song choice, Taylor finally submitted her slip, stopping to take pictures with a few fans on her way back to the table, and she could feel Colt's eyes on her the entire time. When she took her seat, she couldn't help but notice how cozy Chloe and Roman looked as they talked in a corner of the bar, Chloe's body angled toward him. Before the flirting could progress any further, Chloe was called up to sing Whitney Houston's "I Wanna Dance With Somebody."

Taylor pushed out of her seat and stalked across the bar, tapping Roman on the arm once Chloe was out of earshot. He tore his eyes away from Chloe, raising his eyebrows in question.

"Don't hit on my friends, Roman." Taylor shot him a stern look.

He laughed, clapping his hands together. "Get uglier friends."

Exhaling a sharp breath, Taylor shook her head. Whatever. They were adults.

Colt had retreated to his spot against the wall, and she caught his eyes as she sat back down. He smiled that perfect, slightly cocky, eye-crinkling smile, and her stomach exploded into a thousand tiny, fluttering butterflies.

She'd felt sure about her song choice before, but now she was second-guessing it. Maybe it was stupid. Or cheesy. Or desperate. Or obvious. Or an achingly embarrassing combination of all of the above.

But it was Heart, and she knew she could sing the hell out of it, which was the main reason she'd chosen it. Not because it was a song about giving in to the lust and passion between two people. Nope. Not because of that.

Chloe finished her song, and a group of rowdy guys celebrating a bachelor party got up to sing Queen's "Another One Bites the Dust." The waitress came back with a fresh Jack and Coke for Taylor. Maybe the alcohol would help numb the turmoil of emotions churning through her.

She listened to the conversation at their table, chiming in when appropriate, but letting Sierra and Chloe do most of the talking. Between Sierra's engagement and Chloe's movie, there was a lot to discuss. Finally, the DJ called Taylor's name. As she rose from her seat, the bar filled with hoots and hollers, everyone cheering her on. Including Colt, she noticed, and the butterflies fluttered in response. She hopped up onto the stage and picked up the mic, falling into familiar and comforting behaviors.

"How's everyone doing tonight?"

A cheer rose up from the crowd.

"Everyone having a good time?" she asked, louder and with a bit more energy.

The crowd responded with a louder, more enthusiastic cheer. Smiling, she nodded at the DJ, who started the song, the opening strains of Heart's "All I Wanna Do Is Make Love to You" echoing through the speakers. She heard Sierra give an especially loud "Wooo!" and Taylor laughed, pushing her hair over one shoulder. Taking a deep breath, she closed her eyes and listened, not wanting to come in off-key. She opened her eyes and her mouth at the same time and started to sing.

The Brass Monkey erupted with a cheer, and she might as well have been onstage in front of thousands of fans for the rush she got, feeding off of their energy. She did her best to perform, using the entire stage and meeting as many eyes as she could in the crowd, since she knew the song by heart and didn't need the lyric prompts from the screen. But inevitably, her eyes kept snapping back to Colt, whose mouth was tilted up in a half smile, his arms crossed over his broad chest.

She let the energy build over the song, each verse feeding into each increasingly passionate rendition of the chorus. When she got to the part about making love like strangers all night long, she pulled out all the stops, using the full power of her voice to wring as much emotion out of the words as she could, closing her eyes and letting herself get caught up in the song, losing herself in the music. When she opened her eyes, something had shifted in Colt's gaze. Even from all the way across the bar, she could see that the amusement was gone, replaced with something darker and more intense. Something her body recognized instantly as raw desire. If she hadn't been so used to being up onstage, she might've faltered. Instead, she kept pouring herself into the song, keeping the intensity going all the way through to the end. Before the final notes had faded away, raucous cheers filled the bar. She executed a curtsy and then hopped off the stage, tossing the mic back to the DJ.

When she returned to her table, she received high fives from everyone before settling back into her seat and picking up her Jack and Coke. She glanced over her shoulder at Colt, who seemed to have collected himself, and he shot her a thumbs-up along with an approving smile.

Sierra leaned across the table. "Wow. You've got it *bad*."

"Shut up. I know." Taylor glanced once again over her shoulder at Colt, who'd attracted the attention of a pretty brunette. She watched as the brunette swatted at Colt's muscled arm, laughing at something he'd said.

The effort not to walk over there, shove the brunette aside and kiss Colt, right there in front of everyone, was so great that Taylor clenched her fists, feeling as though she were going to vibrate out of her seat. Tearing her eyes away and looking for a distraction, she pulled the songbook toward her, and an idea took root. She'd failed at her Ping-Pong ball prank and needed to find another way to get him back for messing with her phone. She flipped through the book, smiling when she found what she was looking for.

Oh, this was going to be good.

"Are you going to sing another one?" asked Sierra, sipping her wine.

"Nope. Not me." She quickly filled out the slip and handed it in, mischievous excitement prickling over her skin. She signaled to the waitress for another drink to keep her occupied while she waited.

Soon enough, Colt's name was called, pulling him away from the brunette—an added bonus to the prank—and onstage. Initially, he resisted, shaking his head with a furrowed brow, but the crowd's cheers finally coaxed him up on stage, the peer pressure too much to withstand. The look he shot Taylor as he passed was a sexy, teasing "I'm *so* going to get you for this" expression, his eyes narrowed, but a smile tilting up his lips, just slightly. He clearly had no doubt as to who'd signed him up to sing. Taylor suppressed a laugh as she met his eyes and did her best to look innocent.

He tipped his head back and groaned when the DJ announced the song he'd be singing.

The music started, the opening of "SexyBack" thumping through the sound system, and Colt shot her a steely glare. He raised the mic to his lips and started to sing.

And holy hell, he was actually good.

*Really* good.

Taylor's mouth dropped open and Sierra spun in her seat. "Whoa! Bet you didn't see that coming, did you?"

No. She definitely hadn't.

His voice wasn't perfect, but he was hitting all the notes, and his cocky personality shone through onstage. Colt shook his shoulders and hips in perfect time with the music, looking like a seasoned pro, fun and confident. The man could move both in and out of bed, apparently.

Just when she thought his performance couldn't get any better, he dropped to his knees and slid to the front of the stage as he launched into the chorus, giving Channing Tatum a run for his money. He was totally into it, and was killing it up there.

Taylor raised her arms over her head and let out a long cheer, totally surprised by how freaking awesome he was at karaoke. He could sing, he had rhythm, and clearly didn't mind being up there.

He may have thwarted her attempt to prank him, but watching him up there, she didn't even care.

* * *

Around one, the crowd began to thin at the Brass Monkey. After ensuring that everyone had a safe ride home, whether by cab, hired car, limo, or otherwise, Colt led a very tipsy Taylor to where he'd parked the Charger around back, away from the prying lenses of any paparazzi.

He'd tried to cut her off about an hour ago, subtly suggesting that maybe just a Coke without the Jack might be a good idea. She'd shot him a haughty look and ordered another drink. However, despite the number of drinks she'd consumed, she'd behaved herself all night, not causing any trouble. The worst thing she'd done was boo Roman off the stage after the terrible rendition of Madonna's "Holiday" he'd sung, trying to impress Chloe. And even then, she'd only been joking and teasing, not meaning any real harm. Taylor had gone back up onstage once more and she and Sierra had led the bar in a sing-along of "Summer Nights" from *Grease*. Colt had smiled so hard through the whole thing that his cheeks had ached by the time the song finished. Taylor, playing Danny, and Sierra, playing Sandy, had been pretty adorable up there, singing to each other and encouraging the entire bar to join in.

"Did you have fun tonight?" he asked as he held open the passenger's-side door for Taylor. She took a step toward him.

"Shhhhhhhh," she whispered, and sloppily pressed her right index finger against his lips, smushing them together in a smeary motion. "You're so pretty."

"O-*kay*," he said with a chuckle, stepping back and gently guiding her into the car. She tumbled in with a laugh, her eyes bright in the semidarkness.

"So pretty." She sighed and curled into the seat.

Making sure her long legs were safely tucked in, he closed the door and jogged around to the other side. Dropping into the driver's seat, he glanced over at her. To make sure she wasn't puking in the Charger. Not because he couldn't ever seem to keep his eyes off her for more than a few torturous seconds at a time.

"Did *you* have fun tonight?" she asked, swiveling her head around in a lazy semicircle to look at him. "I made you sing." She leaned toward him, as if confiding some deep, dark secret. "And you were really, really good."

He let out a low chuckle. "Well, thank you. I like singing. There was usually a karaoke machine kicking around on base, so I've had some practice. That being said, maybe we should cool it on the pranks, given everything that's going on with your dad, and your stalker."

"Ha! So you're conceding defeat in the prank war?"

"Hey, now. Didn't say that."

She blew out a breath, making a raspberry sound. "Please. Prince Sparklepants? Strippers? I totally win." Before he could reply, she charged ahead on a completely different path. "Let's go to 7-Eleven!" She clapped her hands together enthusiastically.

"For what?"

She shot him a puzzled glare as he pulled out of the parking lot and onto Wilshire Boulevard. "For a burrito. Duh."

"You don't need a burrito."

"Nobody *needs* a burrito. I want one, and there's a 7-Eleven a few blocks up. So. Onward." Leaning back against the headrest, she turned to look at him. "Are you telling me you've never gone to 7-Eleven for burritos after the bar?"

He shrugged. "I guess not."

"Dude, where have you been?"

"Well, there was that time I was in the Army for twelve years."

"They don't have burritos in the Army?" She arched an eyebrow.

He suppressed the smile teasing across his lips. "Not usually."

"Were you ever scared?" she asked quietly.

"Sometimes."

"Did you kill people?"

He turned to look at her, not wanting to get into all of that shit tonight. "Taylor, I don't want to talk about this right now." *Or ever.*

"Oh. Sorry." She turned away to look out the window, angling her body away from him, and he felt like an asshole.

"Don't be sorry. I just…" He swung into the brightly illuminated 7-Eleven parking lot. "It's not something I like to talk about."

"Well." She swung her head back toward him, her blue eyes bright even in the dark interior of the car. "If you ever do feel like talking…" She shrugged. "You could talk to me."

"I appreciate that."

But he wasn't sure she heard him because she'd already pushed open the car door, singing "Burrito time!" in a high-pitched, girly voice.

He really should've tried harder to dissuade her from those last couple of drinks. Shaking his head, he followed her through the parking lot, and held the door for her to go ahead of him into the convenience store. The store was empty, so hopefully they'd be in and out in minutes flat. She took a few steps in before whirling so quickly that he didn't have time to stop, and they collided. Instinctively, his arms went around her to steady her, and she swayed into him.

"I want to steal a burrito," she whispered, her breath hot against his ear.

Gently, he eased her away from him. As much as he might want her in his bed again, tonight wasn't the night. Not when she was drunk.

"No stealing."

She batted her eyelashes at him. "But it would be fun."

"No stealing," he repeated, cutting his eyes at the teenage clerk, who was completely absorbed in his comic book and ignoring them, thankfully. "I'll buy you one. Deal?"

She nodded enthusiastically, her blond waves falling around her face. "Deal."

While he procured her a burrito, he watched as she wandered through the fluorescent-lit aisles, humming to herself and twirling a lock of hair around her finger. Steaming pocket of carbs, fat, and God knew what else in hand, he found her at the back, studying the magazine rack.

"If you had to pick one dirty magazine, which one would you pick?" Her eyes lit up when he handed her the burrito. "Ooh! Thanks." She bit into it and closed her eyes, sighing out a low moan that had blood flowing straight to his dick. She turned her attention back to the magazine rack. "I think…" She danced the fingers of her free hand over the covers. "Oh, this one!" She pulled out an issue of *Camo Cock*, featuring a very buff and oiled-up model wearing nothing but camo-print briefs that barely contained his obviously photoshopped bulge. Colt glanced back at the teenage clerk, whose full attention was now on his phone, unconcerned about his only customers.

"Really? You think that's my flavor?" He crossed his arms in front of his chest and tamped down a smile, trying to look stern.

"Well…" She waved the magazine from left to right, and then through a mouthful of burrito said, "It's military." She turned it toward herself and glanced at the cover. "This isn't what you wear under your soldier-pant things?"

"One: I don't wear 'soldier-pant things' anymore," he said. "Two: Those are definitely not standard issue." He took a step toward her and watched her throat work as she swallowed the last of her burrito. "And three: You're awfully interested in my underwear."

She leaned in, and suddenly their faces were inches apart. "Maybe it's what's *in* your underwear that I'm interested in."

For one long, taut second, their eyes locked, and then she looked down at the magazine, holding it up between them. "I'm gonna steal it for you, because I like you, and it's okay if you're too embarrassed to buy it for yourself."

"For the last time, no stealing. What is it with you? You get drunk and turn into a klepto?"

Blue eyes flashing mischievously, she glanced around the store before starting to slip the dirty mag under her leather jacket. He grabbed for it before it fully disappeared and she laughed, turning away and trying to hold on to it. He circled his arms around her, one hand slipping under her jacket and grabbing the magazine while the other lightly pinched the soft flesh between her ribcage and her hipbone. She shrieked with laughter and loosened her grip on the magazine, and he pulled it free. She spun back quickly to face him, and he held the magazine behind his back, stepping forward and pinning her against the magazine rack with his chest. She scrabbled for it, wiggling against him in a way that had his cock rising quickly to attention, and he dropped it on the floor, the pages fluttering noisily before it landed with a clap against the floor. Before she could maneuver around him, he pinned her wrists to her sides and her eyes found his, pupils wide. She took several rapid, deep breaths that pressed her breasts into his chest, and just as he was about to release her, she tipped her head forward and kissed him.

The feel of Taylor's mouth on his again made every single thought empty from his brain, and he released her wrists and slid his arms around her waist to pull her closer. His hands cradled her back as her lips worked eagerly against his, sucking his bottom lip between hers. Everything about her mouth—her lips, her deliciously sweet tongue—was just as soft and warm as that first night. She moaned softly into his mouth and fisted her hands in his shirt, holding him there, as if she could sense his hesitation. He knew they had to stop, but as her tongue slid against his, he struggled to hold on to the reason why.

Despite all the reasons he shouldn't, he kissed her back

enthusiastically, and she slid her hands up over his shoulders, pulling him tighter against her and rocking her hips against him. She deepened the kiss, opening her mouth to him more, and although he wanted nothing more than to give her everything she wanted, it couldn't be tonight. After savoring the feel of her mouth for a few more seconds, he pulled away, letting his lips linger against hers, not wanting the kiss to be over. He inhaled slowly, trying to get a handle on his breathing. On the lust rocketing through him. On his heart.

She trailed kisses up his neck, and he bit back a groan. "Not like this, gorgeous," he managed, his voice low and a little hoarse.

"Stop talking." She wove her fingers into his hair, and with a gentle tug that had sparks shooting over his scalp, pulled his mouth back to hers, and they melted into each other almost instantly. As wrong as it was, he couldn't deny that he was hungry for another taste of her, and he lost himself in the feel of her body pressed against his, her fingers threaded through his hair, and the sweetness of her mouth as he caressed her tongue with his. She nipped at his bottom lip and he couldn't stop the groan that came from somewhere deep in his chest as he tore his lips from hers.

"Fuck," he breathed, resting his forehead against hers and then nipping at her lips again, just once, in a hungry, biting kiss. He shook his head, trying to find his way back to earth through the haze clogging his brain. This couldn't happen tonight.

"*Fuck.*" He swore again before sliding his hands up to her face, tilting her chin up and closing his mouth over hers. His tongue found hers again, and he stroked into her mouth in a slow, deliberate rhythm. His control was almost gone, and he knew he needed to get hold of himself. If they were going to do this again, they were going to do it right. He knew he couldn't handle being some fuck she'd regret the next morning. Again.

That thought was sobering enough that he was able to summon the last remaining crumb of his willpower and break the kiss.

"No, Taylor. Not like this." He lowered his head and pressed a kiss to her neck. "I want you to be sober when I fuck you again. I want you to remember every single second." He nuzzled into her neck and dragged his lips over the warm skin there. "Every touch. Every kiss. How hard I make you come with my hands. My mouth." He sucked the skin right behind her ear and then soothed it with a lap of his tongue. "My cock. Because I *am* going to fuck you again, and we both know you're going to want to remember it clearly."

"I want all of that tonight. Your hands. Your mouth. Your cock," she said, echoing his dirty talk back to him and arousing him even more. "I want you to fuck me tonight."

A thrill shot through him at her words, and it took everything he had not to pull her back into him and crush his mouth to hers again.

"Not gonna happen." He held out his hand to her. "Come on. Let's get you home." She slipped her hand into his, but didn't move, the light in her eyes shifting.

She bit her lip, looking up at him through her lashes. "Can we...I don't want to stay at my place tonight. With my dad and the sick weirdo..." She trailed off, her shoulders slumping slightly.

He gave her hand a squeeze. "We'll stay at my place, if that's what you want." Fuck, it wasn't going to be easy, sleeping on the couch while he knew Taylor was in his bed, but he'd do anything in his power to make her feel safe.

# CHAPTER 15

Taylor rolled over in bed and slowly peeled her eyes open. Even though the room was still semidark, the light teasing around the edges of the curtains was enough to start a dull pounding in her temples. Groaning, she pushed her face into the pillow, and her stomach churned uncomfortably. The inside of her mouth felt like sawdust, and for some reason, a strange, lingering sense of embarrassment ate at her along with the acid in her stomach. Still facedown, she extended her arms above her head and stretched, noticing that she was still in the same black blouse and jeans she'd worn out the night before, minus the black ankle boots she'd had on. She didn't even remember stumbling into bed.

Holy hell, she'd overdone it last night. She'd tried to drink away the confusing mix of her feelings about Colt, and although she'd succeeded, the relief had only been temporary.

She rolled and pried her eyes open.

This was not her bed. Not her bedroom. No, it was Colt's. She slid her hand across the sheets to the other side of the bed, but they were cool beneath her touch. She blinked several times, trying to think around the pounding in her temples. She flipped over and sat up, making the room lurch in front of her eyes for a second. Pieces of the end of the night started to come back. Her cheeks heated and she curled her arms around herself as she remembered how she'd come on to Colt last night. In a freaking 7-Eleven of all places. God. She'd really let her white-trash roots show, insisting on a stupid 7-Eleven burrito.

And then his words echoed through her brain, sending heat spiraling through her entire body.

*I want you to be sober when I fuck you again. I want you to remember every single second. Every touch. Every kiss. How hard I make you come with my hands. My mouth. My cock. Because I am going to fuck you again, and we both know you're going to want to remember it clearly.*

Oh, hell yes.

Another flash of memory, this one much foggier than the kiss, floated up, and she latched on to it because of the warm sense of happiness it sent coursing through her. It was of Colt, leaning over her and tucking her into bed, smiling as he smoothed her hair away from her eyes and pressed a gentle kiss to her forehead.

Oh, holy Mother of God, was she in trouble. She was already in free fall mode, and they'd barely begun. And yet, a tiny seed of hope took root.

The truth was that with Colt, all of her doubts and insecurities felt unfounded. Her fear felt unreasonable and illogical in the face of just how good he made her feel. Happy. Protected. Worthy. He'd reignited something deep inside her that had been long extinguished, and that had to be worth something.

She reached for where Colt had plugged in her phone on

his bedside table and stopped, her hand suspended midair as a tender pang hit her right in the chest. Beside her phone was an unopened bottle of water, a bottle of aspirin, and a banana. Beside it was a scribbled note on the back of a gas station receipt.

*Thought you might need these. I'm downstairs. —Sparklepants*

A laugh pushed up through her throat and she read the note again, taking in his slightly messy, block-letter scrawl, allowing herself to bask in the intimacy of looking at his handwriting. She twisted the cap off the water and took a long, healthy swallow. Popping open the top of the aspirin, she shook a couple out into her palm, swallowing them down with another gulp of the water. She pushed a hand through her tangled hair before rubbing first one eye and then the other, and the side of her index finger came away smeared with black, since she hadn't removed her makeup the night before. Stretching one last time, she pushed the covers back and padded across the room, poking her head out into the hall, and then darting into the bathroom. With the door latched firmly behind her, she peeled off her clothes and reached into the shower, cranking the water as hot as it would go.

After showering, rinsing her mouth out with mouth-wash, dressing, and forcing down the rest of her water and the banana, she felt semi-human again. Her head was no longer pounding, and her stomach felt much steadier. She left the bathroom, listening for Colt in the house but not hearing anything. She walked down the hall and glanced into the only other room on the upper level, which turned out to be a large, multipurpose loft, with a home office set up by the window, a punching bag and free weights stacked in one corner, and a pool table in the center of the room. She descended the stairs, taking in the rest of Colt's house as she went.

When she'd been here before, she'd barely looked around, and it had been too dark to see anything in detail. But now she had the luxury of both time and daylight, and she took her time making her way through the house. The main floor was open and looked recently renovated, with a cozy living room and eat-in kitchen filling the space. A couple of blankets and a pillow sat on the couch, but other than that, the living room and kitchen were tidy. Being in his house felt...good, actually. She didn't feel like she was intruding or that she didn't belong. She felt cozy and safe.

The coffeepot was still half full, the scent filling the kitchen, and she'd been about to hunt for a mug to pour herself a cup when the faint strains of music coming from the driveway reached her. Glancing out the kitchen window, she saw Colt's Charger in the driveway, the hood propped open.

After retrieving a hair elastic from her purse and pulling her wet hair up into a ponytail, Taylor stepped out of the house and into the bright morning sunshine, squinting slightly as the warmth danced over her skin. Colt's head popped up over top of the hood, and he stepped around the car. Maybe it was a residual effect of her hangover, but her mouth suddenly went dry and her heart fluttered in her chest. She'd seen him in a T-shirt and jeans, in nothing but athletic shorts, and completely naked—albeit in very dim lighting. But this look just might be her favorite.

He dropped a wrench into the toolbox open at his feet and took another step toward her, wearing a pair of black sweatpants with "Army" spelled out in block letters down one leg, and a white tank top stained with black grease. He wiped his hands on a worn blue rag and then tossed it over his shoulder, a smile tipping up the corner of his mouth. A small grease smear adorned one perfect cheekbone.

"How you feeling this morning, gorgeous?"

Oh, yes. Casual Colt, Athletic Colt, and Naked Colt were all nice. Very, very nice. But Mechanic Colt was so gloriously masculine and sexy that she was pretty sure her panties were disintegrating on the spot.

She must've been staring longer than she realized because he leaned his head forward, one eyebrow cocked. "Hello? Earth to Taylor?" Blinking rapidly and giving her head a small shake, she bit her lip and met his eyes.

His phone buzzed and he fished it out of his pocket, glaring at the screen before releasing a tense chuckle. Looking up, he met Taylor's curious gaze. "Roman. I asked him to leave Chloe alone last night, and he's pissed at me."

"Why did you do that?"

"Because I heard you ask him not to hit on your friends." He shrugged like having her back and being on her side was no big deal when really, he had no idea how big a deal that was. She was so used to being on her own, having to tough things out by herself that something inside her melted, turning her insides gooey and sweet. All because he'd cock-blocked a friend for her.

"Colt…" She met his eyes and shivered as the sudden, intense urge to be honest with him hit her. "I'm sorry I got so drunk last night. I was just…I'm scared." Her voice cracked on the last syllable, and suddenly his arms were around her, pulling her against him. She nestled into him, letting his warmth settle over her like a blanket.

"I'm not going to let anything happen to you. Promise." He tightened his hold slightly and some of the tension ebbed out of her muscles. "Shit. I'm getting grease on you."

"I don't care." She slipped her arms around his waist and he stroked a hand up and down her back.

"We should go to the police with all of this."

She nodded against his chest, pulling his scent into her with a deep breath. "I know, but we don't have much to tell them yet. Has your investigator friend found anything?"

"Not yet, but he's running down a few leads. He should have some information for us soon." His voice rumbled in his chest, vibrating against her and she closed her eyes, savoring the feel of his voice, his hands stroking her back, his arms around her. The shelter of him that made her feel safe. Made her feel protected. For a long moment, they just stood in his driveway, Colt's arms wrapped around her as a Bad Company song played softly from the Charger's stereo.

"I'm glad you're here. With me," she said, pressing her face into his neck.

"Until we figure out what's going on, I don't want you out of my sight." He held her away from him and met her eyes. "And once we figure it out, I still won't want you out of my sight."

Her cheeks flushed slightly and she ducked her head for a second before forcing herself to meet his eyes, a giddiness floating through her at his words. "I owe you an apology. For last night, and for what a brat I've been. I was...well—" she forced herself to take a breath before plowing forward "—kind of a mess. I'm sorry if I—"

He cut her off with a gentle kiss, his hand slipping under her chin. His lips moved slowly against hers, and she sighed into him, pressing her hands into his back.

He broke the kiss, and when he spoke, his voice rumbled across her skin, sending ripples of pure, raw hunger dancing over her nerves. "The only reason you didn't wake up naked beside me this morning is because of how much you'd had to drink, and I didn't want it to be like that. Do you remember what I told you last night?"

She nodded against him, breathing him in again as her stomach flipped over on itself. "God, yes."

"I meant it. Taylor, whatever this is between us…" He kissed her again, a brief, sweet caress of his lips against hers. "I want it. I want you." She watched as emotions flickered across his face, barely surfacing before slipping away again.

"Colt." She shoved away the fear knotting her stomach, hanging on instead to the glimmering thread of hope that maybe this time, things could work out. That maybe if she jumped in with both feet, she wouldn't crash and land broken and scarred. That maybe if she let herself fall, Colt would actually catch her. Because she had to admit, everything felt different with him. Bigger, somehow. More real. More vibrant. She couldn't remember the last time she'd felt so *hungry* for someone, and not just in a physical sense. She was hungry for all of him. She wanted to know him, learn everything about him.

"Have dinner with me. Tonight."

She smiled up at him, loving the way his green eyes lit up. "Okay. It's a date."

* * *

Frank stared at the white lines in front of him, perfectly parallel. Each was slightly different from its neighbor, but beautiful in its own way. A Creedence Clearwater Revival song rumbled through the speakers, and he traced a pinky through the white lines, blurring them together only for the pleasure of using his AmEx card to separate them out again. Sorting and organizing them exactly the way he wanted. Simple and clean and pure.

He closed his eyes, took a deep breath, and then brought the rolled-up Benjamin to his nose and bent forward, bumping one of the rails. Immediately, the rush hit him, and he snorted a second line, the buzz fueling his hunger and only making him want more. A calming power flowed through him and he sat back in his chair, the anxiety of the previous moment gone.

Fucking Jonathan Fairfax. Fucking Golden Brotherhood. They'd picked the wrong biker gang to piss off, because he wasn't going to take their threats lying down like some kind of beaten dog. No way in hell. He'd figure out something with the money, but until then, they'd just have to wait. Those fuckers were used to getting their way, but they hadn't dealt with the Grim Weavers before.

The song playing just outside the office door changed, and an intense pang of nostalgia hit Frank like a kick in the gut. Iron Maiden's "Charlotte the Harlot" was now playing over the bar's sound system. It had been Susie's favorite song. It was where they'd gotten Taylor's middle name.

God, Susie. He hadn't thought about her in so long, and the memory of her—her golden waves, her lightly freckled skin, her low, husky laugh—took the edge off his high. He pulled his phone from his pocket and searched for Taylor, bringing up pictures of her. He hated how much she looked like Susie. Hated that Taylor was still here and Susie wasn't.

A series of shouts erupted from the front of the bar, and he hastily dumped the remaining lines of cocaine into a small glass vial and jammed a rubber stopper on the top, then tossed it into his desk. He picked up his Beretta from the desk and made his way out of the office, his skin dancing and his mind buzzing. He fucking hoped someone had come in looking for a fight.

He stepped into the main area of the bar, wincing at the

pain in his left foot, and froze at the press of metal against his neck. He'd felt the barrel of a gun enough times to recognize its kiss against his skin.

"We want our money, Ross," hissed a voice from behind him. Frank stiffened, and the gun pressed firmer against his neck, a strong hand circling his arm. "We figured out who your daughter is. And we've been watching her. So what's it gonna be, Ross? You gonna pay up, or do we need to ask your daughter to pay off your debts?"

Gritting his teeth, Frank spun, knocking the gun away from his neck and pushing the goon up against the wall, the mention of Taylor sending anger and frustration crashing through him. "You think I didn't already try that? She won't give me a fucking cent. And she sure as fuck isn't going to pay you."

"We have ways of making people cooperate."

Everyone else in the bar watched warily, hands hovering inches above weapons, ready to pull them free should a single bullet fly. Frank raised his gun, his thumb poised over the safety. For several seconds, Frank stared the man down, and the atmosphere in the bar shifted from one of intimidation to one of power and authority. "Get the fuck out of my bar. *Now.*"

The goon chuckled, seemingly unconcerned about the gun in his face. "The money. You or her. You have forty-eight hours."

# CHAPTER 16

Colt leaned forward and checked himself out in the mirror in Taylor's guest bathroom, fussing with his hair, brushing at it with the tips of his fingers. Standing up straight, he smoothed his hands down the front of his light gray button-down, which was tucked into black dress pants. Even though they were ordering in—in the interest of safety—he'd dressed up for his date with Taylor. A wave of hot, nervous anticipation washed over him, his pulse pounding in his throat.

He'd gathered several more days' worth of essentials from his place, and once he'd showered and cleaned himself up, he had driven Taylor back to her house. Roman would still be his backup, but no way was Colt leaving Taylor's now. Not after the way she'd curled into him, telling him she was scared, telling him she was glad he was with her.

He'd called Clay to find out if he'd been able to track down any additional information on Taylor's stalker, or any helpful information on her father. Clay had come up blank on both counts, but he was working a few angles and thought he'd have something soon.

Before heading up to her room to get ready for their date, Taylor had spent most of the day in the living room, guitar in hand, notebook open beside her, her gorgeously husky voice echoing through the house. Colt had sat on the bed in the guest room, his laptop in front of him, trying to distract himself with work, but he'd found himself falling into her music, his heart thumping a steady rhythm against his ribs as snatches of lyrics from different songs she was working on floated up to him.

*...you look so good in those worn blue jeans, hottest damn thing I've ever seen....*

*...I like my music like my men, hard, dirty and rough...*

*...I'm living my life, not giving a fuck, I don't play nice, make my own damn luck...*

Giving up on getting any work done, he'd opened a new browser window, clicking through takeout menus from different places. Even though he'd spent several nights in her house, tonight would be the first time that they were actually spending time together. He couldn't seem to get enough of her. That smile. That laugh. Her sense of humor. And now that they were finally letting their respective guards down, he wanted the chance to just...talk. He wanted to spend the evening really getting to know her before hopefully spending the night fucking her brains out.

He dragged himself back to the present, checking his appearance in the mirror one final time before heading down the stairs. He felt like a kid on prom night: nervous and fucking horny. Eager to please. Hopeful and...happy, he realized. God, it had been so long since he'd let himself be happy that he almost hadn't recognized it at first.

The doorbell rang, and he froze on the stairs. He hadn't

ordered the food yet. "You expecting someone?" he called up over his shoulder, and Taylor poked her head around the corner, her long blond hair falling over her bare shoulder.

"No." She frowned and the doorbell rang again, followed by a series of loud, crashing knocks on the front door. Colt strode to the front of the house and looked out, his eyes landing on the gleaming Harley parked in the driveway, and anger beat through him. He pulled his SIG free of his waistband and opened the front door.

"Who the fuck are you?" A sneer turned up Frank's lips as he spat the question at Colt. His leather vest was covered in patches, including ones marking him as a one percenter and as the Grim Weavers' president. His bald head gleamed in the late-afternoon light, the only hair on his face his bushy eyebrows and overgrown light brown goatee. He spit on Taylor's front step and pushed his sunglasses up on his head, then crossed his beefy, tattooed arms in front of him. "Let me guess. Booty call?"

Colt glanced behind him to see that Taylor had followed him into the front hall, and was dressed for their date in a simple, flowing black halter dress that hit just above the knee. Her hair tumbled over her shoulders in loose, golden waves, and she'd done her eye makeup in that way he liked, with the dark, shimmery shadow. Seeing her dressed up for their date, for *him*, sent a wave of possession crashing into him, so intense that he felt it like a punch to the gut. He could feel the anger and fear radiating off of Taylor as he tucked her safely behind him, slipping his SIG back into his waistband and crossing his arms over his chest.

"You need to leave." Colt struggled to keep his voice even, struggled to keep his rising temper at bay.

"I need to talk to my daughter. Fuck off." Frank leveled his blue eyes, so like Taylor's, at Colt in a cold stare before smiling. Frank's eyes, while the same shade of blue, held none of her spark or her warmth, but instead shone with a cruelty that Colt recognized instantly, having seen it in some of his mother's boyfriends. The idea that Taylor had grown up with this man as her father stoked every single one of Colt's protective instincts.

"You look slutty, Taylor." Frank spit again and crossed his arms over his chest, sighing heavily.

Clearly Colt and Frank had different definitions of *slutty*, because as far as Colt was concerned, she looked so beautiful it made his chest hurt a little. Before Colt could answer, Frank nodded. "She always was a little whore." He leaned forward, as if sharing a secret with a friend. "Between you and me, I'd double-bag it with this one." He tipped his chin in Taylor's direction.

"Hell of a way to talk about your daughter," said Colt, beating back the temper rising up in him. He could feel it pushing at his insides, rising higher and higher like licking flames. He wanted to shove Frank, this piece-of-shit excuse for a human being, against the wall, knock his teeth out, and make him sorry he'd shown up at Taylor's. But he knew that wouldn't help the situation. All that mattered was protecting Taylor, and to do that, he had to stay calm and professional.

He had a feeling Frank was going to make that a challenge.

"What do you want?" Taylor met her father's eyes, not flinching under his cruel glare.

"You need to give me money, or we're both fucked."

Colt once again tucked Taylor behind him, deliberately putting himself between her and Frank.

"What did you do?" Taylor asked, resting one hand on Colt's back. Her fingers curled slightly into his shirt and he clenched his jaw, praying for Frank to give him a reason to hurt him.

"I owe some people some money. They figured out you're my daughter. If they can't get it from me, they're gonna get it from you."

Colt's spine snapped straight as realization crashed into him. The van that had been following them yesterday made a hell of a lot more sense now.

"Dad, would you just go? I'm not giving you any money. Figure out your own problems." Her voice was quiet, but he could hear the determination in her tone until the last couple of syllables, when her voice wavered.

"I'm not going anywhere until I get what I came for. Don't you get it? You don't give me the money, they're gonna come after you. I'm trying to help you, for fuck's sake."

"I don't believe you. Who's going to come after me?"

"Does it matter?"

"You're lying."

"Jesus, you really are a dumb bitch."

Something snapped inside Colt, like a rubber band stretched too tight, and he knew his control was slipping. "If you want to keep all your teeth, I suggest you shut the fuck up," he growled, stepping into Frank's personal space. He could feel a muscle ticcing in his jaw.

Frank snorted out a laugh, his eyes narrowing. "Oh, I get it. Boyfriend, not booty call."

"Actually, I'm her bodyguard. And you're leaving." He jabbed a finger into Frank's chest, sending him backward a few inches.

"Not until I get my money."

Smiling, Colt took another step toward Frank, who took a half step backward. "You're leaving. *Now.*"

"Not without my money!" he snarled from between clenched teeth. "That fucking slut owes me. This isn't your fight, buddy. And any fun you might have between this whore's legs isn't worth it."

Colt took another step toward Frank. "Listen up. This is going to end one of two ways. Option one: You turn around, get on your bike, and never come here again. You leave nice and quiet and I won't beat the shit out of you. That sounds like a pretty good option to me, but you might be wondering what's behind door number two, which, by the way, opens in about nine and a half seconds." He closed any remaining distance between them, so that the two men were nose to nose, and Colt chuckled. "Door number two involves me calling the cops and beating the *living fuck* out of you in the fifteen minutes it'll take them to get here. Personally, I'm really hoping you go for option two, but it's your call." It took everything he had in him to step back, and he made a show of checking his watch. "Clock's ticking. What's it gonna be?"

Frank shoved Colt, who didn't move.

"Seriously?" Colt said. "That's all you got?"

Letting out a frustrated grunt, Frank shoved him again, and once again, Colt didn't move, simply absorbing the impact.

"You're gonna have to do better than that. And, oh, look at that. Time's up." Grabbing fistfuls of Frank's vest, he shoved him back against the wall of the porch. "I don't think you know who you're messing with, because I will *fuck you up*. I don't care who you are. No one talks to her like that."

"Dad. Just go." Taylor's voice was firmer, steadier than before.

"Shut up, bitch!" he ground out. "I'm trying to warn you."

"Warn us about who?" Colt shook him, the leather of

Frank's vest creaking in his fists. When he didn't answer, he shook him again, harder. "Who?"

"I can't tell you!"

"Because it's all a lie," said Taylor. "He's not in trouble. He's trying to scare me into giving him money, trying to make me think someone will come get me if I don't pay him. Bullshit! Did you have that van follow us yesterday just to set this whole thing up?"

"You're the dumbest fucking cunt I've ever met."

Frank's words shredded the last remaining scrap of Colt's restraint, and he pulled back just enough to slam his fist into Frank's face. Adrenaline surged through him, and he shoved Frank against the porch wall. Blood tricked from his nose.

"Don't you fucking talk to her that way. Get the hell out of here. If I see you again, I'll break every bone in your goddamn body. You got that?"

Cold blue eyes bore into his before Frank slumped slightly, the fight gone out of him. Colt uncurled his fists and let him go, even though what he really wanted was to pummel him into a bloody pulp.

"This isn't over," Frank spat out before scurrying down the steps and then walking backward to his bike, his arms outstretched. "We're blood. You'll see. I'll get what I deserve."

Taylor laughed, the sound harsh and cold. "I sure hope so. Don't come here again, Frank. *Ever.*" She stood tall, her body stiff, her chin up, as her dad got onto his Harley and pulled out of the driveway, engine growling as he gunned it down the street, leaving a trail of smoke behind him.

Before he could reach for her, Taylor spun and stormed into the house, the delicate fabric of her dress swirling around her long legs. He followed her inside, closing and locking the door behind him. The sounds of her stomping feet and slamming cabinet doors echoed through the house.

He took a few steps inside, sucking in deep breaths and fighting back his temper and the surge of hormone-spiked adrenaline racing through his system. All he wanted was to throw her over his shoulder and find a bed so he could fuck her until neither of them could walk, and as appealing as that idea was, he needed instead to make sure that Taylor was okay.

She leaned against the stainless steel island in the center of the kitchen, two tumblers of amber liquid and a bottle of Jack Daniels in front of her. As he walked into the kitchen, her head rose and she pushed one of the tumblers toward him. Without waiting, she picked hers up and drained it, breathing deeply several times.

"I'm sorry you had to see that," she said finally, pouring herself another drink. She paced restlessly around the kitchen, her hands trembling slightly. Those trembling hands made him want to pull her into his arms, to kiss her, to use his body to make her forget about everything.

He picked up his glass and took a small sip, breaking his "no drinking on the job" rule. He needed something to take the edge off the emotions slicing through him. The protectiveness, and the lust, and the anger, all blending together almost painfully.

"Don't be," he said. "That wasn't your fault. You have *nothing* to be sorry about." He sliced his hand through the air for emphasis.

She nodded, once, still pacing, lips pursed. After several moments, she stilled. "Thank you. For scaring him off."

"You're welcome. I'm glad I was here to help." He took another sip of his drink and forced himself to sit down on one of the leather-and-chrome stools tucked under the island. If he didn't sit down and keep his hands wrapped around the cool glass of the tumbler, he'd leap over the island, pull her into his arms, and kiss her until she forgot there was anything to be upset about. But instead he sat, and sipped, and waited. He only wanted to shelter her, from everything. Her dad, the stalker, the threats, the fear. Shelter her and protect her from all of it. "So you really think all of that was an empty threat?"

She nodded, her lower lip caught between her teeth. "He wants money, and he knows I won't give it to him, so he's trying to scare me. He's a lying, manipulating son of a bitch."

"But someone did follow us yesterday. Someone was watching from that van." Thankfully, the van hadn't made a reappearance today, although if whoever had been driving it knew he'd been made, he likely would've swapped out the van for another vehicle.

"It was probably him, trying to scare me. Or hell, maybe it was just a photographer." She dragged the tip of her finger around the rim of her glass. "Although they seem to have lost interest in me lately. Guess I'm only interesting when I'm getting kicked off planes."

He took another sip of his drink. "I know you think it's an empty threat, but I need to treat it as real. I won't risk not taking it seriously."

"Thank you," she whispered, and she looked up, pain and vulnerability shining in her eyes, all of her shields completely down. "No one's ever stood up to him before."

Unable to stand it any longer, he pushed up from his stool and skirted around the island in a few long steps.

Cautiously, he trailed his hand up her neck and over her jaw, then tucked a strand of hair behind her ear. Fuck, she smelled so good. Like sweetness and warmth. "I told you, I take care of what's mine."

She closed her eyes and pressed her face into his palm.

He was so wound up—from the confrontation, from the surge of caveman-like protectiveness making him want to throw her over his shoulder—that he thought he might split in half.

"I want to be yours."

With her whispered words, it was as though something ignited between them. His lips closed over hers, and her fingers threaded into his hair. The sensation of her tongue sliding against his sent sparks shooting down his spine and straight to his quickly hardening dick. She moaned softly against him before pulling away.

"Let's skip dinner. Right now, I only want you."

Her words slammed into him, and with a growl, he pushed her back against the wall.

# CHAPTER 17

As Colt backed Taylor into the wall, they kissed hungrily and with increasing intensity, tasting and devouring each other like starving people at a banquet. Taylor wanted to gorge herself on Colt and everything he had to offer.

"You sure you're not hungry?"

Not fully removing her mouth from his, she nodded. "Only for you. Sex. Now." After the way he'd protected her, stood up for her and made her feel safe, she wanted nothing more than to give herself to him, and to claim him in return.

He pulled back and leaned his forehead against hers, his breathing fast and shallow. "Tell me if you're not sure, because I'm barely hanging on here."

"What part of 'sex now' wasn't clear?"

He chuckled and tightened his arms around her, pressing his face into her neck. "Just checking."

She closed her eyes, savoring the feel of his mouth on her skin as he kissed and sucked from her ear to the halter neck of her dress. "Such a gentleman."

"A gentleman who wants to bury his face in your pussy."

"God, yes." She grabbed his face and brought her mouth to his again, slipping her tongue in his mouth and kissing him deeply. She lowered her hands, loving the feel of flexing muscle under his shirt as she skimmed her fingers down his wide back. She palmed his firm, tight ass, massaging and squeezing the muscle there as she pulled his hips tight against hers.

"I've wanted to get my face between your thighs again from the second you left my bed."

She whimpered out a moan and rolled her hips against him, already seeking relief for the sweet ache throbbing between her thighs.

"I want to suck and kiss and lick you until you come on my tongue, all wet and swollen."

"Holy shit, Colt." Her voice came out on a tremulous whisper.

"Oh, honey. I think we both know that I'm gonna make you say my name a lot louder than that."

Her stomach flipped and turned, anticipation tingling hotly through her. "I fucking love your dirty mouth."

He grinned and tugged on the string holding the top part of her dress up, undoing the bow in one swift, sure movement. With a quiet rustle, it fell to where her belt cinched around her waist; the airy fabric brushed against her sensitive skin as it slipped down over her breasts. Colt's grin turned into a wide, hungry smile.

"No bra?"

She bit her lip and returned his smile. "No underwear at all."

He slid a hand up under her skirt, the light material bunching as his hand rode up the outside of her thigh all the way to her hip, ripples of pleasure flaring from the friction of his rough hand caressing her bare skin.

He cupped her ass and pressed her back firmly against the wall, raising her up so that her bare breasts were level with his mouth. She wound her legs around his waist just as he took one hardened nipple into his mouth, swirling his tongue over it before gently nipping at it. She moaned and writhed against him, raking her fingers through his soft, thick hair.

"Beautiful," he murmured as he dragged his lips over to her other breast to give it the same attention, hungrily sucking her nipple into his mouth in a hot, open-mouthed kiss. He tormented her nipple, biting it and then soothing it with his tongue, and tension coiled from her breasts straight to her throbbing clit, pulsing in time with each beat of her heart. She tipped her head back as much as she could, pinned as she was against the wall, arched her back, and pressed her breasts against Colt's face, wanting more. Wanting everything. She clenched her thighs around him, sighing out a desperate moan as she tried to put even a little pressure on her clit. He smiled against her flesh, keeping her nipple caught between his teeth. He tugged harder this time, sending sharp pleasure sparking down her spine, and she cried out, her legs trembling around him.

He let her feet slip back to the floor, and still pressing her against the wall, he sucked at the sensitive skin just under her ear as his hands slid up to cup her breasts, the rough pads of his fingers rolling her tight nipples into even tighter buds. Heat poured over her skin as he crushed his mouth to hers again, his tongue finding hers. She started working on the buttons of his shirt, but she couldn't seem to get her fumbling fingers to cooperate, distracted as she was with his delicious mouth on hers, his big hands squeezing and caressing her breasts, playing with her nipples. With a frustrated growl, she grabbed fistfuls of the fabric and tore it open, and buttons popped off and bounced across the floor with quiet clicks.

He pulled back, his green eyes dark and glittering with lust. And then he laughed, a low rumble from deep in his chest, the skin around his eyes crinkling, white teeth flashing.

"Hey, I liked this shirt."

"I'll buy you ten just like it. Off." She pushed impatiently at the fabric hanging from his shoulders, and still chuckling, he slipped a gun out of his waistband, laying it gently on the island behind him. He shrugged out of his now button-less button down, letting it fall to the floor.

His body was incredible, strong and wide and gorgeously masculine, beautifully marked with the Ranger tattoo covering his left pec and the sleeve of feathers covering his right arm from shoulder to wrist. She ran her hands over his pecs, tracing their muscled contours and the edges of his tattoo. She tweaked at his nipples then ran her fingers through the dusting of light brown hair trailing down into his abs. Skimming the firm ridges with the tips of her fingers, she explored his body, reveling in its hard, chiseled beauty. "My God. Look at you. You're perfect."

Tipping her head forward, she licked up his neck and then sucked his earlobe into her mouth, scraping her teeth over his flesh. Trailing her hands even lower, she had less trouble with his belt than she'd had with his shirt, and she had the buckle undone and his fly unzipped in a matter of seconds. She brought her lips back to his, wanting more of his taste, and as he pressed his hands on the wall on either side of her head, kissing her practically senseless, she slipped a hand into his pants.

Skimming over top of his boxer briefs, she ran her palm lightly over his gorgeously thick cock, which was hard and straining for freedom. He flexed his hips into her hand and she stroked him again, with more pressure this time. But when she moved to dip her hand into his boxers, he stepped back, shaking his head. For one terrifying second, she thought he was pulling away from her and from what they were about to do. Instead, he scooped her up and set her on the edge of the island before dropping to his knees in front of her, an adorably naughty smile playing across his lips. She took a deep breath as she looked down at him, never wanting to forget the sight of Colt on his knees in front of her, shirtless and with his pants open, the plump head of his cock peeking out over the waistband of his boxers, his hair a mess from her hands, his cheeks slightly flushed.

It was both sweet and dirty, both tender and erotic. It was a tiny yet perfect moment, and she knew that if she ever had occasion for her life to flash before her eyes, this would be one of the images she'd see.

Exerting gentle pressure on her calves, he hooked her legs over his shoulders and pushed her skirt up, leaving her completely open and exposed to him.

He nipped at her inner thigh. "You're so pink and swollen, gorgeous. So beautiful." Mouth open, she propped herself up on her elbows and watched as he licked the pad of his thumb and then traced a featherlight circle over her clit. Her hips bucked; fierce pleasure shot through her and tightened every muscle in her body.

He looked up at her as he circled her clit again, then trailed his fingers down her slit. Still watching her, he eased a finger into her, slowly teasing it in and out of her. His name fell from her lips in a strangled moan, and she fought to keep her eyes from drifting shut, wanting to watch. After a few strokes, he added a second finger, stretching her. He slipped his fingers out of her and she almost came when he sucked his own index finger into his mouth. He let out a low, gruff moan. "You taste so fucking good."

"Colt, please." Her words came out as a whisper, her throat tight with need.

"Don't worry, gorgeous. I'll take care of you." He gripped her hips, his strong fingers flexing into her. Gently, almost reverently, he pressed a kiss to her clit and then swirled his hot tongue over and around it. Oh, God, this wasn't going to take long. She could already feel her orgasm building, her insides coiling tight. A hot flush spread across her bare chest and up her neck, sweat prickling at her hairline.

"Fuck, Colt. You're so damn good at this," she managed to choke out, her words half moans, half sobs.

"I could do this all night, Taylor. All fucking night." He closed his lips over her wet, sensitive flesh, licking and sucking at her slowly at first, and then with increasing intensity, consuming her with his talented mouth. His tongue traveled down her slit and he lapped at her, drinking in her arousal, groaning out his approval. She ground her hips against him, and her eyes closed, her orgasm shimmering around her, so close. Hot, tight pressure built low in her stomach, and her blood thrummed along in time with her throbbing clit. He sucked her swollen clit into his mouth and she came apart, her orgasm bursting over her like a firework, hot and bright and sparkling and beautiful. She thrust her hands in his hair and rode out her climax as wave after wave of searing pleasure crashed through her, and he kept up his delicious torment, lips and tongue working against her slick flesh. Her muscles started shaking and he didn't stop, only changing his rhythm as he buried his face in her pussy, just as he'd promised. He licked at her clit with slow, firm strokes of his tongue, and she sucked in a sharp breath as another orgasm rode in on the heels of the first one.

"Fuck, Colt!" She screamed as every muscle in her body convulsed and spasmed, leaving her shaking and soaking wet.

He tenderly kissed her inner thighs, her hips, her stomach, as he waited for her to come back to earth. "Bedroom. Now," he said, his voice low and rough. He rose from his knees and slid his arms around her waist, drawing her close as he pulled her down off the island, his hard cock nestled against her hipbone. "I need to be inside you."

Pulling away, she undid the belt holding her dress up and let it fall around her feet, stepping out of it. Fully naked, she grabbed Colt's hand and began leading him up the stairs on shaky legs. She slowed her steps about halfway up and looked over her shoulder at him, her heart clenching and her stomach fluttering at how utterly gorgeous he looked, all disheveled, half naked and ravenous. She felt greedy looking at him, because even though he'd just made her come twice, it wasn't nearly enough.

When it came to Colt, nothing might ever be quite enough.

"God, you're beautiful." He came level with her on the stairs and kissed her, deep and urgent. She melted into him, excitement and fresh arousal zapping through her when she tasted herself on his tongue. "I'm about three seconds away from fucking you on the stairs."

She laughed and resumed leading him up the stairs. "I like that idea, but the condoms are in my bedroom." She quickened her pace and forced herself not to run like an excited kid as she guided Colt down the hallway. She pushed open the door to her bedroom, and the second she did, her feet left the ground as Colt scooped her up and tossed her over his shoulder, making a beeline for the king-sized bed in the middle of the room. She laughed as he gave her ass a playful smack, excited happiness flowing over her like warm, tropical water.

He tossed her down on the bed, and she rolled to the far side, tugged open the drawer on the nightstand, fished out a condom, and tossed the foil square to him. His eyes held hers as he toed off his shoes and pushed his pants and boxer briefs down. His cock sprung free, snapping against his ridged stomach. She bit her lip and sighed out an appreciative moan.

"I don't want to be able to walk tomorrow." She crawled toward him on the bed, watching as he sheathed his gorgeous cock with the condom.

He winked and stroked himself, just once. "That can be arranged."

She flipped herself onto her back and scooted to the edge, letting her legs dangle over the side of the bed. He tumbled down on top of her while leaving his feet planted firmly on the floor, claiming her mouth with his. Scraping her fingernails down his back, she could feel the tension straining the strong muscles beneath his warm skin.

"Oh, God, Colt. I want you inside me."

With a sound like a low growl, he pushed her legs apart and lined up the head of his cock with her slick entrance. Hands gripping her thighs tightly, he eased just the thick head in and then paused.

"I don't think I have it in me to be gentle or go slow."

She found his eyes with hers. "Fuck me, Colt."

With one sure thrust, he slid deep into her and she cried out at the intense pleasure of being stretched and filled to the hilt. The feeling of Colt inside her was pure perfection, and she sighed, every cell in her body full to bursting with lust, happiness, and something more. Something deeper she wasn't fully prepared to name.

"Shit," he ground out, beads of sweat dotting his hairline. He smiled down at her, that cocky half smile she loved. "Don't move, gorgeous. I need a second."

Doing as she was asked, she didn't move her hips, despite the tight ache blooming anew in her core. She swiveled her head up off the mattress, wanting to get a good look at where they were joined. She slid a hand over her abdomen and between her legs, slowly circling her clit with languid strokes.

"Fuck, that's hot." He slid out of her, torturously slow, and then rocked back into her. The sight of him above her, eyes dark, muscles taut and flexing, was incredible. Beyond words.

With his iron grip, he urged her thighs even farther apart, and she complied, loving the feeling of being completely open and exposed for him as he established a deep, hard rhythm, claiming her body with his own. Her head fell back on the bed as she continued to touch herself, urged on by his low, throaty groans. A new kind of pressure began to build, pleasure urged higher with each stroke of her clit, each thrust of his cock deep inside her. She started to shake, her muscles weak with pleasure.

"That's it, Taylor," Colt urged in that low rumble she loved so much. "Come for me. Come on my cock."

Her orgasm spread over her like a crack in a dam, growing and fanning out over her heated skin as the pressure built until finally, with one particularly deep thrust from Colt, it burst over her, flooding her senses with such intense pleasure that she could've drowned in it. She convulsed around him, clenching around his cock.

"Jesus Christ," he ground out, slamming into her once, twice more before every muscle in his body tensed, the cords in his neck straining against his sweat-slicked skin. He was buried so deep inside her that she felt every throb, every pulse of his cock, as he came.

For several seconds, neither of them moved, their bodies still joined. Slowly, Colt opened his eyes and smiled down at her.

"Jesus Christ," she whispered.

Without a word, he slid out of her, eased her farther up onto the bed and kissed her, long and slow and deep, and she ignored the wisp of fear curling its smoky tendrils around her heart.

She'd never survive him, but it was too late. She was a goner.

\* \* \*

Ronnie sat on his bed with his computer in his lap, his limp dick in his hand. He'd thought watching would be a good thing, but he'd been wrong. So, so wrong. And even though he'd known it was a possibility, he hadn't truly expected her to fuck the brute again. Not when she was supposed to be keeping herself pure for him.

He stared out the window into the dark, starless night, wondering if it might be better if he just listened, like he had that first night. But he'd listened to Taylor have sex with that brute—Colt—before he'd taken their relationship to the next level. He'd been watching her for days now. Watching her sleep. Watching her eat. Watching her shower. It was a new level of intimacy, and it was that intimacy, that new sense of ownership, that was making watching her in bed with another man so difficult.

At the sound of Taylor's low, throaty moans, he returned his attention to the laptop screen, forcing himself to watch. He felt like a soldier, training for battle. He watched as the brute slammed into Taylor from behind, one hand between her legs, the other fisted in her hair.

"Are you gonna come?" growled Colt as the pace of his thrusts picked up. Taylor practically screamed, panting out a string of curse words. Colt pulled her hair harder, arching her back. "Come for me, gorgeous. God, you're so fucking wet."

Taylor moaned out Colt's name as her arms started to shake, and then gave out. She collapsed onto the bed, her fists clenched in the sheets as she moaned and gasped.

Ronnie felt as though he were being stabbed in the stomach with a rusty knife, his insides tearing and ripping and spilling open inch by slow, painful inch. With an anguished cry, he slammed the laptop shut and tossed it to the side, not wanting to touch it anymore.

He couldn't live like this. Couldn't live watching the woman he loved savagely taken by a brute who had no business touching what didn't belong to him.

The solution was simple. The brute had to die.

# CHAPTER 18

A few blissfully filthy hours later, Colt lay propped on one elbow in Taylor's bed, watching her as she strode back into her bedroom, fully naked, a bottle of water in each hand. Her hair was a mess, her eye makeup smeared, her lips a deep pink and swollen. A faint love bite was beginning to emerge on the swell of her right breast, and he could see fingertip bruises marking the insides of her thighs, just above each knee.

God damn, but there was a sight he could get used to.

She slid into bed beside him, folding her long legs gracefully under the twisted sheet. With a smile that made him want to bury himself inside her for a fifth time, she handed him a bottle of water and mirrored his posture, facing him propped on one elbow. She clinked her bottle against his, the plastic crinkling quietly.

"What are we toasting?" he asked, twisting the cap off and taking a sip.

Fingers toying with her bottom lip, she took a second before answering. "Amazing sex."

"I will *always* drink to that." He took another small sip before setting his bottle on the nightstand. "So…you want to talk about what happened earlier?"

"You mean the part where you went down on me in my kitchen? Or when you fucked me from behind and pulled my hair? Which I *really* liked, by the way. Or when I let you put your—"

"Taylor." He said her name quietly and laid a hand on her hip. "We don't have to talk about your dad if you don't want to. But I'm here, okay?"

She glanced down, her long eyelashes casting shadows on her cheekbones in the dim room.

He tucked a hand under her chin and gently raised her face. "You can talk to me."

Her features pulled tight in a heartbreaking wince that he felt like a jab to the ribs. He wrapped his arms around her and settled her against his chest, her cheek pressed against his heart. For several minutes, he simply held her, his hands stroking up and down the smooth skin of her back.

She sighed deeply, her body trembling against him, and he closed his eyes against the overwhelming need to protect her. To take all of her pain, all of her fear, and carry it for her, heavy as it might be.

"He…was abusive when I was growing up, verbally and physically. My mom was usually too high to do anything about it, so I was on my own. I tried so hard, Colt. So hard to be good so that maybe he'd stop hating me. And then after my mom died, it just got worse. He took all of his anger, all of his pain, out on me. According to him, I was unlovable, worthless, useless, a waste. A mistake. I'd get slapped, my ass whipped with a belt, that kind of stuff. Once, he stomped on my foot so hard that he broke two of my toes."

She paused, taking a deep, steadying breath. He kissed

the top of her head and tightened his arms around her, waiting for her to continue.

"If I'd been born a boy, he probably would've taken me under his wing, teaching me to ride and fix bikes, bringing me into the Grim Weavers. But they don't allow women as members, so I was worthless there, too. My mom…fuck, she wore this thing called a property patch on her vest so all the other bikers knew whose property she was. The only reason the other bikers didn't touch me was because of who my dad was, but I'm not sure he would've cared. I think my parents sometimes forgot I even existed, and I liked it that way, because when they forgot about me, they left me alone.

"Once, when I was eight, they disappeared for days, off on a ride somewhere, getting high and shit. I watched cartoons and ate cereal, and no one called me names, and no one hit me. I was sad when they came back. So when I hit high school, I started spending less and less time at home, trying to stay away from him. He was getting more and more violent, and I'd given up trying to be a good kid, especially after my mom OD'd. I just wanted to escape, you know? To not feel so constantly shitty about myself. About my life."

"Taylor, I'm so sorry." She'd been on her own in that fucked-up situation, trying to claw her way out of it with no one to look out for her. His mind flashed to Lacey and what her life might've been like had he not been there to protect her, and he shuddered to imagine it. His chest ached, thinking of how alone, how scared, Taylor must've been.

"Thanks." She stiffened and her voice grew quieter. "When I was fifteen, I had a boyfriend. A guy named Jordan, who was cute and funny. I couldn't understand what he saw in some stupid, white-trash girl, so when he wanted to have sex, even though I wasn't sure, I said yes. I wanted to hang on to him so I wouldn't be so alone, you know? Anyway, I waited for a night when I knew Dad wouldn't be home. But he came home early and found me with Jordan."

Colt tensed, his heart thudding heavily against his ribs. "What happened?"

"He broke my jaw."

Colt closed his eyes against the wave of pain and anger slamming into him. "*Motherfucker.*" He pressed his face into her soft hair. "It's probably for the best I didn't know about that earlier tonight, because I would've done a lot worse than punching him in the face."

She looked up at him, eyes shining and full of emotion. Snuggling tighter into him, she laid her head back down.

"Colt, it…was awful. Not only was it—still, to this day—the most painful experience of my life, but I was terrified. I thought he was going to kill me. He told me that if I wanted to be a slut, he knew several pimps who'd be happy to have me."

"What did Jordan do?"

"He was a sixteen-year-old boy. He ran out of the house and as far away from me and my fucked-up life as possible."

He thought back to himself at sixteen, and how he'd done his best to protect Lacey, no matter what. Running had never occurred to him, and it broke his heart and stoked the flames of his protective temper that she hadn't had anyone to lean on. "I'm so, so sorry, Taylor." He didn't know what else to say. He gave her a second before asking, "So then what happened?"

"The neighbors must've heard me screaming, because they called nine-one-one. The cops came, I went to the hospital, and I was put into foster care. Which, really, was for the best. My two foster brothers were rough around the edges, but so was I. I think in some weird, twisted way, we were good for each other. And if I hadn't met my foster brother Alex, I probably never would've picked up a guitar. I'd always liked music, and I knew I could sing reasonably well, but where the hell was I going to learn an instrument? It wasn't even on my radar. But Alex and I, we hung out, and he taught me. It came really easily to me, and music became my dream. Alex played at bars, open-mic nights, and I'd tag along. We had pretty kick-ass fake IDs."

She laughed, remembering. "One night, Alex brought me onstage with him, and once I got a taste of that, I was done. Music became this positive force in my life, this creative outlet that I hadn't even realized I'd needed, you know?"

"Where's Alex now?"

"He's a high school teacher in Fresno. Went to college and everything. Like I said, foster care was actually good for us, in the long run." She looked up at him. "I've never told anyone this shit before, but it feels good. Thank you."

"Taylor, you can unburden yourself with me. I didn't have it nearly as rough as you growing up, but I get it. My dad left my mom when my sister Lacey and I were just toddlers, and she had some pretty shitty boyfriends. Losers, drug dealers, assholes. She was an alcoholic, and she didn't make good choices, for herself or for her kids. She and I aren't in touch." He sighed heavily. "My sister's in the process of reconnecting with her, and I...I'm not sure how I feel about it. A part of me wants to keep her firmly in the past, but another part of me is curious, you know?" He paused, shocked that he'd just spilled his guts like a filleted fish. "I guess what I'm trying to say is, you don't need to carry any of this alone."

"I think if you're curious about your mom, you owe it to yourself to try. If she fucks it up again, then it's on her, not you. And I'm sorry you had to go through that. It sucks when the so-called adults don't have their shit together."

She sighed and then swallowed thickly. "I…I wasn't kidding when I told you that you're the first person who's ever stood up to my dad. Who's ever stood up for me. And it…" She tilted her head up and kissed him with a sweetness that stole his breath. "I don't even have words for how much it means to me."

"I'm not going to let anything happen to you." He kissed her, slowly and tenderly, needing to show her, reassure her. Connect with her. Protect and comfort her. He'd never felt like this before, like he could lose himself in someone else.

Granted, he'd never been with anyone as amazing as Taylor before, either. Strong, and smart, and beautiful, and talented.

She propped herself up, facing him once again, a half smile on her pretty lips. "My turn, since we're having show-and-tell." She traced a hand up his right forearm, and he knew what was coming. "Do you remember that night at the Rainbow when I asked you about your sleeve?"

He nodded, not saying anything, mostly because he was surprised at how much he wanted to tell her.

"You dodged my question, and I let it go." Her eyes met his, and he felt something cold and hard in his chest soften, like a chunk of ice starting to melt. "Will you tell me now?"

He scrubbed a hand over his mouth before speaking. "It's a memorial tattoo. For all the guys I fought with who didn't make it back. Each feather is for one soldier."

Her eyes widened slightly and she bit her lip, studying the overlapping feathers. "But there are so many." Her voice was quiet, full of sadness and respect as she traced the black lines on his arm.

He nodded slowly. "Fifty-eight. Many of them men I was responsible for."

"Oh, Colt." She pressed her fingertips against her mouth,

her eyes solemn. "Scars hidden in plain view," she whispered, again tracing her fingers over the ink, and for the first time in years he could breathe without tasting the pain he kept hidden deep inside, because now someone else understood.

"I have real scars, too," he said, wiggling his eyebrows, deliberately turning his tone flirty and navigating away from the deep waters into which they were quickly headed.

"I noticed that one on your shoulder," she said.

He nodded and turned his shoulder to her, showing her. "Shrapnel from a bomb blast in Afghanistan." He pushed down the sheet and pointed to the faint raised red line right where hip met thigh on his right side. "Bullet graze from my first deployment." Lifting his leg, he showed her the inside of his right ankle, the skin there raised, a mottled pink-and-white. "Second degree burn pulling kids out of a bombed-out school in Iraq."

As good as it felt to talk, to show his scars, he wasn't ready to reveal his biggest one, the one he carried deep down inside him that was completely invisible and yet caused him the most pain. The truth was that he still had nightmares, still hated talking about the shit that had gone down in the Sand-pit, still waged a daily battle against the self-loathing that was always there, simmering just below the surface. It was what the shrink at the VA had called survivor's guilt, a com-mon symptom of PTSD.

She traced her fingers over the scar at his hip. "How many times were you deployed?"

He paused, counting silently in his head. "I was deployed to Afghanistan twice before going to Ranger School. After becoming a Ranger, I did four deployments to Iraq and three to Afghanistan."

Her blue eyes were sad, and her hand came to rest over his heart. "Holy shit. That's a lot of war, Colt."

"I know." He nodded, his head suddenly feeling much heavier.

"I'm sorry." She squeezed his hip, flexing her fingers into him.

"Don't be. I served my country, and I'd do it again."

"So why aren't you in the Army anymore?"

"Time for a change, you know?" Ready to turn the subject away from himself, he skimmed a hand over her tattooed ribs. "Your turn. Tell me what they mean."

She sat up, and he felt blood flow into his apparently insatiable dick at the sight of her breasts bouncing slightly. She swung her feet out from under the sheet and showed him the inside of her right ankle, dotted with tiny music notes. "This was my first one. I think I was…" she paused, biting her lip "…seventeen. For the first time in my life, I'd found something I was good at and that I enjoyed. Making that connection to music…it was lifesaving for me." She flipped over her right wrist, showing a swirled line of delicate black stars. "I don't remember getting this one. I'm lucky it's pretty. I think I was about nineteen." She turned her long, slender back to him and gathered her hair up, exposing the nape of her neck and the Egyptian ankh inked there. "I got this one after White Crown's first album was a success. It's the key of life, and with my music career, I knew I'd found mine." Still with her back to him, she pointed at the gorgeous tattoo covering most of her right shoulder blade, depicting a large feather disintegrating into tiny birds fluttering up to the top of her shoulder. "I got this one after White Crown broke up and I went solo. To me, it represents the freedom I felt striking out on my own."

"And what about this one?" he asked, skimming his hand over her ribs on her left side. In beautiful, scrolling script were the Fleetwood Mac lyrics, "Oh, mirror in the sky, what is love?"

"A reminder." Pain, sadness, loneliness—all of it flashed in her eyes, and it made him want to take on the world for her.

He'd been about to press her further when his stomach rumbled loudly, reminding both of them that they hadn't eaten dinner. Like a switch had flipped, a smile lit up her face.

"Um…" She twirled a lock of her hair around her finger, playing at being shy, and Goddamn, it was adorable. "Do you want to order pizza and have more sex?"

Laughing, he pounced on her with a playful growl, covering her body with his. Looking down at her, he felt so big and warm, it was as though he'd swallowed the sun, and he kissed her until they both forgot about the scars they'd shown each other.

# CHAPTER 19

Rays of pink and orange sunshine were just starting to cut a swath through the layer of smog clinging to the Los Angeles skyline as Colt opened the front door of Taylor's house, letting Clay inside. Clay had called, saying he had information to share on Taylor's stalker and her father, and he'd asked Colt if he could come by. Colt had been reluctant to pull himself out of Taylor's bed—and from the sleeping, naked Taylor in it—but if Clay had intel on Ronnie and Taylor's father, it was worth it.

He hadn't woken her and had left her in bed, looking so gorgeously well tumbled it had physically pained him to leave, even though he was only going downstairs. They'd spent the night talking and fucking like hormone-crazed teenagers. He couldn't get enough of her. And even though he was only going on a few hours' sleep—at best—he felt happier and more alive than he had in...well. In a long time.

Maybe ever. He'd known that they'd had a connection after their first night together, but it had only been physical. Now it was so much deeper. So much more.

Without a word, he motioned Clay inside, and Clay followed him into the kitchen, lagging a few feet behind. Colt took down a couple of mugs and paused when he caught Clay's raised eyebrow.

"Since when do you fucking whistle?" asked Clay, pushing a hand through his messy mane of dark blond hair.

Colt poured them each a cup of coffee, and he couldn't have wiped the smile off his face for every single strip of bacon in Los Angeles. "I'm not allowed to be in a good mood?" he asked.

Clay eyed Colt skeptically, scratching at his jaw, but after a second, he settled himself onto one of the stools beside the island. "Thanks for meeting with me. I was able to get some info on your guy. But first, I have a present for you." He tossed a manila folder onto the island's stainless steel surface.

Colt scooped it up and flipped it open. "How did you get this?" he asked, looking up from the very-hard-to-come-by private military contract in front of him.

"Friend of a friend has a connection. AtlasCorp is one of the biggest private military contractors in the U.S., and they're looking for military or ex-military personnel for a security gig. Stuff like threat assessment, perimeter security, bodyguarding for international corporations and diplomats. It's only a one-year contract, not permanent, but my buddy's connection said they'd likely keep you as long as it goes well. You've got the training, skills, and experience for it, and you've been bitching about how much freelancing sucks. Maybe this is your answer."

Colt's eyes scanned down the page, and he almost inhaled his mouthful of coffee. "This is a huge six-figure salary. To *start*."

Clay nodded. "Plus signing bonus. It's a great position. Long as you don't mind going back to the Sandpit."

Reading further, his heart dropped into his stomach like a brick when he saw where he'd be located: Kabul. He swallowed another mouthful of coffee, hating that fear was his first reaction to the idea of going back there. Hating that he'd reacted like a fucking wuss. He was better than that. Or, at least, he wanted to be.

He kept reading, and noticed that if he took the contract, he'd be expected to work out of the Virginia office when stateside, on the other side of the country from Lacey and the boys.

On the other side of the country from Taylor.

He didn't know exactly where their relationship was headed, but he damn well wanted to find out. After last night, he was in no way ready to walk away from it. From her.

He flipped the folder closed and pushed it to the side, sending Clay a grateful smile. "Thanks, man. I'll think about it." Because despite his reservations, it *was* too good an offer to turn down flat. And the opportunity to get out of freelancing, to prove to himself that he could handle going back into that environment, that he wasn't as fucked-up and damaged as he feared he might be—it was all very tempting.

Clay nodded and pulled another folder from his leather satchel. "I was able to track down your stalker with the info you gave me. Full name's Ronald Baker," he said, sitting back and sipping his coffee.

The top sheet was a full-page color print-out of Ronald Baker's driver's license. Taking a sip of coffee, Colt squinted as he scrutinized the picture. Yeah, that was definitely the guy from the bar. He lived in an apartment on Sherman Way in Winnetka, just north of the Ventura Freeway and only about thirty-five minutes from Taylor's house. Colt flipped to the next page, where Clay had included a standard background check. His eyes narrowed as he skimmed down the page, his heart dropping into his stomach for a second. Baker had been arrested a year ago for trespassing after trying to sneak backstage at one of Taylor's concerts. The security guards at the venue had stopped him, and they'd found a knife on him, as well as a diamond ring.

Shit. This was bad. Colt let the folder fall closed as panic washed over him, tightening his chest. Not only was this guy obsessed with Taylor, but he had violent tendencies and a knack for finding her.

"Guy seems like a whack job," said Clay. "I ran a credit check on him, and he's been making some weird purchases lately, and he took a few big cash advances, too. If you flip the page, you'll see her dad's rap sheet, which is about a mile long. Amazing that he's managed to avoid any major prison time."

Colt flipped the folder back open, turning pages until he was greeted with a fairly recent mug shot of Frank Ross, and his jaw tightened as he scanned down the list of charges. Assault. Mail fraud. Money laundering. Drug and firearm charges. Robbery. Kidnapping. It was a litany of felonies, one piling on top of the next, with a less senior member of the Grim Weavers almost always taking the fall.

"Between Baker and her dad, you might want to consider some backup on this."

"You mean Virtus?"

"I do."

Colt raised an eyebrow and then shook his head. It wasn't gonna happen. Sean Owens had made that plenty clear when he'd fired Colt.

"Yeah, I don't think so, man. I'll figure something out." He had to, because he sure as fuck wasn't going to let anything happen to Taylor. Just the thought sent his heart into a tailspin. He knew he'd never be able to live with himself if she got hurt on his watch. He'd failed so many others; he couldn't fail her.

"Thanks for the intel, man. I owe you one."

* * *

Taylor stood under the hot spray of the shower and stretched, her sore muscles protesting against the movement. She ached all over, and her aches and pains included a particularly delicious soreness between her legs. She and Colt had had sex *six* times, and she'd lost count of the number of orgasms she'd had after hitting double digits. Never in her life had she had a night like that. And given her lifestyle and her proclivity for sex, she'd had some pretty wild nights.

But last night, with Colt? Off the charts. Incomparable, even to their first night together, which had been pretty damn hot. Her heart rate kicked up a notch as she replayed their night and the connection they'd forged. It was physical, but it was so much more than that. She knew she should slow down, take a breath, maybe get some space, but she couldn't. She wanted him—*craved* him—with a fierceness unlike anything she'd ever experienced before. Not even with Zack.

So it was safe to say that if this blew up in her face, it was going to be a fucking mess. No way would she come away from this unscathed if it didn't work out.

It was like staring into a fire. She knew it was hot, that it would hurt if she touched it, but it was so warm and pretty and appealing, that despite knowing better, she was going to stick her hand in anyway and just hope that maybe she wouldn't get burned this time. Because despite her fears, her reservations, her scars, she was already all in with Colt, and damn the consequences.

She'd left the door to the bathroom ajar, and it swung open as Colt stepped in. Her eyes met his, and he yanked his shirt up over his head with a quick and wonderfully masculine tug. He pulled a condom from his jeans pocket and, holding it between his teeth, shoved his pants and boxers down, stepping out of them and sliding the shower door back.

"Morning," she said, running her hands up his gorgeous chest.

He set the condom on one of the built-in ledges. "Morning." The sound hadn't died from his lips before they were on hers, his strong hands circling her arms and pulling her close for a hungry kiss. He kissed his way down her neck, grazing her sensitive skin with his teeth. His hands slid from her arms and down her back to her ass, and he palmed and kneaded the flesh there. His fingers skimmed over the seam where cheek met cheek, and she moaned softly.

"How did it go with Clay?" She reached for the expensive bar of olive oil and honey soap, slicking it down his chest and working up a lather.

He closed his eyes, and his tense muscles relaxed slightly under her touch. "Clay was able to get information on your stalker. He's dangerous, Taylor. He also brought me up to speed on your father. I don't know if what he said about someone coming after you was true or not, but you weren't kidding when you said he was bad news. Real threat or not, I don't want him anywhere near you."

He sighed heavily as she kneaded the muscles of his chest. "We should consider a change of scenery. Maybe get out of town for a while. At least relocate to my place."

She teased her fingers over his flat nipples, pinching them lightly before deepening her massage. "We'll handle it, Colt. I know you won't let him get near me."

"I have to keep you safe." He opened his eyes and cradled her face in his big, strong hands. "I *need* to keep you safe." His voice shook a little on the last word, and then he crushed his mouth to hers.

Her heart unraveled like yarn and tangled back together into something bigger and stronger than it was before.

Massaging in gentle, thorough strokes, her hands slipped lower and lower until she circled her fingers around his cock, teasing him with light, soapy touches. Cupping his heavy balls, she began pumping her slick fist up and down in a slow, easy rhythm, loving the way her hand didn't quite fit all the way around him.

"God, that feels good," he groaned, his eyes closed, his head tipped back. She continued stroking his cock as she pressed her face into his neck, kissing his warm, wet skin, savoring the taste of him on her tongue.

He gathered her into his arms, their bodies winding closely together as he kissed her, deep and with a hot, possessive urgency. His hands roved over her body, playing in her hair, tracing the crease of her spine, slipping over her ribs and hips. Breaking the kiss, he dipped his head lower and sucked a nipple into his mouth, lightly scraping his teeth over it and then soothing it with his tongue.

She rolled her hips into him, and she was starting to go boneless under the wicked torment of his mouth. Once he'd discovered that her breasts and nipples were extremely sensitive, he'd paid them extensive attention, as evidenced by the multiple love bites dotting her pale skin. It had been years since she'd had a hickey or love bite of any kind, and she was surprised at how much she liked it. At how much she liked being marked by Colt.

She felt his hands tremble against her skin, and she pulled back, cupping his face this time. "Hey. I'm okay."

"And you're gonna stay that way." He spoke the words against her mouth, his arms wrapped around her as the warm water slithered over them, steam billowing around their entwined bodies. He dipped a hand between her legs, parting her lips with sure fingers. Carefully, he eased two fingers into her, resting the heel of his palm against her sensitive clit. "Not too sore?"

She didn't quite trust her voice to work properly around the unexpected lump in her throat at Colt's tender concern, so she simply kissed him and rolled her hips against his hand, grinding her clit into his palm. She was sore, yes, but the ache to have him inside her, to be connected to him again, was far greater.

He pulled away only long enough to tear open the condom with his teeth, his mouth back on hers as he rolled it on and guided her back against the shower wall. Hooking an arm under her right knee, he gently lifted her leg and wrapped it around his waist. His cock slid against her wet folds, teasing her.

"I need you inside me. Please," she whimpered, clutching at him, feeling needy and desperate.

His eyes held hers as he inched the head of his cock inside her. "God, Taylor. You feel amazing. Fuck." The last syllable came out on a reverential whisper as he slid into her, and she felt instantly calmer. "I promise I'll keep you safe. I take care of what's mine."

"Yours," she echoed back to him as he began to thrust in and out of her in those hard, deep strokes she loved so much. Their sighs and moans mingled with the patter of the water, echoing off the tile and glass enclosure and muffled by the steam. The scent of soap and sex filled the humid air as skin met skin in soft, wet claps, and that gloriously hot pressure began to twist deep in Taylor's stomach.

Colt slowed and tore his mouth from hers, trailing kisses down her neck. He pulled out of her and dropped to his knees in front of her, guiding her raised leg onto his shoulder. Ravenously, he closed his mouth over her swollen clit, scraping at it delicately with his teeth and sending searing shocks of electricity coursing through her.

With a few embarrassingly short sweeps of his tongue, she came undone, the pressure snapping and giving way to hot, heavy throbs. Her hips bucked against him, and he held her steady as she shook.

And then he was on his feet again and back inside her, stoking the flames of her orgasm and prolonging it with his hard strokes. She slid her arms around his broad shoulders, because even though it was physically impossible, she wanted him even closer. He dug his fingers into her hips hard enough that she knew she'd have more bruises, and he buried himself to the hilt, groaning her name as he came hard. Little by little, he relaxed, his forehead pressed to the wet tile beside her head.

He traced his knuckles over her cheek. "I think I'm addicted to you."

She kissed him, running her fingers through his hair, sending drops of water falling onto his shoulders. "I know the feeling."

* * *

Colt sat on Taylor's bed, a towel knotted around his hips, his hair still wet and dripping onto his shoulders. They'd spent nearly an hour in the shower together, touching and tasting, kissing and exploring. He couldn't get enough of her; the feel of her skin beneath his fingers, the scent of her hair, the taste of her mouth, the sound of her voice. Each gorgeous thing about her fed into the next, stoking something deep and primal in him. The need to protect her. The need to cherish her. The need to just fucking *be* with her, in every sense of the word.

With Taylor still in the bathroom, he'd snagged his phone from his pants, wanting to check his messages and make a few calls. He raised the phone to his ear, waiting to connect to his messages. There was a slight gap in the call, and he frowned when he heard a faint but distinctive ticking on the other end of the line. It sounded almost like a faraway, fuzzy turning signal. His voice mail box connected, but he ended the call, frowning.

Colt pushed off the bed and redialed into his messages, putting the phone on speaker and waving it in a slow path back and forth in front of him, walking through the room. In the few seconds of silence on the line, the ticking grew stronger and clearer as he approached the television. Bending forward, he scrutinized the TV and the DVR box, his skin prickling. Biting back a curse, he jogged back to the guest room and grabbed a flashlight out of his bag, hanging on to the towel around his hips.

He rapped quickly on the bathroom door, and Taylor poked her head out. "Yeah?"

"You got an empty toilet paper roll in there?"

She stared at him with one eyebrow arched, and he swallowed, trying to get his heart to slow down.

"I think I might've found something."

"What?"

"A hidden camera."

Her eyebrow dropped back down, and her mouth fell open in a small, surprised O. "What?" she repeated, much quieter this time.

"In your DVR, I think."

She pulled her own towel tighter around herself and swung the door open. Dropping to her knees by the toilet, she fished a toilet paper roll from the small garbage bin.

"Stay in here and turn the lights off," said Colt, and she nodded as he pulled the door shut, entering her bedroom again. Hastily, he closed the automated blinds and pulled the curtains shut, making the room as dark as possible. Clicking the flashlight on, he held the cardboard tube to one eye like a telescope and stalked toward the DVR, slowing as he approached. In a slow, deliberate path, he swung the flashlight across the front of the DVR, pausing when the telltale wink of a camera's charge-coupled device flashed back at him for a fraction of a second.

Anger shot through him, stealing his breath for a second, at the realization that Baker must've installed the cameras—it was the only logical explanation. Not only that, but he'd enjoyed a front-row seat to Colt and Taylor together last night. Fury seared through him. His skin suddenly felt too tight as the knowledge of the violation crackled over him. And it wasn't the violation of *his* privacy that he cared about. No, he didn't give a shit about that. But the fact that this psycho creep had seen Taylor, naked, and...fuck, it made him want to smash things.

"Son of a bitch!" He ground the words out and bent forward, bringing his face within inches of the DVR. "I know you've been watching, you sick fuck, and when I get my hands on you, I'm gonna turn your fucking face into a goddamn abstract painting, you hear me? You listening, Baker? Fuck!"

Unable to fight back the anger coursing through him, he yanked the DVR free with a violent tug and smashed it on the floor.

# CHAPTER 20

Taylor stared vacantly out of the Charger's window, not really seeing the trees, buildings, and cars as they blurred by on Fountain Avenue. She tucked a strand of her still-damp hair behind her ear, curling the end around her finger and wrapping it as tight as she could, cutting off the circulation to the tip of her finger, watching as it turned bright red. Wanting to feel...something. Anything besides the sickening, slimy mixture of anger and numbness that had taken over as soon as Colt had told her he'd found a camera.

After Colt had smashed the DVR, they'd both quickly dressed, and she'd followed him from room to room as he'd scanned every object and every surface with the handheld radio-frequency-signal detector he'd retrieved from his car. He'd located two more cameras, one each in the living room and the bathroom. When he'd pulled the small camera—no bigger than a guitar pick—from the vent in the bathroom's ceiling, she hadn't been able to hold back the revulsion crawling through her like maggots, and she'd flung herself in front of the toilet, heaving until her stomach was empty and her throat was raw. Colt had held her hair and then brought her a cool cloth, wiping at her face tenderly. It was that small act of tenderness that had broken her completely open, and he'd sunk to the floor beside her, pulling her into his arms as she'd cried.

They'd gone to the police, and she'd officially filed a report about her stalker, giving the police the information Clay had found on him, the spy cameras Colt had found hidden in her house, the creepy card that had come with the flowers, and her own account of what had happened that night at the Rainbow. That, coupled with his previous record of trying to get backstage at her concert with a weapon, was enough to file for a temporary civil harassment restraining order. She'd have to go to court to get a more permanent one, but in the meantime, the creep would be served with the restraining order and told to stay the hell away from her.

There wasn't enough evidence to bring him up on stalking charges—after all, there was no proof it was Ronnie who'd put the spy cameras in her house, although the cop had agreed that it had likely been him—but the investigation would continue. They'd also told the cops about her father's threats and the altercation last night and filed a separate report about that.

After leaving the police station, they'd gotten back into the car, and instead of heading back toward the Hollywood Hills and home—the *last* place she wanted to go—they'd gone south to Fountain Avenue and were now turning left onto Vine.

"You okay?" asked Colt as he swung the Charger through the turn.

She shrugged, her arms wrapped around herself. "Not really. We have no idea how long those cameras were there. I don't know how many times he watched me change,

watched me shower. He could've watched us…last night…"
Her voice caught on the last syllable, and she cleared her
throat, through with crying. She laid her hand on Colt's
thigh, and he glanced at her for a second before returning
his attention to the road. She cleared her throat again before
continuing. "It meant something to me. And I hate that
there's this shit hanging over it."

He slid a hand from the steering wheel and laid it over
hers. Big and warm, it anchored her as he laced their fingers
together, and she took a deep breath. "It meant something to
me, too, Taylor." He squeezed her hand and glanced at her
again. "So fuck him." He eased the Charger to a stop at a red
light. "Last night was about you and me, gorgeous. Not him.
You and me."

Her throat thickened, and she nodded, blinking furiously
against the tears stinging her eyes. Colt drummed his fingers
on the wheel and then rubbed a hand over his mouth before
continuing. "So, listen. Until we get all of this resolved, I need
to make sure you're safe. And as much as I hate to admit it, I
don't know if Roman and I can handle this on our own."

"So what do you want to do?"

"I think you know I used to work for Virtus."

She'd glanced away from him to look out the window and
whipped her head back around at the name. "Yeah. Sierra
mentioned it."

"Has she talked to Sean about…me, working for you?"
His knuckles were white against the steering wheel, she noticed.

"I asked her not to."

"You need to know that I…a job went wrong because I
made a mistake, and I got fired. But if anyone can help us,
it's them." He swallowed, his Adam's apple bobbing in his
throat.

As they drove up Vine, a high-rise office tower that she knew housed the Virtus Security offices came into view. She licked her lips, wishing she had a bottle of water. Wishing she could ask him about getting fired, but she knew now wasn't the time.

The last thing she wanted was for Colt to feel like he had to do something that would make him uncomfortable. She could at least try and protect him from that, even if it was too late to protect him from all the other shit he'd been through. Going to the man who'd fired him had to cost him, mentally and emotionally. "Listen, Colt, we don't have to—"

But he cut her off, his voice a little rough. "I promised I would keep you safe. And I will."

She nodded, swallowing around her thickening throat. "So, uh, in the spirit of honesty…" She hesitated, fiddling with the hem of her shirt, her face hot and prickly. "I used to date one of the guys there." She ran her tongue over her teeth, hoping he wouldn't ask for details. Hoping that Zack wouldn't be there, and that she could avoid that whole messy situation.

For a reason she couldn't quite name, she didn't want Colt to know that Zack was the one who'd hurt her so bad. She already felt so transparent with him—he'd barely known her, and he'd known she'd been pushing him away because she'd had her heart broken. And although things were going well between them, she still felt somehow compelled to hold little bits and pieces of herself back, almost as though she were doling out parts of herself as rewards the longer he went without hurting her.

Colt let out a long breath, shaking his head slightly. "Well, isn't this just going to be a fucking party."

* * *

Colt didn't let himself hesitate as he pulled open one of the glass doors leading to the Virtus offices on the tenth floor of the office tower at the corner of Sunset and Vine. It didn't matter that this was the last place he wanted to be or that the last person he wanted to ask for help was Sean Owens. Keeping Taylor safe was the only thing that mattered, and as much as it killed him, he didn't want to risk trying to take on her psycho stalker and potentially a biker gang by himself. Sean might hate Colt, but that didn't mean he was an asshole. No, if anyone was the asshole, it was Colt.

A rolling wave of heat churned through his stomach as he ushered Taylor into the offices, and it hit him how much he fucking missed this place. He missed working with a team, and he missed the steady, secure paycheck. He glanced over at Taylor, who was pale, her bottom lip caught between her teeth as her eyes scanned the space. Her fingers were wrapped tightly around the strap of her purse, her knuckles snow white against her skin.

She was looking for him, the guy she used to date. Mentally, he went through the roster of guys. He knew it wasn't Owens, and it likely wouldn't have been Ian MacAllister, given that he didn't date, ever. It could've been Jamie, but wouldn't he have mentioned that at the poker game when he'd clued Colt in to Taylor's Virtus connection? So that left Carter, which wasn't impossible. The ex-NFLer was a good-looking guy, single, smart, good sense of humor. There was also the possibility it was someone Colt didn't really know, or someone who'd started after he'd been canned. His stomach churned harder, and he pushed down the surge of jealousy washing over him as he took a few steps toward the circular stainless steel reception desk. But before he got there, he heard his name from several feet away in a deep, Scottish-accented voice.

"Priestley? You doaty bastard, that you?"

A wide smile spread across Colt's face as he turned, shaking his head at former SAS paratrooper and medic Ian MacAllister. He and Ian had bonded over old war stories and scotch, and had worked dozens of jobs together. They'd fallen out of touch after Colt had gotten fired.

"You son of a bitch," said Colt by way of greeting, and Ian clapped him on the shoulder, sending him a rare smile. "This is my..." He cleared his throat as he gestured toward Taylor. "This is Taylor Ross. She's my client." Fuck, she was so much more than that, but this wasn't the time to get into it. Not when she was pale and quiet, her eyes still roving over the modern, sleek, open-concept office space.

"Aye, we've met. How are you, Taylor?" he asked, and Colt couldn't stop his eyes from darting between them, wondering briefly if Mac was the Virtus guy she'd dated.

But before he could observe any further and let his jealousy flare up again, one of the glass office doors to the left of the space swung open, and Sean Owens stepped out, one eyebrow cocked as he approached them. His gaze flicked from Taylor to Colt and back again, and a frown creased his face. "I was wondering when I'd see you." Owens, his hands on his hips as he came to a stop, towered over all of them by at least a couple of inches. He cut his eyes from Colt to Taylor again. "Don't be mad at Sierra, but she told me what's going on."

"She did?" Taylor asked, frowning slightly.

Sean nodded. "She's worried about you, and so am I." He shot Colt a pointed glare.

"We talk in your office?" asked Colt, tipping his head in the direction Sean had just come from. Taylor looked shaky, and he wanted her to sit down, maybe have some water. Wanted to shoulder everything he could for her, and he was suddenly glad that, although walking in here had meant swallowing his pride, he was able to do it for her. Sean nodded again, pushing a hand through his hair. Colt ground his teeth together when Sean put an arm around Taylor's shoulders and pulled her in for a hug, whispering something Colt couldn't hear into her ear. Taylor just nodded and let Sean lead them into his office, Colt trailing a few feet behind. He tipped his chin at Ian as he walked away, trying to process everything. Being back in the Virtus offices. Taylor. The immediate situation at hand. The past. All of it was slamming together, making it impossible to tease any one part away from another.

A row of offices, all walled in glass, filled the left-hand side of the bright, open space, and Sean led them to the one second from the back, ushering them inside. He didn't say anything until he'd settled himself behind his desk, his fingers tented in front of him. He looked at Colt and then Taylor, who seemed slightly more relaxed.

"So. Let's hear it," he said, meeting Colt's stare.

"She's got a psycho stalker. We filed a restraining order and all of that, but he's been arrested for trespassing at one of her concerts before. The guy's been obsessed with her for a while now and is potentially dangerous. When he was arrested, he had a knife on him, and he's shown a pattern of escalating behavior.

"On top of that, her dad—who happens to be the president of the Grim Weavers—has been harassing her, trying to scare her into giving him money. He tried to convince her that there are some people after him and that they'd come after her if she didn't help her pay them off. Not sure if he's telling the truth or not, but until we know more, I'm not taking any fucking chances. I need backup on this." He looked at Taylor and shot her a half smile. "That about sum it up?"

She smiled, nodding. "Perfectly."

Sean studied them, an unreadable expression on his face. He glanced away, curling one of his hands into a fist. "I wish you'd told me about this sooner." He sighed heavily before turning to Colt. "I'll need all the intel you've got on this situation so I can brief the team. We'll take it from here."

"Colt stays." Taylor's voice was low and quiet, but firm.

"Did he tell you that he used to work here? That he got fired?" asked Sean, a challenge gleaming in his eyes.

"I did." Colt crossed his arms over his chest.

"Did you tell her why?"

Colt shook his head, glancing down at the floor before meeting Taylor's curious gaze. "He and I were assigned to guard this hip-hop star. The guy was an idiot, looking for trouble wherever he went. Thought it made him a badass or some shit. He'd already spent some time in prison on weapons and drug charges. Anyway, one night he started a fight in a nightclub and…" he shrugged "…things went sideways."

"Things went *sideways*?" Sean let out a sharp laugh. "Another couple of millimeters and I could've lost an eye, thanks to you. I had the situation under control. I was breaking up the fight, and then this idiot jumps in and escalates things. I took a beer bottle to the face because of him."

"You make it sound like I'm the one who stabbed you in the face." Colt clenched his jaw, fighting back his rising temper.

"Taylor, let us help you. You don't need him."

"Enough!" Taylor stood, glaring at each of them. She wheeled on Sean. "*Colt stays.* I trust him, and that has to be enough for you."

Sean met Taylor's gaze. "Fine. If that's what you want." He paused and sighed heavily. "If you trust him, I can work with that."

"That's...thank you."

She sat back down and reached out, lacing her fingers through Colt's.

Well, well. Everything was out in the open now, wasn't it? The corner of Colt's mouth twitched up as he rubbed a thumb back and forth over Taylor's knuckles.

Sean blew out a breath as he pressed his thumb and index finger to his brow and then slowly shook his head. "I don't even want to know how you two found each other." He held up a hand. "It doesn't matter. You know, Priestley, you could've gone to any security firm for backup. Why here?"

Colt ground his teeth before answering. "Because you guys are the best. And I want the best for Taylor." Her fingers tightened on his. "I'm still the primary on this, but I do need backup. Even with the restraining order, that psycho's still out there, and I don't feel like taking on the Grim Weavers by myself."

Slowly, Sean nodded, his expression completely unreadable. "You're primary on this, but any situations that require a second or a third, call in, and I'll send someone or come myself." He shot Colt a pointed glance. "This doesn't mean you're getting your job back. This is temporary until we get Taylor sorted out. Understood?"

Colt nodded, relief flooding him that he'd have help—the best help—keeping Taylor safe.

# CHAPTER 21

"You sure you want to play?" asked Colt, one eyebrow raised as he chalked the end of his pool cue. Taylor wrapped her fingers around her beer bottle, the glass cool and wet against her fingers. For the past several days she'd been cooped up at Colt's, alternating between working on her music and fucking Colt until she couldn't even remember her name. And while both of those activities were both fun and fulfilling, she was starting to feel a bit stir-crazy. She'd begged Colt for a night out, to a bar, a movie, anything, but he'd refused. She had, however, managed to talk him into a game of pool at the table in his loft.

Taylor took a long pull on her beer and then nodded as she swallowed, smiling at him. "Yeah. I haven't played in ages, but I used to be pretty good."

The corner of Colt's mouth quirked up in that cocky half smile that made her want to drag him into the bedroom and fall to her knees in front of him.

"Oh yeah? Why don't we make it interesting, then?" he said.

She took another sip of her beer and then brushed by him, grabbing a cue of her own. She glanced over her shoulder. "Interesting how?"

He leaned back against the pool table and slipped an arm around her waist, pulling her against him. "I win, I get to tie you up."

She leaned into him and dragged her lips over the shell of his ear, her stomach exploding with butterflies at the idea of being bound for him. "Fine. But if I win, you have to do a striptease for me. And I get to pick the music."

He pulled back, his green eyes glittering. "Deal. You want to break?"

"Sure, but I'm not very good at it," she lied. "Will you rack them for me?" She sipped her beer, watching, with pure, female appreciation, the way Colt's forearms flexed as he racked the balls. She walked around to the other side of the table, cue in hand, and bent forward, loosening her grip on the cue as she lined up her shot. She glanced up at Colt through her lashes, biting her lip as she pulled her cue back. She took her shot, which just barely grazed the cue ball and sent it rolling slowly into the side rail. "Shit. Does that count?"

Colt smiled at her, wolfish and hot. "Why don't you let me break?" He repositioned the cue ball and broke smoothly, scattering the balls across the felt. As ZZ Top played on the stereo, Colt proceeded to sink ball after ball, while Taylor sunk a couple of balls but flubbed the majority of her shots.

As Colt bent over the table, he shot her a glance, one eyebrow raised. "I thought you said you knew how to play," he said just before he sunk an impressive bank shot.

"I do! I just haven't played in a while. Give me a round to shake the rust off." As the game progressed, she let herself sink a few more shots, just so her losing wasn't so obvious.

Several minutes later, Colt sunk the eight ball, winning the game, and he closed the distance between them, pinning her against the pool table. Before she could say anything, he kissed her, slow and deep. "I'm going to make you so happy you lost," he whispered, his lips brushing against her earlobe.

"Mmm," she purred, knowing he was 100 percent right about that. "Want to play again?"

He chuckled, the deep sound rumbling over her skin. "Sure, gorgeous. Same stakes?"

"How about double or nothing? If I win, I get to tie *you* up." She felt his dick twitch against her hip and knew he was just as into that idea as she was.

"Deal. You want me to break again?"

"Nah. Lemme try again." He stepped back and let her walk around to the end of the table. Instead of using the rack to organize the balls, she gathered them all at the end of the table and then used her forearms to rack them into a perfect triangle in seconds flat. She bent forward, lining up her cue with the cue ball and she glanced up, winking at Colt before she broke with a blistering crack, the balls shooting out across the felt. Colt stood still, staring at her with a half-pissed, half-turned-on expression on his face.

She tipped her chin at him. "Hey, we gonna play? It's your shot."

Grumbling under his breath, he took his shot, but within a few minutes, Taylor had sunk all of her balls. Only the eight ball was left, and she took a sip of her beer before leaning forward and lining up her shot. Her cue poised in her hands, she looked up at Colt, who was watching her with a mix of admiration, lust, and the tiniest bit of irritation.

"I'm gonna make you so glad you lost," she said, right before she sunk the eight ball and won the game.

He opened his mouth to reply but was cut off by the doorbell, and he held up one finger in a "hold that thought" gesture. "That's probably Carter. Sean said he'd be by to pick up the copies of my files I made for Virtus."

"Oh, well, I want to come say hello and thank you. I always liked Carter."

Colt studied her for a second, but with a tip of his head, he turned and left the room, Taylor following closely behind.

Colt glanced through the peephole and frowned. "Who is it?"

"Zack De Luca from Virtus. Carter had something come up with his kid, and he sent me to get the files," called Zack through the door, his deep voice as familiar as ever. "Here's my ID. I can wait while you call into the office to verify."

"Do you know him?"

She froze as her heart plummeted like a stone into her stomach, her eyes glued to Colt's front door as though, if she stared hard enough, she'd be able to see the man on the other side. She managed to nod weakly. "He's legit."

Yeah, she knew him. Zack, the man she'd been hoping to avoid. Zack, the man who'd sent her into this little tailspin to begin with.

Tracking her gaze with an arched eyebrow, Colt turned to look at the door. He opened it, and Zack held out his hand to Colt. Colt shook it, glancing once again from Zack to Taylor. Zack zeroed his dark brown eyes in on her, rubbing a hand over his thick, dark brown hair. A layer of stubble clung to his jaw, framing his thick lips. "Hey, Taylor. It's, uh, been a while."

Taylor glanced at Colt, whose eyes were bouncing back and forth between Zack and Taylor, and the line of Colt's shoulders tightened slightly, his expression darkening almost imperceptibly. Taylor knew, just looking at him, that he'd put two and two together and figured out that Zack was the guy she'd dated.

She straightened, and Colt clapped Zack on the shoulder, maybe a little harder than was necessary. "Colt Priestley. I don't remember you from when I was at Virtus." Colt crossed his arms over his chest, studying Zack.

Zack rubbed a hand over the back of his neck, and Taylor noticed the scrapes on his knuckles, probably from training. Zack's dream was to be a professional mixed-martial-arts fighter, and he was actively pursuing it, training almost every day and fighting professionally in one of the bigger fight promotions in Southern California.

"Oh, yeah. I think I was your replacement. After you… after you left."

"And you know Taylor." It wasn't a question.

"Zack and I dated," said Taylor, wanting to get it out in the open. To get the honesty over with. She forced herself to meet Zack's eyes, just for a second, and then she looked down, brushing an imaginary piece of lint off of her jeans. "Hey."

Her mind flashed back to when she'd told Zack she was in love with him, and he'd told her that he cared about her, but he wasn't in love with her. That he was sorry if she'd gotten the wrong idea, but they were just casual, having fun, not serious. That he wasn't looking for anything permanent, or long-term. The subtext, of course, was that he wasn't looking for anything serious, permanent or long-term *with her*. She'd handed him her heart, damaged and messed up as it was, offered it up to him, and he'd handed it back. It hadn't been good enough.

"Hey," Zack answered, studying her the way a veterinarian might study a wounded tiger, wary and cautious. "It's good to see you. Sorry to hear about all the shit happening."

She shrugged. "Thanks."

"I'll go grab those files," said Colt. "Be right back." He slipped an arm around Taylor's waist as he passed and pulled her into him, planting a hot, hard kiss on her before releasing her and heading up the stairs.

He'd staked his claim, and damn if she didn't like it. More than like it.

She felt the weight of Zack's gaze on her, and after a deep breath, she met his eyes. She braced herself, but she was relieved when she found that her heart didn't flutter, that her breath didn't catch, that her skin didn't hum and vibrate when she looked at him. It used to. Now, looking at him, gorgeous as always—ridiculously gorgeous, really—she only felt a dull, residual ache, like a bruise that was almost healed, but was still a little sore if you pressed on it. An ache coupled with the heaviness of shared memories, both good and bad.

"I wasn't sure if I'd see you," she said, her voice coming out quieter than she'd intended.

"I wanted to see you," he said, leaning against the door-jamb, his hands shoved into the pockets of his suit pants. "When I heard about what was happening, I wanted to make sure you were okay."

She nodded, letting his words settle over her.

"For what it's worth," he continued, "it was supposed to be Carter tonight, but he had something with his son, and I volunteered. Sean didn't want me on the rotation."

"Thanks. That's, uh, nice of you to care."

He rubbed a hand over his hair. "Taylor, I do care. I always have." He shoved his hand back in his pocket. "I know I've said this before, but I need you to hear it. I'm sorry that I hurt you. I never meant to. I wish things had gone down differently." He sighed heavily. "I let things go too far, and

I don't expect forgiveness. I just want you to know that I didn't want to hurt you. That I do care about you."

"You didn't want to, but you did hurt me, Zack. You did. But I know you didn't mean to. The whole situation got away from us, and for a while, I hated you for it. But as much as I wanted to hang on to that anger, to believe that all of this happened because you're an asshole, I know that's not true." She felt lighter as the truth she hadn't known was buried deep inside her flowed free.

"Do you still hate me?"

She swallowed, mentally poking around through her baggage for the answer, for the truth. She looked at him—*really* looked at him—and shook her head. "No, Zack. I don't hate you."

He nodded, the lines of his face softening a little as some of the tension left him. "Maybe if the timing had worked out differently, or...fuck, I don't know. I'm just sorry I couldn't love you the way you deserve." Tentatively, he reached out and laid a hand on her shoulder. "Because you deserve it all, babe. You deserve someone who can love you so big and so hard that you don't even know what to do with all of it. More than anything, I just want you to be happy."

Her throat thickened, and she swallowed, blinking away the tears stinging her eyes, threatening to fall. He'd never be able to undo the damage he'd caused, but hearing the words helped. Not just hearing them, but actually believing them, turning them over and examining them, and keeping them.

Colt came back down the stairs, and their eyes met. Her heart didn't flutter; it grew wings and tried to fly into his hands. Her breath didn't catch in her chest; it couldn't, because there was no oxygen in the room. Her skin didn't hum and vibrate; it caught fire and burned, every single cell in her body blooming into flame for him.

"Okay?" He mouthed the question as he walked toward her.

Taylor smiled and nodded, but her smile dropped away when she noticed that every line of Colt's body had gone hard and tense. Zack's hand went to his hip and the gun holstered there. Three men in suits had emerged from what looked like an armored Lincoln Navigator that had pulled up, and they were now making their way up Colt's driveway. Colt pulled his SIG free of his waistband and stepped in front of Taylor, shielding her with his body.

"Give us the girl, and no one gets hurt," said the biggest of the suited men, his deep voice booming. Colt and Zack looked at each other, eyebrows raised. Zack gave the tiniest nod and took Colt's place in front of Taylor as Colt approached the trio. Taylor's mouth went dry as she wrung her fingers together, trying to anchor herself against her furiously pounding heart.

"Yeah, that's not gonna happen." Colt studied the men, and Taylor had no idea how he could be so calm. Especially when the men advanced farther onto his property as though they hadn't even heard him.

"Your daddy owes us a lot of money, sweetheart," said the tall one, his dark brown hair pulled back in a ponytail. "Money he doesn't have. But you have it, don't you? So you're going to come with us and get us our money. Simple."

Well, shit. For once in his goddamn life, her father had been telling the truth. He owed these guys money, and he'd tried to warn her that they'd come after her.

"How much does he owe you?" she asked from behind Zack.

The big one shrugged casually. "Well, once you factor in the forty percent interest and the late payment fee, his tab's up to $500,000. It was supposed to be more, but our boss likes round numbers."

Taylor's stomach swirled uncomfortably, and she thought she might be sick. "I...I don't have that kind of money," she said. Her entire net worth was just over three million dollars, and a lot of that was tied up in her house and the few investments she had. It had been years since she'd last had a hit record, and although she'd seen success, success didn't always mean crazy wealth. She didn't have half a million dollars cash on hand, and even if she did, she sure as hell wasn't going to use it to pay her father's debts.

"That's why you're gonna come with us, so we can work something out," said Ponytail, and they started to advance. Colt aimed his gun at the closest man, who looked like a version of Homer Simpson come to life, bald and overweight.

"Not another fucking step," Colt ground out, his voice almost a growl. "De Luca, get her inside."

Zack's hand closed around Taylor's arm, and he tugged her quickly back into the hallway. He pulled her up the stairs and into the loft over the garage, with its front facing windows. His own weapon drawn, he peered out the window.

"You can't just leave him," Taylor whispered, hot, itchy panic shooting through her.

"No." Zack handed his gun to Taylor. "You stay here, out of sight, and don't hesitate to pull the trigger if one of them gets past us and tries to grab you. Call nine-one-one." Leaving his weapon in her hands, he disappeared from the room, his footsteps thundering down the stairs. She sunk to the floor, the gun clutched in one hand as she fished her phone out of her back pocket and dialed. A trickle of cold sweat slid between her breasts, and she thought her heart might explode as she listened to the phone ring. She crawled toward the door, cracking it open the tiniest fraction of an inch. She could barely hear the 911 operator over the blood thundering through her ears.

"Nine-one-one. What is your emergency?"

"Men are trying to kill us. They have guns," she whispered, her voice shaking.

"Miss, where are you?"

She gave Colt's address. "Please hurry. Please. They're going to kill us."

"I'm sending someone now. Please stay on the line with me, okay?"

Taylor knew she should hide, stay out of sight, but she needed to see what was going on. She crept to the top of the stairs just as the big man charged into the house. Colt fired, narrowly missing. The sound exploded through the house as the man took Colt down in the living room, knocking his gun from his hand, and Taylor's heart vaulted into her throat.

Colt rolled with him and pulled a knife from his boot, shooting quickly back to his feet. Zack tackled Ponytail, taking him down to the ground as another gunshot rang through the house. Taylor cowered behind the banister at the top of the stairs.

Knife in hand, Colt ducked and then grabbed his opponent's arm, twisting it behind him and causing him to drop his gun. The big man reared back and smashed his head into Colt's face, and Colt let him go. Blood flowed from Colt's nose as they circled each other, finally trading a flurry of punches before the big man grabbed Colt and threw him into the coffee table. Taylor cringed as glass shattered, but Colt rose quickly to his feet, seemingly unfazed by the blood trickling down his face from cuts near his hairline and across his cheekbone.

From behind, Zack put the big man into a chokehold, wrestling him to the ground and holding him there as the man's face turned red. Ponytail came at Colt and grabbed for his knife, but Colt took the man's arm, spun him, and slammed his elbow into Ponytail's temple. He fell into a limp heap on the floor, and Colt turned, wiping blood out of his eye as he turned to face the fat, bald one, whose attention was focused on Zack.

The big man on the floor with Zack stopped struggling, and Zack quickly slipped a hand into his pocket, fished out some zip ties, and bound the man's hands and feet. The bald man drew his gun and aimed it at Zack, his finger on the trigger. Before Taylor could call out, Colt closed the distance between them and took out the bald man's knee with a vicious kick. He cried out and spun, and Colt's fist connected with his face, sending him back a few inches. Colt landed a hard kick in the man's flabby stomach, which caused him to drop his gun, but he absorbed the impact with a grunt and came back at Colt, fists swinging.

Colt ducked and grabbed the man's shoulders, bringing his knee up into the man's face with a sickening crunch. The man straightened and Colt punched him again. The man staggered back a few steps and glanced at his two incapacitated companions, clearly weighing his options.

Zack took advantage of the tiny pause and picked up a potted plant off the floor. He threw it hard and fast, and it shattered against the man's shiny, bald head.

"Fuck!" the man screamed, his legs wobbling. Colt grabbed him and slammed him into the wall, his heavy fist making contact over and over again. Ponytail began to stir, and Zack used more zip ties to bind his hands and feet.

Colt wrestled the bald man to the floor and pressed the tip of his knife against the man's throat, pinning him down with his knees on the man's chest. "Who are you?" He ground the words out, his voice rough and dangerous, his chiseled features grim and dark. He added pressure to the knife, and the man squirmed, sweat streaking across his bald head in narrow rivulets. "Answer me!"

The man mumbled something Taylor couldn't hear. Colt and Zack exchanged a look across the living room just as the sound of sirens split the night open.

# CHAPTER 22

Colt tightened his grip on the Charger's steering wheel and checked the rearview mirror for what had to be the two hundredth time since they'd left Los Angeles, just after dark. They'd hidden out in a hotel after the attack last night and waited until nightfall tonight to head out, because they'd be a lot harder to follow under cover of darkness. He'd done a sweep of the Charger with his radio frequency signal detector, but the car was clean.

He glanced over at Taylor in the passenger seat, her chin in her hand as she gazed out the window at the starless night. She must be tired. She hadn't slept last night after the events at his house. He knew, because he hadn't, either.

Colt hadn't believed it when he'd heard it from the guy's mouth. His words, barely a whisper: "It's the Brotherhood, man. And we'll keep coming."

The cops had rushed in, and once the three attackers had been arrested, Zack, Colt, and Taylor had all gone down to the station for questioning. Taylor had told them everything about her dad, his harassment and his threats, and everything had clicked together.

The Grim Weavers were rumored to be dealing drugs for the Golden Brotherhood, a powerful, underground, organized-crime ring so legendary in its activities it was almost mythical. Hell, before last night Colt had thought the Brotherhood was made up, or that if they were real, their reach, influence, and power were severely exaggerated.

He'd been wrong.

Now, with the mounting evidence and the arrest of three key Brotherhood enforcers, the LAPD were planning raids on both the Brotherhood and the Grim Weavers. And until everything settled down, Colt's focus was getting Taylor somewhere safe and keeping her that way. Everything else was in the hands of the police now, but her safety was still his responsibility, and he wouldn't want it any other way.

He clenched his jaw tightly as he thought of how close she'd come to getting injured or worse last night. So first thing this morning, he'd called his sister and asked if he could use the cabin she and Paul owned just outside of Big Bear Lake. While they laid low, Sean had assured Colt he'd stay in touch with the LAPD about the status of the investigation and keep an eye out for any suspicious activity.

As Colt drove, he didn't give a shit about the pain from his face, his knuckles, and the various bruises and scrapes on his body. They were nothing, because *she* was here, beside him, safe and whole. Staring out at the night, he made a silent vow that he'd do everything in his power to protect Taylor, no matter the cost.

* * *

Ronnie hefted the cleaver in his hand and brought it down hard on the flesh in front of him, a slight shiver teasing through him as he worked the knife through skin, fat, muscle, and sinew, all of it parting under the steel in his hand. He glanced up at the clock on the wall in the walk-in refrigerator where he worked, and his stomach roiled, not because of the meat—no, the meat was beautiful, the only thing keeping him together right now—but because his visitor would be here any minute.

He'd made up his mind several days ago and had reached out to his black market contact again, but he didn't want more spy equipment this time. No, he needed something darker, something harder to come by. At the thought of the spy equipment, anger gripped him. The way the brute had taunted him, had practically flaunted the vulgar way he was treating Taylor—it made Ronnie want to scream. The brute had no claim to her. She belonged to Ronnie. And he was getting fucking sick of her pretending that she didn't. That she wasn't supposed to be at his side, bearing his children, giving him everything she had. Her body. Her mind. Her spirit. Everything.

If she wasn't his, why had she written all those songs about him? About *them*? If she wasn't his, why did he hear her voice in his head, whispering promises? She was the Juliet to his Romeo, and the harder the world struggled to keep them apart, the more his love, his passion, and his need for her grew.

And he'd show them all. He'd make them sorry they laughed. Sorry they doubted. Especially Frank. Ronnie had joined the Grim Weavers over a year ago now in an attempt to get closer to Taylor through her father, but he'd been dismayed to learn that they didn't have a relationship. He'd tried on several occasions to broach the subject of Taylor with Frank, but Frank had always waved the topic aside, more concerned with bikes, women, and drugs than his daughter, and the man who loved her.

A knock at the back door sent a quiver through his muscles, and he set the cleaver down, wiping his hands on his apron and walking across the space, nudging the door open with his shoulder.

"You Baker?" asked the man, who Ronnie was both relieved and disappointed to find looked completely normal. He was of average height with a large build, probably in his early forties, and had thinning sandy hair and a neatly groomed goatee. He wore a red long-sleeved shirt and khakis with sneakers. He could've been anyone. A dentist. A teacher. The guy next door.

He certainly didn't look like a man who killed for money. But he'd come highly recommended and had fit Ronnie's budget.

"You have what I asked for?" the man asked as he stepped through the door.

Ronnie nodded at him and pulled the envelope from his pocket that contained $10,000 cash—his entire savings, plus money he'd borrowed from the bank—and a photo of the brute. He held the envelope toward the man but pulled it back at the last second. "And my terms? That I come with you to get the woman while you take care of the target?"

The man nodded, took the money, and pocketed it. "You know where they are?"

"His sister has a cabin near Big Bear," he said, immensely proud of himself for having the foresight to hire a private investigator to dig up as much information on the brute, his family, and his friends as possible. "I know they left town, and I think they went there. The address is in the envelope."

The man nodded and opened the door. "We'll go up soon. I'll call you when it's time."

He stepped through the door into the bright sunshine and disappeared as quickly as he'd arrived.

Soon, she would belong to Ronnie forever.

* * *

The cabin was glorious. Surrounded by towering pines and snow-capped mountains, it felt as though it were on the other side of the world from Los Angeles, despite the fact that the drive had only been about three hours. The night Taylor and Colt had arrived, they'd settled into the small cabin quickly, storing the groceries they'd stopped for along the way. Colt had gone through the cabin, checking the locks on all the doors and windows, making sure he had cell reception, and changing one of the outside lightbulbs that was burnt out. He'd also set up a basic alarm system. It wasn't fancy, but it was the best he could do on short notice.

The cabin itself was small but cozy. The exterior was a mix of logs and stones, and while it was older, some of the fixtures, like the windows and the kitchen appliances, were newer. The front door entered into the living room, furnished with beat-up leather couches covered in plaid blankets and throw pillows and facing a fireplace with a flat-screen TV mounted above it. The living room opened onto the small kitchen, and a door off of the kitchen led to the outdoor space at the back, which featured a deck with several Adirondack chairs, a fire pit, and a spectacular view of Big Bear Lake, the water a glimmering cobalt. A hallway ran along the back of the cabin, and it led to two bedrooms and a tiny but newly renovated bathroom, with a walk-in shower, toilet, and sink.

It was their own tiny oasis, a stunningly beautiful and peaceful cocoon from the outside world. She felt safe—

and yes, the cabin and its location had something to do with it, but mostly it was because of Colt. From the night they'd arrived, he'd kept her close, protecting her with his body, holding her as she slept, with his strong arms wrapped around her and her face pressed against his chest. That first night, she'd fallen into a deep sleep after they'd made love, not having slept much the night before. She'd found almost immeasurable comfort in the scent of Colt's skin and the warm, steady thump of his heart against her cheek. But before that sleep, they'd been desperate for each other, and with their limbs intertwined, sweat glistening on his skin, he'd shattered her, over and over again. The second time, deep in the middle of the night, when she'd woken and reached for him, had been slower, sweeter, his fingers laced with hers as he made love to her, his body over hers as he'd kissed her until neither of them could breathe.

Until she forgot where she ended and he started.

Now she sat with her acoustic guitar in her lap, picking out Beethoven's "Moonlight Sonata" while she watched the sun set over the lake. Colt grilled hamburgers and corn on the cob on the barbecue, and she thought back to the first morning she'd woken up here, a couple of days ago. Days that felt like years. Days bathed in warm, golden sunlight and capped with magical, silvery moonlight. Days where the fact that multiple psychopaths were after her didn't matter. Colt, and making music, and the beauty surrounding them. That was all that mattered.

That first morning, she'd flung an arm over her eyes and then turned her face back into the pillow, the sun barely peeking in around the curtains, and she'd forgotten for a second where she was. Before she'd opened her eyes, Colt had pulled her close and kissed her temple, his stubble rasping against her skin. She'd turned into him, throwing her leg over his.

"Morning." She'd buried her face in his neck, breathing in his warm, comforting scent.

"Morning, gorgeous." He'd threaded his fingers into her hair, brushing her tangled locks away from her face.

"Don't get up yet," she'd mumbled. "I know you're an early riser, but stay with me."

He'd laughed and brushed his lips against hers before he'd flipped her on her back. His mouth trailed over the sensitive skin just below her ear as their legs tangled together.

"I am an early riser." He'd pulled back and wiggled his eyebrows. "A big one."

She'd laughed, and she'd felt as though she were floating off the mattress and melting into Colt. "So humble."

He'd kneed her legs apart and she'd felt his cock, hot and hard, slide against the inside of her thigh. "It's not bragging if it's true."

She'd laughed again and wrapped her legs around his hips, sighing and arching up into him as he took her nipple into his mouth. "Mmm. Can't argue with that."

But instead of reaching over to the nightstand for a condom as she'd expected, he'd settled beside her and slid a hand down her body, over her breast, her ribs, into the dip created by her hipbone. "I'll stay with you as long as you want, gorgeous. As long as you want." His hand had slipped between her parted thighs, and his fingers had brushed gently against her lips. With sure movements, he'd eased her lips apart and slipped a finger into her. She'd clenched around him, and he'd smiled, pulling his finger out and slicking her wetness over her, his fingers rubbing a slow, teasing circle over her clit. She'd let out a soft moan, and he'd repeated the motion, adding a bit more pressure as her hips rose to his touch. He'd moved his fingers in a sure, steady rhythm, doing nothing except stroking her clit, until she fell apart in his arms, her legs shaking, her muscles rigid, his name falling from her lips in breathy gasps.

"You are so beautiful when you come," he'd said, his deep voice rumbling across her oversensitized skin. He'd looked down at her, a smile pulling up one corner of his mouth. It was then that he'd reached for a condom while her stomach let out a long, loud grumble.

"Let's get you fed first," he'd said and winked. "I need your energy up for what I have planned for you."

An unwelcome rush of cool air had tingled across her skin as he'd pushed up off the bed. She'd watched with pure female appreciation as he'd bent and scooped his boxers off the floor, yanking them on and then his jeans, his muscles flexing and bunching beneath his taut, tattooed skin, his big hands pulling his pants on. With possessive satisfaction, she'd noticed the red lines down his back, scratches from the night before.

Her stomach had grumbled again, and with a sigh, she'd levered herself upright, swinging her legs over the side of the bed. She'd extended her arms above her head and stretched, the afterglow of her orgasm still tingling through her.

She'd heard a low, gruff moan of appreciation from behind her and glanced over her shoulder. Colt stood with one shoulder against the wall, arms crossed over his bare chest, a thumb resting against his bottom lip.

She'd bit her lip and smiled. "Enjoying the view?"

His eyes had crinkled as he smiled. "Always, gorgeous."

"Back atcha."

Her stomach growled loudly again in the quiet room, and he laughed, bending to pull a clean shirt out of his duffel bag. "Come on. Breakfast. Then, I promise, we'll go back to bed."

He'd kept his promise.

Bringing herself back to the present, she let out a sigh as she strummed her guitar idly, watching the sun sink into the trees, casting dreamy pink and orange light over the lake.

For the first time in weeks, maybe even years, she felt peaceful. Happy, despite everything going on. And she knew it was because of Colt.

\* \* \*

"I want to suck your cock." Taylor's husky voice sizzled against his ear as she slipped her arms around his waist from behind. He paused with his hands immersed in warm, soapy water, a sponge in his hands as he washed their dinner dishes. He pulled his hands out of the water so fast that he flung suds against the window above the sink. He spun and pulled her against him, slamming his mouth into hers.

Tongues and lips melded together instantly, and she let out a breathy moan that sent even more blood flowing to his cock. Her mouth was warm and hungry against his, her breath sweet and addictive. He kissed her with abandon, losing himself in the perfection of her mouth.

"I love how you taste," she breathed in a husky voice, her lips moving against his as she spoke. "And I want to taste all of you."

"Fuck, yes."

With a sweet smile, she sank gracefully to her knees. She looked up at him through her lashes, her blue eyes slightly hooded and dark with lust. Without a word, she undid his pants, the metallic zip echoing in the kitchen as she lowered his fly, and then she slipped his cock and balls through the fly of his boxer briefs. The fact that they were both still fully dressed with only his massive erection and heavy, quickly tightening balls protruding from his pants was a hell of a turn-on.

Her eyes locked with his as she wrapped one hand around the base of his shaft and licked the clear bead of moisture from his swollen head. She hummed out her approval. "So good."

His hands found their way into her golden waves, holding her hair back from her face in loose fistfuls. She dipped her head slightly, sucking one of his balls into her mouth and swirling her tongue lightly over it before releasing it and tracing her tongue up the underside of his shaft in one long, slow lick.

"Fuck, gorgeous," he whispered. She slicked her tongue over her palm and stroked him, just once, and then pressed the head of his cock against her lips. Just when he thought the visual couldn't get any more perfect, she smiled and enveloped him in the wet heat of her mouth. He fought the urge to tip his head back and close his eyes, because he needed to watch every single second of Taylor on her knees with his throbbing cock in her mouth. She teased the head, swirling her tongue over it, sucking it, pressing it against the inside of her cheek. The pleasure of it, hot and intense, was tearing him into little pieces, shredding him from the inside out until he had to remind himself to breathe. She pulled back, stroking him a few times, slicking the moisture from her mouth over him. Heat pulsed low in his gut, electric tension radiating through his muscles and across his skin.

"I love how you feel in my mouth," she murmured. He'd been about to reply with something dirty and encouraging but was only able to let out a long, low groan as she filled her mouth and throat with his pulsing dick, taking him far, far deeper than he'd have guessed she could. Wet heat engulfed him, her mouth deliciously tight around him. She anchored her hands on his hips and began bobbing her head in a sure, steady rhythm.

He fought the urge to move his hips, but as though she could sense what he needed, she moaned and picked up her pace. His vision narrowed, almost fading in and out at times. Probably because his eyes were on the verge of rolling back into his head.

"Fuck, Taylor," he managed, his hands tightening their grip in her hair. "Your mouth feels so damn good. Holy shit."

She slowed her rhythm and looked up at him, her blue eyes bright with lust and arousal. God, she was enjoying it, and fuck if that didn't make what was already the hottest blow job of his life even hotter. When she looked up at him like that, his cock filling her pretty mouth, he felt like a fucking god. A god who would do anything for her.

His balls tightened with a sharp, sweet twinge, and he knew he was going to come soon. Very soon. Searing pleasure radiated from his balls and up his cock, intensifying with each sweep of her mouth up and down his shaft. Pressure built, an incredible sensation of fullness swelling his cock almost to the bursting point.

"Taylor, I'm gonna come, so if you don't want…" His voice was hoarse and shaky, but it didn't matter. He wasn't able to finish his thought because she sucked him hard and deep, and he hit the point of no return. All other sensation in his body dropped away, and his entire existence narrowed to his cock.

He ground out her name as he felt the first intense throb of his orgasm blast through him. With his hands wound tightly in her hair, he came hard, pulsing his release into her beautiful mouth. With half-open eyes, he watched her swallow down everything he had, knowing the moment would be forever burned into his brain.

She slowed her movements, giving him a few seconds to ride it out. A heavy numbness invaded his limbs, his dick warm and tingling from the release. With an adorable, self-satisfied smile, she tucked him back into his pants and stood, smoothing her hands down the front of her shirt. Hoping he could trust his legs to support him, he pushed off the counter and circled his arms around her waist, pulling her into him and kissing the soft, warm skin at the juncture of her neck and shoulder.

"That was fucking incredible. Thank you."

She pulled back and smiled, biting her lip. "You can pay me back later."

"Trust me, it's at the top of my to-do list." He pressed his face into her neck, trailing kisses across her throat. "*You* are a very naughty girl, and I fucking love it."

"Mmm. Maybe I need to be spanked."

He spun her around and leaned her over the counter, his hands dropping to her ass. He caressed the supple flesh and then roughly squeezed, a hand on each cheek. "You're trying to kill me, aren't you?" Because despite the intense orgasm he'd just had, he was beginning to stir in his jeans at the thought of bending her over and marking the pale flesh of her sweet little ass with his hand print. Marking his territory and claiming it for his own.

"But you'll die such a happy man," she said, pressing her ass against his hands.

"God, you've ruined me for other women." He meant it as a joke, but his heart stuttered, tripping over itself, stopping and then restarting with a jolt as the truth of that statement washed over him.

"Good." She drew in close, her breath hot on his ear as

she wound her arms around his neck. "I don't want there to be any other women. Only me."

"There aren't; only you. No other men?"

She pressed her forehead against his and shook her head. "Only you. I only want you."

Even with a gun to his head, he couldn't have stopped his wide smile from surfacing. "You and me, gorgeous. It's you and me."

She sighed, and he felt a tremor pass through her. "I really like how that sounds."

"No one else. Just you and me." He cupped her face, tracing his thumbs over her cheekbones. When he kissed her, he tried to pour everything good that was filling him up into the kiss. Everything he was too scared to voice. The hope. The happiness.

The feeling that maybe he'd found home.

# CHAPTER 23

"Tell me something you've never told anyone before." Taylor pressed her face into Colt's chest, breathing in the clean cotton scent of his T-shirt. He pulled the blanket tighter around them and slid a hand up and down her back. She tilted her head slightly, pulling the fresh, cool air into her lungs as she took in the star-speckled night, thousands of stars hanging in the dusky indigo sky, spread like diamonds against velvet.

LA's night sky was blank, void. A nothing sky. But here, looking at the thousands of stars with Colt, it felt as though the sky hanging above them held everything. Beauty and promises and love. Everything good and pure, twinkling back at them. It was their sky, the two of them together.

They'd grabbed pillows and a blanket and climbed up onto the cabin's flat roof, something that had quickly become part of their nightly routine. They'd lie on the roof and watch as the sky darkened and the stars switched on, talking about anything and everything. Every night, she learned new things about him, and it only made her hungry for more. He was like a map of a new, uncharted continent; she was exploring and slowly discovering all of his hills and rivers, his oceans and borders, and filling his map as she learned new and amazing things. What made him laugh, what made him moan, what annoyed him.

But even more, it was the little things. Like that he preferred jam on his pancakes instead of syrup. Or that his first celebrity crush was on Cameron Diaz. And that he was really, really good at beer pong. That his biggest regret was that he hadn't gone to college. That if he had gone, he would've maybe liked to be a teacher. She took it all in with a voracious hunger, wanting everything he'd give her.

And then there was last night, where, as they'd lain in each other's arms, he'd confessed that he pictured himself with kids someday, even though he wasn't sure he'd be very good at it. She hadn't trusted herself to say anything, hadn't trusted her voice to even work, so instead she'd just kissed him, slowly and tenderly, trying to show him that she wanted that, too, for herself and for him. Trying to show him that she understood how he felt, because she had the same damn reservations about herself. But maybe, with the two of them, it could work. Being with him was easy, because her broken pieces fit perfectly with his, and when she was with him, she actually liked who she was.

"Something I've never told anyone before?" he asked, and she nodded against him. The lake lapped quietly at the shore, the blackened tops of the pine trees poking up into the sky. "A happy thing, or…something else?"

"How about one of each?"

His chest rose and fell underneath her cheek, and she trailed her hand over his stomach, which was hard and firm, waiting quietly while he thought of an answer. He cleared his throat softly before answering. "Sometimes, I don't understand why I'm here. Why I—out of all the guys I fought with—why I'm the one who made it back. Some of those guys died because of me, because it was up to me to protect them and I failed. Guys who had a hell of a lot more to come home to than I did. Girlfriends and wives. Parents who loved them. Babies. Futures."

Her arms tightened around him, this man who was so strong, so brave, and who carried so much pain around.

He continued, his voice rumbling over her. "I feel so damn guilty that I'm just here, alive, breathing, when those guys aren't. I don't…it hurts, sometimes, Taylor. It's too much, and when I start to really think about it, I just…I can't. I don't deserve to be alive any more than they deserve to be dead."

"You deserve to be alive," she whispered. "You do, Colt." She raised herself up onto one elbow and kissed him, wanting to comfort him, to take some of his pain and help him carry it.

When she pulled back, he smiled, cupping her cheek with one, big strong hand. "You keep telling me that, and I might start believing you."

"Good." Their eyes met, and something passed between them, shimmering like the stars surrounding them.

"Your turn. Tell me something that you've never told anyone before."

"You never told me your happy thing."

He wound a lock of her hair around his finger. "I'll tell you after. Spill."

She sighed and laid her head back down on his chest, loving how perfectly she fit against his strong, sturdy body. How safe she felt in his arms, his heartbeat pulsing against her, seeping into her skin. "You're gonna laugh at me. It's stupid."

He tipped her chin up and kissed her. "I won't, and I bet it's not. Tell me."

"I'm not the kind of girl who grew up planning her wedding. But I've always thought, if I ever do get married, that I want to go to the Little White Wedding Chapel in Vegas."

He pulled her tighter against him. "With Elvis and everything?"

She nodded. "And I want to walk down the aisle to 'Can't Help Falling in Love with You.'"

He kissed the top of her head. "Didn't peg you for an Elvis fan."

"My grandpa—my mom's dad—was. He looked after me sometimes when I was little, and whenever we drove anywhere in his big boat of a car, there was always an Elvis cassette playing." She took a breath. "He died when I was nine. Heart attack. Sometimes, when I think about my fucked-up family, I try to remember him, and that maybe there's something good in me."

"Gorgeous, there's a lot of good in you. You're smart, and talented, and strong. You're funny and beautiful. That's a hell of a lot more than just good."

She inhaled sharply, trying to get her erratic heart under control. "Tell me the happy thing you've never told anyone before."

He looked down at her, the starlight highlighting his cheekbones and the chiseled planes of his gorgeous face. "I'm falling for you, Taylor. Hard and fast, and I don't want to stop."

Her heart stopped completely and she pulled him down, their mouths crashing hungrily together. Her fingers went immediately to his belt buckle, needing more than anything to have him inside her, to wrap his body with hers and never let him go.

His tongue stroked hers, and with his belt buckle and fly open, he came down on top of her. Her legs wound around his waist, and she pushed up into him, desperate for more.

"Show me, Colt. Make me feel it," she whispered against his mouth, and he rose up just enough to push his pants and boxers down. She shimmied out of her jeans, gasping out a sighing moan as he came back down on top of her, his hard cock sliding against the insides of her thighs.

"I want to show you everything, Taylor. I want to give you everything." He pulled a condom from the back pocket of his jeans and rolled it on. She could've sworn that his hands were trembling. He lined himself up at her entrance, already slick and aching for him. She seemed to be in a perpetual state of semi-arousal around him. "Look at me," he said, his voice low and rough, and she tore her eyes away from his cock. She met his gaze, and everything in her went completely still.

His eyes glittered and held hers as he slowly pushed into her. "It's you and me, gorgeous. Always." He buried his face in her neck and thrust into her, hard and deep. She dug her fingers into his scalp and wrapped her legs tightly around his pumping hips, holding him close with her body. With her heart. Taking everything he had to give and letting it fill her up like gold, warm and pure.

"I love you," she whispered, but the words were lost against the night breeze and the sounds of their bodies coming together.

\* \* \*

Frank spit out a mouthful of blood and glared up at Jonathan Fairfax, who wiped his hands on a white handkerchief.

"What are we going to do about this, Frank? Hmm? You

don't have the money you owe us. You stole our drugs. Now, I know that I can't get blood from a stone, but you understand that I can't just let this slide, right?" Fairfax paced the small room, shaking his head. "What kind of message would that send, if I let someone who stole from me, someone who couldn't pay his debts, just walk, no consequences?"

Frank didn't answer, knowing that Fairfax didn't really want to have a fucking conversation.

"We tried to talk to your daughter, but that didn't work out so well. Now three of my guys are in jail, and she ran off somewhere to hide."

"What do you want, Fairfax? Spit it the fuck out already."

"Well, I want my money. You don't have it, but your daughter does. So you'll need to figure out a way to get it from her. Here's a little preview, on the house, of what you can expect if I don't get my money." He tipped his head at someone behind Frank. A huge man holding a sledgehammer emerged, smiling grimly at Frank.

The sledgehammer swung down, and Frank screamed.

* * *

The sound of knocking woke Colt out of a sound sleep, and he rolled to his feet, grabbing his SIG from the bedside table. He yanked on a pair of boxers and then stood still, listening. He glanced over at Taylor, still asleep, her golden hair spilling out across the pillow.

The knocking sounded again at the front door, and he quickly pulled on sweat pants and a T-shirt. He glanced at Taylor again before opening the bedroom door, pulling it slowly to avoid making a sound.

Flipping on lights as he walked through the silent cabin, his SIG tucked into the waistband of his sweats, he slowed as

he approached the front door. He glanced through the peephole, staring at the man on the other side. He was midforties,
plain looking, wearing a pair of jeans and an old USC sweat-
shirt. Colt unlocked the front door and opened it, resetting
the alarm as he stepped outside.

"Can I help you?" asked Colt, his voice rough with sleep.

The man nodded. "I'm so sorry to bother you, but my car
broke down and my cell phone's dead. I was hoping you'd
have a phone I could use." He glanced up and down the de-
serted road. "You're the third cabin I've tried. The others
seem to be empty, and I'm kind of stuck here."

Colt narrowed his eyes, glancing between the house and
the man's car, which sat on the side of the road, the hood
propped open. A creeping sensation prickled up his spine,
and he crossed his arms in front of him.

"Don't have a phone, but I can take a look at your car
for you. Might be able to get you going." He tipped his head
in the direction of the man's car, not wanting him near the
house, or Taylor. Just wanting him gone.

The man smiled. "I'd appreciate that. Thank you."

They started down the driveway, and Colt studied him, on
high alert for anything suspicious. "Where you headed?"

"Not far. I'm supposed to be meeting some friends for the
weekend. Took a wrong turn, ended up on the wrong side of
the damn lake. Next thing I know, car dies on me."

Colt tipped his head, relaxing slightly the farther he got
the man from the house. His brother-in-law had a small toolshed near the end of the driveway, and Colt stopped there
to grab a toolbox and a flashlight. The man made idle conversation about the weather and how nice it was up here,
away from the city. When they arrived at the man's car, Colt
leaned forward, bracing his hands on the front fender as he
took a look.

The man shifted behind him, and the hairs on the back of Colt's neck stood on end. He spun to face him, just in time to see the man swing a heavy wrench at him. It connected with Colt's temple, and he slumped against the car, his vision fading around the edges. Gritting his teeth, he started to reach for his gun, but the man swung again, and darkness fell.

# CHAPTER 24

Taylor sat up in bed, pulling the sheet around her. Something had pulled her from sleep, and she flung an arm out, only to discover that Colt's side of the bed was empty. She turned on the bedside lamp, pushing her hair out of her face as she listened for running water, for the toilet flushing. Maybe he'd had one of the nightmares he'd told her about, and he'd gone into the living room to watch TV for a bit.

But his gun was gone. Her chest tightened, and cold sweat broke out on her palms and feet. Why would he have—

The alarm began to shriek, and seconds later, Ronald Baker—the man from the bar, the man who'd sent her flowers, the man who'd stalked and spied on her—walked into the bedroom.

With a small flick of his wrist, he locked the bedroom door and leaned against it, a smug smile on his face, his arms crossed over his chest.

Oh, God, where was Colt? What had Baker done to him?

With a sickening lurch, her brain scrambled as she tried to figure out what to do.

Willing herself to stay calm, she smiled weakly while adjusting the sheet around her, keenly aware of her nakedness and trying desperately not to give any indication of how scared she was. The last thing she wanted to do was antagonize him. Her mind flashed back to the bar, to how quickly he'd become agitated.

"Ronald, baby," she purred, biting her lip coyly. "You're not supposed to be here." She feigned surprise, her eyes wide. His eyes skated up and down her body, and a wave of nausea rocked her. She swallowed, dots pulsing in front of her eyes as her blood hammered through her temples.

"I know. And it's all his fault."

She nodded, bobbing her head up and down, trying to disguise the fact that she was looking around the room, trying to figure out if she could get to her phone, if she could use the lamp as a weapon, if she should just scream for help. She clenched her hands in the sheets, hoping he couldn't see them shaking. She didn't know what would set him off. "You know, I'd hate for you to get in trouble. Maybe you should head out, and I can come meet you later. What do you think?"

"No. I've got you all to myself now. I've waited so long to be alone with you. You're so fucking special, Taylor. You have no idea the lengths I've gone to for you." His voice shook with emotion as he closed the distance between them and dragged his fingers over her cheek. Her stomach churned, and she clamped her jaw against the fresh wave of nausea rolling through her at his touch.

"You're so beautiful," he breathed, stroking her face again, while she held as still as possible. "My angel. Too pretty for this world."

Where the hell was Colt? Panic spiraled through her, making it hard to breathe, and she glanced at the door.

Baker chuckled, a sad little sound, as though he were disappointed in her. "He's not coming. He's dead."

\* \* \*

Colt blinked, trying to focus his eyes. He forced a deep breath into his chest. Pain shot through his legs, and he realized that he was on his knees in the toolshed. The light was too bright, and every movement of his head, even his eyes, sent the room spinning sideways.

He slumped over, his shoulder slamming into the workbench. With a mumbled curse, he tried to push up to his feet but found that his ankles were bound together with a heavy layer of duct tape. Groaning as pain throbbed through his temples, he sank down onto his ass and pulled his legs clumsily in front of him, reaching forward to pull at the duct tape. But his arms wouldn't cooperate, and it took his brain a few seconds to realize that they were duct-taped behind him. Forcing himself to concentrate, to coordinate his movements, he rolled onto his stomach. From there, he curled into a fetal position, got his knees under him, and hopped to standing.

His eyes roved the toolshed, looking for a knife, a saw, anything. The sound of the cabin's alarm reached him, and Taylor screamed. The sound tore through him like a jagged knife. He moved toward the door, and it swung open. Pain exploded across his face as the man stepped into the toolshed. Colt fell back and slumped to the ground.

Colt began to struggle back to his feet, but the man pushed him down and drew a gun from his waistband, then pressed it to Colt's temple.

Taylor screamed again, and the remaining fog in Colt's mind seemed to clear. Getting to Taylor was the only thing that mattered. He'd made her a promise that he would keep her safe, that she could trust him to protect her.

Ignoring the gun pressed to his temple, Colt ducked and slammed his head into the man's groin, causing him to shout and kick Colt in the chest. Adrenaline surged through Colt, and he pushed to his feet, squatting down as fast as he could and shearing apart the duct tape binding his ankles with the force of his movement. The man fired the gun, narrowly missing Colt as the sound exploded through the tool shed. As hard as he could, Colt kicked the man in the stomach, sending him crashing backward. Colt quickly slipped to the ground and managed to step through his bound wrists, shorn duct tape still trailing from his ankles, but before he could work the duct tape around his wrists free, pain seared through his back, and he felt the warm gush of blood. The man loomed over him with a knife, now stained red with Colt's blood, in his other hand. Ignoring the burning pain, Colt rammed his joined wrists against a wood beam, shearing the duct tape around his wrists. His assailant used the opportunity to slam his gun into Colt's face, and Colt felt the skin over his cheekbone split open. Then the man leveled the gun at Colt's chest.

Taylor screamed again, and Colt knew he had to take this chance to get to her. He pivoted and grabbed the man's hand, turned the barrel of the gun toward the man's chest, and wrenched the gun out of his hands. Colt pointed the gun at the assailant, who charged at him with the knife.

Left with no other choice, Colt aimed and pumped two shots into the man's chest.

* * *

Rocks tumbled against each other in Taylor's stomach, her vision narrowed to pinpoints, and her heart shredded itself into tiny little pieces. Baker grabbed her, his fingers like slimy steel bands around her upper arms as they dug into her skin. Her heart thundered in her chest, sending blood pounding against her temples with such speed and force that it almost hurt.

She opened her mouth, trying to think of something to say, something to do, but she couldn't seem to get her tongue and brain to connect. Her arms and legs started shaking, and he loosened his grip.

"You're scaring me," she whispered, hoping to appeal to anything human that might exist in him.

"You've been a bad girl. Maybe you deserve to be scared." He rubbed his hands up and down her arms. "Look at your skin. So perfect and soft." He released her and pushed her down onto the mattress, stripping the sheet away and pulling a knife out of his pocket. She tried to stand, not caring that she was completely naked, but a wave of dizziness forced her back down, and then suddenly he was on top of her, his weight pinning her as he straddled her.

Something burst in her chest, and she began to struggle in earnest. She felt as though she'd been underwater in some kind of nightmare that couldn't actually be real and had just surfaced into reality. Anger surged through her as she fought to shove him off of her, screaming at the top of her lungs.

"Get off me, you fucking creep!" She clawed at his chest, his back, his arms, but he kept her pressed into the mattress, his knees digging painfully into her stomach as he shifted his weight onto her. Still, she struggled, lashing desperately at him until she felt the cold, sharp press of metal against her throat. She stilled, fear seesawing with anger.

"Don't deny me what's mine. I don't want to hurt you, but I will." He trailed the knife down her throat and over her breasts, flicking it against her nipple. She bit back a whimper, not wanting to give him the satisfaction of reacting. "You'll never have our baby if you don't let me fuck you. I'm your husband. It's my right." He shoved a hand between her legs, cupping her. "This is mine."

"You're a fucking psycho. I hope you rot in hell, you bastard." She ground the words out through clenched teeth, keenly aware of the knife pressed against her.

He leaned over her, his face inches from hers as he rubbed his palm against her, his other hand still brandishing the knife against her breast, right over her heart. And then he laughed, a cold, mirthless snort. "This beautiful body is mine, and you're going to do what I say. I've played games long enough. I've waited long enough. I tried to be nice, to get your attention the old-fashioned way, but it didn't work. You were too busy playing slut with that brute. You want to be a slut? I can treat you like a slut."

Her teeth clamped down on her lip, and she felt a tear cut a hot swath over her cheek. She squeezed her eyes shut. She let loose another wordless scream, putting everything she had into it. Baker yanked his hand from between her legs and closed it around her throat, the knife pressing in harder, hard enough that she knew he was breaking the skin, could feel the wet bead of blood sliding down over her breast. A gunshot echoed through the night, and her heart burst right along with it. *Oh God, Colt.* Tears burned her eyes.

"Don't you dare scream again, bitch."

Spots danced in front of her eyes as she scraped at his hand around her throat. He let up just enough that she was able to gasp in a single precious breath before he resumed his choke hold. He sat back a bit and looked thoughtful, studying her as though she were an experiment or a crossword puzzle he just couldn't solve. He took the knife and, with the very tip of it, carved something into the skin just above her heart, loosening his grip on her throat.

She sobbed at the burning pain, struggling harder to get away from him. She could feel the warm blood trickling across her skin, and suddenly he slapped her, so hard that the room spun for a moment. The taste of blood filled her mouth. She screamed again, pouring everything she had into making as much noise as possible, and the sound of two gunshots exploded through the night.

"You promised me!" He screamed the words into her face. "'Let me be your snow in July, / waiting for you in a world gone mad, / because I promised you forever, / and forever doesn't mean good-bye.'" He recited her own lyrics back to her, his eyes glittering and dark and wild. "That was for me," he whispered, his voice fierce, and the knife dug in a little more. "That was about us. It's our song. You wrote it for us, and you're a lying bitch if you deny it. I know it. You know it. I want everyone to know it."

He released his grip on her throat and she coughed, gagging on the air flooding her lungs. "I fucking hate you!" She sobbed out the words, her voice hoarse and raw, and began struggling again.

Hard, heavy footsteps pounded through the cabin, and the door burst open, splintering in the frame. Lightning-fast, Colt was there, and a sharp, metallic click reached her ears as he pressed the barrel of his gun to the back of Baker's skull.

"Don't *fucking* move, asshole."

Baker froze, shocked fury contorting his features into an

ugly snarl. At the sight of Colt, her muscles melted, relief rushing through her veins, sucking the tension out of her body and leaving her limp.

"Drop the knife. Now!" Colt barked the words out, steady and sure, his eyes narrowed to angry slits. Blood seeped through his T-shirt, and trickled from several cuts on his face.

Baker closed his eyes, his nostrils flaring. Slowly, he unwrapped his fingers from around the knife's handle, leaving it lying on her chest. Time kept speeding up and slowing down, and suddenly it felt as though everything were moving at double time. In one swift movement, Colt scooped up the knife and slammed the butt of his gun into Baker's head, sending him crumpling to the floor in an unconscious heap. Grabbing zip ties from his pocket, he fastened them quickly around Baker's wrists and ankles.

Taylor let out a strangled cry, her breath coming in shaky, nearly silent gasps as her entire body shook uncontrollably. She wanted to breathe but couldn't seem to get her lungs to inhale properly, could only get them to stutter and stop and jolt. Colt sank down onto the bed beside her and wrapped a blanket around her, covering her. He gathered her into his arms, pulling her into his lap and cradling her against him. With his solid, sturdy warmth around her, she let go, giving in and letting the sobs rack her body. He was covered in blood, and her heart caved in on itself at the sight.

"I'm so fucking sorry, Taylor." Colt's voice was an intense, passionate whisper, and his apology only made her cry harder.

"N-not your f-fault," she managed to choke out, convulsing against him.

"Yes, it is. I fucked up. I let my guard down."

"You saved me." She buried her face in his chest, inhaling the warm, comforting scent of him, listening as he dialed 911. For several minutes, maybe longer, she cried into his chest and he held her, stroking her back, his lips pressed to the top of her head. The steady rhythm of his heart, the deep rise and fall of his chest, calmed her until she couldn't cry any more. Until the fear and the anger had been wrung out of her, and all that was left was exhaustion and relief.

"What happened to you?" Her voice felt like sandpaper scraping against her throat as she spoke, partly from crying and partly from Baker's choke hold.

"Baker brought someone with him, and he jumped me. I could hear you screaming, and I had to get to you." He took a deep breath, his voice low and gravelly when he continued. "I think I killed him. The other man. I think he's dead." He went very still and very quiet for a moment before she heard a whispered curse, and his arms tightened around her.

"Oh, Colt," she whispered, knowing what killing that man had cost him.

"I'd kill him again to save you, Taylor." He closed his eyes and blew out a breath and then gently tucked a strand of hair behind her ear with a shaking hand.

"Hey." She dipped her head, forcing his eyes to meet hers. "I'm okay. We're okay." Her throat thickened again, and she couldn't say anything else.

# CHAPTER 25

Colt sat at the desk in his home office, tipping back in the black mesh office chair. The floorboards creaked softly under the plastic wheels, the only sound in the dark house.

After everything had gone to shit at the cabin, Baker had been arrested, and while Colt had had plenty to answer for—he *had* shot and killed a man—ultimately, they'd let him go. The man he'd shot had been an alleged contract killer wanted by the FBI, and Colt had killed him in self-defense.

A contract killer. Baker was so fucking psycho that he'd hired a hit man.

It was the first—and only—time Colt had ever killed someone on American soil. He looked down at his hands, half-expecting to see blood, to see gunpowder residue, to see something marking him as the killer he was. As a failure, as the monster he was.

Another nightmare to add to the menu.

They'd come back to his house from the cabin, and the word from the cops was that Taylor's dad was in the wind, probably long gone, running from the Brotherhood. But until they knew the Brotherhood issues were completely resolved, she needed protection. Maybe she needed better protection than what he could provide.

Taylor had retreated into herself after the attack. She was pretending she was fine, but he knew she wasn't. Maybe because he'd been putting on the same kind of front, pushing down pain, fear, and scars and slapping on a smile for years. Faking it so he wouldn't have to talk about any of the shit he didn't want to talk about. It was classic avoidance, and he was well versed in the techniques.

Back in LA, they'd settled in at his place; security was doubled by the presence of Virtus guards. After discovering the surveillance, she still didn't feel at ease at her house. He was pretty sure she didn't feel safe here either, but she hadn't wanted to go to a hotel. Mentally, he added it to the list of ways that he'd failed her. Tonight, three days after the attack at the cabin, he'd made sure Taylor had fallen into a deep sleep, and then he'd slipped out of bed, grabbed the bottle of Johnnie Walker from the kitchen, and made his way through the dark house to the office.

Not bothering with a glass, he screwed the top off and tipped the bottle to his lips, relishing the burn as the scotch sluiced down his throat. He curled his fingers around the bottle, clinging to it like an anchor in a storm. He tilted his head back and closed his eyes, blowing out a long, slow breath. His brain buzzed and snapped with an anxious guilt, and he knew he wouldn't be able to sleep right now. Especially not beside Taylor, pretending he had any business curling his arms around her and pressing kisses into her hair.

He scrubbed his hands over his face and then took another pull on the bottle. Massaging his fingers over his forehead, he tried to block out the truth whipping through him.

That he'd tried his best to keep her safe, and his best wasn't good enough for Taylor.

That she was vulnerable, and he'd taken advantage of that.

That he'd failed to protect her when it was the only promise he'd ever made her.

She'd gotten hurt on his watch. It was his fault, and he'd carry that with him for a long time. Probably forever, and that couldn't be helped. It was done. But he could make sure it didn't happen again.

After another fortifying swallow of scotch, he pulled open the bottom drawer of the desk and lifted out a thick manila folder. One ankle propped on his knee, he leaned back in the chair and thumbed through the contract Clay had given him a few weeks ago. Before he could talk himself out of it, he picked up a pen and signed it, then tossed the pen back on the desk with a resigned sigh.

He rubbed a hand over the back of his neck as his stomach churned with doubt.

No. Running wasn't the answer, was it? Was that who he'd become? Frowning, he stared at his signature on the page, and shaking his head, he dropped the contract back into the drawer and kicked it shut.

If running wasn't the answer, what was?

Maybe taking the contract was what was best for both of them. A job for him, freedom for her. He'd hand over her protection to Virtus, remove himself from the situation, and protect her from any further damage in the process.

"Fuck," he whispered in the dark, hating the tightness in his throat. He took a long pull on the scotch bottle, trying to ignore the burning in his eyes. If he stayed, he'd inevitably hurt her in the long run. But if he left, he'd hurt her, at least in the short run. The plain truth was that she couldn't escape from him unscathed.

If that wasn't proof of what an asshole he was, he didn't know what was.

A heavy guilt sat on his shoulders as he ran through his litany of failures. Of all the times he'd tried to do the right thing but had fucked it up. Had caused hurt, pain, and suffering. It was an inescapable truth that his main talent was letting people down. His mother. Lacey, when he'd gotten himself kicked out of the house. The guys under him who had trusted him and had come home in body bags. Owens, and the guys at Virtus. Now Taylor.

And hell, he loved her, which meant he owed her better than to keep deluding himself that he could give her the future she wanted and deserved. He just had to figure out what would cause the least amount of damage.

But fuck if he knew what that was.

* * *

Three days of distance.

That was how Taylor felt about the seventy-two hours following Baker's attack. And it wasn't due to any seismic shift in how Colt acted toward her. No, he still touched her, kissed her, held her at night when she couldn't sleep. When she couldn't get the images of Baker, his hands around her throat, out of her mind. But it was as though a thin shield had gone up around him, and although everything seemed the same, there was a tiny bit of space that hadn't been there before.

It was the way his smile didn't quite reach his eyes. She hadn't seen them crinkle in days. It was the way he touched her—delicately, as though he were scared of breaking her. When he laughed, there was a hollowness to the sound.

And despite the fact that they'd slept next to each other for the past three nights, he hadn't once tried to initiate sex. Granted she hadn't, either, but still. It was very un-Colt-like, and she couldn't help but think that he saw her as damaged now.

Well. *More* damaged. And she couldn't help but wonder how much damage she could sustain before she became an unsalvageable wreck.

He was pulling away from her ever so slightly. And damn, it *hurt*.

And now, here they were, entering hour seventy-three, sitting together but apart on his couch, eating In-N-Out burgers while she took a break from working.

For what felt like the hundredth time, she opened her mouth, having almost worked up the courage to say something. But every time, fear stopped her, and she shoved food into her open mouth instead.

What if she worked up the guts to ask and then didn't like the answer? What then? A tiny flare of resentment sparked through her at how vulnerable the doubt made her feel. She didn't usually pussyfoot around what she wanted to say, but the last time she'd had this feeling, this niggling, burrowing shard of worry digging through her brain, she'd come away wishing she hadn't said anything. Wishing that she hadn't told Zack she loved him just so he could rip her heart to shreds, confirming that a man like him would never, ever, really love a woman like her, with her history and her scars. Sex? Sure. Fun and games? No problem. Love? Get real, sweetheart.

A chill frosted over her skin as she wondered if she was misreading the entire situation. Maybe this wasn't about the attack. Maybe this was about her. About how unlovable she was. She didn't want to believe that he was just like every other man in her life, who'd used her and then thrown her away when her usefulness had run out. But it was hard not to wonder, given the empty space expanding between them.

* * *

Chords running through her mind, Taylor peeled open her eyes, humming the tune she'd found in her sleep. She sat up, glancing at the empty space in the bed beside her. She could hear the shower running, and she pushed her hair off her face, her shoulders slumping a little. With a sigh, she grabbed her phone from the bedside table.

She swiped her finger across the screen, but it remained black. Dead. Of course. She'd been so distracted with everything that seemed to swirl constantly through her brain—Colt, the attack, her music, everything—that she'd forgotten to plug it in last night before crashing. But she needed to write down the chords before they vanished and floated away like a dream. She threw the covers back and then kept humming the wistful D-B minor-E minor-A progression so she wouldn't lose it as she made her way to Colt's office.

The hardwood floors creaked under her bare feet, overly loud in the quiet room, and the noise made her feel as if she were intruding on Colt's space, a feeling that had been growing over the past few days. Maybe it was time to go home, to stop clinging to him, get one of the guys from Virtus to stay with her. Still humming, determined not to lose the tune, she hurried over to the desk by the window, skimming her fingers over the felt of the pool table in the center of the room as she passed by it.

She smiled as she took in the desktop, which was military-precision neat, just like the rest of Colt's house. The simple black desk had only a computer monitor, a printer without any paper in it, and a white mug with a few pens and pencils. No notepad, no scrap paper. Not even an old bill. Looking for a piece of paper she could use, she sat down in the chair and tugged on the top drawer, but it didn't budge. Locked. Knowing Colt, there was probably a gun stashed away in there. She opened the second drawer, which was filled with hanging files, each with a name and number scrawled across the top in Colt's slightly messy block lettering. She flipped through them quickly and saw that they were client invoices, tax forms, and other stuff related to his business, so she slid the drawer closed. Fingers crossed, she opened the third drawer. A pile of printer paper sat under a few file folders.

"Bingo," she sang in tune with the song that was still running through her mind, and she started to pull the stack of blank, white pages free, knocking open the top manila folder in the process.

She hadn't been trying to snoop, but when she saw Colt's name at the top of the page, in his own writing, just under the AtlasCorp logo, she paused. Before she realized what she was doing, her eyes skimmed down the page.

"What the hell?" she whispered, the song and its chord progression pushed from her brain. She set the brick of printer paper down on top of the desk with a soft thud and pulled the folder out of the drawer, then quickly paged through it. All the blood drained from her head and pooled thickly in her limbs, making her feel as though she weighed a thousand pounds. For a brief second, the room closed in around her, making everything tilt and slide.

She shook her head, trying to focus, and the words

danced in front of her unfocused eyes. One-year contract…
top-level security…high risk…Richmond, Virginia…threat
assessment and protection…diplomatic specialized guard…

Kabul.

And worst of all, Colt's signature at the bottom of the last
page. Flipping back to the first page, she noted the date on
the contract.

He'd had this for weeks. *Weeks.*

Her eyes stung and blurred as she let the pages flutter to
the floor. She slumped in the chair, shoulders hunched as she
tried to curl into herself and away from what she'd just read.
Away from the hurt, the humiliation, the stunned confusion.

He was leaving. Leaving LA. Leaving her. Just like that.
Without even talking to her.

Oh, God. She'd done it again.

Just like with Zack, she'd completely misread what was
between them. Sad, lonely, abandoned puppy that
she was, she'd mistaken friendship and great sex for
something more, something deeper. She'd let herself fall,
confusing lust and a bit of temporary fun for a real connection and love. Her heart thudded sluggishly in her
chest as wave after wave of naked humiliation crashed
into her, leaving her dizzy and wrecked. Suddenly the distance she'd felt over the last few days made a lot more
sense. He was formulating his exit plan, trying to free
himself from her. He was leaving her in his dust.

"Fucking idiot," she whispered, her voice shaking as she
dropped her head into her hands, her elbows digging into her
thighs.

She'd let herself fall for someone who didn't want her.
Who didn't love her. Again.

She'd thought maybe this time was different, what with
the "it's you and me" and the "I'm falling for you" stuff, but

she'd obviously misread that, too. He'd probably just wanted to make sure she wasn't fucking anyone else.

Why would he leave if he loved her?

Swallowing against the thickness in her throat, she forced herself to take a deep breath. She'd deluded herself into thinking this was more than it was. Because if it was more, he wouldn't be leaving. He wouldn't have spent the past several days putting distance between them, bit by bit.

She clenched her teeth as the first pulse of anger beat through her, heating her blood.

Fine. If he wanted out, she'd fucking let him out. Better to beat him to the punch than let him humiliate her any more than he already had. He'd played her like a fucking song, but the concert was over. Now. God, when had she gotten so soft? So trusting? So blind?

She heard the shower shut off, a dull thud echoing through the pipes. Squaring her shoulders, she picked up the pages of the contract from the floor and pushed out of the chair, striding through the house. She would *not* let him see the damage he'd caused.

The bathroom door opened, and Colt emerged, a navy blue towel knotted around his hips. "Hey, I..." His voice trailed off weakly when he saw the folder in her hand.

"I didn't mean to snoop. I was looking for a piece of paper."

He opened his mouth, but nothing came out. He rubbed a hand through his hair, sending droplets of water chasing one another down his torso, but she refused to let her eyes follow them. A thick silence hung between them as his green eyes held hers, shining with something that looked a lot like regret.

"You want to tell me what the hell this is?" she asked, waving the folder at him before slapping it to the floor. Her temper sparked in her chest, and her heart was so brittle and dried up that it was in danger of igniting and burning to ash.

He let out a long breath, his hands pressed to his hips. He closed his eyes for a second, and when he opened them, he wouldn't look at her.

"It's exactly what it looks like, Taylor."

"You're leaving." Her tone was flat, a statement, not a question.

He shrugged, looking at the ceiling. "Guess so."

"Well." She flared her nostrils, forcing back the tears she refused to let fall in front of him. He didn't deserve her tears. Not when he couldn't even meet her eyes. Not when he'd played her. Not when she'd given him something true and real and vulnerable that he clearly didn't want. "That's probably for the best."

His eyes snapped to hers, and he frowned, his brows drawn together in a tight, anxious line.

"If that's the way you feel." He spoke cautiously, his voice quiet.

"We both knew what this was." She shrugged, trying to keep her cool and not make a fool out of herself. She'd done enough of that, and fuck if she'd give him any more of herself. Thankfully, she had years of experience hiding pain.

"We did?" His eyebrows shot up, and just for a second, hope rocketed through her as she thought he might challenge her on that. That he might actually fight for her. She gave him several long seconds but nothing more came out of his mouth, so she nodded, needing this to be done. Now. Wishing life came with a fast-forward button.

"Let's just call this an extended one-night stand. Nothing more."

For one brief slice of a second, he looked as though she'd

slapped him. But then, just as quickly, it was gone. He shook his head, his jaw tight. "I wish it hadn't gone down this way. I…" He looked as though he wanted to reach out to her but stayed where he was, silhouetted against the bathroom door. "I didn't mean to hurt you, Taylor. I never wanted to hurt you."

"Don't worry. You didn't," she lied, rubbing at her nose. "Besides, I'm the one breaking up with you."

He rubbed a hand over the center of his chest. "We… I…let this go too far, and I…" He swallowed hard. "I'm really sorry this couldn't work out."

"So I guess that's it then, huh?" Her chest tightened and then expanded, the pain almost too much to contain. Too big for this absurdly calm conversation. It was as though someone had dipped her heart in liquid nitrogen and crushed it into a million pieces. Shards of what used to be her heart stabbed her lungs, making it hard to breathe.

She'd wanted him to deny it, to fight for her, to promise he'd stay, to tell her that he loved her as much as she loved him. Instead, he'd let her push him away with surprising ease, almost with *relief*. Which was only proof that getting out now, before the scar he'd leave got any uglier, was the smart thing to do.

God, she was so fucking stupid. Stupid, stupid, stupid. She'd let her loneliness and her hormones scramble her brain. She'd thrown herself off the same cliff twice now, and only had herself to blame now that she'd landed broken against the rocks at the bottom for a *second* time.

She wasn't sure if she wanted to laugh, scream, cry, or punch something.

He nodded slowly, watching her intently. "Yeah. I guess so. I'll call Owens, have Virtus take over your security detail. I think that's best."

She wasn't sure how long they stood there, watching each other, because time seemed to have stopped.

"Fine." She forced her legs to move, despite the weakness in her muscles. "I'll get my shit." She brushed past him, and the shower-fresh scent of his skin twisted her entire chest into a knot of pain.

As fast as she could manage, she gathered up her clothes and toiletries, shoving them carelessly into her bag. She could hear Colt on the phone with Sean, his deep voice rumbling through the wall and slamming into her. She sat on the bed, her bag beside her, her hands plunged into the mounds of fabric as she clenched and unclenched her fists, just trying to breathe.

"Owens is on his way to pick you up. He'll be here in ten." He was still in nothing but a towel. Still not fighting for her. For them. For what they'd shared.

"I'll wait downstairs." She stood and shouldered her bag. She was going to cry, but she'd be damned if she was going to do it front of him.

He snagged her arm as she walked past him. "I'm sorry, Taylor."

She nodded, gingerly extracting her arm. "Good-bye, Colt."

# CHAPTER 26

Colt stood in his kitchen, staring unfocused at the coffee-maker as it spit and sputtered coffee into the glass carafe. He braced his palms against the counter, holding himself upright against the waves of shock and pain crashing into him.

He'd done the right thing. He needed to believe that. Because otherwise he didn't know how to cope with the pain he'd seen in Taylor's big blue eyes. She'd put on a brave front, but he knew he'd hurt her. Just like he'd predicted, she hadn't been able to escape unscathed. Even on her own terms.

She'd ended things between them, and even though it had gone against everything he had in him—his brain screaming at him to tell her he loved her, that he wouldn't leave, that he needed her—he'd let her walk away. It didn't matter what it cost him; he'd made a promise that he'd protect her from anyone or anything, no matter what. And he had by letting her go, by handing her over to Virtus. He was protecting her from himself.

He'd done the right thing.

He knew now that he'd been so fucking reckless. None of this should've ever happened. He should've never slept with her, never duped himself into thinking he could actually be good enough for her. Then, at least, he wouldn't be standing in his kitchen, trying to remember how to breathe.

But he needed to let her go. He hadn't known what to do: if he should end things, if he should take the contract, if he should be a selfish asshole and tell her that he was in love with her…He leaned on the counter, shaking his head. The fact that she'd found it even though he hadn't left it out in the open had to be some kind of sign from the universe. Like she'd said: Ultimately, it was for the best.

He scooped up a mug and hurled it against the far wall, watching as it shattered and landed in shards on the floor.

"Fuck!" He slammed his fist against the counter, rattling dishes in the cupboards above. He grabbed a second mug, but before he could throw it against the wall, his phone buzzed. He set the mug down clumsily, yanking his phone out of his pocket as hope soared through him.

But it wasn't Taylor. He swiped his finger across the screen to answer his sister's call.

"What?" He grimaced at the gruffness in his voice and forced himself to take a breath.

"Uh, hi. Bad time?"

"No. Sorry. What's up?"

"Just calling to remind you about Ben's birthday party this weekend. Are you still planning on bringing Taylor?"

He picked up the discarded mug and squeezed it so hard that the handle snapped off. "No. That's…We…No. Just me."

"Oh, okay." And then softer, "*Oh*. I'm sorry, Colt. You okay?"

"Fine."

"You don't sound fine."

"Lacey." His voice low, he turned her name into a warning.

"Okay. Well. I'm here if you need me. See you Satur-day?"

"Sure. Saturday."

They hung up and he smashed the mug, watching it ex-plode into pieces in a violent reflection of the pain slicing through his chest.

* * *

Blue balloons emblazoned with a white "6" bobbed cheer-fully in the warm breeze as Colt pushed open the gate to Lacey's backyard. He tightened his grip around the handle of the gift bag containing a Lego Batman set, took a deep breath, and plastered a smile on his face that he hoped didn't look as phony as it felt.

A few of Ben's cousins—nieces and nephews from Paul's side—ran around the yard screaming, playing the world's loudest game of tag. Seeing him at the gate, Lacey came over, a smear of what he hoped was chocolate frosting across the front of her jeans.

"Hey," she said, giving him a quick hug and pressing a firm kiss to his cheek. "Let me take that." She reached out a hand for Ben's present, and he let her take the bag. She stood awkwardly in front of him for a second before smiling ner-vously, her eyes darting back and forth between Colt and the house. "So, listen. Don't be mad."

He closed his eyes briefly and blew out a breath, planting his hands on his hips. "What am I not supposed to be mad about?"

She chewed her lip and looked up at him, suddenly look-ing much younger. "I invited her."

"Her who?" Colt's heart leaped and clenched in his chest

at the absurd hope she'd somehow contacted Taylor and brought her here. Even as he thought it, he knew it was ridiculous, but he could feel his chest filling with the idea anyway.

"Mom."

With one syllable, she knocked him flat on his ass, deflating all of that hope and letting it escape through the puncture wound she'd just created.

"You invited her? *Here?*" He jabbed a finger in the direction of the house, glad Lacey had taken the bag from him, because he really wanted to smash something. His garbage bin at home was full of broken mugs, plates, a lamp, and the glass shards of more than one empty Johnnie Walker bottle.

Five days. Five days since he'd let her walk away. Five fucking miserable days. He'd alternated between beating the shit out of his punching bag, going on punishing runs, and drinking until he was so numb he couldn't even feel his own skin. He was trying to pulverize the pain, to drink it into submission. And when that failed, he simply sat in his office, staring at the contract, trying to figure out if he should just take the job and leave.

Lacey nodded quickly and grabbed his arm, knowing he was about to bolt. "She's changed, Colt. She's sober. She's trying."

"And what is this? A stop on her 'making amends' tour?"

"She wanted to be here for Ben." And then, her voice quieter, "And the chance to see you."

"I can't believe you pulled this crap on me, Lace. You could've at least warned me. Given me the option."

"But then you wouldn't have shown up at all."

"And what does that tell you?" he whispered fiercely, trying to keep his voice down. "I don't have time for this shit."

Her face crumpled, and her lower lip trembled. "I'm sorry, Colt. I was just trying to…" She trailed off, hands fluttering helplessly in front of her. "Please don't be mad."

At the sight of tears threatening in her eyes, his anger dissipated, and he pulled Lacey in for a hug. "I'm not mad. But I can't do this." Not only had he shut that door a long time ago, but he wasn't anywhere near the right frame of mind to deal with his mother. "Tell Ben I said happy birthday and that I'm sorry I had to go." He kissed the top of her head, pulling away from the hug.

"Please don't leave on my account. I'll go. You stay."

His head snapped up at the low, feminine voice that he recognized instantly, even though he hadn't heard it in over fifteen years. His mother took a tentative step toward where he and Lacey stood, her eyes shining as she studied him. Her auburn hair was streaked with gray, but still hung in long, thick waves around her shoulders. Delicate lines framed her eyes and mouth and traced gracefully across her forehead, and her frame was smaller than he remembered. Smaller, but also stronger looking. Healthier.

Lacey backed away, and his mom took another step forward. Carefully, as though she were reaching her hand into a lion's cage, she curved her hand up and cupped his cheek. Her touch was warm and gentle. "Look at you," she whispered, and with a slow blink two tears broke free, racing each other down her cheeks. "So handsome. So strong."

Despite his best efforts, something in him gave at his mother's touch. He took a breath, and then another as they studied each other.

"Hi, Mom," he finally managed. He hadn't expected to feel so overwhelmed at seeing her. Overwhelmed with what he'd lost—any chance at a decent childhood, all the years he'd gone without a parent in his life—and with the happiness and relief at seeing that she really was okay. He couldn't remember the last time she'd touched him so tenderly, and it felt…right.

"Can we go somewhere and talk?" she asked. "There's so much I need to say to you."

He nodded, not trusting his voice to work properly through the surge of emotions clogging his throat. Anger. Hope. Grief.

He led her into the house, through the kitchen, and into the living room. He sunk down on the far end of the sofa, unable to take his eyes off of her. Unable to believe how healthy and whole she looked. And yeah, it was good to see her like that, but fuck, it also made him angry. She'd taken so much from him, and she got to be okay. When did he get to be okay? He was the one who'd had everything taken away, who'd sacrificed and fought and struggled, and what did he have to show for it? PTSD, and a broken heart.

He sat back on the couch, his arms splayed over the back, one ankle propped on the opposite knee. Trying to look calm and in control.

She met his eyes and took a long, deep breath. "Colton, I'm so sorry. I screwed up. I should've never kicked you out all those years ago. I know you were only trying to do what you felt was right, and that you were trying to look out for me and Lacey. I wasn't…making good decisions then. For you or Lacey, or for myself. You kids deserved so much better than I ever gave you, and for that I'm so sorry. I understand if you don't want anything to do with me. I just needed you to know that none of what happened was your fault. It was my fault, and mine alone."

He nodded slowly, not really knowing what to say. "Okay. I…thanks. For telling me that."

"I can't tell you how deeply I regret the way I treated you. You're my son. I love you. I will always regret that I was so awful to you. I don't expect you to forgive me, and I'm not asking you to. I just wanted you to know." She shrugged, one slim shoulder rising. "And I wanted to see the man you'd become so that I could tell you how proud I am of you. Lacey told me about your military service. That you were awarded a Medal of Honor."

He almost snorted. He'd been awarded the medal "for extraordinary courage and selflessness" even though he'd been one of the only surviving members of Delta Company to make it out of that mission.

He swallowed thickly and rolled his neck to one side, her words easing into him. He'd carried the weight of her rejection, of his failure as a son and a brother for so long that he'd forgotten it was there. But now that it was starting to lessen, just a little, he felt a thousand pounds lighter.

"So you don't blame me for..." He didn't finish his thought, not wanting to rehash everything.

She pressed a hand to her chest, pain flashing in her green eyes. Green eyes just like his. Just like Lacey's. "Oh, God, no. Colton, no. I don't blame you for anything. It was all my fault. I was the screw-up. Please don't think it was you. I would hate for you to blame yourself for my actions. *I'm* responsible for my actions. Not you."

He closed his eyes and took a deep breath, trying to pull her words as deep into him as possible.

"Lacey said that you're a bodyguard now?" she asked after a long silence.

He blew out a breath and allowed himself a small smile. "Personal security expert, yeah. For a couple of years now."

She smiled warmly at him, pride and hope shining in her eyes. "You were always so concerned with protecting everyone around you." Her voice softened. "Even at great personal cost to yourself. Sometimes at too great a cost."

The ache in his chest flared up again.

"How long have you been sober?" he asked.

"Five years now." She pulled a small bronze coin out of her pocket and handed it to him. It was adorned with an embossed *V*, and Colt turned it over in his fingers, examining it briefly, before handing her five-year sobriety chip back to her.

"Good for you." And he meant it.

She nodded. "I hope that you're happy, Colton. You deserve so much to be happy. My wish for you"—she laid a tentative hand on his tattooed arm—"is to rise above the damage I inflicted on you. You're strong, and smart, and worthy of happiness and love and everything good. *Because you are good.* There's nothing bad in you."

He'd imagined coming face-to-face with his mother countless times over the years but never had the conversation gone like this. He opened his mouth and spoke words he never thought he'd say. "I forgive you, Mom." It was stunning how freeing uttering those four words was. Freeing and...peaceful. As though something that had been twisting and churning in him for years was finally still.

\* \* \*

Taylor's phone buzzed for the tenth time that night, and she pulled it out, already knowing what she'd see.

Colt: Can we talk?

She stared at the message, her thumb poised over the screen, hovering between replying and deleting it. She lay sprawled across her bed, right in the center of it, taking up as much room as possible so she wouldn't notice how empty it was without Colt in it.

Dropping the phone down onto the pillow, she pulled the covers tighter around her, the silence of the house pressing down on her. Ian—whom everyone called Mac—was in the guest room. The room that Colt had occupied not that long ago. He'd been staying with her for a few days now, keeping an eye on everything, but there'd been no sign of her father, and her stalker was in jail.

She hadn't felt like trying to make forced conversation with Ian, so she'd gone to bed at an absurdly early hour, only to lay in bed, staring at her phone, watching Colt's text messages come in. She couldn't figure out what she wanted to do. If she should text him back. If she wanted to see him. It was hard to think in the quiet house. Hard to feel anything but numb.

Although she had enough songs for the album, she'd picked up her guitar earlier, hoping to sort out her thoughts with her fingers on the strings, but nothing had come. Colt had taken everything and left her empty.

Her phone began to vibrate on the pillow, and she snatched it up, her heart slowing when she saw Jeremy's name on the screen. She swiped her finger across the screen to answer it.

"Hey, Jer."

"Taylor? Are you all right? You sound funny."

She sat up and pushed a hand through her hair. "I'm fine. What's up?"

"I have good news. I just had a meeting with Ernie Glick, and he listened to several of the demos you've recorded." He paused for dramatic effect, but Taylor couldn't muster up the energy to care. She'd handed in a bunch of songs about a man who didn't love her. Fuck, she didn't even want to release the album anymore, but she knew she didn't have a choice. An album full of songs that were nothing but lies. The prettiest illusions.

"Yeah?" she prompted, wanting to get off the phone.

"He *loved* it. Said it was some of your best work. Heartfelt, and real. They want to put a major marketing push behind this."

"Awesome. Great. Can we talk later? I have a headache."

"Oh. Um, sure. Yes. Feel better. And congratulations. This is going to be the biggest album of your career."

"Thanks. Night, Jer." She hung up and squeezed her phone tight to her chest, the plastic creaking ominously under her grip. Her eyes burned, tears filling her eyes. She wanted to scream, smash things, and get drunk, but with Ian around, she couldn't really do any of those things. But she couldn't stay here, in this deadly silent house, in her cold, empty bed. She felt as though she couldn't breathe.

A drive. That was what she needed. And she knew it was better, easier, to ask for forgiveness than permission. Suddenly energized by the idea, she quickly made her way down the stairs, grabbed her keys, and pulled out of the driveway in seconds flat, hoping that she'd be long gone by the time Ian noticed she'd ditched him.

She rolled down the window, letting the fresh night air pour into the car, and cranked the volume on the radio, feeling some of the tension ease out of her with the rumbling of the Corvette's engine. As Journey's "Wheel in the Sky" blasted through the speakers, she angled the Corvette farther up into the hills, not caring where she was going, just driving.

For a second, she debated turning toward Colt's house, but she knew it wasn't a good idea. In the name of self-preservation, she needed a clean break. She'd been stupid enough to give him one chance despite all the warning signs, and she'd be a damned fool to give him another. She already hurt too much; she couldn't handle any more.

And yet, she missed him. She missed him so much that it overwhelmed her, obliterating everything else. Her ability to think, to breathe, to exist. Gone. Because he was gone. Because they were over.

Because he hadn't fought for her. Hadn't fought for *them*. She'd trusted him, been vulnerable with him, given him her heart, bruised and battered though it was, and he'd let her walk away as though it were nothing.

And maybe to him, it *was* nothing.

Maybe she wouldn't know the truth if she didn't at least hear him out.

She wove her way along Mulholland for several miles, letting her brain work while the hum of the engine, the cool night air, and the music calmed her. With her hands wrapped around the Corvette's wheel, she felt more like herself than she had in days.

She turned right onto Franklin Canyon Drive, heading down toward the reservoir. A pair of headlights flashed in her rearview mirror and she frowned, tightening her grip on the steering wheel. Before she could react, the car slammed into her from behind.

The Corvette careened off the road, and she yanked the wheel, trying to regain control. The car slammed into her a second time, and this time there was nothing she could do but brace herself as the Corvette came to a crashing halt against a pine tree.

Panic flooded her, and for the first time since she'd left the house, it hit her just how alone and vulnerable she was, driving at night, not telling anyone where she'd gone. She pressed a hand to her forehead, a dull throb beating through her skull, and her fingers came away wet with blood.

The driver's-side door flew open, and she didn't even have time to react before her father's fist connected with her face, sending her sprawling back against the seat as pain exploded across her cheekbone.

"Today's the day I get my money, bitch," he snarled and yanked her out of the car by her hair. She scratched her nails down his face, but he didn't let her go and slammed her face into the body of the Corvette. The coppery taste of blood filled her mouth as black dots pulsed in front of her eyes. Frank's arms tightened around her from behind, squeezing all of the air out of her lungs. She kicked and struggled helplessly, her mind reeling with fear.

"Get the stuff!" he called over his shoulder. She struggled, knocking her head against his and earning a punch in the stomach that made it impossible to breathe for a second. Pain erupted through her torso, pulsing in time with the throbbing in her skull.

"Here! Take it!" she heard another man's voice shout and suddenly her mouth and nose were covered with a sweet-smelling rag.

She fought, holding her breath for as long as she could, but eventually her world went dark.

# CHAPTER 27

Colt's phone rang, and he snatched it up from where it sat on his kitchen counter. He'd texted Taylor at least a dozen times after his nephew's birthday party. He needed to talk to her. Needed to make her understand that although he'd failed to protect her when he'd promised to keep her safe, instead of punishing both of them for his failure, he wanted the chance to make it up to her. He wasn't sure he deserved a second chance, but goddammit, he *wanted* one.

Maybe wanting to be with Taylor didn't make him a selfish asshole. Maybe he was good enough. And if he wasn't, he wanted to keep trying to be.

God, he'd fucked up so huge letting her walk away. Biggest mistake of his life, hands down, and he was damn well going to fix it. He loved her. He didn't have a choice.

He glanced at the display on his phone, tempering his disappointment when he saw Clay's name flash on the screen.

"Hey, man," he answered, leaning against the counter.

"Hey, listen. I just heard from a pal at the LAPD that your buddy Baker got sprung earlier today."

Colt stood up, his spine snapping straight with tension. "How the fuck did that happen?"

"He got sprung on bail. And you're not gonna fucking believe who paid it."

"Who?" asked Colt, the hairs on the back of his neck standing at attention.

"Frank Ross. Taylor's stalker got sprung courtesy of the Grim Weavers. Something's going down. Wait, what?" There was a muffled murmuring from the other end of the line. "Hang on."

Colt's heart slammed violently into his ribs, pounding a mile a minute as he waited for Clay to come back on the line.

"Colt…Taylor drives a red 1970 Corvette Stingray, right?"

"Yeah. Why?" he asked, the words sticking in his mouth like sawdust.

"I just found out that someone called in a 1970 Corvette Stingray, red. Crashed into a tree on the side of a road just outside of the Franklin Canyon Reservoir. No sign of the driver."

"You get a plate?" he managed to choke out.

"Yeah."

Colt stopped breathing as Clay read the plate back to him, a series of numbers and letters that told him the only thing that mattered: Baker and Ross had gotten their hands on Taylor, and he needed to find her.

"Thanks, man. I owe you." Without waiting for a response, he hung up on Clay and called Taylor, fingers tapping restlessly on the counter as it rang. And rang. And rang. Finally, her voice mail came on, and he hung up without leaving a message.

Panic surging through him, he made a second phone call, this time to Roman.

"Yeah?" he answered.

"Baker's out on bail. He's part of the Weavers. Frank paid his bail. Taylor's car was found, crashed just outside of Franklin Canyon Reservoir. We have to find her."

"I'll head out to the canyon, see if I can pick up anything."

"Keep me posted."

Colt hung up and called 911, notifying the police that Taylor was missing and possibly abducted. As soon as he'd hung up with the operator, he dialed Owens.

"Owens."

"It's Priestley. Taylor's missing, and Baker's been sprung from jail. He has a connection to her dad and the Grim Weavers. Not sure who was supposed to be with Taylor tonight, but her car just turned up, crashed on the side of the road near the Franklin Canyon Reservoir. She's not answering her phone, and I'm in a full-on fucking panic here."

"Shit." Owens blew out a breath. "Mac's at her place right now. I'll call him. But…" he paused before continuing "…if Baker's got her, where do you think he'd take her?"

"There are a few options. His apartment, or maybe her dad's place." He grabbed the file Clay had put together on Frank and Ronnie and paged through it.

"Okay. Anywhere else? What does your gut tell you?"

Colt flipped another page in Baker's background report and froze. His vision narrowed as he stared at the name and address on the page.

"The butcher shop where Baker works." Colt answered without hesitating. "He doesn't know I have this background report on him. His place and Taylor's dad's place are too obvious. But this? It works. It's clicking for me."

"I'll send guys to check out Baker's place and Taylor's dad's, and Ian and I will meet you at the butcher shop. Text me the address."

* * *

People were wrong about hell. It wasn't hot. It was cold.

So, so cold.

Taylor's head lolled against her chest as she struggled to open her eyes. Her eyelids felt thick and heavy, and her hands and feet were numb. She managed to pry her eyes open, and her vision swam as she pulled her head upright. She blinked slowly several times, and once her vision righted itself, gave her head a slow shake, trying to dispel the tapping sound rattling through her skull. A few more blinks, and then she realized the tapping was the sound of her teeth chattering.

She moved to wrap her arms around herself, but her wrists only jerked helplessly behind her. With a wave of nausea, what had happened came rushing back. The crash. Her dad. The sickly sweet smell. And then nothing, like a scene missing from a filmstrip.

She glanced around at the concrete walls, the harsh fluorescent lights searing her sensitive eyes. She jerked again, panic mounting when her eyes landed on the rows of animal carcasses hanging from hooks, some pink, some bloodred, some with bones sticking out at odd angles. They hung together, almost touching, a macabre row of death preserved.

She took several fast, ragged breaths, and a cold, iron-like smell caused her to gag and twisted her stomach into a knot. She tried to push up from the freezing metal chair, but found she couldn't move her legs at all. More and more alert with each heartbeat, she looked down and found her knees and ankles duct-taped together, and then again to the chair.

She licked her lips, took a breath, and screamed for help as loud as she could.

She tried to kick against the bindings, and the metal chair

scraped roughly against the concrete floor. She screamed again, and a door at the far end of the meat locker opened, cutting a swath of light through the room and across the lifeless pigs hanging from hooks, their ribs exposed like grotesque xylophones.

She stilled, shock and fear pinning her in place as Baker entered, a meat cleaver in one hand. She tried to blink, to look away, but found she couldn't tear her eyes from the glinting metal.

"I thought—" she began weakly, but she didn't have the fortitude to keep speaking. Her fear drained everything from her, and the room spun for a second.

"—that I was in jail? I was. But your old man bailed me out. Us Grim Weavers, we stick together."

"Give me a second with my daughter," came a familiar male voice from behind Baker, and her father stepped in beside him, patting him on the shoulder. Her breath hitched in her chest, and she couldn't get enough air. She wanted to close her eyes, to wrap her arms around herself, to run, but she couldn't. Her muscles tensed against her bindings.

Baker nodded and stepped out, leaving the door ajar. A stream of warm air flowed through the crack, but it wasn't enough to calm the violent shivers wracking her body.

"Here's how this is going to work, sweetheart. You're going to pay your own ransom." He crouched in front of her, his voice lowered to a whisper. "See, Ronnie's been a member for a long time now, and I know about his obsession with you. I knew if there was anyone who could find you, it'd be him. And sure enough, he led me straight to you. And now, he and I, we both get what we want. I get my money, and he gets you. Why anyone would want a whore like you is beyond me, but to each his own, right?"

She tried to straighten in the chair, anger warming her

bones. "How *the fuck* do you plan on getting away with this?"

"You pay me, and I pay my debts. Then I hand you over to Ronald. You don't pay me, I kill you. Pretty simple. Even you should be able to follow that." His fingers traced around her throat and over the marks that had almost faded. "What he does with you once I've got my money...Fuck, I don't really care."

Her mind reeled as she processed the information. Her dad was working with Baker. Baker was part of the Grim Weavers. "I hope you fucking rot in hell, you piece of shit," she stammered out through clattering teeth.

His eyebrows popped up. "So where's your pretty boy? He get bored with easy, tired pussy and go off to find something better?" He cackled to himself, rubbing a hand over his stomach.

Pain that had nothing to do with the cold cracked through her chest at the thought of Colt. At the thought of what she'd lost. The truth in her dad's words—that Colt had left to find something better—burst through her, pressing everything except pain and loneliness out of her chest until she felt like nothing but an empty shell.

"I'm not giving you a goddamn *cent*, asshole."

"You'd rather die than help your old man out? You really are the dumbest bitch I've ever met. I'm embarrassed that you're mine."

"Fuck you." She spat the words out as forcefully as she could with her numb lips.

He slapped her, a hard backhand across the face that had her vision fading in and out. He laughed, and then hit her again, and she sunk back into darkness.

\* \* \*

Colt cut the lights on the Charger as he pulled into the otherwise empty parking lot of Bobby's Meats in Reseda. He
parked in the far corner of the lot, and a pair of headlights
flashed at him. Grabbing his gun, Colt raised a hand and met
Sean and Ian in the middle of the parking lot.

"You bring your picking tools? Front door's locked," said
Ian, tipping his head in the direction of the dark building.

Colt nodded and pulled his lock-picking set from his back
pocket.

Moving as fast as he could, he set to work on the front
door, working as quietly as possible, not wanting to tip off
Baker and Taylor's stupid asshole father that they had company. Slipping in the long, narrow tension wrench and then
hooking the L-shaped wrench in after it, he began to turn
them, listening for the soft click indicating the release of the
pin tumblers. Sean stood a few feet away, giving him space
to work while surveying the parking lot, his Glock drawn
and ready.

Ian did a quick perimeter check of the building and came
jogging back a minute later. "Two bikes parked round back."
He met Colt's eyes in the darkness, and Colt could practically smell the guilt coming off of him. "I'm sorry, mate.
This happened on my watch."

A couple of years ago, Colt would've been tearing Ian a
new asshole over his mistake. But now, after everything he'd
been through with Sean, and with Taylor, he knew how easily a mistake like this could happen. He also knew how guilt
over a mistake could eat at a person, and he didn't want that
for Ian, who had enough of his own shit to deal with already.
"This isn't on you. The only people to blame are the two assholes inside."

Sweat pricked at Colt's hairline as he returned his attention to the lock, intent on opening the door and getting to

Taylor. After a few minutes, the deadbolt slid back with a metallic scrape.

Colt, Ian, and Sean all nodded at each other, and Colt pulled his SIG from his waistband. Taking care to make as little noise as possible, he slowly pulled the door open just wide enough to slip his arm through. Reaching up, he closed his hand around the bell to stop the clapper from chiming. He stepped inside, holding the door for Sean. Ian remained outside, watching the parking lot for any company.

The front of the butcher shop was completely dark, save for the dim light filtering in from the parking lot. The only sound in the room was the soft hum of the refrigerated display case. Silently, he motioned to Sean to move forward. Moving through the space, they checked the front of the store, the small office, and a bathroom, but all were empty and dark.

Colt's blood froze in his veins.

*Oh, fucking hell. The meat locker.*

* * *

Taylor grimaced against the sharp pains shooting up her legs, cramping from having been taped to the chair for...how long now? After she'd woken up the second time, she'd been alone, her muscles stiff and sore from shivering, her bottom lip cracked and swollen. She was so cold that she just wanted to sleep, but she knew she had to stay awake. Unable to pinch herself, she bit the inside of her cheek, trying to snap some alertness into her brain with a fresh shot of pain.

It worked for a few seconds, but before she could stop them, her eyelids were slipping back down like heavy curtains. With another bite to the inside of her cheek, she snapped her head back up and wanted to cry, because it couldn't be a good sign that she was hallucinating.

That was the only explanation for the sight of Colt easing his broad shoulders cautiously through the door, his gun cradled in his hands. His eyes locked on her, and he lowered his gun.

"She's here. Call nine-one-one," he said softly to someone behind him before holstering his gun and closing the distance between them with wide strides. Pulling out a pocket knife, he started working on her restraints, slicing through them with quick, sure movements. And then Sean was there too, helping to free her.

She couldn't talk. Her brain couldn't move fast enough to actually latch on to any of the feelings floating through her and turn them into words. Before she could stop them, the tears started coursing down her face, her silent sobs making her shake even harder.

Colt paused in freeing her, just for a second, rubbing a tear away with his thumb. "Shhh, gorgeous, it's okay. You're okay. Shhh." The last of her binds finally broke free, and it felt as though her brain were finally working, just a little. Enough that she could shout out a warning: "Behind you!"

Her voice came out like a strangled croak, but it was enough. Colt whipped around just in time to see Baker approaching with a gun leveled right at Sean's head. Lighting fast, Colt dove forward, pulling Sean to the ground milliseconds before Baker squeezed the trigger. A seam of blood beaded and welled on Colt's arm where the bullet had grazed him before disappearing into one of the pig carcasses behind him.

Still half on top of Sean, Colt shouted "Ears!" and she watched, frozen and dumb, as Sean clamped his hands over his ears and twisted away just as Colt yanked his gun from his waistband and fired two quick shots, hitting Baker in the arm and side. At the sound of the shots, Taylor's father came running, his own gun drawn, but before he could do anything, Colt fired at him as well from his position on the floor, hitting him in the shoulder.

"Get Baker!" Colt shouted to Sean as he pushed up from the floor and advanced on Frank, his gun trained at him. Taylor's head snapped back and forth, watching Sean pull zip ties from his pocket and use them to cuff a moaning, whimpering Baker, and watching Colt, who'd cornered her father.

Taylor crumpled back into the chair, too overwhelmed to stand.

* * *

After giving his statement to the police, Colt sat against the hood of the Charger, watching as paramedics loaded a barely conscious Taylor onto a stretcher and then into the waiting ambulance. One of the paramedics approached, a med kit in his gloved hands.

"We're taking her to Cedars-Sinai. Sir, can I take a look at your arm?"

Colt glanced down to where his gray T-shirt was glued to his bicep with dried blood. He nodded and let the medic clean and dress the wound, which, thankfully, was only a graze and would heal quickly, leaving only a minimal scar.

"She's gonna be okay?" he asked, watching as the paramedic carefully taped a gauze bandage in place.

"I'd think so. Mild hypothermia, a few cuts and bruises, possibly a minor concussion, but nothing life threatening. You saved her life. She could've frozen to death in there."

Colt just nodded, pulling his shirtsleeve back down over the bandage.

"That makes two." Sean's voice came from behind him. "You saved my ass back there. That bullet had my name on it."

"Don't mention it." Colt shrugged, watching the ambulance disappear down the street, its red and blue lights swirling against the dark.

"Colt. I'm going to fucking mention that you saved my life."

Colt shot him a half smile. "Anytime, man."

Sean returned the half smile and shrugged. "There's a job at Virtus for you, if you want it."

Colt's eyebrows shot up. "Really?"

Sean nodded and shoved a hand through his hair. "Yeah."

They stared at each other for a few seconds before Colt nodded. "I *am* sorry. About what happened. It was my fault."

Sean nodded again. "I know. But you've earned this second chance. More than earned it."

Colt watched the tiny lights of the ambulance, and he hoped Sean was right.

# CHAPTER 28

Taylor didn't care where she was. She didn't want to know. It didn't matter because she was *warm*. Slowly, like swimming to the surface of a deep pool, she regained consciousness and dared to crack her eyes open. Soft beige walls, dim lighting and a flat-screen TV mounted to the wall greeted her. Frowning, she tried to sit up but found she couldn't quite manage it, wrapped up as she was in heavy, warm blankets.

"Hey, don't try to move."

She swung her head too fast at the familiar low rumble, and dots danced in front of her eyes for a second.

Colt pushed out of the gray armchair by the window. "Just relax. How do you feel?"

"Better. Tired, but warm, at least. I'm in the hospital?"

"Cedars-Sinai. You've been asleep for a little while. Do you remember what happened?"

He cupped her cheek, and it was hard to think with his warm, callused palm on her skin. She finally managed to nod. She remembered. She had a feeling she'd never forget.

"How did you find me?" she asked, closing her eyes and pressing into his touch.

"Clay called when he heard Baker had been sprung by your dad. He saw the police report about your car. I figured out the rest."

"Help me sit up?"

He raised the bed to a more upright position, rearranging the pillows behind her so she could recline comfortably, still swaddled up like a baby. God, it felt good to be warm. Warm, and safe.

Colt sat on the edge of the bed, his hand still gently cupping her face. His green eyes held hers as he spoke. "Taylor, I'm so sorry. I shouldn't have let you walk away. Letting you go was the biggest mistake of my life. I should've fought for you. For us. I screwed up. I'm so sorry. Please forgive me for hurting you, gorgeous."

"Why should I?" she asked in a shaky voice. Her pulse throbbed in her throat as her heart tried to leap right out of her body and into Colt's waiting hands.

"Because I'm so in love with you that I can't even breathe right without you."

She sucked in a breath, the power of his words rocking her. "But it's so complicated with us. There's so much damage," she whispered.

"I want complicated. I want damaged. I want it all, as long as it's with you." He pressed a soft kiss to her temple, his words flowing over her like warm water.

"Colt," she said, barely able to get the single syllable of his name out.

"I love you so much, Taylor. I love the good parts and the broken parts, and I want all of them, if you'll give me another chance. I don't want to give up on us."

She stared at him as her chest filled almost to bursting with happiness and love. Relief and forgiveness.

"Taylor, please say something," he whispered, his brows drawn.

"What about the contract?"

He shook his head. "I'm not going anywhere. Sean offered me my job back." He bent forward and kissed her softly on the lips. "It's you and me, Taylor. Always."

*It's you and me.* His words, golden and pure, shimmered around her as life poured back into her.

She freed her arms from the pile of blankets and wrapped them around him, pulling him close and pressing her face into his neck to hide the tear slipping over her cheek. Could she trust him? Trust the words that were melting her broken heart so that it could be re-formed into something new?

Could she give him another chance to get it right? Could she forgive him?

Yes. A hundred times, yes.

Slipping her arms around his neck, she kissed him with everything she had. Kissed him and melted into him. "I love you," she whispered against his lips, and he moaned softly before deepening the kiss.

"I love you," he whispered back. "More than anything."

* * *

Taylor couldn't remember the last time she'd been this happy as she watched Sierra and Sean dance together in the ballroom of the Four Seasons Hotel in Santa Barbara, celebrating their engagement. The past few weeks had gone by in a blur, but for once, it was a good blur. The label was beyond happy with the songs she'd written for her new album, and she was set to start recording it next week. Baker and her father were both going to prison for a long time, and the Grim Weavers were under investigation by the FBI. They hadn't been able to connect them to the elusive Golden Brotherhood in any way, but the investigation was ongoing.

She still wasn't sure how to feel about everything that had gone down with her father. She'd known that he'd resented her, maybe even hated her, but he'd tried to kill her. Her own father. It would take time to sort through everything, to come to some sort of peace with what had happened.

Colt, on the other hand...She knew exactly how she felt about him. She was head over heels in love with the man. When she'd been discharged from the hospital the morning after the attack, he'd come home with her, and in the weeks that followed, he hadn't left. He'd gone back to work at Virtus. And when he wasn't at work, the two of them were starting to build the foundation of a life together. A normal, coupled-up life. Going to movies. Family dinners.

Having incredible, toe-curling, soul-nourishing sex on a daily basis.

Alexa sidled up beside her, a glass of wine clutched in one hand. She tucked a strand of her chin-length blond hair behind one ear and let out a sigh as she watched the couples on the dance floor. "They all look so happy, don't they?"

"Mmm-hmm."

Taylor watched as Alexa's eyes drifted from the dance floor to the bar, where Zack stood with several of the guys from Virtus, laughing and talking. Alexa glanced at Taylor and promptly returned her attention to the dance floor.

Taylor smiled. "He's pretty hot, huh?"

Alexa's fair complexion turned bright pink. "Oh. I... um...Zack...hot..." Her disjointed train of thought derailed as she looked at Zack again, who'd noticed Alexa's attention, and smiled. Alexa's blush deepened from rose to crimson.

Colt strode over, his hands tucked into his pockets. "I think they're playing our song," he said, pulling her out onto the dance floor before she could protest. Slipping his arms around her waist, he buried his face in her neck, and they began to sway together as Elvis's "Can't Help Falling in Love With You" floated out from the speakers. He turned them in a slow circle, and she breathed him in, feeling all light and shimmering at just being near him.

"Having a good time?" he asked, his voice rumbling across her skin in a way she'd never stop savoring.

"Yeah. But this is the highlight so far."

He kissed the spot just behind her ear that always made her melt. "Oh, gorgeous. The night is young."

She shivered and pressed herself closer to him, wanting to imprint the moment on her brain. Good memories to chase out the bad.

As the last strains of the song faded away, replaced with something more upbeat, she slipped her hand into his. "You wanna get out of here?"

"You read my mind."

Quickly, they wove through the crowd, everyone too caught up in their own good time to pay attention to Taylor and Colt. They'd booked a room in the hotel for the night, and Taylor planned to make good use of it. The hotel's elevator doors had barely closed behind them before he had her backed up against the wall, his mouth working urgently against hers.

"God, I've been waiting all night to do that," he breathed, nipping at her ear before kissing a hot trail down her neck.

"Me too." She tipped her head back as his teeth scraped

along her jaw, his hands skimming up over her breasts, teasing her nipples through the delicate silk chiffon of her dress. The elevator doors parted, and she led him down the hall to their room, fumbling for her key as Colt stood behind her, his hands around her waist, his mouth warm and soft as he pressed kisses to her shoulders.

"Hurry, gorgeous. I'd hate to rip your beautiful dress."

Finally, she managed to get her key card to work, and they stumbled into the room, a clumsy mess of arms and mouths as they consumed each other. He picked her up and tumbled down onto the bed with her, already pushing his suit jacket off and tossing it to the floor.

"Flip over," he said, his voice low and hoarse. Doing as she was told, she flipped onto her stomach. With his hands around her hips, he pulled her up onto all fours and then eased her zipper down her back, pushing the straps of her dress down over her shoulders as his mouth trailed across the sensitive skin at the nape of her neck.

She lifted her knees and managed to wriggle out of her dress, and before she could change positions, his mouth was on her, scorching a path up the back of one thigh, his teeth sinking into her ass cheeks as he teased a finger over her wet and swollen folds. And then his tongue was on her clit, one long, slow, teasing lick. "I love how you taste. I will never get enough of this."

Her arms shook as she struggled to keep herself upright under the onslaught of pleasure weakening her muscles. Her insides tightened, but before she could let go, he pulled away. "I want to be inside you when you come."

She collapsed onto the bed and watched as he quickly stripped, pulling a condom from the pocket of his pants.

She pushed herself up onto one elbow. "I thought maybe we could…not use that tonight."

He paused, the foil square still in his hand. "Are you sure?"

She bit her lip. "I don't want there to be anything between us. I just want it to be you and me, nothing else."

"Are you sure?" he asked a second time, his green eyes dark and glittering.

"I'm on the pill. I want you bare inside me."

He crawled on top of her and caught a nipple between his teeth. "Fuck yes, Taylor. Do you have any idea how hot this is? How much I want this?" he asked as he lined up the bare head of his cock with her slick entrance.

"Trust me, I'm right there with you," she moaned, angling her hips up to meet him. He leaned his forehead against hers and slid into her, fully connected, nothing between them.

He thrust once and then paused, his jaw tight. "Holy shit. I didn't think it was possible for you to feel even more incredible." He thrust again, deeper this time, and slid his hands up to entwine with hers. "You are so goddamn beautiful. I love you so much, Taylor."

"I love you, too, Colt. Now fuck me."

He let out a low growl. "Yes, ma'am."

\* \* \*

"Hey. Taylor."

"Mmm." She pressed her face into Colt's neck, savoring his warm scent and the feel of his solid body under hers. God, she loved him. Loved him and needed him and wanted him. Colt. This incredible, gorgeous man who made her laugh, who protected her, who curled her toes and who owned her heart completely. Who saw her for who she was, scars and all, and loved her in return.

She pressed a lazy kiss to his collarbone, the salt of his skin lingering on her lips. The sun was just beginning to peek over the horizon, bathing their naked, sweat-streaked bodies in a warm pinkish-orange glow. She'd lost count of how many times they'd made love last night, talking and laughing in between. She couldn't get enough of him.

"Wanna go to Vegas?" His voice rumbled against her skin.

"Sure, but—"

He cut her off with a kiss, stealing her breath along with her thoughts. "Marry me." He spoke the words against her mouth.

"What? You're crazy." Her heart thundered to life in her chest, taking off at a hundred beats a minute.

"I know. Marry me. At the Little White Wedding Chapel. Today."

She swallowed, her mouth suddenly dry. "If this is a prank, you're a dead man." Despite her threat, her voice was barely a whisper as every cell in her body shook and trembled with how desperately she wanted to say yes.

He chuckled and kissed her again. "Not a prank. In fact…" He leaned over and pulled a small velvet box from the pocket of his discarded suit jacket from where it lay on the floor. He flipped the box open, revealing a black diamond surrounded by tiny white diamonds set in a white gold band.

"And it's not going to turn my finger green?" she asked, her eyes stinging and her throat clogging.

"Would you just say yes already? You're killing me here."

She cupped his face and pressed a trail of kisses along his jaw. Finally, she reached his mouth, and by the time she did, she couldn't speak around the happiness swelling her chest and making it impossible to breathe.

"I want you to know that you can trust me," he said. "That

I'm not going anywhere. That even though I'll fuck up, I love you more than anything. I figured this was the most efficient way to show you that I one hundred percent fucking mean it."

"How can I say no to that?"

"That's a yes?"

"It's a huge hell yes."

He slipped the ring on her finger and brought his mouth down on hers, kissing her as though his life depended on it.

A couple of hours later, they drove off into the desert together, the Rolling Stones' "You Can't Always Get What You Want" filling the Charger. Taylor basked in the hard-won happiness coating her like warm sunshine as she laced her fingers through Colt's. The scars, the damage, the baggage—none of it mattered, because their broken pieces fit perfectly together.

For the first time in a long time, they were both whole.

Former child star Sierra Blake is making a stunning Hollywood comeback—and attracting a scary amount of attention. From the moment she sets eyes on her indecently sexy new bodyguard, Sean Owens, Sierra's thoughts are anything but professional.

Look for the first book
in Tara Wyatt's Bodyguard series,

## *Necessary Risk.*

An excerpt follows.

# CHAPTER 1

Sierra Blake glanced up at the bank of lights, and tiny dots danced in front of her eyes. People didn't often realize just how hot stage lights could be. The expression "basking in the spotlight"? That stray *s* had to be a typo, because it was more like "baking in the spotlight."

"Sierra, what do you think separates you from other child stars?" The 90's Con panel moderator directed the question at her, smoothing a hand down his tie as he glanced at the index cards clutched in one hand. She took a breath, the prickling threat of sweat teasing along her hairline. God, was she relieved she didn't have to do this daily anymore. She smoothed her hair over her shoulder and ran her hands over the skirt of her cream-colored silk dress. Hundreds of eyes locked onto her, and a zing of adrenaline shot down to her toes.

She bit her lip and fingered the shooting star pendant at the base of her throat. "You mean, how did I avoid living 'la vida Lohan'?"

Laughter bubbled up from the audience, and she relaxed

a little. Although it was par for the course at events like this, she'd always hated that question and the quagmire of emotions it dredged up.

She took a deep breath and dove in. "Quite frankly, being a child star is pretty messed up. You're working with adults, keeping adult hours, making adult money, and trying to live up to the expectations of everyone around you. Any kid would find that kind of pressure confining. And that's where the rebellion comes in. Drinking and drugs and sex. And all of this is happening when you're trying to figure out who you actually are. How are you supposed to do that in that environment?" She paused, contemplating how much to share.

"But you didn't go down that road," prompted the moderator.

"I didn't. I think part of the reason is that *Family Tree* was an ensemble show." She looked across the stage at her former costars, smiling warmly. "There wasn't one star carrying everyone else. We were a group, and the older actors looked out for the younger ones. I think the shock of suddenly being in the spotlight was easier to absorb when it was shared between all of us."

"That's definitely true," interjected Rory Evans, one of the other stars of the show. "We all bonded in that environment, and we became a pretty tight-knit group. We were a support system for each other without really even realizing that's what we were doing."

"Totally." Steven Simmons nodded. "We were a crew. No one had pressure on his or her shoulders to make the show a success. I think part of the reason it was a success was that the bond Rory mentioned shone through on the screen. We were all friends."

"We're all *still* friends," said Rory, taking a sip of his water. And it was true. Rory was a good friend, who'd seen her through the loss of a parent, through a change in career, from her teens to her thirtieth birthday just a few months ago.

"For sure," said Sierra, grateful that she hadn't had to shoulder the question on her own. "I can't speak for everyone else, but I think if I'd started in movies instead of on a TV show with the cast we had…" She shrugged. "Well, I don't know. I might've given Lindsay a run for her money."

"We all might've. In fact, some of us tried," said Steven, looking around innocently and drawing laughter from the audience. Although he had it together now, the antics of his early twenties were well documented.

"We did," said Sierra, her fingers once again straying to her star pendant. Rory reached over and squeezed her knee, giving her an encouraging nod. "You know the drinking, and the drugs, and the sex that I just referenced? All of that was true, at least for me. There was a period, between when *Family Tree* ended and when I started working on *Sunset Cove*, that I…" She trailed off, her fingers knotted together. "I lost control. I was seventeen, and my dad was dying of cancer. I was trying to figure out…well, everything, I guess. I was lost. Scared. So I drank, and I partied, and I hooked up with boys, trying to find a way to quell the fear that my world was about to end. Keep in mind that I also lived in a world that completely facilitated this behavior. It didn't matter that I wasn't legal, I had no issues getting into bars, finding someone to sell me pot, or getting boys' attention. That whole Hollywood world was so toxic. I didn't realize it at the time, but it was. Especially for a scared, lost kid. Everything came crashing down when my dad died, and then I had a pregnancy scare."

She forced herself to take a breath, and Rory gave her knee another squeeze. "I'm telling you all of this to partly explain that in some ways, I'm not so different from other child stars. I was messed up. And that toxic environment is why I'm not really in that world anymore.

"When I thought I was pregnant, I went to Choices. For anyone who doesn't know, Choices is a nonprofit organization that provides confidential reproductive, maternal, and child health services at low or no cost, and has centers across the country. I didn't know where else to go. I didn't want to tell my mom. I didn't even know if I was pregnant, and I was too chicken to go buy a pregnancy test. What if someone recognized me?

"I was able to take a test there, and it turned out that I wasn't pregnant, which was a relief because clearly I would've been ill equipped to deal with an unplanned pregnancy at seventeen. I didn't have my own life together. How could I even think about a baby's life? The support I received at Choices played a huge role in turning my life around. They offered me counseling, birth control, and support at a time when I felt alone and scared. So after I finished working on *Sunset Cove*, I went to college, and now I work for Choices. I'm proud to be their spokesperson, because I know firsthand what a difference they can make in someone's life. Frankly, I—"

"Shut your fucking mouth, whore!" A male voice erupted from the crowd, and stunned silence fell over the audience. Sierra froze, her mouth still open. A chill ran up her spine as a feeling of naked vulnerability engulfed her, pinning her in place. Rory's hand tightened on her knee and she scanned the crowd, but with the bright stage lights, she could see only the first few rows of people. Everyone else was hidden, shrouded in the shadows and beyond the reach of the lights. She glanced at Rory and the panel moderator, unsure what to do next. She'd spoken about Choices in public dozens of times, and no one had ever hurled obscenities like that at her.

And that's when something heavy, soggy, and cold slammed into her chest. It was as though someone had hit the slow-motion button on her life, and she felt as though she were suddenly underwater, dizzy and unable to get enough oxygen. Slowly she looked down, and all she could see was red, blooming in large patches on her dress, soaking it through. She ran her trembling hands down her torso, trying to figure out where all the blood had come from. But there was no pain, and the blood was cold.

Not her blood.

Shaking, she stood, and that's when she saw it, crumpled at her feet. A diaper with an exploded red dye pack. It was supposed to look like a bloody diaper. And someone had thrown it at her. A boiling anger ate at her chest, and her cheeks burned with humiliation. She clenched her jaw against the hot, stinging tears prickling her eyes.

"Oh my God, are you OK?" Rory's hands were on her shoulders, and the slow motion of the moment morphed into fast-forward. She shook again, a shiver racking her as a wave of dizziness washed over her, making the room tilt nauseatingly for a second. She nodded, her chest tingling hotly as her mind scrambled to make sense of what had just happened. The overwhelming urge to get the hell out of there took over, and she spun, almost tripping over the chair she'd just been sitting in. Shoving it aside, she ran offstage, needing to get away from the lights, away from the exposure.

Just away.

\* \* \*

Sean Owens pulled his sunglasses from his face, squinting against the bright Los Angeles sunshine as he strode toward the back entrance of the convention center, slipping them into the pocket of his suit jacket. He scanned the small aboveground employee parking lot, on the alert for any unusual activity, but nothing stood out. The standard perimeter check complete, he reached into another pocket for his phone, ready to check in with De Luca, the new guy on his team, before heading back to the office.

Before he could send the text message, the nondescript door at the back of the convention center flew open, slamming against the brick wall with a sharp bang, and he tensed, his hand edging toward the Glock 19 in the shoulder holster under his suit jacket. A woman came rushing out, one hand clutched to her chest, her face pale.

She was covered in blood.

Ten years of training and carefully honed instinct kicked into high gear, and he rushed toward her, his legs kicking into motion before he even had time to think about it. He raked his eyes over her tiny body, trying to figure out where all the blood was coming from, and if it was hers. She wasn't moving as though she was injured. She almost collided with him, but he anticipated her and braced his hands in front of him, his fingers curling lightly around her upper arms to steady her. She gasped and looked up, and a pair of bright-green, terrified eyes met his. Immediately he looked behind her, trying to determine if someone was pursuing her.

"Are you hurt? Is this your blood?" he asked, keeping his voice calm as he held her steady, his eyes still scanning the area for potential threats.

She shook her head, the ends of her golden-brown hair brushing against his fingers.

"No," she said, her voice strained. "It's dye."

He frowned and once again scanned the area behind her as he swapped places with her, putting himself between her and the door.

"Are you all right? You're not hurt?"

She laughed, the sound shaky and hollow. "Am I all right? Not really. But I'm not injured."

Sean's heart eased out of his throat from where it had leaped at the sight of a woman covered in blood running out of the convention center. But only slightly.

She pulled away, moving back a little. "I need to go."

He nodded, wanting more than anything to help her. "Where? I can drive you."

She took another step away from him, one eyebrow arched, a frown on her face. "Yeah, I don't get into cars with strange men, but thanks for the offer." A bit of color returned to her cheeks, making her green eyes look even brighter.

"Understandable. My name's Sean, and I'm a security expert." She eyed him warily, and he continued. "A bodyguard. I'm here at the convention to check on a new member of my team, see how he's doing with a client." He slipped his hand into his pocket and fished out a business card, handing it to her, wanting to earn her trust. Even though she was uninjured, his instincts told him that she needed him. She studied the card with narrowed eyes for a second before crossing her arms over her chest.

"This doesn't prove anything. You could've had these made."

He bit his lip, trying to suppress the smile he knew wouldn't get him anywhere. But he couldn't help it. Not only was she cute, she was smart.

"I just…" She toyed with his card, running it back and forth over her knuckles. "I just need a minute."

"Why don't you sit down?" He gestured to a bench several feet away. She glanced from him to the bench before finally nodding. Still keeping himself between her and the door, he let her lead the way. She sat down heavily, her elbows on her thighs, her face in her hands. He eased down beside her, sitting so as to block her from view of the convention center's back door. He watched as she took several deep breaths, and his chest tightened slightly. She was scared, and upset. Even if she didn't trust him, he could protect her from whatever had her so upset, and no way in hell was he going to leave her on her own. He couldn't. Not only was it his training, but there was something about this woman. He couldn't put his finger on it, but he felt drawn to her. Wanted to protect her and look after her.

The parking lot was quiet except for the distant rush of traffic from the front of the convention center, the rustling of the leaves of the trees lining the parking lot, and a bird chirping softly somewhere above them. Her slender shoulders rose and fell as she took several deep breaths, and he said nothing, giving her space. After a few moments, she straightened and leaned back against the bench, smoothing her hands over her stained dress that had once been white or yellow. It was so ruined, he couldn't tell for sure. Her eyes raked over him, and he let her look, hoping to put her at ease. Finally her eyes met his.

"What happened?" he asked, needing to know so he could keep her safe.

She sighed heavily, and her shoulders relaxed, easing down from around her ears. "I was speaking at the convention," she said, gesturing to the building behind them, "and someone threw a diaper full of dye at me."

"Someone attacked you with a diaper?"

She nodded, her bottom lip caught between her teeth. She looked up, her eyes once again meeting his, and there was that tug in his chest again. That pull.

"Why would someone do that?" he asked, propping one ankle on his knee and threading his fingers together, forcing his body into a relaxed posture to hide the tension radiating through him.

"I guess because I have some unpopular opinions."

"About?"

"Equal access to birth control and family planning. I'm a spokesperson for Choices, the women's health nonprofit." She looked down at her splotchy dress and sighed again, rubbing a hand over her face.

"Ah. Explains the diaper." The knot between his shoulders loosened just slightly. Chances were this was nothing more than idiot protesters, looking to make a point by embarrassing her. He looked back at the door again, but there was no sign of anyone following her.

Her lips moved, a tiny ghost of a smile. "I'm sorry I kind of accused you of…lying, or whatever. I didn't mean to be rude. I'm just…"

He held up a hand. "No apology needed."

She glanced down at his card, still clutched in one hand, now slightly crumpled. "I've heard of Virtus," she said, referring to the security company he ran with his father. The blue-and-gray logo was emblazoned across the top of the card he'd given her. She extended her hand across to him. "I'm Sierra, by the way."

He nodded. In the back of his brain, he'd recognized her almost immediately, but his concern for her had taken precedence over everything else. "I know. I'm Sean." He enveloped her small, delicate hand in his, and a warm, electrical tingle worked its way up his arm. Slowly she pulled her hand back, and damn, the friction of her skin against his felt good.

"I know." She held up the card.

He rubbed a hand over his cheek, his closely cropped beard bristling against his fingers. "Right. So, any idea who might've attacked you?" He scanned the quiet parking lot again. No way in hell was anyone getting close to her right now.

She blew out a slow breath and shook her head. "Not a clue." Some of the color dropped out of her face again, and he knew he needed to keep her talking. The urge to comfort her was nearly overwhelming. He couldn't change what had happened to her, but he could try to make the present suck a little less. He wanted to ask her about her own security, if she had anyone working for her, but thought that might come off like too much of a sales pitch, and that wasn't what she needed right now. So he headed in another direction.

"Were you on a panel?" he asked, tipping his head toward the convention center.

She nodded. "Yeah. *Family Tree* reunion. We do it every year for 90's Con."

"I remember that show. You were cute."

She smiled, fully and genuinely this time, and that smile aimed in his direction felt just as good as the slide of her hand against his. "Thanks. It was a long time ago. I'm surprised people are still interested in it twenty years after the fact, to be honest. Surprised, but glad."

He tilted his head, considering. "People grew up watching that show. I know I did."

Her eyebrows rose, and she leaned toward him slightly. "You did?"

"Sure."

"I guess I thought…I don't know. That it was mostly dweebs who watched it. It was kind of a goody-goody show." She shrugged, wrinkling her nose. Fuck, she was cute. His chest tightened again, but this time there was something else there along with the protectiveness.

He arched an eyebrow. "Who's to say I wasn't a dweeb?"

She laughed. "I seriously doubt that." Her eyes skimmed down over his body again, this time leaving a trail of heat in their wake.

"And why's that?" His eyes met hers, and a flush crawled up her neck and to her cheeks. Her eyes dropped to his mouth, just for a second, and something hot and thick pulsed in the air between them. She tucked a strand of hair behind her ear, and his fingers itched to repeat the motion.

Damn. She wasn't just cute. She was gorgeous.

"You don't look like a dweeb," she said softly.

Several feet away the door swung open again, and Sean leaped to his feet, putting himself between whoever had emerged and Sierra. She stepped out from around him and into the arms of Rory Evans, her former costar and...what, exactly?

"I've been looking for you. Are you OK?" he asked as he held her.

She nodded, and Sean was surprised at the jealousy swirling through him at the sight of this woman—who was pretty much a stranger—in someone else's arms.

"I'm OK. I just needed some air."

Rory smoothed a hand over her hair, completely ignoring Sean. "The police are here, and they want to get a statement from you about what happened."

She nodded again, and started to walk back toward the convention center. Turning suddenly, she laid a hand on Sean's arm, giving it a squeeze. She smiled up at him and it was as if someone were squeezing his heart with a fist.

"Thank you, Sean." Her hand lingered on his arm for a second, the air between them once again thickening.

How good would it feel to pull her into his arms the way Rory had just done? At least there she'd be safe. "You're welcome. Listen, if you ever...need anything, give me a call." He pointed at the card still in her hand, reluctant to let her go, but knowing he needed to get back to the office. Trying to reassure himself she'd be all right, with her *friend*, or whatever the hell Rory was to her, and the police. "You sure you're OK?" he asked, wishing he could go back inside with her to keep an eye on her. Not wanting to let her go. It felt...wrong.

Another fierce tug yanked at his chest.

"Yeah. I am." Her eyes held his for a second, and then she turned, slipping her arm into Rory's.

Sean pushed a hand through his hair as he watched Sierra walk away, his heart punching against his ribs as she glanced back over her shoulder at him one last time before disappearing back into the convention center. He took a deep breath, and then another, and then he walked back to his SUV. He looked back over his shoulder, contemplating going inside, just for a few minutes, just to make sure everything was under control...yeah. It couldn't hurt. He'd taken a few steps back toward the convention center when his phone rang, vibrating in his pocket.

"Owens."

"Who are you sending on the Robinson job?" his father asked, no greeting, just a barking question. Typical.

"Davis and Anderson. Why?" Sean's jaw tightened, tension seeping down his neck.

"You don't think it needs a third?"

Sean shook his head, irritated but not surprised that as usual, his dad was questioning his judgment. "It's a pretty standard job, so no. I think Davis and Anderson can handle it just fine, and keeping it to two keeps it within Robinson's budget."

"Uh-huh," said his father, sounding unconvinced. "This goes wrong, it's on you."

"It'll be fine. They've got it, and I'll check in with them regularly," said Sean, yanking open the door to his SUV and dropping into the driver's seat. He rubbed a hand over his mouth, used to his dad's blaming him for everything that went wrong. But just because he was used to it didn't mean it went down any easier.

Especially the blame he deserved. After all, it was his fucking fault his mother wasn't around anymore.

Phone jammed between his ear and his shoulder, he pressed the ignition button and tugged his seat belt on.

"You check on De Luca?"

Sean grimaced. "Didn't get the chance. Something else came up, but I'll check in with him by phone. I'm sure he would've made contact if there were any issues. I'm on my way back to the office now. Did you get the proposal I sent about the revised marketing plan?"

His dad sighed heavily. "It's a waste of fucking time. Not to mention money."

Sean leaned his head back against the seat, his jaw clenched tight. Nothing was ever good enough. "Let's talk about it back at the office."

"Fine. But it'll take a lot to convince me you can pull it off."

Sean almost snorted. Story of his fucking life, right there.

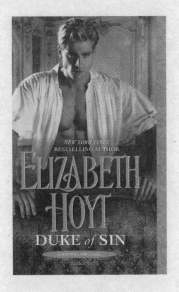

**DUKE OF SIN**
**By Elizabeth Hoyt**

Valentine Napier, the Duke of Montgomery, is the man London whispers about in boudoirs and back alleys. A notorious rake and blackmailer, Montgomery has returned from exile, intent on seeking revenge on those who have wronged him. But what he finds in his own bedroom may lay waste to all his plans.

*Fall in Love with Forever Romance*

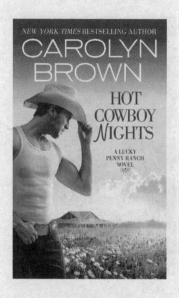

**HOT COWBOY NIGHTS**
**By Carolyn Brown**

*New York Times* and *USA Today* bestselling author Carolyn Brown brings us back to the Lucky Penny Ranch for some HOT COWBOY NIGHTS. Toby Dawson never was and never will be the settling-down type. But what harm could there be in agreeing to be Lizzy Logan's pretend boyfriend? They'll put on a show so all of Dry Creek knows Lizzy's over her ex, then be done. Yet the more Toby gets to know Lizzy—really know her—the harder it is for him to keep his hands off her in private.

*Fall in Love with Forever Romance*

**PRIMAL INSTINCT**
**By Tara Wyatt**

When Taylor's record label hires a bodyguard for her, she's less than thrilled to find it's her one-night stand, ex-army ranger Colt, who shows up for the job. But as danger from an obsessed stalker mounts, crossing the line between business and pleasure could get them both killed. Perfect for fans of Suzanne Brockmann, Pamela Clare, and Julie Ann Walker.